ALAS FOR CHOMA'S CHARGERS

Screeching and howling, Choma's Chargers came clanging through the woods.

Then Ruek's foot hit the first trip-cord. He went sprawling—and a tree fell on him. Choma fell across the tree. Somewhere nearby, brass carriage bells tinkled madly.

Traps! Choma had time to think. *Alarms—*

Then Vona's own fire lit the earth. Flames exploded from the ground, accompanied by a roar like thunder and clouds of smoke. Ruek screamed once, then went silent. Having just stumbled to his feet, Choma now fell backward, clawing at his flare-blinded eyes. Around him, the others screamed in terror, turning to run, falling against unseen trees.

And then the arrows came. The Thona brothers howled and died. Dak stumbled off blindly through the trees, then fell. Choma, crawling away through brush and jabbing tree-roots, heard him screeching for a long time.

They really were wizards, Choma thought inanely. *They really were. . . .*

C.J. Cherryh
Leslie Fish

A Dirge for Sabis

Book 1 of
The Sword of Knowledge

A DIRGE FOR SABIS:
THE SWORD OF KNOWLEDGE, BOOK I

A Baen Books Original

Baen Publishing Enterprises
260 Fifth Avenue
New York, N.Y. 10001

First printing, June 1989

ISBN: 0-671-69824-9

Cover art by Stephen Hickman

Printed in the United States of America

Distributed by
SIMON & SCHUSTER
1230 Avenue of the Americas
New York, N.Y. 10020

1042   **From founding of Sabis**

PART I

Fire

1

"Fire ready!" Sulun shouted warning.

"We're safe," and, "Go ahead!" came two muffled voices from the trench behind him.

In the middle of the dirt courtyard, a careful arm's length from the metal tube posed on its wooden mount, Sulun hitched the hem of his tunic above his knobby knees and inched the glowing end of the lighted reed toward the waxed string fuse.

The flame caught, sputtering a bit, and the fuse began burning toward the hole. Sulun dropped the reed, turned and ran for the trench. Omis's fire-scarred arms caught him as he tumbled in.

"Shhh!" snapped the burly soldier beside them. His studded leather armor creaked as he peered over the trench's edge. "It's burning, almost there . . ."

The other two stuck their noses out of the trench and watched as the sullen little flame worked its way up the fuse, across the base of the squat iron tube and into the narrow hole.

Nothing happened.

A snickering came from the windows of the mud brick house that closed the courtyard behind them. The apprentices.

"Don't laugh yet," snapped Omis, looking over his shoulder. "I've seen fire play worse tricks—"

A roar came from the bombard. Smoke and flame belched from its raised mouth, and a rattling something whistled out too fast to see.

" 'Ware 'low!" bayed the soldier, as he always did, as if this were an ordinary catapult.

"Going out to mid-river," Sulun noted, peering after the whizzing projectile as the crooked smoke trail arced out the ruined garden wall between two eight-story apartment buildings, and across the dike and moored rowboats.

"Kula, Mav and Deese of the Forge, let the seams hold!" Omis was praying.

The little gang of apprentices cheered and whistled from the house behind them. Neighbors on either side shouted and swore, heads came out of apartment windows, and the neighbor next door threw some garbage out his window. Out on the river a sudden waterspout rose, crested, and fell back.

"Within a yard of the buoy!" Zeren the soldier announced, standing up and starting to climb out of the trench.

"Not yet!" Sulun caught him by a booted foot. "We have to inspect the tube first."

Zeren waited, grumbling. Ordinary catapults weren't so temperamental; once fired, they were done. This iron bombarding tube of Sulun's seemed as fractious as a bored palace lady.

But oh, if she could be made to perform reliably . . .

Big Omis reached the bombard tube first. He inspected it anxiously, peering at the welds, poking at the touch hole and patting the base of the tube to check its heat. "She seems to be holding," he shouted back. "I think that lard-flux weld is just what we needed."

"Will she fire again?" Zeren shouted, scrambling up from the trench at Sulun's heels.

"Should," Omis said.

Sulun, likewise patting the tube to check its heat, cautiously waved toward the house, toward youngsters clustered in the courtyard doorway.

His apprentices came tumbling out like puppies, toting the necessities in a proud little procession: tall, twenty-year-old Doshi hefting the stiff leather tube of round stones; Yanados with the measured bag of firepowder, swaggering enough to show the width of her woman's hips under the man's robe and cape; skinny little Arizun bearing the fuse and the reed and the tamping brush in his arms as if they were sacred symbols in a temple procession.

Omis chortled at the show, but Sulun scarcely looked up.

First he took the brush Arizun offered and worked it cautiously down the tube's barrel, feeling for obstructions. Next he took the new fuse and worked it carefully into the touch hole. Then he pulled out the brush and delicately poured the black firepowder into the tube, at which point everybody else took a respectful step back.

He reinserted the brush, tamped firmly twice, and withdrew it.

Last came the greased leather cannister filled with stones. He struggled, lifting the heavy container so as to position it into the muzzle of the bombard tube. Failing to do that, he set it down and prepared to try again.

Omis stepped forward and shoved him grandly aside. "Here," Omis laughed. "That's another job for the blacksmith." Omis picked up the cannister in one hand, hauled it up, and shoved it smoothly down the barrel.

"Still, better let me do the tamping," Sulun insisted, taking up the brush again and pulling the tattered ends of his flapping sleeves up to his elbows. "After all this time working with firepowder, I've learned a certain touch for it . . . Ah, there!" He tamped carefully, withdrew the long brush, and checked the fuse. "Ready, test two!"

Everybody but Sulun ran for cover in the house or the trench.

"Now where's my tinderbox?" Sulun searched among the half-dozen pouches on his belt.

"Here." From the trench, Omis clambered out of his refuge with the little box in hand. "You dropped it when you fell on me."

"Oh. Um. Yes." Sulun scratched repeatedly at the box's scraper, lit the whole tinder compartment, then realized he didn't have the reed ready to hand. Inspired, he shoved the burning tinder at the end of the fuse. It caught.

Fast.

"Fire ready!" Sulun squeaked, scrambling for the trench. Once more he dived in headfirst, and once more the blacksmith caught him.

"You've left your tinderbox up there," Zeren commented, watching the fuse burn. " 'Ware 'low!"

The back door of the house slammed. Yells. Arizun's voice protesting.

The bombard fired with another roaring belch of fire and smoke.

Again the cannister whistled off toward the river, leaving a snaking trail of smoke between the buildings, and finally landed, sending up a geyser of muddy water and reed.

"It hit the marking buoy!" Zeren crowed, starting to his feet. Omis jerked him down.

Again the neighbors swore and yelled, "Noisy wizards!" Another load of garbage came flying out the window over the south wall, this one containing parts of a freshly slaughtered chicken.

Once more the engineer, the blacksmith, and the Emperor's soldier inched out of their safety trench and went to inspect the bombard.

"I don't know, I don't know," Omis fussed, brushing his curly black hair out of his eyes. "The seams look all right, but she's hotter this time, I think . . ."

"Best wait till she cools a little then," said Sulun, fumbling around in the weeds after his dropped tinderbox. "Hmmm. Of course that could be a problem in actual combat. . . ."

"No worse than reloading and rebending a catapult." Zeren waved the objection aside. "We'd have a whole battery of these things, half a dozen at least, shooting off one after the other! By the time the last one shot, the first would be cool again. Definitely faster than catapults, Sulun! And the distance! Given a dozen of these pretty bitches, we could retake the whole north country. . . ." His pale eyes, seeing a vision far beyond the muddy Baiz river, held a look of quiet, infinite longing.

"Don't count your conquests yet," Sulun said, waving for his apprentices and their gear. "We're still not sure this model can withstand repeated fire."

"Good ten-times-hammered iron!" Omis snapped, indignant. "And fluxed with lard in the mix, this time! Those welds could hold an Eshan elephant!"

"But it's not an elephant they have to hold," Sulun muttered, peering down his long nose into the barrel of the tube. "I suspect we're dealing with forces stronger than any beast that walks, any whale that swims or wind that blows—"

"Magic!" Arizun chirped at his elbow, handing him the tamping brush. "*True* sorcery!"

"Natural philosophy," Sulun corrected him, plying the brush. "Sorcery deals with spiritual forces. I deal only with material—Hoi, Omis! It's snagged on something!" He poked it again with the brush.

Omis took the tamp into his hands and tried it, then pulled it out. "Obstruction," he said gloomily. "About halfway down the barrel. And I left my tools back at the big house."

"Let me." Zeren drew his sword in a quick, smooth

motion, and poked its satiny gray length down the tube. "Ah, there. Soft . . . Just a second. Ah, there!" He pulled the sword out, held it up, and displayed the blackish lump stuck on the end. "What in the hells is this?"

Sulun rolled his sleeves up above his bony elbows and took a close look at the thing.

"Mmm, some sulfur? Perhaps not mixed smoothly in the grinding?"

He shot a look at his apprentices. Twelve year old Arizun looked indignantly innocent. Yanados shrugged and shook her head, denying responsibility. Doshi looked hang-dog guilty, but that proved nothing: Doshi always looked guilty when anything went wrong, no matter whose fault it really was.

Sulun studied the mass again. "Huh, no . . . I think it's a piece of charred leather from the cannister. Ah, *that* would mean that the stones weren't contained. They spread in a wider pattern. No wonder the buoy went down!"

Omis, busy with the tamping brush, didn't notice. "It goes all the way down now," he announced. "Do we try again?"

"Yes." Sulun straightened up and reached for the bag of firepowder. "We've got to. The whole point is, we've got to be sure this design holds repeated firings."

"Better than the last one, anyway," Zeren muttered, shaking the lump off his sword as he headed for the safety trench. He called back, "That one peeled like an orange at the second blast!"

The apprentices fled. Omis took cover beside Zeren in the trench. This time Sulun took care to have the reed ready, lit it off the tinder, closed the tinderbox, and put it away before he lit the fuse. Once more he shouted warning and ran for the trench. Once more the door banged, everyone ducked, watched and waited.

Nothing happened.

They waited longer.

Still nothing happened. Smothered chuckles from be-hind the wall and opened shutters above told that the neighbors were listening. A knot of local boys leaned out the windows of the left-hand apartment building, throwing out catcalls, jeers, and one or two empty jugs.

Still nothing.

"Hex," Zeren whispered. "Dammit, the neighbors—"

"Hex, hell. Hangfire," Sulun whispered. "It hasn't caught yet, that's all, it's just smouldering."

"Hex," Zeren said.

Possibility. If the neighbors got a pool together, they might afford someone potent enough.

Or if their master Shibari's fortunes were truly slipping . . .

Sulun ran his fingers through his wiry bird's-nest of dark hair, bit his lip, then scrambled for the rim of the trench.

Omis grabbed him by the tail of his tunic. "Uh, I wouldn't go out there yet."

Sulun sank back again, unnerved. Hex or not, dealing with a smouldering waxed wick in the touch hole was not a comfortable situation.

And even a little hex could overbalance an already bad situation.

With firepowder involved . . .

"Oh, piss on it!" Zeren picked up a stone from the bottom of the trench and threw it toward the iron tube, striking it neatly at the base.

The bombard tube exploded. With the loudest roar yet, the flames and smoke erupted from the mouth and center of the bombard, throwing stones, leather shreds and splinters of hot iron skyward. Quick thunder echoed off the surrounding walls. Dark orange flame lit the ground and the weeds of the garden court, making new shadows where the sun should have painted light. Thick yellow-white smoke rolled outward, filling the yard with heavy, dry mist that made everyone cough.

The echoes faded, leaving a shocked silence. Even the river birds were struck dumb. Then shutters opened in the haze of sulfur reek and a ragged cheer went up from the neighbors, followed by applause, more catcalls, whistles and laughter from the apartment buildings. The southside neighbor threw a whole cabbage over the wall.

Sulun and Omis climbed gloomily out of the trench and plodded over to study the damage. Zeren didn't bother to watch them. There was no bombard. There was no firepowder. Therefore there was no danger. The apprentices had figured it: the house door had opened. Zeren tromped toward it, collared Doshi, clapped some copper coins into his palm and sent him off to fetch some wine at the tavern on the corner. Arizun, after a moment's look at the disaster, scampered back into the house to get clean cups.

Yanados, out in the yard, commented to anyone listening that the cabbage was big enough and clean enough to make part of a consolation supper.

The neighbors, seeing victory, slammed shutters against the stink of smoke and went to gossip.

The bombard tube was ripped open along one side and bent by the force of the explosion. Ragged shards of iron jutted from the gaping tear, and the wooden mount was splintered.

"May as well use this for firewood," Sulun noted, picking up the shattered mount.

"It was the seam," Omis said gloomily. "I've tried everything I can think of, or ever heard of, and nothing holds. Maybe it *was* a hex."

"Hex or firepowder, it'll still blow at the weakest point. It's always the weakest point. It can't *have* a weakest point. We'll fix it. We'll come up with a new design." Sulun gave the twisted metal a kick. "No point wasting all this good iron."

"How do I make a tube without a seam?" Omis grabbed and tugged his woolly hair, staring at the mess. "*How?* Out of solid iron?"

"Doshi's back with the wine," Zeren announced.

Sulun shouldered the firewood, Omis gathered up the ruined bombard—at least the major pieces—and they went inside.

"How do you make a tube without a seam?" Omis was asking for the fourth time, over his third cup of wine. In the dimmed afternoon light his bearded, spark-scarred face looked flushed and boyishly distressed, and he drew admiring looks from Yanados, across the table, that were much out of character with her apprentice boy's disguise. Sulun smothered a wry laugh behind his hand; Omis was not above twenty-five years of age, remarkably *un*-scarred for his trade, and certainly handsome enough under the frequent layer of soot.

Omis was also busily and happily married, another of Shibari's freedmen working mostly at Shibari's house. A shop uptown, a wife, couple of kids in the estate itself—Yanados didn't have a chance there.

Yanados, now . . .

Sulun turned the half-full cup in his hand and studied her over its rim.

In the four years since he'd left old Abanuz's tutelage and applied to Shibari as tutor, philosopher, and sometime (more frequently lately) naval engineer, he'd learned that Yanados's case wasn't unique; a young woman with no family, no dowry, she had few choices in Sabis—or anywhere else for that matter: prostitution, slavery, thieving, begging . . .

Young men, however, could enter the various guilds as apprentices and work their way up to a respectable trade. And disguise, at least as regarded the public eye, was easy. Take off the clattering jewelry, flounced dresses, filmy veils, headdresses, face-paint; take away the willowy poses, fluttery gestures and giggles. Put on the simple tunic, hooded cloak, plain sandals of a boy of the trades; lower one's voice, stride straight, bind the breasts if need be, swear a little—and behold, a young man.

How many males one passed on the streets, Sulun wondered, weren't? Who could tell? Who even knew to look?

A master would. A master might exact convenient bargains for keeping her little secret. So might other apprentices. But everyone in Sulun's workshop knew about Yanados, and Sulun took no such bargains, nor did anyone else—not even Zeren. Master Shibari had no idea. Neither did Shibari's other servants and freedmen and retainers—which, given Yanados's not uncomely lines beneath the man's garb, argued that a servant was a servant even to other servants. Odd notion! Sulun wondered if anyone in Sabis these days bothered to look beneath the superficial things, like dress, like manner, like social status.

"If we report another failure to master Shibari," Doshi mourned over a slab of bread and cheese, "he'll probably turn us all out. Reckoning how bad his finances are these days . . ."

"So we won't tell him," Arizun piped up, helping himself to another cup of barely watered wine. "What the nobles don't know won't hurt us."

Sulun grinned. Best of friends, total opposites, that pair. Tall, pale, rawboned Doshi was a farmer's son from the Jarrya grain belt, tinkerer, dreamer by nature, with frustrated hopes of becoming a scholar in the city. The Ancar invasions that had driven his family out of their farm and south

to Sabis had likewise given him his chance of apprenticeship—but it had ruined the rest of his farmer kin, and *that*
stroke of fate left Doshi permanently guilty of something,
anything, everything around him so far as Doshi's thinking
went, poor lad.

Now Arizun—small, dark, eternally cheerful Arizun—
never felt an instant's remorse for anything that *was* his
fault. Arizun had been working a street magician/fortune-
telling racket in the Lesser Market when Sulun had first
seen him—little scamp pretending to a wizard's talent,
petty hexes for a few pennies—hexes the effectiveness of
which nobody could prove yea or nay. A little sleight of
hand, a lot of glibness, a clearly brilliant, and thanks to
someone, even literate street urchin who plainly deserved
better circumstances—as Arizun himself had pointed out.
Sulun had offered him an apprenticeship, and Arizun had
jumped at the offer: no relatives to notify, nothing to pack
but the clothes he stood in, no regrets and not a single
glance backward.

So now the boy made an honest living, mixing firepowder
and learning chemistry, making tools and learning mechanics,
running errands and teasing poor Doshi for his gloom and
his bookishness—and Doshi seemed to enjoy the association
thoroughly. Fair trade: Doshi helped Arizun with his reading
and his math, and Arizun taught Doshi a hundred and one
tricks of survival and success in the ways and byways of the
city—many of them legal. With any luck, Sulun reckoned,
they'd stick together, maybe set up shop as a partnership
when they finished their apprenticeship in Shibari's house.

"The best of weapons, if it doesn't come too late," Zeren
was muttering to himself, leaning on Omis's shoulder. "If
we'd had it twenty years ago, Azgunedes wouldn't have
fallen. Of course I wouldn't be *here*. D' I ever tell you my
family were educated folk?"

"Oh, yes," Omis sighed. "Many times."

"We owned two thousand hectares above the southern-
most loop of the Azesu." The mercenary had that sad,
faraway look in his pale eyes again. "A good villa—smithy,
tannery, potter's shop, ever'thing. In a good year, we sent
ten wagon loads down to the capital. In a bad year we
never needed set foot off our own lands: we could make
everything we wanted. There were tutors taught all the
kids on the estate. A respectable library. Even the cook's

boy could read." Zeren peered into his winecup. "D' I ever tell you, when I was a boy I wanted to be a philos'pher?"

"*Natural* philosophy?" Sulun pricked up his ears. "Is *that* why you hang around our little studio?"

Zeren shrugged, looked away and reached for the salad bowl.

"Then why'd you become a soldier?" Doshi asked, all innocence, around a mouthful of bread.

Yanados glared, and must have kicked him. Sulun winced.

Zeren favored Doshi with a fast, angry glance, then looked away again, raking salad onto bread.

"Really, Doshi," Omis said.

"Really what?" Doshi asked, looking from side to side.

Sulun said, under his breath, "Everybody knows what happened to Azgunedes."

"Well, of course," Doshi said, rubbing his leg under the table. "The Armu horde—"

"Doshi," Sulun said.

"The Azesu river," Zeren said quietly, looking out the window. "We saw them coming—could see it from the villa wall, the dust they raised. They came wading across the ford half a day north of us, so many they made the river run mud. One day was all the warning we had. One day to pack everything we could carry, herd in all the cattle we could reach, and move everything down the road—right through the troops coming up from Zebes. And the army commandeered half the cattle, right there on the road. We got to the city with almost nothing, and the general ordered every able-bodied man we had pressed into the army—including me."

"I'm sorry," Doshi whispered, staring at the tabletop.

"Wasn't a bad life," Zeren said. "Oh, the food was terrible and the officers were worse, but at least I could strike back at the Armu. We had some hope we could throw them back, at least turn them, establish a new border—at first we thought that, anyway. I didn't see the fall of Zebes, never found out what happened to my family. It was just fighting and running, grabbing what supplies we could, fighting and running again, all the way into Murrek. Those of us who were left signed up with the Murrekan auxiliaries. . . ."

Yanados cleared her throat and offered a lighter tone, "Didn't know Murrek ever had the money for auxiliaries."

"Murrek didn't have shit." Zeren gave two syllables of a sour laugh and leaned back, easier. "Except for brains. Orders and officers changed every fortnight, and the royal house wasn't much better: assassinations, coups, intrigues under every table—total confusion. The wiser heads in Murrek packed up and ran for the south, even before the hordes took Sefet. I figured it was better to join them. South, all the way to Halas, where I joined the King's Own cavalry regiment." Zeren poured the last of the jug into his cup. "The things I saw, the stories I could tell you about Halas, about the whole south coast, in fact. I must have soldiered for every king and lordling clean across to Mez, right in front of the tide—and it just kept on coming. Kingdom after kingdom. Never served in anything could hold it back—till I got to Sabis."

"Well, Sabis won't fold." Yanados tried to sound cheerful. "They've hit us before. We're still here. And you're doing all right second captain of the City Guard—"

"I'm not sure even Sabis can hold out." Zeren sighed, refusing now to be cheered. "Good gods, look around you. Who's on the throne? A nine-year-old child and his aging grandfather. Who rules the court? An army of courtiers and clerks and dotty wizards, the whole court worm-eaten with its own petty intrigues—"

"Zeren, be careful!" Arizun glanced significantly at the windows.

"So who bloody cares?" Zeren growled.

"Nobody but our neighbors," Doshi said.

"Gods know, they probably tell worse on us. Hell with the court. Taxes on everything. All of it to feed an army that's full of outland mercenaries like me! *I* make no claims for any great virtue, but most of them are far worse, and far stupider, than I am. Gods, I've seen them back stab each other for pennies, mutiny, duck out of fighting whenever they can, never stop to think this is the last, the last damn place that's got a chance to hold out! If the cities north of here fall, it goes; and their money won't buy them anything—not the court, not the mercs. Not after that."

"Ah . . . should I go out for more wine?" Arizun asked, neatly snagging the empty jug.

"Hell, yes!" Zeren threw him a silver coin. "Keep the change."

Arizun grabbed the coin and darted out the door.

Silence lingered.

"Well," Yanados said cheerfully, desperately. "Well, half an army's better than none. With the Armu busy tearing up the east, maybe it'll be barbarian against barbarian a while; maybe nobody else will push toward Sabis. Why attack the sheepdog in a field full of sheep?"

"Not just the Armu now." Zeren glowered at the dropping level in his wine cup; took another drink. "The last few pushes—the ones that took north Jarrya—"

Doshi winced, and took a drink himself.

"—were from a new tribe, these damn Ancar you've been hearing about. Not Armu. Who, d'you think, pushed the Armu hordes south in the *first* place?"

"We always thought it was the drought," Doshi muttered. "Those bad years in the north, Grandpa always said—"

"Bad weather pushed the Ancar. The Ancar pushed the Armu. The battle of the Gor kicked the Armu eastward then, they came down on the south—but the Ancar still kept coming. They're two hundred leagues south of the Gor already, that's what the scouts say. That's what they're not telling out in the streets—yet. Ancar's hell and away a worse enemy than our grandfathers fought in the Armu wars, and Sabis's hell and away a lot weaker now. Lost the east to the Armu, north's already going. What in hell are we going to do with the Ancar?"

"Oh, come, come," Sulun felt obliged to put in. It was all getting too grim, too desperately grim. "Sabis's got more people now than it did then. A bigger army than it's ever had. You can't say it's weaker."

"Where'd it get those people?" Zeren gave him a sad half-smile and idly brushed bread crumbs off the leather strips of his armor skirt. "Same place it got me. Collapsing borders. Lost provinces. Where's the trade that used to feed the world, with the east torn up by invasions and internal squabbles and border wars? Where's the food coming from now? Jarrya-south. Jarrya-north is gone. And overseas from the south. But where's the sea trade in general, with that rat's nest of pirates raiding everything that comes near Sakar?"

Yanados flinched visibly; drew her arms off the table. "What choice did the fleet have?" she snapped. "When the old navy was betrayed in that damned Pergian coup, who offered to pay them? Who offered them a port? Where else could they go?"

Sulun raised an eyebrow. Stranger and stranger things, on this inauspicious day. Just how, he wondered, did his apprentice Yanados happen to know so much history—and so much about the lamentable affairs of Sakar? Yanados never had really said much about where she had come from when she turned up asking apprenticeship with Shibari's house tutor-cum-engineer. She had just given the general impression that her family had been merchants in Cerinde, or maybe Alise. But what if . . ?

"Doesn't matter now," Zeren said. "Fleet's gone. What does matter is that Sakar harbors a legion of pirate ships, and they've sliced a good piece out of the sea trade, no matter if they're hunting supplies or just damned well looting. Just ask Sulun how much your master Shibari's lost this last year on pirated cargoes."

Yanados fell silent. Shibari was indeed neck deep in clamoring debts. And that was something none of them liked to think about.

There was profit to be had. Sulun knew, for instance, there was a big cargo coming in from Ista—*big* cargo, big profit in the shortages that plagued Sabis.

But even if the ships clung to the south coast all the way up to the coast of Mez, there was still the risk the Sakar pirates would raid them.

And if that happened, if Master Shibari lost *that* investment—

"The point is," the soldier went on, "Sabis is poorer and weaker today than it was when the Armu came down. Fifty years ago the center of the Empire fought off the invading barbarians, but is it going to be lucky twice?"

"There's still the wizards!" Doshi said.

"There's *their* wizards," Zeren said. "Who're you going to bet on?"

Worse and worse. A man who worked with firepowder didn't like to go far down that train of thought. The poets made stories about wizards who could rain down fire and smoke on their enemies, but that wasn't real. What was, was your wizards sat down and ill-wished your enemies and good-wished *your* side, and *their* wizards sat down and did the same thing only in the other direction, and if your wizards were more powerful than their wizards, then everything that could go wrong on their side went wrong and everything that could go wrong on your side didn't.

If a piece of harness had a flaw, if a wheel could come off, magery could find it—and there was no way to tell when a wheel fell off your cart whether it was bad luck or somebody's bad-wishing; if a spark was remotely possible, for instance, too close to the firepowder. . . .

Sulun gave a little shudder.

Not that he *believed* the neighbors could or would hire anybody . . .

Not that he believed that anybody they could afford was more than Arizun had been; or even, if that Anybody had real magery, that that Anybody could out-mage master Shibari's house wizard . . .

Which ought to let a man stop worrying and do his work, and not think about things like that. *Natural* philosophy didn't have to compass magery; by its very definition, natural philosophy didn't have to worry about things like that. The wizards did, and because they did, you just did the best you could in the natural world and didn't leave any flaws for the mages to get a foothold in; that was the first and best defense.

Of course, if you worried that a hex could hex you right into making a flaw in the first place . . .

A man could go crazy down *that* track. So a man didn't think about it when he struck a spark from the tinderbox.

". . . still wizards," Zeren scoffed. "And *they* have wizards." The soldier drained his cup and swept the room with a long, sad glance. "Sulun, my delightful little philosopher friend, Sabis desperately needs one wizard-factor that will give it the advantage over a vast horde of dangerously good foot soldiers. Some wizard-factor like this little toy of yours. Give me a hundred of these, a hundred that can be fired over and over without blowing themselves to the nine hells, and I could turn even the Ancar."

There was a long moment's silence, wherein Omis kept running his fingers through his curls, and saying over and over, "It's the seam. The seam never holds. But how do you make a tube without a seam?"

And Yanados said, "And where do we get enough firepowder for a hundred bombards? Charcoal, that's no problem. Saltpeter in every old dungheap. But sulfur, now . . ."

Doshi pushed his cup across the table. "Omis?" he said timidly. "Maybe like this?"

"Huh?" Omis asked. "Like what?"

"A tube. Imagine this cup deeper, longer, more of a tube. There's no seam in it. Look."

Omis picked up the empty tin cup. "No seam, true. But it's only half a ball shape, hammered out of a flat sheet onto a form. Tin-smithery. You couldn't hammer it much deeper, let alone in a tube-shape. You stretch it. You fold it . . ." He turned the empty cup in his hand, studying its shape and its construction. "Thin metal. Bending metal. Thin enough to hammer around a form is thin enough to burst in the charge. But if it wasn't hammered . . ."

"Where do you find sulfur?" Yanados was wondering. "I know you mine it. But from what sort of land? Mountains? Seashores? Where do they find it?"

"Near certain kinds of hot springs," Sulun said absently, scratching his chin. He had an appointment with Shibari: he had to shave, go back up to the big house with the accounts and *explain* his expenses. Shibari was anxious about today's trial. Shibari was anxious about mounting expenses and little return from this house Shibari's dwindling resources maintained for Sulun and his disciples and hangers-on in this waterfront neighborhood—a laboratorium, as Sulun had called it in laying out his plans and his diagrams and his financial requirements, in a neighborhood, as Sulun had also put it, more tolerant of the unusual and the noisy. Sulun's stomach was upset.

Yanados: "What kind of hot springs?"

"Hot springs in certain mountains," Sulun said, thinking still about those accounts, "the sort where one also finds black glass."

"Maybe not hammered at all," Omis murmured, turning the cup faster and faster in his hands. "Cast? But you can't get the impurities out without hammering. Got to start with twenty-times-hammered iron, a sheet or a rod or a block . . . Maybe drilled? But what could drill iron?"

"Find your answer soon, friends," Zeren muttered under his breath, "find it soon or not at all."

2

The great houses hove up in splendid independence on the heights of Sabis—occupying the hilltops, generally, set to catch the wind in their upper tiers. The block-long apartment buildings that were the lot of the most of Sabis' citizens occupied the low ground of the riverside and the valleys between Sabis's fair hills, territory prone to settling (and unheralded building collapses), prone to stale air and river stench (and the stink of other things, since the city provided sewers to the street, but not to the buildings), lately prone to overcrowding, since the city had become, over fifty years of dwindling provinces, the refuge and the economic hope for the world (the sink of all the sewers of the earth, the late Emperor had said on his deathbed—so the story ran).

There were Houses and there were *Houses*, and Shibari's was, like the family, old, well-suited, and cracking in its walls. It sprawled over a large area of the hill of Muzein, with a splendid view of the river and the poor district of warehouses that had grown up in a utilitarian age more dependent on trade than on a warrior aristocracy.

It overlooked the warehouses, it lived off the warehouses, now that the world went as it did. No more divine right for lords: just the Emperor—on the highest of all hills, outside town—and the Emperor's soldiers, also mostly outside town. Sabis had become increasingly polyglot, the old Sabirn aristocracy increasingly strangers in their own city, in the ascendancy of the nine year old son of a provincial-born general and his Sabisan maternal grandfather—who had been a gentleman farmer and an atrocious poet before he became a regent.

So, in the modern city, the old House of Shibari survived—in the neighborhood of woodcarvers, a couple of taverns, three slightly seedy apartments and a wineshop of odd and criminal patronage barely down the street from its vine-covered walls and sheds and its still-magnificent front entry, its plaster pillars incised more with accidents—the bash of a cart here, the knock of a box-edge there, over the centuries—than with the graffiti that scored the walls in the poorer areas just slightly downhill from here.

18

The front doors were still bright; the fish-tailed, twenty-breasted goddess Ioth on the right, and snake-tailed Baiz, pouring the waters of his river from a bottomless jar, on the left. The sea and the rivers indicated an ancient past, a claim on Sabis's long past, when the Sabisi had come in from the sea and conquered the peninsula, when the sea-lords had become the first lords of Sabis, the aristocracy of the aristocracy that arrived later and settled at its skirts.

Of that most ancient past, Shibari was one of the most ancient, perhaps—certainly no one of this nervous age dared speculate—with an ancient claim on imperium, on the throne itself.

But mostly Shibari just struggled, like any house however noble, to pay its war-tax, and struggled with business decisions (because the great Houses traded nowadays; the Emperor had confiscated too much of the land in too many previous rebellions, and doled too many holdings out to new favorites, and levied too severe a tax on old wealth for a House to live on past glories.)

And business decisions, Sulun knew, trudging up the cobbled, littered street toward that facade and an unwelcome necessity to confess his results—business decisions were what had to prevail, increasingly.

"Sulun! Sulun!" It was a swarm of youngsters, inside the marble hall, with the sea-goddess frescoes and the bronze figure of a ship prow for a centerpiece—ties to the sea, always, where Shibari's fortunes had begun. And always the children: Omis's three, the cook's two, several slave kids, Shibari's own four—voices pealing off the high ceilings, small feet pattering on the marble. . . .

He used to make fireworks, little poppers, paper rolls with just enough firepowder to make a flash—to the annoyance of Shibari's house wizard, whose daughter Memi had been no less a participant in the fireworks.

Memi stood at the back now: a quiet, sullen child.

"Did it work, did it work?" Tamiri asked, clapping her hands. Omis's daughter, who had seen the bombard in its forging, who had, at least to her own estimate, considerably helped Omis work the bellows.

"Mostly," Sulun said. It was terrible enough to face the children. But he had to walk down the hall, shake off his young escort, and walk in on Shibari in his study, accounts in arms, and stand there until Shibari, in a spindly chair at a desk piled high with codices and scrolls, realized he had a visitor.

"Sir," Sulun said, finally, and cleared his throat.

Shibari looked at him most carefully in a troubled way, as if he could read everything in Sulun that he possibly wanted to know today.

"A failure?" Shibari said.

"Not unqualified," Sulun said.

"Not unqualified." Shibari sighed and shook his head.

"Four firings and *accuracy*, sir—"

"Accuracy where? Expensive fire tubes, apt to explosions? Four strikes at the barbarians and an explosion wreaking havoc in our own lines?"

Sulun squared his shoulders. "Still four to one, sir."

Shibari's mouth stayed open.

"That was the way a soldier put it to me, sir," Sulun said.

"Zeren. Zeren's a *mercenary*." Disgust came through: the old-line aristocrat against paid soldiers, against foreigners, against a world quite, quite changed from honest, honorable ways. "Blow up one crew, hire another—I suppose that's very easy in Zeren's accounting. I tell you—"

The door opened. Mygenos insinuated himself through the door. "My lord."

"Come in," Shibari said, and Sulun folded his arms protectively across his account book and regarded Mygenos with a scowl. Memi's father. Mygenos the wizard. Mygenos the very well-fed, sleek and comfortable wizard. Mygenos never had to beg for funds. Even if a house was in Shibari's financial straits, it *paid* its wizard, and paid two of them if it could afford it—the best wizards it could find.

If he's so damn good, Sulun thought, not for the first time, *why is the house in this mess?*

But of course he didn't say that. He bowed to Master Mygenos. Mygenos bowed to him with a frown that became a sweet, unctuous look the instant he turned his face Shibari's way.

"I'm very sorry," Mygenos said smoothly. "I was in the garden."

"Master Mygenos asked to be here," Shibari said. "He's quite concerned about this for another reason."

"My lord." Another bow in Shibari's direction, a straightening of the body and a folding of the arms when he looked Sulun's way. "I hope you'll understand, Master Sulun, I bear you no personal ill will, all our differences aside. It's merely a matter of priorities, and I *can't* advise my lord to pour more resources down this rat hole, granted, *granted* you've made minor progress with your fireworks—"

"*Not* fireworks, Master Mygenos. The salvation of this *house*, Master Mygenos, *and* the Empire."

"The damnation of this house, Master Sulun! I must be blunt with you; you are a liability! I am a professional in my trade; I assure you I understand the principle of risk and reward, and in that professional capacity I have to advise my lord that the risk, in your case, is constant! I have a considerable ability, Master Sulun, I would say a *very* considerable ability. I serve this house with no help, no relief, and I extend my abilities to all my lord's enterprises, which encompass an extraordinary range of territory. I do not mind the sleepless nights and the magnitude of the burden, but likewise I must advise my lord when a disproportionate amount of my effort is drawn away from critical matters, by an enterprise which involves a very poor return on a very high expense—not only of money, Master Sulun, but of my energies! In short, you are exhausting me, Master Sulun. I cannot cover the things that truly affect the welfare of my lord against all his purposeful enemies, and against the pirates at sea and the chances of weather. All these things, I say, *are* my responsibility; but I am being drained by *your enterprise*, Master Sulun, which, even if successful, is years away from any useful application. It is a *luxury*, Master Sulun, for a time less dangerous and less critical to our lord. I protect you as I can—I cannot avoid protecting you, considering the possibility of *lawsuits* and loss of life and limb which could be ruinous to this house—"

"I hope your protection of our lord is more effective!"

"I am a wizard, Master Sulun, not a blacksmith! *If* your devices are grossly flawed, I am doing all I can to prevent loss of life and property! If you *will* work with firepowder, you can expect I will concentrate my primary effort on preventing your device working destruction on the city and on this house, and *then* I will worry about your personal safety, and *then* I will worry about your personal pride and the integrity of your abominable instrument! But I prefer not to continue to do so!"

Sulun waved his account book. "I require a minuscule amount of support compared to your budget, Master Wizard, and by *your* counsel, this house would venture nothing, run no risks and make no profits whatsoever! For centuries, Shibari has stood for explorations and enterprises the monuments of which decorate this house, Master Mygenos, and our master is no less than his illustrious ancestors!"

Argue with the house rhetorician, you fat-bottomed, overpaid son of an ape!

Predictably, Shibari's color came up a bit, his shoulders squared a bit, he took a larger breath and looked a half a hand taller.

But he still looked like a worried man.

"I never implied otherwise!" Mygenos was shouting. "I also know our master is not a fool like some I could name! He's been entirely too generous, and you trade on his good will! I wonder where a good part of this money is going!"

"Enough!" Shibari said. "Enough!"

Sulun folded his arms again and bowed. Mygenos bowed.

"I will support this, three months more," Shibari said. "And then I'll see."

"My lord," Sulun said fervently, with another bow.

"My lord!" Mygenos protested. "I feel I have to talk frankly here about due compensation! I've refused offers of a third again what you pay me! And this tinkerer supports a staff of apprentices, diverts your smithy to his own work, appropriates materials, entertains mercenary soldiers and gods know what *other* hangers-on with funds that I'm sure don't appear with the morning dew!"

"Three months," Shibari said, with that jut of his aristocratic jaw that meant Interview Ended.

"My lord," Sulun said, another time around the courtesies. "Thank you."

"My lord," Mygenos said.

And outside the door, in the marble hall with its goddesses and its bronze ship: "You son of a whore," Mygenos said. "You'll cross me once too often."

Ordinarily a man was afraid of wizardly wrath. A man worried about accidents.

This wizard, on the other hand, was Mygenos.

"Somebody'd better be seeing to this house's welfare," Sulun snapped, nose to nose with him. "You don't look like you've spent many sleepless nights, Mygenos, *or* missed any meals lately!"

He really shouldn't have said that, he thought on the way back into the estate storerooms, searching through his belt and the leaves of his little account book for the list he was sure he had brought somewhere about his person. Damn! If he could keep track of things . . .

But a man only got a few good openings with Mygenos. And wizards, they said, couldn't hex against their own work. He *was* right, he *was* going to succeed, he *was* going to do everything he promised, and the very fact that he didn't break his neck going down the steps, for instance, argued that, like it or not, Mygenos had no power to harm him.

Very complicated thing, magery. A *natural* philosopher was quite glad just to keep the wizards all in balance so that good science worked.

Omis held the burin steady with a block of wood and the pressure of his hand while Doshi worked the leather strap that spun it, back and forth, drilling the bolthole. Sawdust made clouds in the light of sunset streaming through the window.

A simple repair on the worktable this time. The aged legs had gone; too much hammering and sitting on it. Sulun tucked himself up in a chair in a sunny patch, working on his notes and his sketches while the repairs proceeded.

"Here, let me," Zeren said, pushing Doshi aside. With the blacksmith holding the drill steady this time and Zeren's strength doing the pulling, sawdust poured, making a little pile on the dirt floor.

And proliferating in the air. Sulun wiped his nose and sneezed suddenly, convulsively.

"Bless!" said Yanados, worriedly looking up from her grinding and mixing. Not only sawdust smell permeated the room—there was also sulfur.

"Umm," Sulun said, and wiped his nose again. "If that's old Mygenos ill-wishing me, all he can manage is a tickle."

"Don't joke!" Yanados gulped.

"Mygenos *is* the joke," Sulun said. "Poor Memi. The poor child used to be a nice little kid." Another pass of his arm across his nose. "She looked like a scared rabbit."

"Old Myggy didn't take it real well," Omis said, "that it was *his* precious daughter dropped the poppers in the cistern."

"Wonderful bang," Yanados said. "Tremendous echoes."

"Water tasted of sulfur for a month," Doshi said.

"Memi's changed," Sulun said. "Gods know what he did or what he said. That son of a bitch. Fortunately Shibari didn't listen to him. One of my better—"

The door banged open. Arizun ran in, gasping for air, stirring up a cloud of sawdust. Light from the window showed him as pale as his olive complexion could get.

"Sulun!" he panted, and stabbed a finger toward the door. "The word just came—down on the river. A ship got in! Shibari's ship was lost—pirates got it! The cargo, the ship—*everything!*"

"Gods," Yanados said. "Shibari's creditors—"

"They'll eat him alive," Zeren said.

"His whole household will go up on the block!" Yanados said. "What will that mean for *us?*"

Sulun found himself on his feet. In his mind he saw the ravening creditors running through the house. "They'll strip the laboratory," was the first thing he thought of.

"Nine hells, they'll do worse than that," Zeren said, grabbing his helmet. "They'll seize all the household slaves, too—and gods help the servant who can't prove he's a freeman. I've seen it happen!"

"Oh, gods!" Omis howled, diving for the door. "Vari! The children!"

"And his forge," Yanados exclaimed, scrambling after him. "He can't carry that away and hide it! All his tools—"

"Save what we can," Doshi gasped, hiking up the long skirts of his tunic and following. But Sulun was out the door in front of him.

3

Only Arizun remembered to latch the door behind them. Their little party went skittering up the street, right turn at the main avenue, up the hill toward Shibari's house at the best speed they could make. Zeren led the pack for the first few streets, but by the time they reached Shibari's walls, Sulun had passed him.

They scrambled to a halt as they sighted the front doors and saw the small but noisy mob gathered there—assorted money-lenders, peddlers' agents, even a cloth merchant or two, all waving pieces of parchment and yelling angrily at the closed wooden doors, while a pair of city guardsmen were glumly hammering on the panels with the butts of their swords.

"Gods," Zeren muttered. "Let me get to the guards, and I can hold off the looting for awhile." He turned to face the rest of the interrupted party. "There must be a back door. Take it. Get in, grab everything you can, get out again and hide until the vultures are gone. And hurry." He turned back toward the crowd at the gate, spread out his cloak so that it flapped behind him like vast red wings, and marched off at his best parade ground strut toward the guardsmen at the gate.

Sulun and Omis traded glances, then turned back and slipped around the corner of the wall. The three apprentices tiptoed after them.

Beyond the corner lay a narrower street, fronted with small shops that backed against Shibari's wall. A dozen shops down, a narrow alley zigzagged between the outer buildings and appeared to end at the wall. Little light reached here, even by day, and in the deepening dusk the whole alley was clotted with shadows, but Sulun's pack knew the way. Down to the wall they ran, quietly as they could, and ducked under the side eaves of the offside shop. A blank wooden door stood there, almost invisible in the dark, featureless save for a knothole close to the top. Sulun reached up, poked two fingers through the hole and scrabbled for the latchstring beyond it, choking off a curse as he missed. Arizun glanced about to see if any of the neighbors had noticed, but the surrounding buildings were silent. In the desperate quiet they could hear the yattering noise from the front gate, topped off by Zeren's voice bellowing about "—must prevent unlawful disposal of property and any possible bloodshed." The crowd howled furiously in return.

"Hurry!" Omis whispered, dancing from foot to foot.

Sulun's fingers found the latchstring, and pulled. The unseen latch released and the door creaked open. Sulun almost fell through, onto the rising stairs. He felt for the uneven plank steps in the dark and scrambled up them, the others crowding close behind.

The stairs opened out onto the shop's flat roof, beside the peeling wall. A few steps further on, a line of hand- and footholds climbed to the wall's top, some ten cubits higher.

Someone was already up there. A small, curly-headed child in a smudged tunic straddled the top of the wall, feeling for a toehold on the near side.

"Tamiri!" Omis shoved Sulun aside and reached up for the little girl. "Come to Papa, darling."

Tamiri squeaked with joy, dug her toes into the footholds, and scrambled down the wall as nimbly as a monkey. "Daddeee!" she squealed, throwing herself into Omis's burly arms. "Mommy's down there trying to get Mido to climb up, but he won't 'cause he's too scared, and Mommy's got her hands all full of the baby, and there's all the bundles of our clothes and things—"

Sulun was already clambering up the wall, Arizun and Yanados right behind him.

"Vari!" Omis wailed below them. "Help her! Get the children!"

Doshi plucked Tamiri out of the blacksmith's arms. "I'll watch her," he promised. "Go on over. Bring back a rope, and we'll pull up the bundles from here."

"Good thought!" Omis levered himself up the wall after Sulun's party.

At the top of the wide wall, each of them paused in turn to look down into the grounds below. Directly ahead lay the tall hedge that cut off all sight and reach of the kitchen garden from the main formal gardens; under its shelter scurried house slaves and free servants, running for boltholes, trampling the planted onions in their haste. The formal gardens on the other side of the hedge stretched empty and silent save for the drifting noise from the front gate. Further ahead loomed the whitewashed bulk of the house, equally silent and empty, like a fresh corpse awaiting the descent of the blowflies. Brief flickers of firelight from the front windows gave the only hint of life remaining inside.

"But where's Shibari?" Sulun wondered. "Where's his family?"

"Who knows?" Yanados grunted, swinging off the top of the wall onto the hand- and footholds below. "Let's get down and grab what we can."

"Sulun!" wailed a familiar voice directly below, over the sound of a baby squalling. "Come help! And where's Omis?"

They looked down, and saw Vari standing at the foot of the wall, buxom and pretty as ever, but more flustered and disheveled than they'd ever seen her. She was surrounded by lumpy bundles tied up in hastily-knotted sheets, clutching the baby, with two year old Mido clinging to her skirts like grim death and whining to be picked up. Sulun wondered how on earth she'd managed to get this far with all that, and how she'd expected to get everything over the wall once she reached it.

"Vari!" Omis shouted. "Wait right there, love! I'm coming."

He started climbing down the wall after Yanados. Sulun and Arizun scrambled after him.

At the wall's foot, Omis managed to clutch and kiss Vari for only a moment before she shoved the baby into his arms and ordered him back up. Yanados and Sulun grabbed up bundles. Arizun ran to the gardeners' shed and came back with a small coil of thin rope. Omis carried the baby and the rope's end up the wall, handed them over to Doshi and scrambled back down while Yanados tied on the first bundle. Vari took up the howling two year old and climbed the wall with him. Omis would have followed, but Sulun grabbed his sleeve.

"The equipment!" he panted. "Your tools, mine, everything we don't want the creditors to get—"

"Gods, gods!" Omis groaned, "How do I carry off a forge and an anvil?"

"Take what you can. I have to get—"

"Sulun!" Doshi yelled down from the top of the wall. "Look at the house! The front windows—look!"

They all turned, looked, and froze.

The second-story windows toward the front of the house flickered with far too much firelight for lamps, torches or braziers. Thickening smoke rolled out of them, followed by a cloud of sparks. The first tips of flames peeped above the window ledges, too widespread, far too many.

"Oh gods, my books!" Sulun ran for the house. "My patron!"

The others pounded after him, dodging fleeing servants, trampling more rows of onions.

At the kitchen door they had to fight their way through a mob of escaping cooks and scullions to get in. Once past the kitchen they split up, Omis running for his forge, Sulun and his apprentices heading for their workshop. The fire hadn't reached this part of the house yet, but the smell of smoke grew heavier in the air. Arizun and Yanados yanked the curtains off the wall brackets and spread them on the floor. Sulun grabbed armloads of books and threw them onto the curtains.

"Books, notes, sketches, models," Yanados panted, tying the first loaded curtain into a bundle. "What else?"

"The tools, the lenses . . ." Sulun looked about him. Damn, no, he couldn't take the lathe: too heavy. So much was too heavy, too big, too cumbersome for three people to carry out, much less over the wall—but much of that was replaceable, even cheaply. Shibari could . . . "Shibari! We have to find him!" Gods, to be patronless in this city was the ninth hell. "Get the bundles out. I'll find Shibari."

Sulun dashed out the door and down the long corridor that led to the Family's part of the house. If he could reach Shibari, help him escape the horde of creditors with the family coffers, the master could set up elsewhere— possibly overseas, more likely up in Jarrya, under another name. The household would be smaller but still intact, still capable of maintaining a small host of craftsmen, and Shibari would be grateful to those loyal servants who had helped him. They could get back to work on the Bombard Project within a few months, with luck.

Beyond the heavy door that marked the end of the servants' quarters, the smoke was ominously thick. Through watering eyes and increased coughing, Sulun searched from room to room. The chambers were empty: no sign of the children, or their tutors or nurses, or Mistress Nanya, or Shibari himself. The clothespresses had been opened and ransacked, but to judge from the clothes scattered about, almost nothing had been taken. Perhaps this meant that Shibari and Nanya had had the sense—for once—to seize only necessities: a few plain travelling clothes, jewelry, money, easily carried valuables. Maybe they'd already made their escape under the confusion of the fire.

But how could they have fled so fast?

Shibari was famous for doing everything with slow majesty and proper gravity, which always took irritating amounts of time. The man was addicted to Reputation, to the point of spending himself into debt rather than reducing the splendor of his household, which was how he'd backed himself into this wretched position in the first place. Had Mistress Nanya made plans for such an escape when the debts first began to soar? It was possible, but didn't seem like her; as far as any of the servants knew, which was much. Maintaining the household's appearance absorbed all her attention. Possibly one of the upper house servants, the butler or housekeeper or secretary, had made the contingency plans after a passing word from Shibari; the gods knew, the master quite often tossed ideas to his servants and then forgot them himself until presented with their accomplishment later. The problem was, both Shibari and Nanya resented being outthought by their servants, and often resented or rejected out of hand good advice and good projects offered by their underlings.

Sulun hitched his shoulders higher, remembering a few times that had happened to him. The steam powered engine, for example: Shibari had been delighted at the little model, its water-laden globe spitting steam from its four angled jets and spinning merrily on its axle above the brazier, making a grand impression on the dinner guests—but when Sulun later presented him with the list of costs for making a larger version, including a diagram for a small ship powered by the engine, and even some clever suggestions on how the money could be raised, Shibari promptly and sourly lost interest. (Sulun still couldn't understand that. Shibari made most of his money by shipping; why couldn't he see the value of building ships that could outrun any pirate craft, sail straight against the wind and even drive through storms without the rowers collapsing from exhaustion?) The man's pride thoroughly outweighed his common sense, and in that respect his wife was worse.

So where had they gone so quickly? Not in the sewing room, the herbarium, the bath, the small dining room, the bedrooms or the study—and the smoke was much thicker here. Sulun could hear the flames crackling now, mostly upstairs in the house servants' rooms, but some seeming closer. The fire must have started down here, in the front of the house, then spread directly upstairs by way of the drapes. How fast was it spreading on the ground floor? How close was it?

Sulun leaned on the study wall for a moment, and felt that it was hot.

On the other side of the wall, he remembered, lay the formal dining room. In it stood the family altar, the ranked busts and portraits of Shibari's ancestors, the canopied great-couch from which the master and his wife dined on such formal occasions as their wedding feast or the first-blessing of their newborn children. Of all the house, that was the room most completely dedicated to family pride.

And the fire was there.

"Oh, great gods!" All the details suddenly snapped into place, and the final picture was monstrous.

Sulun ran for the door, pausing only to feel it, making certain it wasn't hot, that he wouldn't open it to face a sheet of flame, and yanked it wide.

The fire was at the outside wall, a blazing sheet that engulfed the floor-to-ceiling tapestry, climbed the curtains to the window beams, and crawled across the ceiling. By its light, Sulun saw the great-couch, and its occupants.

Shibari lay to the left, his body formally arranged though dressed in his ordinary clothes. His bloodless hands were folded neatly on the hilt of a short sword that protruded from his blood soaked breast. He had, clearly, been dead for at least an hour.

Beside him, as precisely posed as an effigy on a tomb lid, was Nanya. Her hair was impeccably coiffed, as always, and she was dressed in her best formal dining gown and jewelry. Her stiffening hands clasped a small glass bottle.

Around the two of them, likewise dressed in their best,

though sprawled in attitudes of natural sleep, lay their four children.

A blackened brazier, deliberately placed against the blazing tapestry, showed how the fire had started.

Coughing furiously against the smoke, throwing silent curses and pleas at every god he could think of, Sulun ran to the couch and gripped Nanya's wrist. No pulse. He sniffed at the glass bottle, then turned away, sickened.

"Gods, not the children too . . ." Sulun poked among the small, tumbled bodies, feeling at wrists and jaw-hinges. The twin boys were still, lifeless. The pretty elder daughter was warm to the touch, but after a moment Sulun realized that was only because she lay closest to the fire.

The younger daughter was still breathing.

"Teigi . . ." Sulun whispered, dragging her off the couch. Her body seemed so light. How old was she, anyway? Nine? Despite her small size, she'd always seemed older than that: always sneaking into the workshop, staring fascinated at the engines and workings, poking into the books and actually reading them. . . .

The child's eyes fluttered open. "Mama," she whimpered. "It tastes nasty. I don't want to—"

A shower of sparks brought Sulun's attention back to the fire. It was creeping across the ceiling panels, almost directly above them. The roof could fall in at any moment.

"Out!" Sulun coughed in a sudden gust of smoke. He pulled Teigi onto his shoulder and scrambled for the door.

Behind him, with a roar like Omis's forge, the fire caught the couch canopy.

"Mama!" Teigi shrieked, staring back.

Sulun ran down the corridor, heading for the back of the house and the still-safe exit. Above him he could hear the fire growling. There! The door to the servants' quarters—and some fool had shut it! He tugged furiously at the handle. Gods, the air was like an oven back here.

A sudden rending crash and flare of light filled the corridor behind him. Teigi screamed. Sulun half-turned and saw, horrified, that part of the corridor ceiling had come down, bearing a load of burning rubble with it.

Blinding smoke and a near solid wave of heat rolled toward him. A rain of sparks and small coals peppered his head and shoulders. Teigi howled again, batting at sparks caught in her clothing.

Sulun wrapped both hands around the handle of the heat-jammed door, and pulled like a madman.

With a sullen groan of protest, the door came loose and swung open, Sulun dived through it and ran down the main hallway of the servants' quarters, half blinded with smoke. There, the kitchen, and there, thank all the gods, the kitchen door. He plunged through it, missed the step, fell rolling. Teigi yelped at the impact, and went limp.

Sulun staggered to his feet and stumbled out into the kitchen garden. He could hear shouts and wails, but couldn't see anybody. From the outside front of the house he could hear, above the steady roar of the fire, Zeren's voice bellowing instructions to what seemed to be a quickly organized bucket brigade.

Either the fire or the creditors would be on them soon. Where the hell was the wall?

"Sulun!" A long hand grasped his wrist. Yanados. "This way, and fast. We got everyone over the wall except you. All the books, the notes, the diagrams, some of the tools, some of the models . . . Who's that?"

"Teigi," Sulun coughed. "She's the only one left. Shibari stabbed himself. Nanya poisoned herself and the children, and started the fire. Teigi didn't swallow enough—"

"Gods, we're patronless!"

"Teigi—"

"A child! And female. No property of her own, but she'll be liable for Shibari's debts, being the last of the family. Gods help her if the creditors find her."

"Gods . . ." Sulun echoed. He hadn't thought of that. He was too tired to think of all that. "Hide her. Hide us. The lab by the river."

"Good enough. We can decide what to do tomorrow. Here's the wall." Yanados guided his fumbling hands to the climbing holds. "Can you manage, carrying her?"

"Think so."

He managed. Teigi lay like a grain bag on his shoulder, neither help nor obstruction, her small weight growing heavier with every step. By the time Sulun reached the top of the wall and flopped over it, he was as exhausted as he'd ever been in his life. Multiple hands pulled the child-burden off his shoulder and helped him down onto the shop roof below. He flopped among the piled bags and panted. Arizun wordlessly handed him a wineskin.

From beyond the wall came a vast roaring crash, and a soaring column of flame and sparks.

"There goes the roof," Omis mourned from the wall top. "No saving anything now."

"Let the damned creditors pick through the ashes," Vari sniffed. "Ah, gods, what to do now that we're patronless?"

"We go to the workshop by the river," Yanados reported. "We can all stay there tonight, at least."

Sulun pulled himself to his feet and tottered up to the rest of the party—himself and his apprentices, he noted; Omis and his wife and their children, and now Teigi. Vari was crouched over the unconscious child, carefully rubbing her face with a wet cloth.

"How is she?" he asked. "Can she travel?"

"There's no injury I can find," Vari murmured, patting over the girl's head. "I think it's just smoke and fright."

"And a touch of tincture-of-poppy juice," Sulun added gloomily. "Well, if need be, Omis can carry her. Doshi can carry your boy, and you take the baby. The rest of us can manage the bundles."

Vari nodded agreement. "We'd best go soon, while everyone's busy with the fire. We don't want to be caught by patrols looking for Shibari's runaway slaves."

"No fear of that," Arizun put in from the top of the wall. "Look: Zeren's got them all busy putting out the fire. I think they might save the back part of the house, our workshop, the forge—"

"And the creditors will seize it all," Omis groaned. "How will I make a living without my forge?"

"And what will we do without the big workshop?" Doshi added. "We couldn't get everything out, had to leave most of the models. Without those, how do we make a good enough impression to get a new patron?"

"Tomorrow," Sulun snapped, impatient with fatigue. "We'll deal with that tomorrow. For now, let's get to the river workshop and get what rest we can. Omis, can you carry Teigi that far?"

Before the blacksmith could answer, the child woke up—and howled. "Mama! Mama, no! Not fire!" She struggled out of Vari's startled grip and crawled blindly across the roof. "Where are you? Where?"

Omis caught her before she'd gone more than a few steps. "Hush, you're safe," he said, swinging her up in his

burly arms. "We're on the roof of the house next door. I'm
your papa's blacksmith, remember? We're all your papa's
people, and you're safe."

"Mama," Teigi sobbed, refusing comfort. "Where's
Mama?"

The adults looked at each other, wondering what to say.

"She's dead," little Tamiri cut in brutally. "She was in
the house, and it's all burned up."

"Who asked you?" Vari snapped, aiming an outraged
swat.

"She did," Tamiri chirped, ducking the swinging hand.
"The house is all burned up. You can see it from the top of
the wall."

"Let me see! Let me see!" Teigi struggled in Omis's
grip.

"You may as well let her look," Vari sighed. "Go ahead,
lift her up."

Omis shook his head, but lifted Teigi up to where she
could see over the wall. Firelight reflected off her face as
she watched the flames, the smoke, the fire-brigade working below—and the collapsed, burned-out front of the
house. She watched until Omis' arms grew tired, very
quiet and still.

"There now," Omis said gently, putting her down. "Your
mama and papa are gone, but we'll take care of you. We'll
take you to a new house. Do you think you could walk a
ways?"

Teigi said nothing, only shook her head.

"Well, that's no trouble. I'll carry you." Omis picked
her up again.

"Best cover her with a cloak, too," Arizun pointed out.
"In those fancy clothes she doesn't look like a blacksmith's
child. We don't want to draw attention."

"Good thought." Vari dug among the clothing bundles
for a cloak.

"How fast can we leave?" Sulun asked, eager to be
gone. "Let's get out of here before the patrols start
searching."

The rest of the group caught the mood, and began
picking up various bundles and children.

"The models gone, the forge, the workshop," Doshi
muttered, trying to manage Omis' two year old and a
bundle as well. "How will we make a living?"

"Cheer up," Yanados offered. "It could have been worse."

"Oh? How?"

"Well, what if we'd kept the firepowder in there?"

"Oh."

Doshi cheered up considerably, or at least pretended to, and the small caravan cautiously made its way down the stairs.

4

The little workshop had never been more crowded. Vari marshalled the apprentices to clear and sweep the floors, hunt up and spread a modicum of straw, and finally stretch out the salvaged bedding. Omis tended the children, trying to get a smile or at least a few words out of Teigi. Sulun gloomily inspected the salvage from the house and tried to imagine how to make a living from it.

"It'll be crowded, but there's bedding for all of us," said Vari, inspecting her finished work. "Is there any food in the house?"

"Some bread, I think." Arizun padded off to the cupboard. Teigi began crying again, very softly.

"Ah, there now, dear . . ." Vari rummaged in one of the opened bundles. "Are those burns paining you? Here, they're not very big. Let me put some salve on them."

The little girl kept crying, not noticing her blisters or Vari's ministrations.

Sulun vividly remembered that last look backward at Shibari and his family, and the flames devouring the canopy of the couch. Gods, yes, that would be pure hell for a child to remember. He sidled closer, and draped a cautious arm around Teigi's shoulders.

"They were already dead," he said quietly. "They died of the poppy-juice tincture, long before the flames reached them. They never felt an instant's pain; it was just like going to sleep."

Teigi sobbed louder. "It tasted nasty. I spat it out." She rubbed a grubby fist across her eyes. "She turned her back, and I spat it out."

"Good thing you did, or you would have died too."

"I should have!" Her sudden howl echoed off the walls. "I should have gone with them!"

The others looked up, startled.

"Whatever for?" Doshi asked. "What good would that have done?"

"Honor," Teigi hiccupped.

Arizun made a rude noise. "What sort of honor kills little children? Destroys whole families? Leaves the servants to run or be burned to death? Ha! Honor's a slaughterer, no different from the Armu barbarians—don't they do the same?"

Teigi only shook her head and cried.

"Now hush that silliness," Vari said, slathering on the burn ointment. "I'll tell you what your real honor is, child. You're the last of your family now, the last of Shibari's ancient and honorable blood. That's why the gods spared you, you understand?"

Gods nothing, Sulun grumbled to himself, *I dragged you out of there—and only in hopes of keeping a patron. And, admit it, because I like the little girl. And because I wouldn't leave anyone to a death like that. Gods? Well, if the gods are no more than human greed and human pity, then I suppose Vari could be right.*

Teigi was sobbing a little less, and listening closely.

"Now what you must do," Vari went on, artfully pouring out a spoonful of hemp-seed syrup from her supplies, "is hide your true name until, hmm, the omens are better. Then, when you're old enough to marry, you will refound the family of Shibari. You must live to have children of your own, do you see?"

Sulun raised an eyebrow at the elegance of that argument. Vari held out the spoon and neatly fed its contents to the girl.

Teigi swallowed, then protested, "Papa's creditors . . ."

"She has a nice grip on essentials," Yanados murmured.

"Don't worry, they won't find you." Vari put the spoon and bottle away. "We'll hide you among our own children. Hmm, we'll have to give you a new name . . ." She looked around for suggestions.

"Male or female?" asked Yanados. "If we're going to hide her from Shibari's creditors, best to disguise her sex as well."

"Good thought," Omis rumbled. "As a boy, she could pose as an apprentice. Hmm, but I don't suppose, child, you have the muscle to work as a blacksmith . . ."

"Sulun." Teigi turned tear-wet and disconcertingly bright eyes to him. "I could be his apprentice."

"Wait a minute—" Sulun gulped.

"Of course she could." Vari clapped a firm hand to his shoulder, leaned close and whispered fiercely in his ear. "Don't discourage her. The child needs some hope to live for, and my silly story won't support hope very long."

"Uh, yes—yes," Sulun stammered, feeling as if the floor were sliding out from under him. "I can always use another apprentice."

Yanandos and Arizun smothered explosive snickers. Doshi only looked pained.

"It would look strange if a blacksmith's son were apprenticed to anyone but his father. Er, I'll say you're a cousin of mine." Sulun looked around wildly for inspiration. "What'll we call her—him? What's a good name?"

"Aziya," Teigi piped up. "I used to have a puppy named 'Ziya, but he ran away . . ." The rest of her tale was smothered in a yawn.

"Hmm, Ziya it is, then," Vari soothed. "Come lie down—Ziya."

"Now that we have that matter settled," said Arizun, handing the scant bread around, "what shall we do about making our living, now that our patron's gone?"

Instant silence fell.

Sulun heaved a sigh of fatigue and impatience. "Come, come. Someone must have some ideas. Suggestions?"

Omis shook his head. "Without my forge and anvil, I can't set up a free shop. I'll need to find some other blacksmith who needs a partner, if any such exist in the city."

"We're in much the same kettle," Yanados pointed out. "And I don't know of any natural philosophers who need partners."

"It is a rather specialized field of endeavor," Doshi said dourly.

"If we could get across the straits to Esha, we could set ourselves up as a college of magicians," Arizun offered. "Outside the port city, it's a wonderfully backward place. We could dazzle the locals with our knowledge, perhaps even get a position in the king's court—"

"I thought you said you came from Mez," Yanados sneered. "The king of Esha is only a puppet of Sabis, and not a terribly wealthy one; he'd spend no money on luxuries such as us. Besides, with the little we've saved from the house, what do we have to impress a patron?"

"Besides that," Doshi added, "do we have enough money to buy passage for all of us across the straits? Or to feed us afterward?"

For a moment everyone stopped and thought, for the first time that night, specifically about money. The adults promptly checked their belt-purses. Arizun also peered into one of the bundles he'd salvaged from the house, and came up with a lame-looking smile.

"Among us all," Sulun concluded, "we have perhaps enough to feed us for a tenday. I think we must forget about crossing the straits."

"There's plenty of employment in the army," Yanados grinned, "Or among the pirates out to sea."

"I rather doubt they'd take a horde of children," Vari sniffed. "What would we do about the children?"

Sulun, who'd been briefly fancying himself as a pirate, came back to earth on that question. What about the children, indeed? For a moment he seriously considered sneaking out of the house before dawn, signing up in the army or going to the docks, leaving his apprentices and friends to manage for themselves. But without his cumbersome books and notes and tools and models, what could he do? He'd make a poor soldier, and a worse sailor, the sort that didn't survive for long. He'd do better begging in the streets of Sabis.

"There's no other way," he said with a sigh. "We simply have to find a new patron, and quickly. Any suggestions?"

There was a long moment's silence.

"Well," Vari finally offered, "Perhaps those very creditors who are hounding after us."

"*What?*" Omis squawked. "Those vultures picking the house bare already?"

"Think!" Vari insisted. "With the house burned, and the money and servants gone, how will the creditors regain their loans? They'll all come up short, and they'll all be greedy for more. Well now, we have skills to sell, don't we? That makes us objects of value that formerly belonged to Shibari, doesn't it?"

Everyone thought that over for a long moment. It was a grim suggestion, but nobody could find fault with it.

"It would have to be a rich creditor," Arizun said slowly, "One who could afford to take on all of us. Otherwise we'd be separated—and then, who knows when we'd get the Bombard Project done?"

Nobody could fault that either.

"How do we know who Shibari's wealthiest creditors were?" Doshi protested. "Only Shibari himself—and maybe his secretary—knew. Shibari's dead, and the gods only know where the secretary is."

"Probably halfway across the straits by now." Arizun considered.

"How do we find out?" Yanados asked. "Perhaps the Hall of Records—"

"Any one of us who shows his nose there might be recognized and seized for Shibari's debts," Doshi warned. "Anyone seized would have to prove he wasn't one of the household slaves. How does a servant prove he's not a slave?"

Another long silence followed.

Omis shoved a set of tongs aimlessly back and forth, then smiled suddenly as inspiration came. "I know who could find out for us—walk right into the Hall of Records and ask to see anything, even bully the clerks around if they don't move fast enough."

Everyone caught on at once.

"Zeren!"

Unnoticed, Teigi/Ziya snored gently in Vari's lap.

5

It was a long, crowded, largely sleepless night, and Arizun was stumbling and yawning when Sulun sent him out in the morning. It was another sweaty, hungry, apprehensive hour before Arizun came back with Zeren in tow. The burly captain strolled through the doorway, surveyed the little bivouac in the middle of the workshop, and shook his head.

"You do look a mess," he grinned. "Still, I'm glad to see so many of you got away—and with how much gear?"

"Not enough to complete the Bomabard Project without another patron." Sulun cleared off a table and two relatively clean chairs. "That's what we want to talk to you about. Arizun, did you pick up the food and wine?"

"No, he didn't," Zeren cut off the apprentice's reply. "I told him to save his money. You're all coming to my house for breakfast and, hmm, a bit of a visit."

"And a bath?" Tamiri asked.

"Bath first!" Zeren laughed. "Come along, the lot of you. Pick up the gear and the children; it's not that far a walk."

He was right; being a mere guard captain and not an aristrocrat, Zeren lived in a modest house much closer to the river than Shibari's manse. Nonetheless, by the time the little party had moved themselves and their gear there, washed, changed clothes and eaten, it was close upon noon. Zeren's lone servant, an aged housekeeper, took one look at the invading mob and discreetly vanished. Vari hustled the children off for a nap, leaving Omis, Sulun and his three regular apprentices alone with Zeren. The others, for all that they'd helped form the plan, were quite content to let Sulun do the talking.

Zeren heard him out, then leaned back in his chair and thought awhile.

"The problem is," Zeren said finally, "that getting a list of Shibari's creditors isn't easily done. The creditors would have gone to court, to our own dear Minister of Justice, to get permission to seize the property. The Minister of Justice wouldn't handle such petty business himself; he'd shuffle it off to one of his secretaries, and there are at least a dozen of them. The secretary would pass it on to one of his clerks, and there are hundreds of those. As a mere guard captain, I couldn't approach the Minister; he wouldn't give me an appointment—at least not for months, not without a substantial bribe of money or information to interest him."

"I suppose the possibility of the bombard wouldn't be information enough," Sulun groaned.

"Indeed not. He's not interested in things military anyway, looks down on soldiers, considers himself something of a pacifist." Zeren drained his cup and refilled it with half-watered wine. "Of course, that's a fashionable attitude uphill. Folks there can afford enough guards that they need never take a weapon in hand to defend themselves. They assume everyone can do the same."

"Ye gods!" Sulun tugged at his hair. "Are all the wealthy and powerful so brainless?"

"Damn near." Zeren munched absently on a cucumber slice. "That means I'll have to go from secretary to secretary to learn which one got the appeal from the creditors. Hmmm, just as well that Shibari was a noble; if he'd been a common man with common debts, the writ would have gone straight to some minor clerk, and stayed there. Then I'd have to question my way through all several hundred of them, which could take weeks."

"*Weeks?*"

"If not months. Then again, such a search would be cheap; as a captain of the city guards, I'd have enough power to bully the clerks into giving me the list without having to pay them anything. As it is, I'll have to work my way through a dozen or so secretaries, which should take no more than a day or two. However, I don't outrank that sort; I'll have to pay some sort of bribe: money, or lucrative information, or the promise of possible money to be gained otherwise by helping me. Now, I'm not wealthy enough to bribe a dozen secretaries, and the gods know how many I'll have to go through before I find the one who has, or had, the list."

Sulun rested his head on his hands, and swore.

"Perhaps just the gratitude, and potential favor of a guard captain would be enough to content them. I wouldn't rely on that alone, though." Zeren leaned forward and fixed Sulun with an intent look. "What sweetening can I offer, what information that would seem valuable to a city courtier, a secretary in the Ministry of Justice? You'll have to tell me. I'm a soldier, and no politician, and I've no idea what that sort would believe."

"Good gods, how would I know?" Sulun groaned. "I'm no courtier, only a philosopher. Petty nobles are as alien to me as they are to you."

"Money and power," Yanados murmured in the taut silence. "They all chase after money and power. How might giving you the list repay some secretary in money and power? Think hard."

"Money and power? Out of the creditors?" Doshi asked, scratching his blond stubble. "Well, any of them has more of either, now, than Shibari does."

"Thieves," Arizun spat, as emphatically as any adult. "Hmm. Maybe a falling out among thieves? A little thief holding out on a big thief? And the big thief offering a reward . . . Damn, no, that would still require money—which we don't have."

"Still," Sulun considered, "you may have an idea there."

Zeren strolled through the Hall of Records, Division of the Ministry of Justice, with his polished parade armor clashing softly. The loftily impassive look on his face was beginning to slip into grim boredom, despite his best efforts. He'd been through three secretaries so far, was on his way to see the fourth, and already devoutly wished he were out in the clean stink of the streets. At least by now, he had his carefully rehearsed lines as well memorized as any actor in the city could do. He pushed open the fourth ornate door of the day.

"Guard Captain Zeren Roshi's-son, to see His Lordship, Master Secretary Yidar Fiblen's-son." That part he could practically do in his sleep, especially the salute.

"Indeed?" The wizened petty noble behind the wide table had a manner reminiscent of a lizard. It matched his face and hands, if not his overdecorated robe. "Er, do sit down, Captain."

Stage two: getting comfortable already. A good sign. Zeren sat with an unfeigned sigh of relief, and rubbed a little obviously at his knee. "Ah, thank you. Good to get off my feet."

"Some refreshments, Captain?" the master secretary offered, reaching into a closely placed, and well-stocked, wine cabinet.

Wine already? Better and better. This interview might go quickly. "Don't mind if I do." Hmm, well-made goblets, and not a bad vintage. "Thank you much. This is a finer wine than a poor soldier's used to."

"And may I inquire what brings you to my office? No problems with any escaped prisoners, I hope?"

Ah, so that was his worry. Possibly worth looking into later. "Oh no, nothing like that. It's this matter of Shibari's estate, and his creditors. No doubt you heard of what happened last night?"

"Oh, of course. Tragic business—and so unnecessary." Yidar leaned closer, much like a lizard creeping up on a fly. "Were any of the, er, strongboxes recovered?"

Better and better. "That's exactly the problem, Master Secretary." *Now put down the cup and fix the old reptile with an eagle-eyed stare.* "We have reason to believe the fire was indeed deliberately set, but not by Shibari himself." *Which indeed it wasn't. Poor Nanya.*

"No?" *Ah, see him hesitate, slowly ease back, uncertain.*

"No, indeed." *Very stern, now.* "We suspect that the fire was set as a diversion, by one of Shibari's creditors who had entered the house earlier and found what he wanted."

"Good gods." The master secretary plumped back into his seat, thinking that over.

"Yes. I suspect that said creditor either found Shibari and his family already dead or else . . ." *Pause ominously.* ". . . helped them prematurely into that state—and then searched the house at his leisure."

"W-what—" *How breathlessly eager!* "What do you think he found?"

"Considerably more than enough money and valuables to recover his loan." *Now smile, grimly.* "I suspect he discovered where Shibari's real treasure might be found—and determined to keep it all for himself." *Now wait, watch for his reaction.*

"Good *gods!*" the secretary spluttered. "You don't think I had anything to do with that, do you?"

Better than we'd hoped! But keep calm. "Certainly not. You weren't one of Shibari's creditors—were you?"

"Absolutely not." The secretary smiled with reassured confidence. "I could show you the official listing of Shibari's creditors, if you like."

"Hmm, yes, I would like a copy of the listing, if you please." *Don't seem too grateful for it, not yet.*

"Nothing would be easier." Yidar scribbled briefly on a waxed tablet, then rang a small bell. Almost instantly, a well-trained clerk came in. The master secretary shoved the tablet at him. "Go fetch this document and have it copied, quickly."

The clerk bowed and left. Yidar settled back into his chair. Studying his smile, Zeren would have bet his commission just then that this particular master secretary was skimming sizable sums somewhere out of the Ministry of Justice. Independent debt-recovering, perhaps? Or was it something to do with those missing prisoners he'd mentioned? Worth checking into later.

"Could you tell me, Captain," Yidar leaned forward again, "just how you intend to find . . . the miscreant?"

Now. Drop it now. "I myself was at Shibari's house last night, first making some sort of order out of the crowd of creditors demanding justice, and afterward organizing the fire brigade. I had much opportunity, as you can guess, to see just who was present at the front gate when the fire broke out." A grim smile again. "I intend to go visit everyone on this little list of yours and see which ones I recognize on sight—and which one I don't."

"Er, don't?"

"My dear Master Secretary, it must be obvious that whoever was inside setting the fire could not have been outside at the front gate."

"Ah! Process of Elimination!" Yidar seemed terribly proud of using that term. Clearly he'd had some tutoring in proper logic and rhetoric, as befitting a gentleman. "Hmm, and tell me, once you identify the miscreant, what then will you do with him?"

Oho, see him sniffing the bait! "Why, bind him over for trial, of course." *Now shrug, look unconcerned.* "I leave it to persons more skilled than myself in such matters to extract confessions."

"And to discover the whereabouts of Shibari's treasure?"

Bait taken! "Certainly. It's most important that the debts be settled."

"But you have no idea of the whereabouts, or nature, or total amount of the treasure?"

See the gears engage, as Sulun would put it. "None whatever." *Shrug again.* "But then, that's not my department. My business is to catch the thief—and possible murderer—and hand him over to the Emperor's justice. Let others do the clerical work; I'm a guardsman."

"Yes indeed." Yidar smirked. "And a most dedicated one, too."

See him thinking: what a fool, what a dumb clod of a soldier. May the gods help any of Shibari's creditors who fall into the hands of the Ministry of Justice for the next year or more. This lizard will borrow the Emperor's own torturer if he must, hunting for treasure.

Who would believe that Shibari's only surviving treasure is Sulun? Sulun and Omis, and their cleverness, and what they might yet create to save all of Sabis, and more.

The clerk knocked discreetly at the door, then tiptoed

in and handed over a short document with its ink still wet. Yidar took it and studied it, frowning in concentration.

"Let me see the original, for accuracy," he snapped.

The clerk looked offended, but handed over another, longer parchment.

The master secretary looked from one to the other, and smiled. "There, you see?" he said, displaying them both to Zeren. "All the names and addresses and amounts are there, as is the complaint. It lacks only the clerk's statement and seal."

Zeren was careful to take the copy without snatching at it. "Hmm, yes. I see I'll have a lot of walking and interviewing to do." Gods, yes, there *were* a lot of them. "Thank you greatly for your help, Master Secretary. I'll remember it."

"Your gratitude is my reward," Yidar almost purred. "You will keep me informed of the progress of your investigation, won't you?"

"I'll certainly let you know when I've caught the wretch," Zeren promised, easing out of his chair. "Now, seeing how many faces I have to go study, I'd best get on with it. Thank you once again for your invaluable help." He clasped arms formally with the master-secretary, (noting that his arms *felt* like lizard-skin, too) rolled up the document, and left as quickly as he could.

A single glimpse back from the corridor showed that Yidar was studying the document, memorizing the names of Shibari's creditors, already trying to guess which one of them knew the secret of the dead noble's missing wealth.

Zeren hurried down the corridor, out of the Hall of Records, into the clean city air.

6

Idleness was too much a burden for any of them. Vari vented her impatience by marshalling a cleaning-party to dust and scrub Zeren's house. The housekeeper beat a hasty retreat to the tiny kitchen garden. Omis got the duty of marshalling the small children, which was exhausting enough to keep him from undue worry. Arizun and Yanados went out to ply Arizun's old trade of fortune-telling;

with a little luck, and the credulity of the average Sabisan citizen, they might charm up enough money to purchase a decent dinner. They would certainly pick up an earful of the latest news about Shibari's creditors and the hunt for the missing servants. Doshi took the opportunity to catch up on some sleep—until Omis, worn out with babysitting, woke him up and gave him the job instead. The children, finding out that Doshi was wonderfully teasable, enjoyed him immensely. Teigi, clinging fiercely to her new purpose and new identity, practiced—with variable results— disguising herself as a boy. She insisted on being called Ziya now, and a single scuffle with Tamiri convinced the smaller child of two things: the point was not arguable and Ziya was not safe to tease.

Sulun inspected and reinspected the gear saved from Shibari's house, wandered about Zeren's spartan rooms for a time, then went to commiserate with Omis about being skilled craftsmen bereft of their tools.

"But you still have the working model of that steam engine, don't you?" Omis noted. "That's an advantage—a pretty enough toy to impress the superficial sort, useful enough to impress the practical. You can win a patron with that alone. What do I have?"

"Oh come, now, you or Vari must have grabbed some of your pretty knives and cookware, at least. The masters of the house will be impressed by the one, and his wife or housekeeper by the other. Don't worry." Sulun clapped him on the shoulder. "You're a good craftsman, and it shows plainly."

"I hate patron-hunting. How long before we can get back to the Bombard Project?"

"I suppose that depends on what else our patron will want us to do."

"If he's an ill-tempered sort, we'll never have the time to work on our experiments." Omis pounded one fist on his thigh. "Gods, how wretchedly our business is arranged. There must be a better way than this!"

"There must be," Sulun agreed, lured off into a daydream of some fanciful kingdom where enlightened patrons provided their philosophers and craftsmen with necessities and otherwise left them alone, left them to experiment and study to their heart's content, without interruptions or demands for frivolous work. The gods knew what might be invented then!

The sound of the main door opening interrupted his speculations. Zeren stepped over the threshold, glittering in his parade armor, and halted in something like dismay as the smaller children descended on him with squeals of delight. Tamiri and Mido danced around him like moths, grabbing playfully at his hands, swordbelt and armor skirt, until Vari came to shoo them away. Sulun choked back a whoop of laughter at the sight of a captain of the City Guard of Sabis brought to a standstill, and very nearly routed, by a small gaggle of children.

Zeren shook his head and took another few steps, recovering his balance. "I'd forgotten what it was like," he muttered, then bellowed, "Buna! Get in here and start supper, with wine. No, bring the wine first." He tugged off his helmet and turned to Sulun. "Gods, I've got to get the taste of parchment dust out of my mouth. Go collect the others; we may as well discuss this over a good comfortable supper."

The housekeeper scurried in, threw Zeren a reproachful look and hustled off to the kitchen. Sulun collared Doshi and sent him out to find Yanados and Arizun. The others went to help marshal the children and set up for supper.

Zeren dropped into the nearest chair and began removing his formal armor, marvelling to himself at how different the house looked, sounded and felt when it was full of friends and children.

Dinner consisted of wine, sweet and sour breads, boiled white beans with cheese, a large salad, a modest baked fish and a large roast duck—the duck provided by Arizun, who didn't mention how he'd got it, and Yanados wasn't telling. The pair also brought in a respectable purse of mixed coins and a bigger bag of gossip.

"The old house has been stripped to the walls," Arizun reported around a mouthful of sweet bread. "I even saw charred timbers from the roof being sold for firewood."

Sulun, noticing how Teigi/Ziya winced at that, thought to ask, "Has anyone performed the proper rites for Shibari and his family?"

"Oh yes. The burial society of the Temple of Inota took care of that. The old master certainly paid them enough in his lifetime to cover the cost of the urns and the prayer service and maintaining the tomb. Nobody had to pay for the cremation, of course, but—Ow!" Arizun rubbed his ankle where Yanados had diplomatically kicked it.

"Yes, we should go to the tomb and pay our respects as soon as we can," Vari said, keeping an eye on Teigi/Ziya's set face.

"We heard that at least two of the creditors are fighting over the house and grounds," Yanados put in. "Some of the house servants have been caught, and the guards are supposed to be searching for the rest."

"Not too hard, I'll wager," Zeren commented over his wine cup.

"Without the family records, the law clerks can't tell the slaves from the free servants. It's a wretched mess." Yanados sighed. "We'd best not be seen too much outside, not until we get another patron."

"Or we could all be enslaved," Doshi added.

Teigi/Ziya shivered, but otherwise kept very still.

"Speaking of patrons, Zeren . . ." Sulun hinted.

The burly soldier pushed his plate aside, pulled out a sheet of parchment and spread it on the table. "The good news," he said, "is that I've tracked down all of Shibari's creditors, even learned which one took the lion's share. He has your forge and tools, and yes, he's rich. Very rich."

The apprentices couldn't keep from cheering, and the children joined in.

"The bad news is, he's Entori of Funay."

Instant silence fell. Omis broke it with a faint groan of, "No, not Entori the Miser!"

"Entori the slave-maker, you mean." Arizun shuddered. "The last debtors who couldn't pay him lost everything but the clothes they stood up in—and then they were sold at slave auction."

"How desperate could our master have been," Vari asked softly, "to risk falling into the hands of Entori the Infamous?"

"The gods know," Sulun murmured. But now he knew why Shibari had fallen on his sword, why his wife had killed herself and their children and burned the house.

Doshi said it for all of them. "Gods, must we put ourselves into the hands of our master's worst enemy? The man Shibari died to escape?"

Zeren leaned back and looked around at the doleful

little company. "There are a few other rich men on that list," he said, "but none so rich as Entori. Any of them might be willing to take on either a blacksmith or an engineer, complete with dependents, but none of the others would be inclined to take you both. Entori already has your forge, your lathe, all your large tools and supplies. He may be a wretched man to work for, but he's your best hope. I'm sorry."

There was a longer silence as the others thought that over. It ended in sighs of resignation.

"Ah, well," Sulun made it formal, "I suppose we'd best plan how to persuade him. Any suggestions?"

7

Entori's house was almost invisible from the street, hidden behind its high wall and skirts of wall-front shops. The front door crouched at the end of a shallow alley between a potter's and a rug merchant's. Small spy-windows flanked the plain doorway, one of them opening when Zeren pounded on the blank, bronze-sheathed door. Omis and Sulun traded worried glances while Zeren bawled out his name and business at the barely visible doorman. What manner of house was this, they wondered, that hid itself from all sight and disguised itself in a screen of the houses and bodies of the poor?

The spy-window snapped shut and the door creaked grudgingly half-open. Zeren, Omis and Sulun stepped from shade to shadow, into a dim bare corridor scarcely wider than the door, smelling faintly of dust and mold. The doorman, a palsied ancient in a threadbare tunic worn as gray as the rest of him, hurried to close the door behind them. In the deepened gloom, the pale sunlight at the far end of the corridor beckoned like mirage.

Sulun and Omis traded looks again. They hadn't known what to expect of the house of Entori the Infamous: perhaps furnishings of boastful, overwhelming, barbaric splendor; perhaps manacles and whips mounted on the walls, or portraits of all the victims Entori had brought low in his long career. The last thing they could have imagined was this vast, quiet, dusty barrenness.

"Stay here," Zeren barked at the servant. "I know the way." He led the others boldly toward the dim light.

All the way down the corridor they heard no sound but their own footsteps, saw no decorations or lamps or god-shrines of any kind, met no other living thing but a single wayward moth. Sulun felt oddly grateful for the presence of that moth; without it, he might have imagined that he was walking into a tomb.

The room led out into a small courtyard with a square rain-pool in its center. The surrounding walkway, its walls interrupted by closed doors and curtained windows, was covered with slanting tile roofs that aimed toward the pool.

Entori the Miser wasted not even rainwater.

"Is the whole place a silent warehouse?" Omis muttered under his breath. "How can people live like this?"

At the far side of the rainwater pool, in a narrow bar of sunlight, sat a woman in a plain dark dress, reading a book-sized scroll. She glanced up, frowning slightly, as the trio approached.

Zeren, having no idea who she was, but noting that she didn't strike the usual posture and attitude of a servant, gave her a polite, half-formal salute and repeated the party's names, titles and business. Omis noticed that she had a most intriguing face: the straight dark hair, almost black eyes, delicate bones and pointed chin usually associated with the old Sukkti blood; not a young or conventionally pretty woman, certainly, but interesting. Sulun peeked at the book in her hands, and saw that it was a treatise on ancient history by a respectably honest author; it was the most encouraging item he'd seen so far in Entori's house.

"My brother is in his study," the woman said, waving a languid hand toward the mouth of another corridor behind her. "Second door on the right." Her eyes were already straying back to her book.

Sulun glanced back at her as the three resumed march. He hadn't known that Entori had a sister, much less that she was of a scholarly turn of mind. He just might have a possible ally in this place.

The next corridor led into the formal dining hall, a vast and shadowy room filled with enough banners, tapestries, lamps, cabinets of ancestral busts and bits of statuary to have furnished all the rest of the house they'd yet seen. Zeren rolled his eyes at the clutter, searched his way to an ornate door on the right, rapped on it and announced the party for the third time.

"Enter, enter," snapped a dry, gravelly voice.

Zeren pushed open the door, which did not creak, and led the others into Entori's lair. Sulun and Omis stifled a gasp of surprise at the sheer amount of parchment: countless sheets and scrolls of it, filling and jamming the cubbyhole cabinets that climbed the walls, cluttering the massive table that commanded the center of the room, intermixed with clay tablets, wax tablet-books, weighing-scales and weights of assorted sizes, stylus shafts, pens, inkwells and an abacus or two—enough for the records room of a small tax-office. A large strongbox behind the table completed the illusion, though Sulun guessed that the bulk of Entori's ready money was concealed elsewhere.

The room was lit by thin sunlight through the window behind the table, and by a single bronze oil-lamp set like a wave-washed rock in that parchment sea. The flickering yellow light picked out a circle of account records, a pair of thin hands resting on them, a heavy carved chair, a thick fur robe, the bald head and blinking dark eyes of an indeterminably-aged man who could only be Entori the Miser. The thick white ruff of the fur robe, much too heavy for this weather, gave his thin bald head and narrow hands the unflattering suggestion of a vulture.

"Yes?" His voice added to the impression.

This, Sulun thought, *is he who destroyed our master and all his house.*

Zeren pulled out his own bit of parchment and opened it with a flourish. "You are Entori, Yeshinan's-son, creditor of the late Shibari to the amount of 27,382 silvers?"

Entori blinked. "Yes . . ." He quickly added, "And I did not recover the full amount of the debt."

"But you did recover—" Zeren pretended to check his sheet of parchment again, "one blacksmith's forge and anvil, with sundry related tools, one mechanic's lathe, with sundry related tools, plus several mechanical devices in various stages of completion. Not so?"

"Er, yes . . ." Entori rattled his fingers on the tabletop, clearly dying to see what else was on that list. "But that doesn't begin to cover the debt! Those things are of no use to me, and where can I sell them? And when? And for how much? A pittance, five hundred silvers at best—no, no, they don't begin to cover the amount of the debt."

Omis squirmed, biting back considerable words. Sulun elbowed him still.

Zeren tucked the parchment back in his belt and leaned forward, smiling. "Still, I think there may be a way to give you some satisfaction," he purred. "You know, we're trying to settle this business as thoroughly as possible for all concerned."

"Satisfaction?" Entori asked, edging further into the lamplight.

"Shibari did leave so many debts unsettled, especially with the house burned and its contents largely destroyed. We're trying to give the creditors as much value as possible, you know—"

"Satisfaction?" Entori nudged.

Spring the trap, Sulun thought, biting his lip.

"As you said, the tools are useless to you." Zeren straightened, snapping out the words like numbers in an account list. "Likewise, Shibari's displaced craftsmen are useless without their tools—like farmers without land, or land without farmers to tend it."

Entori blinked again, registering the truth of the analogy.

"Now, put the craftsman and his tools together, and one might see some profit out of this lamentable business." Zeren leaned closer. "I have it on good authority that these particular craftsmen were working on some most valuable devices when Shibari made his ill-advised sea trade venture. Some of them—" He dropped his voice to a conspiratorial whisper, "—were of . . . interest to the military. They might still be so, if properly developed. Do you take my meaning, good sir?"

Entori took the hint, at least. One hand slid upward to rattle thoughtful fingers on his chin. "And of course," he murmured, "the officer who presented these . . . profitable devices . . . to the right eyes could expect some expression of gratitude from them?"

Zeren smiled like a tradesman closing a deal. "I see that we understand each other."

Entori nodded thoughtfully, and rolled expressionless eyes toward Sulun and Omis. "I assume these are the craftsmen in question?"

"The two masters," Zeren corrected. "There are also their assistants."

Omis crossed fingers for luck behind his back. Technically, the apprentices all belonged to Sulun. Only a long stretch of the imagination could label Vari as a blacksmith's assistant, to say nothing of the children.

Entori's eyes narrowed. "Just how many extra mouths will I be taking into my household?" he asked.

'Will be taking' . . ? Sulun dared to hope.

"Hardly extra," Zeren snorted. "A grand total of ten—"

"Ten!"

"And a bargain, at the price of their keep." Zeren shrugged with elaborate unconcern. "Of course, if you'd rather not gather the harvest for the price of the seed, I'm sure Shibari's other creditors—"

"Not so fast, not so fast." Entori raised a birdlike hand. "I didn't say I wasn't interested. . . ." He cocked a cold eye at Sulun and Omis. "But of course, I wish to know what value I can expect to receive for taking on this . . . seed money expense."

"But of course." Zeren waved theatrically toward Sulun and Omis, and stepped aside.

At the cue, the two bowed formally. They straightened, whipped two large baskets out from under their cloaks, and opened them together. Sulun pulled out the little bronze steam engine model and placed it on the clearest section of the table. Omis produced a small brass firecup filled with treated charcoal, and slid it under the globe of the engine.

"My design," Sulun intoned, pointing at the assemblage.

"My workmanship," Omis echoed.

The words sounded natural and unforced, as well they should after yesterday's hours of practice. Omis even managed a suitably impressive flourish as he whipped out his flint and steel striker and lit the charcoal.

The distilled wine fumes caught at the first strike, shooting up impressive yellow and blue flames. Omis tossed a really unnecessary cue-glance at Sulun, and stepped back. Now for the distracting patter while waiting for the water to boil. If only he could manage this without fumbling his lines. *Gods, why should I have to play an actor, too?* Sulun complained to himself as he struck an orator's pose and began.

"Know, oh most wise and honored host, that this is but a small version of that which might be." *Pray it so, or ten desperate people might soon be out in the street again.* "As you see this little globe rests, like a wheel, upon an axle whereby it might spin." *And hope the water boils soon!* "Within it lies a small quantity of water, easily replaced."

But how would one replace the water at a steady rate in order to keep the globe spinning? Design problem: deal with it later.

"The fire heats the water, making it boil unto vapor." *Boil soon, dammit!* "This vapor, being closer to that divine state of the spirit than is mere fluid or gross earthly matter, seeks to rise toward heaven."

Seeks to expand, actually, and spirit has nothing to do with it, but this is no time to argue with common misconceptions.

"Yet first it must escape this imprisoning globe, and what escape may it find save through these three identically curved little pipes?" *Nudge one of them, encourage the fool toy to spin.* "Thus, escape it does, so fiercely seeking its freedom that in leaping outward toward the free air it doth thrust backward against the door of its former prison."

There, is that a faint wisp of escaping steam? Please? "Even as a sailor, stepping from a small boat to the dock, doth thrust the boat away from him with his lattermost foot . . ."

Yes! Steam, at last!

"So this backward thrust presses the pipes away from the direction of the escaping steam, er, vapor . . ." *Move, dammit!* "And as the pipes are firmly affixed to the globe, which in turn rests upon its axle, the globe hath no choice save to . . ."

There it goes!

". . . Spin."

Sure enough, the little globe spun: slowly at first, then faster, whirling merrily in its soft halo of escaping steam.

Entori peered closer, fascinated, his dark eyes very wide and round. *Quick now, before the water ran out or the man's normal suspicion reasserted itself.*

"Consider, milord, a much larger globe spinning thus. Picture it standing upon the deck of a ship. Picture the axle extended over the sides of the vessel, and wheels attached. Picture the wheels rimmed with oars reaching into the water. Consider, oh most wise and far-seeing, how fast and steadily such a ship could go—regardless of the vagaries of winds or fatigue of rowers."

Now hit the conclusion good and hard.

"A ship driven by such an engine would be mistress of the seas, fearing no storm nor dead winds, nor pirates.

"How wealthy would her master be?"

Entori nodded slowly, a smile spreading widely across his face, as the vision took hold. "Tell me," he murmured, "did Shibari commission the building of such a ship?"

"No, milord. He considered it too newfangled and undignified." *Well, that was half the truth anyway.* "Also, he would not spare the time required to build it, preferring to gamble on quick profits with existing ships." *That, too, was part of the truth.*

"Shibari was a fool." Entori sat back, folded his hands, and turned his attention back to Zeren. "I agree, Captain, that there are possibilities here. Yes, I'll take in these craftsmen of yours. When we have ships of the sort that will interest the officers of the Imperial Navy, I will certainly inform you."

Zeren gave him a smile and a slight bow. "I have no doubt that there will be other such profitable developments," he purred. "I'll send the craftsmen and their assistants to you before the day is out."

"I'll have rooms prepared," Entori murmured, reaching for a stylus and tablet. "Good day, Captain."

Omis and Sulun suppressed sighs of relief as they turned and followed Zeren out the door. Only when they were out in the corridor did Omis dare to speak.

"We're out of the cookpot, but maybe into the fire. Sulun, it will take months to build a big steam engine, much less mount it on a ship, test it, get it seaworthy. And there are certain design problems. And when will we have time to work on the bombard?"

"We'll manage," Sulun promised. "At least now we'll have the tools, and a roof over our heads."

'I wish," Zeren muttered, "that you'd had a model of the bombard instead. Sabis needs land defense more than fast ships."

*   *   *

The little company arrived, bags and baggage, children and all, shortly after noon. The porter let them in at once, led them down a different set of gloomy corridors and into their new quarters chattering all the way, quite garrulous now that there were none but other Entori house servants to overhear.

"Well, well, well, so you're the new craftsmen of the house! All of you, then? Hah, I didn't think so. Can't quite see the babies hammering iron, eh?"

"Give them time," Omis huffed.

"Oh, yes indeed, yes indeed. Meanwhile, best keep them out of the master's sight, or else put 'em to sweeping floors or some such harmless work, keep 'em looking busy. Master doesn't like to pay for useless mouths. Clever idea, though, claiming four apprentices instead of a wife and three children; he set aside full three rooms for your lot, and as much for goodman Sulun and his. How d'ye like the furnishings, eh?"

Omis and Vari surveyed the first of the three cubicles, and bit their respective tongues.

"Not much cabinet space," Vari dared to comment.

"Eh, well, you can always get more cabinets out of your pay. Don't go borrowing bits of furniture from storage without the mistress's express permission now, tempting as it looks. Always remember Master Entori may run the business, but Mistress Eloti runs the household. 'Tis a fine point in your favor that she likes you."

"Likes us?" Sulun put in. "I didn't know she'd even seen us."

"Oh, she did. She has her ways. Heh-heh! Yes. Master wanted to hire you, right enough, but the expense worried him, so he talked to Mistress about it. When he stopped for breath she put in a word. 'Hire them,' she said. 'Good investment,' she said. Then he went back to talking and rattled on for another good half-hour, and finally concluded by saying he'd go ahead and hire you all. Then it was a question of what to pay you."

"Really?" Sulun said. He hadn't dared bring that up himself; it wasn't seemly for an unemployed craftsman to bargain with a master who was graciously consenting to save him from begging on the street. Zeren hadn't dared to bring up the subject either; it would have seemed out of character, considering his argument for Entori hiring the lot of them in the first place. "And what did they decide?"

"At first Master rattled on and on about the expense of feeding ten new mouths, plus added costs of lamp oil and laundry soap and all like that, and said you should be grateful enough for that and allowance for materials—"

Behind them, Arizun snorted, loudly.

"But then Mistress pointed out that unpaid hirelings tend to steal, and unpaid craftsmen tend to pad their budgets for materials, and that better paid servants tend to keep their mouths shut about their master's business. Master thought about that for a bit, and suggested that two silver pieces a month should buy proper secrecy—"

This time it was Doshi who did the derisive snorting.

"But Mistress pointed out that there's many who would pay far better to keep so valuable a secret as that steam powered ship engine, and she argued for a full gold piece per month. Master ranted and raved a bit, then thought it over, and finally agreed on one gold for each master and eight silvers for each apprentice, which isn't too shabby, especially for so . . . ah . . . economical a household as this one."

Sulun shrugged. No, that wasn't too shabby for this household, and he could make up the differences needed by padding his requests for materials.

The apprentices were already unloading their personal gear in their assigned cubicles, already arguing over who got which bed, which drawer, which clothespress.

"Now, the workshops are down this way."

"This way" led down another corridor, past rooms choked with piles of furniture, parchment, household furnishings, odd tools, clothing, bags of grains, sealed jars of wine, oil and spices, assorted arms and armor, crates and sacks and barrels of unidentifiable goods—loot from unnumbered debt forclosures. Omis found the sight infinitely depressing, while Sulun took notes.

Then out into a back courtyard near the wall, a courtyard filled with larger spoils, heavy equipment, bigger tools: and to one side of the tangle sat Omis's forge and anvil, and Sulun's lathe. Omis fell upon the anvil with a cry of joy, and hugged it to his muscular chest. Sulun only frowned.

"It'll take days of work to make a proper workshop out

of all this mess," he pointed out. "Just clearing space. And where can we put all this other junk? And there's no roof. We'll need to set up a canopy—"

"I'm sure ye've enough apprentices to do it," the porter sniffed. "And there'll be room for storage in the eighth room down the hall, once Master sells that lot—say, another two days."

Sulun and Omis looked at each other. Plainly they'd be given no help settling in or setting up. On the other hand, they'd be left alone to arrange the workshop as they pleased and, incidentally, to explore the other tools and engines in that pile.

"Very good." Sulun put on that polite, politic smile that was becoming easier with practice. "We'll set up the rooms tonight and start on this after breakfast tomorrow. How long until dinner?"

Dinner was at sundown, in the chill formal banquet room lit with a few sullen lamps. The half-seen statuary lining the walls seemed alternately to glower or smirk in the uncertain light. At the high table sat Entori, still wearing his fur-collared robe, and his sister Eloti, to his left, wearing another, equally subdued, dark dress. The entertainment consisted of harp-twanging by a skinny youth who, so Vari whispered for her husband to pass on, spent the rest of the day as a sweeper. A scullery maid doubled as server to the high table.

At the lower table sat Omis and his family, Sulun and his apprentices, the porter, a disturbingly slender cook, another slatternly maid, a sour-faced elderly woman who described herself variously as housekeeper/seamstress/lady's maid, a drowsing ancient dressed in the robes of a third-level mage, and three burly, inexpressive men whose duties were not described but who wore heavy truncheons at their belts. The food was plain, so was the servants' livery, and conversation was subdued.

Noting all the covert glances his party got from the other servants, Sulun could barely wait for the dinner to end, the master and mistress to depart, and the usual after-dinner servants' gathering to begin. There was much he needed to learn here.

He noted that the servants were dawdling over their food.

Dinner seemed interminable, though the master of the house ate fast. Entori gulped at his food like a well-trained but hungry watchdog, with no spattering or notable haste, but with no wasted motion. Mistress Eloti ate with a similar economy, but with less speed. Entori finished well before her, and sat rattling his fingers on his winecup as if debating whether or not to have more wine. Eloti, if anything, slowed down. Entori gave up and had his cup refilled. They finished their last mouthfuls at almost the same moment, and Sulun wondered which of them had timed it that way. Entori stood, obliging the rest of the household (except the harper) to rise too, then swept out the door with his sister on his arm.

"At last," muttered the serving girl, as the rest of the servants sat down again.

"Hush," the old housekeeper snapped. "Wait."

The others gulped their food but kept quiet, watching the door. Sulun's gang traded bewildered glances.

The harper stopped in mid-note and came over to the table, casting a quick look down the corridor as he passed the door. "They're gone," he said, shoving into an empty seat. "Pass the beans."

"Hell, pass the wine!" rumbled one of the house-guards.

"Amen," mumbled the house wizard, holding out his cup.

The serving girl came over, grinning, and the supper promptly became more lively.

Omis gulped at his refilled cup, and made a face. "Gods! Is this stuff half vinegar, or what?"

The guardsmen laughed. "Entori buys cheap," one of them chuckled. "But don't worry; we've a way to get at the better stuff, once this is gone."

"Hush," snapped the housekeeper again, glaring side-long at the wizard. "No sense encouraging such things."

"Oh, why not?" Another guardsman laughed. "Let Aobi tell it. Our Terribly Important new friends will find out soon enough, anyway."

"Important?" Vari puzzled in mid-bite.

"Of course," sniffed the housekeeper. "The master hired the whole lot of you at once, and at good money too, after talking privately with a commander of the City Guard. That, from a merchant and moneylender who never parts with a copper bit unless he's weighed it first. We can all make good guesses."

Vari turned a bewildered glance to her husband, who bounced it to Sulun.

"Engine-makers," the wizard hiccupped. "More damned protection for fires—"

"As I was saying," Aobi the guardsman resumed, "the Old Man has barrels and barrels of wine in the cellar, but he hardly touches it himself. Always hoping to trade it for something better, he is. Now the stuff he's had there the longest—and I swear, he has a good lot that's been down there more than four years—might rightfully be expected to have turned sour by this time."

The other servants at the table snickered and grabbed at the wine ewer.

"Now Gipu here—" Aobi nudged the guard next to him, "can tell you about the empty jars he found in one of the storerooms. Enough to hold a barrel's worth of good wine, eh?" He nudged Gipu again, who chuckled mountainously around a mouthful of stew. "Why let the poor things stand about empty, says I. As for the barrel, we refilled it with good wine vinegar, bought with our own pay. Does the Old Man ever tap that barrel, he'll find the wine's turned too sour to drink. Oh, pity. He'll probably sell the vinegar for a better price than we paid."

"Meanwhile," Gipu added, "we get to drink better than this swill. Jug empty yet, Loac?"

The third guard upended the ewer in his cup. "Finished," he announced. "Get the good stuff."

The maid grabbed the jug and ran off giggling.

"So," Aobi purred at Omis, leaning closer, "just what is it that makes your lot so valuable to the Old Man, eh?"

"Ten of you, for such good money," Loac added, favoring Sulun with a thoughtful eye. "A blacksmith, maybe, one could understand. But so many?"

Sulun glanced around, seeing all the servants' eyes on him and Omis's almost desperate look, and realized how close he was to arousing the enmity of his new household. This miserly household thrived on secrets, and he'd best give these people a convincing one. Simply calling himself a Natural Philosopher wouldn't do.

"Engines for ships," he offered in a properly conpiratorial tone. "Ships that can sail against the wind, or outrun pirates. We know how to build them."

The servants traded glances, nodded in understanding, and smiled.

"If you need any help," Aobi offered, "Just ask."

"Forges, fires . . . more damned work," mumbled the wizard. "Where's that wine?"

The maid came back with the ewer full of better-smelling wine, and dumped a generous dollop in Sulun's cup. The other servants promptly clamored for her attention.

Omis took the opportunity to whisper in Vari's ear. She nodded, got up from the table and began collecting children. "Time the little ones went to bed," she explained sweetly to any who might care to listen, then hustled the children and herself safely out and away.

Omis stuck out his cup for a refill, and grimly prepared to make a long night of it.

8

"Sulun!" A fierce whisper, followed by a heavily shoving hand. "Sulun, get up! The sun's high, and we've much to do."

Sulun opened one eye, closed it again, and groaned.

"Here, drink the winterleaf tea." Omis's calloused hand shoved a steaming mug close to Sulun's nose. "The wife says it's good for wine-head. Drink, and get up."

Seeing that there was no help for it, Sulun drank the foul-tasting stuff and managed to roll himself upright. Omis held out a plain robe, and after a moment's hesitation Sulun struggled into it. "Gods," he muttered. "Remind me never to drink more than four cups at one sitting again. How did you survive?"

"There's more of me to saturate than there is of you. Try eating more. Hmm, do you want breakfast?"

'No!" Sulun pulled on the robe, hauled himself to his feet and stumbled to the pitcher and washbasin in the corner. "Gods, gods . . . was it worth all that wine? I can't remember."

"Oh yes." Omis sat down on the bed Sulun had just quitted. "We learned a great deal indeed. First, the master leaves all the running of the household to his sister, who manages surprisingly well, but is something of a mystery to everyone. Second, the Old Man resents the noble families terribly; it appears that they don't accept him socially, though they're friendly enough with men not nearly so wealthy. The servants think it's because he's such a mean and miserly sort that he can't possibly amuse them; he thinks it's because he's descended from one of the old Sukkti houses, if you please."

"Sukkti?" Sulun puzzled as he dried his face on a threadbare cloth. "I didn't think there were any of the old race left. How many centuries has it been since the conquest?"

"Six at least. Who cares? One doesn't have to be pure Sukkti to have a bit of the old blood, as surely half of Sabis must. I'm just telling you what the servants say the Old Man believes." Omis cracked his knuckles noisily. "But to get on, Entori is the sort who nurses a grudge. He intends to buy that power which he can't win with his personal charm, and for that he needs money—always more money."

"That, we knew," Sulun grumbled, reaching for his comb.

"It doesn't end there. The Old Man cares not overmuch how he makes his money or who he deals with to get it." Omis leaned forward, making the bedwebbing creak. "Nor does he care how his servants are treated, so long as the money comes in. Consider, friend Sulun, that galley slaves on his ships tend to die off at a higher rate than usual."

"The steam engine . . ." Sulun frowned, yanking the comb through his woolly tangle of hair.

"Yes, the steam engine for ships. It gets more interesting still. Entori's business has suffered from the loss of the northern trade as well as from the piracy out at sea. Many of his creditors have gone down, leaving him with cartloads of goods that he has trouble selling. He hopes to make up for this by—listen well—supplying the army and navy. You see where this leads?"

Sulun put the comb down and looked about for his sandals. "Does Zeren know this?"

"If he didn't before, he does now." Omis sat back with a satisfied grin. "I sent Arizun scampering off to him with a message, just after the morning report."

"Morning what?" Sulun asked, fumbling his way into his sandals.

"Another little custom of the household. Every morning— early, mind you—all the servants are required to show up in the master's office and give brief, concise reports about their work and the condition of the supplies. All the rest of us went this morning, and we had difficulty enough explaining why you weren't present. You'll have to be there tomorrow, and with something to report."

"Report?" Sulun forced his aching brain into action. "By tomorrow morning? We'll be lucky if we have half the shop set up by then. What, in the name of all the gods together, are we expected to report?"

"We'll have to think of something." Omis pulled himself off the bed and offered a hand to Sulun. "Shall we begin?"

Two hours further into the morning, the task seemed just as formidable, even with the help of all four apprentices and two of the interested house-guards. The storerooms and back courtyard of Entori's house contained an incredible amount of hoarded junk.

There were also a few unsuspected treasures.

"Sulfur," Yanados whispered in Sulun's ear while the guards were busy on the far side of the courtyard. "This room, here—Arizun made the map—by the back wall there are five big grainbags full of sulfur. The dust is so thick on them, I'll wager Entori hasn't seen or thought about them in ten years."

"I'll go see them at lunchtime," Sulun whispered back. "Don't let anyone see that map." Gods, the Bombard Project! He'd almost forgotten it.

Yanados nodded, rolled the parchment quickly, and scurried off. Sulun caught Teigi—no, think of her always as Ziya—watching him, and quickly touched a warning finger to his lips. Ziya looked at her feet, frowned, and trudged off after Yanados.

Then Omis came rolling up, looking harried but somewhat pleased. "I've found most of the tools," he reported, "plus some oddments I never used before. Given a half-moon's time, I think we really can assemble a workable shop."

That struck another memory. "Omis," Sulun asked very quietly, "do you think we can assemble enough money to keep paying the rent on that workshop down by the river?"

Omis thought a moment, cast a quick glance around the yard, and whispered back, "Ask Vari, at lunch."

Sulun grinned agreement and took the tools off to the cleared space around his forge.

Next came Doshi, pausing for a moment in the task of clearing the useless bits of debt plunder out of the courtyard. "Master Sulun," he murmured, keeping his voice as low as the others had, "in one of those storerooms I found some old maps—merchants' work, I think—of the north country: Torrhyn, Jarrya . . . lands long gone to the barbarians. I recognized some of the old hills, the streams . . ." He shook his head quickly, as if fighting off tears. "Beautiful work. I wonder if I might have time and parchment to copy some of them."

"Certainly," Sulun promised. "We'll discuss it at lunch." Money for good parchment? When they might need every last copper to keep the riverside workshop? But it would keep Doshi happy, and everyone's spirits were unsettled now. . . .

Then came Arizun, toting a basketful of oddities. "Master Sulun," he chirped, not caring if the guardsmen heard him, "we've found some good canvas sheeting, enough to make a sun roof over the forge if Master Entori will allow it. And what in the nine hells are these?" He held out his basket.

Sulun looked in, pawed among the glittering assemblies of metal, and stifled a gasp of recognition. "Valves," he whispered, almost reverently. "Good, solid trapdoor valves. The kind used for piping steam into bathhouses. And a ball-and-socket joint. All made of good brass . . ." A genuine inspiration, breathed of smiling gods, settled gently as a sacred dove on his shoulder. He stood up, smiling. "Yes, I think we'll have something of value to report tomorrow morning."

Lunch was a simple affair of bread, cheese, dried fruit and thin beer, eaten out in the courtyard under pretext of not slowing down the work. The guards, chuckling at such unnessary dedication, went inside to eat where the noon sun wouldn't bother them. Sulun's gang huddled together and spoke in low voices.

"A wretched, dusty place," Vari was grumbling. "Nowhere to dry the laundry save up on the roof, and I fear the mildew will get at it. So little light gets in through those miserable, tiny windows, one can barely see to clean. And the dust! Dust everywhere, especially near those storerooms, where cleaning is just impossible. I said as much to Mistress, when she came up on me in the hallway, and she said there was no help for it and I must do the best I can."

"The Old Man seems to like his house dark and musty," Doshi muttered. "I fear to think how we'd fare if plague came through the city. Plague demons could thrive here."

"Keep out in the sunlight whenever possible," Yanados advised. "We've excuse enough, with the workshop here."

"Speaking of workshops," Sulun cut in, frowning over the figures on his waxed tablet, "we'll earn enough to keep the workshop by the river, but that won't leave us much money else."

"None for the bombard, you mean?" Omis laughed bitterly. "Easily answered; add to the list of expenses for the steam engine."

"That, at least," Sulun agreed. "How much iron will you need to make another bombard? How much will that cost us?"

"We can always do a bit of work outside," Arizun offered. "I can go back to telling fortunes in the market, and Yanados could always work as a hired sword." He dodged fast as Yanados aimed a swat at him.

"I don't suppose we could spare a few coppers for parchment," Doshi sighed. "Those beautiful maps . . . I wonder how the old country has changed."

"Just take the damned maps," Arizun snorted. "If the Old Man ever remembers and wants them, he'll send one of the servants to get them—and the folk in this house tell each other if they find anything missing, long before they'll tell him. You'll have plenty of time to sneak them back."

"True." Doshi brightened.

"And we have the sulfur now," Sulun went on, noting how the others pricked up their ears and Yanados grinned. "Five full sacks of it, lying unnoticed in Entori's storehouse for enough years to collect a thick furring of dust. I doubt he even knows what it is, let alone what its properties are."

"Rest assured, he'll notice if any of it goes missing," Doshi commented. "From what the servants tell, he keeps tally of every ounce of straw in a bale."

"But recall the servants' trick with the wine," Sulun

reminded him. "Do we replace any sulfur we take with some other yellow powder, and he can be persuaded that the 'mineral salt' has gone bad—soured, like the wine."

Omis guffawed. Vari shushed him, casting nervous glances back at the near doors and windows.

"So we have sulfur," Yanados agreed. "But how shall we purchase charcoal and saltpeter? Can we pad our budget enough to cover that?"

"And flux, for my ironworking?" Omis added.

"Most probably, we can ask for it outright. Do we say we need it for making the steam engines, he'll agree to the purchase."

"In any event," Omis considered, "we'll need to show him good progress on the steam engine. We'll not have the shop ready to work for a few days yet. What shall we tell him tomorrow morning?"

"I'll rehearse my speech tonight," Sulun promised, "rather than stay late after dinner again."

Everyone else chuckled at that.

"Another way to cut our actual expenses . . ." Sulun pulled the two brass valves out of his robe and held them up. "Be certain the Old Man doesn't know what these are. Do we ask for time, money and good brass to make valves for the steam engine, we can apply it to other things—and then use these."

Doshi and Yanados recognized the objects, and laughed agreement. The others looked puzzled. Omis took one of the valves and turned it over and over in his hands, studying its construction. Sulun handed him the ball-and-socket joint as well.

"If you can drill that out and attach a sizable funnel, we'll have a means to keep the steam engine steadily supplied with water."

"Aha!" Omis caught on, peering closer at the brass joint. "If I need to excuse all my ironworking for the bombard, I'll make the funnel for this out of iron. She'll rust, of course, but the Old Man won't know that until later."

"We can do it, then." Doshi actually grinned. "Entori will have his engine-driven ship and Zeren will have his bombard. How long will it take, think you?"

"Oh, that reminds me," Arizun put in, "I took your message to his house. He should give us some answer by tomorrow."

Vari, Sulun noticed, wasn't listening; she was watching Ziya, hitching closer to her, reaching tentatively for a bowed shoulder. Now that he looked, Sulun saw that the child was crying silently, face hidden under the raised hood of her robe. Sulun recalled, with a twinge of remorse, that he'd barely spoken to the child in the past two days.

"Eh, Ziya," he offered, clumsily patting the girl's nearer shoulder, "I hadn't meant to neglect you. What did you wish to say?"

Ziya pulled a deep breath, which caught and then rushed out again bearing a ragged spool of words. "Ohhh, it's all so shameful!"

"Huh?" Sulun couldn't imagine what she meant.

"Shameful!" Ziya gulped again. "All of you plotting lies and tricks to rob your master. Did you serve my father so?"

The others gnawed their lips and looked at each other. Yes, in truth they had played a few such games on Shibari. Not many, not so many as this, but they had done it.

"Not at all," said Vari, sounding utterly sincere. "Your father was a good master, not at all like this one."

Ziya hiccupped, rubbed her nose, and sat up a little straighter.

Sulun gave Vari a quick look of guilty gratitude, which she barely acknowledged. He understood. It wasn't the first time, nor would it likely be the last, that they'd used well-meant lies to give the child some hope, some reason not to roll over and die of misery. If ever she learned the truth, would she forgive?

For that matter, Sulun wondered with a shiver, did the gods do the same to men? If so, could mankind ever forgive the gods?

Then Ziya sniffed and spoke again. "Do bad masters always make their people bad?"

Even Vari couldn't answer that one; she threw Sulun a look of silent appeal. He could feel the weight of everyone else's eyes, and Ziya's question, fall on him.

Well, hang it, couldn't he justify himself in words so simple that a child could understand them?

"No, child. Bad masters only make it difficult for their people to be good."

There. Chew upon that, you gods.

Ziya turned wide, wet eyes up to him. "But not impossible?" she asked.

"No, not impossible. Just . . . difficult."

The child nodded acceptance and went back to munching on her bread and cheese, sorrow passing like a quick summer storm. The others dug into their food, as if determined to finish fast and get back to work.

Sulun pulled up the hood of his robe and glanced suspiciously at the half-clouded sky, wondering why he felt as if he'd just made a pledge before heaven.

9

Early next morning Sulun stood in line with the other yawning and bleary-eyed servants, awaiting the audience of accounting with Master Entori. Omis stood behind him, the apprentices in a cluster beyond, after them Vari and the children. They'd all been up long after dinner, rehearsing their lines. Sulun and Omis carried waxed tablets scribbled with lists and figures, Vari would rely on her excellent memory, the apprentices and children would merely look respectful and nod agreement with their elders. The other servants apparently used a similar method, for Sulun noted all three of the house-guards entering the master's office together, just ahead of him.

Given his own gang's agreed tactics, Sulun didn't know whether to hope the guards would stay closeted with Entori for a brief while or a long one. Meanwhile, he pored through his notes one more time.

The guards' interview proved to be a short one, and they came out together looking bored. A good sign, Sulun dared hope. The door remained shut for a few moments more; then the small bell sounded from beyond it, summoning the next in line. Sulun drew a deep breath, pushed on the heavy door, and entered.

Entori sat at his littered table, just as Sulun had seen him first, save that he wore a different dark, heavy robe. He raised his eyes from his pen and freshly marked ledger to acknowledge his latest servant and demanded, simply: "Well?"

Sulun bowed formally, lifted the first of his tablets and

began. "Tools for workshop: nearly assembled save for forge-bellows, estimated at five coppers; double-span tongs, estimated seven coppers; twenty-weight of brazing flux, eight coppers two irons . . ." Sulun carefully made his voice a soothing drone, the reading of the list reminiscent of a prayer-chant.

Entori began fidgetting with his pen, but his eyelids refused to droop.

No, best not to ask for too much new iron today.

Sulun switched to the second tablet. "Now, concerning the first try at a full-sized engine, a small cargo vessel should be used. No sense buying more brass than we need before we've determined the proper ratios and balances . . ."

"I can obtain the loan of a fifty-tonner," Entori cut in.

"Hmm, so . . . It will not be necessary to take the ship out of service at once, not until we have the engine ready for testing. We need only measure and chart the ship before then, which may be done in a few days. We shall need carpenters to assemble the paddle wheels also. I have here the design, with tentative measurements that can be revised after we've inspected the ship." Sulun handed over another tablet. "We assume that building the engine shall require some five tons of brass, at—"

"Five tons?" Entori sat up jowls darkening.

"Er, one tenth the weight of the ship, we presume," Sulun managed to keep his voice calm, philosophical, unruffled, despite the sweat gathering on his back. "Surely no more than that, possibly less, but we must be sure—"

"Five *tons!*" Glowering, Entori pulled a short whip up from his lap.

"Master," Sulun bowed low, shivering. "This engine uses forces of great power, and we must take great care to contain them. Better to make the parts too strong than too weak, lest they break—disastrously."

"But five tons?" Entori fingered the thongs of the whip.

"In the event that lesser weight is required, the excess brass will, of course, be applied to the building of the next engine. If Master has any brass already in store, naturally, that could be used first."

"Not five tons."

A muffled sneeze sounded nearby.

Entori gave Sulun a sudden, hard look. The two of them

were quite alone in the room, and neither of them had sneezed.

"Damned sneaking servants!" Entori sputtered, clambering to his feet. He came fast around the table, giving Sulun barely time to jump out of his way, ran to the door and threw it wide.

No one stood there but Omis and the rest of the line, looking puzzled, a respectable ten paces away. Entori glared at them, then shut the door and stamped back to his table. "The lout must sneeze like an elephant," he muttered, settling into his heavy chair.

Sulun said nothing, but thought much. Omis, he knew, did not sneeze as loud as an elephant. Neither had that sneeze come from beyond the door. He could have sworn the sound came from somewhere toward the left wall, where stood nothing but stacks of parchment-laden shelving.

"Enough of this," Entori grumbled, reaching for his pen. "Just leave me your lists there, and get on with work."

Sulun bowed again, set his piled tablets on the least littered corner of the table and bowed his way out, closing the door behind him.

Omis tossed him an enquiring look as he passed, but all Sulun could give him was a shrug. He paced carefully down the corridor, trying to measure the walls. There had to be a room on the other side of Entori's study, but who would be in there at this time of day? And why? And why so close to the wall that a sneeze might be heard right through it?

An intriguing mystery, that sneeze. What a pity he had really no time to solve it.

Omis, with his mercifully short list of requirements, had better luck with the Old Man; Entori curtly gave him leave to use the canvas in stores to make his workshop pavilion, as well as all the charcoal he could find.

The little company was just putting up the canvas when Arizun came scampering up with a short note from Zeren. Sulun read it quickly, stuck it in his robe without comment, and went on with the business at hand.

At lunch hour he warned the others to keep to the courtyard, retraced his way through the house and headed out the front door. The ancient porter demanded to know why he was leaving, where he was going, for how long, and had the Master been informed? Sulun restrained his annoyance, remembering that the porter really bore him no ill-will and was most probably just following the Old Man's orders.

"I'm off to the coppersmiths' street," Sulun replied pleasantly, "to consult with some smiths there about present prices and qualities of brass. I'll return at the end of the lunch hour, and you can inform the Mistress for me."

"Oh, the Mistress?" the porter cackled. "Aye, I'll tell her and none other, right enough. Heh-heh!"

Sulun shook his head and walked out the door. The whole house appeared to run on petty intrigue. Where did the Mistress fit in?

He did not, of course, go to the market. A few minutes' walk brought him to Zeren's house, where the housekeeper let him in and took him at once to the small dining room. A small meal waited there, and so did Zeren, who had already started on the light wine. He had loosened his working armor, dumped his swordbelt unceremoniously on the floor, and looked distinctly morose.

"Welcome, friend philosopher," he greeted Sulun with a raised cup. "Come, honor my humble table, and we'll trade sad stories. How are you and yours faring in House Entori?"

"Gods!" Sulun dropped into the empty chair and reached for the wine. "It's unbelievable." He gulped down half the cup before he caught himself.

Zeren laughed coldly. "You knew the man was a miser when you went to him. I told you I could do no better for you."

"I know, and rest assured I'm utterly grateful." Sulun set down his cup and dug into the dish of olives. "What I didn't know, couldn't have expected, was how terribly the man's stinginess warps the character of his entire household. One simply can't live there without resorting to theft and intrigue. Oh, let me tell you—"

"In detail," Zeren murmured, pouring himself another cup.

Sulun told, in detail, at length, until the food was gone. Zeren listened quietly, eyes wandering to distances again, until his guest ran out of words.

"So," he said finally, "how long, think you, before you can finish the Bombard Project?"

Sulun stared at him for a moment. "I haven't even mentioned it to him yet. Good gods all, I daren't suggest a new project before the Old Man's seen some profit from this one, and the gods alone know when that will be. Perhaps if you come visit him with more suggestions he'll show interest, but otherwise—"

Zeren heaved a sigh that seemed to come all the way from his boots. "My dearest philosopher friend, I greatly doubt that I could play the same trick twice with Entori the Miser. Quite right, he'll make no new speculation until he's seen profit from this one. Give him his wretched engine soon, I pray you. Soon."

Sulun ran his fingers through his hair. "But there's so much I don't know. I'm only guessing at the proper size for a ship's engine. I've some idea how to keep the steam flow steady, but how can the engine be started and stopped on command? Or reversed? How much fuel will it need? How long to heat enough water? How should it be attached to the ship? How to keep the fire pot from scorching the deck? I should experiment with the model first . . . Oh, it may take years to learn everything!"

"And the bombard?"

"Friend commander, unless I can steal the money and supplies out from under Entori's nose, I have no idea when we can build a workable bombard."

Zeren rubbed his eyes hard, then took a deep breath and sagged back in his chair. Sulun saw that the man's eyes were very red. With an oddly slow sense of shock, he realized that Zeren was either very morosely drunk—at noon, on a working day—or else that he was fighting back tears.

"Sulun, my beloved philosopher." His voice was perfectly calm and level. "You have less than a year, perhaps only half that, to bring me a reliable bombard and the skills to make more. After that, nothing will matter. Nothing."

Sulun shivered, and felt obliged to whisper. "Why?"

"Because I've read the latest reports from the frontier patrol officers. Because I know what they foretell, even if the Emperor himself can't. Because I've seen this happen before, and before, and before—"

"What?" Sulun snapped, hoping to the gods that Zeren was only drunk.

"Another fall." Zeren fixed him with perfectly sober eyes. "What remains of Jarrya is being overrun. Within less than a moonspan, the Ancar will be at Sabis's northern borders. With what army and supplies Sabis has now, we can last no longer than a year."

"A year?" Sulun set his cup down on the table, very slowly, as if it were made of thin glass instead of good, sturdy bronze. He knew Zeren—his skill and wit and knowledge—too well to doubt this. The unbelievable could happen. Sabis could be invaded. The queen of cities could burn. He must make himself think about this, try to understand it, believe it.

"No more than a year," Zeren repeated. "Unless the gods open the sky and grant us a miracle. Or unless you give us a weapon that can stop an uncountable invading horde. The bombard. Do you understand?"

"Gods!" Sulun gripped a double handful of his wiry hair and tugged hard enough to hurt. "How? How, when I have to sneak every copper piece past this wretched miser? Tell me how!"

"Steal," said Zeren. "Cheat. Intrigue. Find another patron in secret. I wish to all the heavens and hells that I could do it for you, but none of the nobles, not even the City Guard Commander, will listen to me. Be as ruthless as you must, Sulun, for worse is coming. Worse than you or I or even Entori could ever be. I know. I've seen it. So many times over—"

"Gods, I must . . ." Sulun scrambled away from the table. "Must go back, before I'm missed. I'll find a way. Less than a year, perhaps only half . . . Gods!" He hurried to the door, too distracted for proper farewells, mumbling to himself about sulfur and saltpeter.

Zeren watched him go, then turned back to study his almost empty wine cup. "Vozai, my patron god," he murmured, "why are wise men enslaved to fools? Why do the fates of a hundred thousand innocents rest upon one wretched servant? Why do you play such insane games with us?"

The cup didn't answer.

Zeren sighed, and drained it.

"Not enough." Omis sighed, peering again at the figures on the wax tablet. "I can get the iron, tomorrow maybe, but this just isn't enough for the flux and the firepowder ingredients."

"I know, I know," Sulun groaned, tugging absently at his hair. "And before you ask: no, there's no point asking Master Entori to take on the Bombard Project openly. I've tried hinting delicately, tried asking the other servants for advice, and no luck to it anywhere. He's a little man with big fears and big resentments; he hired us to do one project for him, and he won't take risks on anything else. No money for anything more, not until he sees some profits on the engine."

"We could always make haste slowly. I won't have the new iron for a few days anyway. We could put off getting the flux until next new moon, then—"

"No, no time!" Sulun ran his gaze around the room as if looking for omens in the cracked plaster. "The bombard can't wait. We *must* start it as soon as possible. There must be more money, some way—"

"I know of one." Vari leaned over to trim the oil lamp, almost catching her long untied braids in the guttering flame. "The Mistress."

"Eloti?" Sulun sat up, pulling back his ragged sleeves. "How could she help? And why?"

Vari peered out the door, making certain they weren't overheard, before answering. "I've heard she has some money of her own, often funds quiet little projects of her own, without Entori's knowledge. It's a legend among the servants. The difficulty lies in persuading her, and it's said to be worth one's neck to try and fail."

"Worth all our necks anyway," Sulun muttered. Then, aloud: "How do I approach her?"

"She takes evening promenades alone in the third court-yard, every night. But, Sulun—"

"Every night? Would she be there now?"

"Why, yes. But, Sulun, why the haste? This is dangerous!"

"Everything is dangerous now." Sulun stood up, straight-ened his robe and made a quick study of his appearance in the mirror. "Third courtyard, you said?"

"Yes." Vari stepped back, watching him. "But are you so sure you can persuade her?"

"Of course." Sulun marched determinedly to the door, and out, and off down the corridor.

Behind him, Omis and Vari stared at each other in dismay.

"What," Omis asked feebly, "has got into the man? Does he realize what he's risking?"

"Something's frightened him," Vari concluded, "Frightened him too much to reveal it to us. And that, love, frightens *me*."

The third courtyard was small and swept clean, containing only a small central fountain and narrow rows of herb beds, circled with a cobbled path. In the lights of the sickle moon the surrounding walls and path and fountain shone dull white, the herb beds and pooled water and shadows dead-black. Eloti in her dark dress was likewise a sketch in faint white and black, pacing almost automatically around and around the pool, eyes distant and expression blank.

She could almost be a sleepwalker, Sulun considered, watching from an archway. Best to approach with dignified slowness, let her see him as soon as possible, give her time to travel back from her unguessed mental distance. He waited until her round brought her almost facing him, then stepped out into the open air.

She saw, and stopped, and awaited his approach with no change of expression.

Courage, Sulun reminded himself. "Lady," he began quietly, "may I walk with you?"

"Why do you disturb my evening walk?" she asked calmly, the faintest ghost of a frown creasing the inner edge of one eyebrow.

"I mean no disturbance, Lady Entori. I've come to bring an urgent warning to your ears alone."

"Walk with me, then." The ghost-frown vanished. Eloti resumed her stately pace about the fountain, allowing Sulun to match her stride. "What warning, sir?"

Sulun drew a deep breath. "Within five days, Lady, news will come that the north riverlands have fallen to the barbarians. Sabis will be shaken to its rooftops, trade will be shaken also, and I have no doubt that many of the wealthier families will begin fleeing south across the straits."

Eloti did not so much as slow her steps. "So? And is there any more?"

"Indeed there is." Sulun marvelled at her composure. "The Ancar will sweep down the river valley and take

Sabis within the year, unless some great change comes to halt them."

Eloti flicked her vision once toward the sky, then back to her path. "You are telling me only that the sun will rise tomorrow," she said, "and set, also."

"And set indeed," Sulun murmured, watching her. "Do you care nothing for these things? Would you wish to live in a city while it is sacked by the Ancar?"

Eloti paced on, implacable. "When life becomes insupportable, there is always the quick knife, the quiet poison." An ironic smile touched her lips, ever so faintly. "We all die. What changes?"

"Lady, given the chance, *I* could change this!"

Eloti stopped in midstep. "You?" A slight but distinct tone of interest tinged her voice.

"Yes, I could," Sulun gulped. "I know the means to make a weapon that could defeat the Ancar. Given the equipment to make it, the space to test it, I and my friends could make this weapon within . . . um, one moon's time. My Lord your brother, unfortunately, won't hear of this. He wants his ship engines, and will spare no coppers for anything else."

"Ah, so you come to me." Eloti resumed her pacing, a definite smile on her face now. "You want money."

"Yes, Lady," Sulun answered, unashamed. "Enough to pay the rent on our workshop by the river. Enough to buy the flux for Omis's iron. Enough to purchase the saltpeter, sulfur and charcoal for the powder. Enough for the leather cannisters of shot. Not cheap, Lady, I admit—but less costly than the quick knife or the quiet poison, I dare say."

Eloti actually laughed, a low and quiet sound. "You intrigue me, sir, I admit. Yet I've seen that you're honest enough."

"I've no time for anything less, not knowing what I know. I've no wish to endure the fall of the city."

"Nor I, actually." She glanced once at the silver moon. "I've wagered before, the gods know, and for poorer stakes. I shall give you my answer tomorrow."

"Thank you, Lady."

"You may g—Htcha!" she sneezed.

Sulun, already backing away, suddenly remembered where he'd heard that exact sneeze before. He turned and hurried off through the archway, mind rolling with possibilities.

In the morning, after a mercifully brief report of purchases to the master of the house, Sulun chivvied his crew to work with a ferocity that was rare for him. They assembled a small procession of carts and went down to the smeltery to fetch Omis's iron and Sulun's brass, headed home by the emptiest road and managed to get the whole shipment into the courtyard by lunchtime. Vari was waiting for them there, holding something wrapped in a napkin, looking very thoughtful.

"Here." She handed Sulun the bundle. "Mistress came up to me while I was at the scrubbing, handed this to me as quiet as you please, says to bring it to you quietly and adds that she'll want an accounting later. I haven't dared look. Sulun, what have you gone and done?"

Sulun said nothing until he'd unwrapped the napkin, opened the small drawstring bag he found there and looked inside. Sunlight caught on the edges of wide gold coins. He stared blankly for a moment, then pulled the bag shut and stuffed it quickly into his robe.

"I've managed to persuade the Mistress," he said, feeling the smile stretch across his face. "How soon can we have those carts ready to go again?"

"An hour! An hour!" Doshi wailed. "Let the poor beasts have their meal—and us, too."

"An hour, then," Sulun agreed, "But no more."

The afternoon passed in purchases of odd minerals and tallows and odd cuts of leather, plus a side trip by Arizun and Yanados to pay the rent on the riverside shop. On all but the latter, Sulun dickered fast and furiously, and kept careful track of the money spent. Not so much as a copper piece went to anything outside of the Bombard Project, though Solun did yield to pressure from Arizun and Doshi and bought some cut-rate sheets of parchment for diagrams. They came dragging the carts home barely in time to unload, no time to wash and dress before supper. They looked a tired and well-worked lot at the table, and more than once Sulun caught Mistress Eloti giving him and his crew appraising looks. She must guess, he considered, that they were giving her full value for her money.

After dinner conversation at the servants' table was unduly full of comments on their industry and devotion to their tasks. Aobi went so far as to growl at them: "Don't work so blazing hard, you lads; you'll make us all look lazy, and the old goat will take it out of our hides."

"It'll go slow after this," Omis predicted, thinking of the days of forging and hammering ahead of him.

"Entirely too slow," Sulun muttered, imaging the gods' hourglass hanging, invisible, over Sabis.

Vari and the apprentices exchanged worried glances, and excused themselves early from the party.

10

"Enough of that." Entori cut off Sulun's droning report of items bought and progress made, shuffled through a teetering pile of waxed tablets, pulled one out and shoved it across the desk. "The fifty-tonner *Yanira* sits at fourth dock south, unloading this morning. Here are the directions." He handed over a scrap of folded and sealed parchment as well. "Here is my note to the captain. Take as many of your . . . scholars as you need, and go make your measurements."

"I beg pardon?" Sulun fumbled, caught off balance by the change of subject.

"The ship you wanted," Entori snapped, impatient. "Go measure it for your engine. It's docked and idle for the day."

"Oh. Yes, of course. Today."

"You have until evening, when she'll be loading again. I trust the time will be sufficient."

"Er, yes, Master. It should be." Sulun ran his eyes once more over the wall behind Entori, wondering where the spy hole was and if it was occupied.

"Then go to it, and don't waste time. Next!" Entori rang the small bell on his desk and turned his attention back to his pile of parchments.

Sulun backed away, bowed, turned and went out, almost colliding with the three house guards on their way in. He hurried back to the workshop-courtyard, wondering when, if ever, he'd have time to explore the house thoroughly and discover just where the spy hole was hidden. Not that it really mattered; the lady was his ally, for the moment at least.

Omis already had the forge lit and working, with Doshi pumping the bellows and Ziya shovelling in wood. "Gods!" he wailed at the news. "I can't go now! I'm about to start the first heat, and the forge is nearly ready."

"And no doubt you'll need Doshi and Ziya," Sulun added. "Don't trouble yourself, then. I'll take the others. Where are they?"

"Back courtyard, hitching up the donkey cart. They've already heard the news."

"What? How?"

"By being earlier in the morning line than you, lay-a-bed." Omis grinned without looking up. "Ziya, hand me that first iron billet."

Sulun shook his head, and went off to fetch his measuring tapes.

A seagull creaked and wheeled overhead, throwing its shadow across the deck. Sulun eyed it warily; he'd been splattered once already by the pesky birds, much to the amusement of the two sailors idly guarding the ship.

"Twenty cubits, two spans," Arizun duly reported from the other end of the tape.

Sulun scribbled the figures on his tablet, and took his foot off the near end of the tape. "Roll it up," he said, searching down the column of notes to see if any were left unfilled. None were. "I believe we've finished."

Arizun and Yanados gave sparse cheers and began stuffing the tapes and instruments back into their basket. Sulun stuffed the tablet in his bag beside the others, tried once more to pinch the pervasive stink of tar and rotting fish out of his nose, and headed gratefully for the gangplank. The others caught up to him at the donkey cart.

"It isn't going to work," Yanados whispered in his ear.

Sulun started to turn, then caught himself. The sailors, or anyone, might be watching. "Why not?" he asked, just as quietly.

"Look at the whole length of the ship. Look at the length of the boom and the sweep of the tiller. How much space lies between them?"

Sulun looked, for the first time that day seeing the little ship as a complete unit. A good, low, wide design, he thought: sleek enough for speed, but stable in the water. A well-set long boom, and the tiller's sweep— "Oh." He saw it. "Maybe five cubits," he said, sighing. "No room for the engine. Very well, the sweep and boom will have to be shortened." But how many cubits? He measured it with his eyes, trying to guess at the right size for the engine.

"Another problem." Yanados pulled out a tablet of her own, showing the basic sketch of the ship mounted with its two side-set paddle wheels. "Were you planning to run the axle straight across the deck?"

Sulun was about to say, "Of course, and why not?" but stopped, reconsidering.

"Yes," Yanados caught the unspoken words. "How would the sailors get past it?"

"So be it!" Sulun flapped his hands in resignation. "The axle and engine should be mounted under the top deck, on that second level, the . . . uh . . ."

"Captain's quarters, crew's quarters and ship's stores?"

Sulun tugged at his hair, briefly wondering if he saw a few gray threads in it. "It shouldn't take that much room. Hmm, put the supply room behind it, under that last hatchway. A bit inconvenient, but workable."

"True. Now we come to a tougher nut to crack. Sulun, once the engine begins spinning, how can it be stopped quickly? Or made to run backward?"

"Why . . . It can't."

Yanados rolled her eyes skyward. "Then we must devise a way to disengage the engine from the paddle wheels, even turn it around and reengage, and that, speedily. Otherwise, once started, the ship can neither stop nor maneuver."

"Oh." Sulun gave her a sidewise glance. "Forgive me, but I don't believe I've ever so much as set foot on a ship before."

Yanados shrugged and looked away.

Arizun, who'd been impatiently holding the donkey's bridle, asked if they intended to stand there until dinnertime. The other two turned and climbed into the cart quickly, without speaking. Arizun scrambled up beside them, took the reins and fly whip, and chivvied the donkey into a slow but steady walk home.

The other two didn't speak for most of the ride, and Arizun, guessing that something was wrong, didn't prod them for conversation. Halfway past the market, though, Sulun drew out his last unmarked tablet and began sketching a new design.

"This isn't what you showed me before." Entori frowned across his table in the dim light. "What are all these complications?"

And how much will they cost? Sulun finished for him. "What I showed you earlier, Master, was a simple illustration of how the engine works. This is the full and complete version, designed to fit the needs of the ship. The finished version is always more complicated than the basic model, just as a painted portrait is more complex than the original sketch. Once we've completed a working model, we can demonstrate for you—"

"Designs! Models!" Entori shouted, his face turning purple. "Do you think I'm a fool to be misled by toys? Waste no more of my money on such playing! Make the engine for the ship, and that right quickly! Do you hear me, servant?"

Sulun only gaped at him.

"Do you hear me?" Entori bellowed.

"Er, of course, Master." It was the only safe thing Sulun could think to say.

"Then get out of my sight, and do it!" Entori lifted the bell's striker as if he might use it on Sulun's head.

Sulun bowed quickly, turned and fled.

A faint sniff sounded behind the wall, but Entori, grumbling and shuffling parchment sheets, didn't hear it.

"Unbelievable." Omis put down his hammer and wiped his forehead. "You'll make the model anyway?"

"Of course." Sulun sat down on the nearest pile of iron billets and laced his shaky fingers together. "Yanados is carving the ship model right now, and Arizun's measuring out the drawings for the engine parts. We'll simply have to hide what we're doing, and make the usual excuses."

Ziya threw him an unfathomable look, but said nothing.

"Just how complex is the improved design?" Doshi asked.

"With the perpetual feeding assembly, it looks like a hoo-raw's nest," Sulun groaned. "I don't blame him for being perplexed by the drawing, but to think we can proceed without a model for testing . . . How can the man be such a fool? Is he mad?"

"He's probably never dealt with any sort of engine work before." Omis picked up another billet with the long tongs, and shoved it into the glowing heart of the forge. "He's used to haggling and debt collecting with tradesmen and creditors. It never entered his thoughts that metals are less pliable than men; they have no ears to hear threats or promises, no greed to entice, no minds to change. Therefore, smithing can't be hurried, nor engine crafting either."

"Metals have more honor than men," Ziya murmured, dumping more wood into the furnace."

Sulun hadn't the heart to even try answering.

"Enough wood, Ziya," Omis mercifully cut in. "Come here and tend the bellows awhile. That's a good lad. Doshi, put your gloves on and hold these tongs."

Sulun pulled himself to his feet and shambled off to his drawings. Best give Arizun some help finishing them. Time, time, not enough time: two projects to finish, one of them secret and one half secret, and all of Sabis was running out of time.

The bad news came to Sabis with a blare of trumpets in the early morning, a knot of troopers bringing back wagon-loads of wounded at the north gate, and a horde of desperate refugees behind them. By noon the word was everywhere: the north had fallen. The riverhead lands were lost, including the last of Jarrya, and where would grain, wool and mutton come from now? Prices jumped and bucked and jumped again like colts feeling the saddle for the first time.

At noon Arizun ran into the back courtyard of Entori's house with a minimal bundle of purchases, a blanched face and an earful of news. All the others clustered around him to hear it, repeat it, demand details. Yes, the north was gone. No, nobody knew when the Ancar would come down the river valley toward the city. Yes, there were refugees, many now and more coming, all of them desperately poor. Yes, there was talk of another draft in the city to raise troops for the fighting northward. No, nothing had been heard of the northern army except that it was in retreat. Yes, the docks were crowded with panicked Sabisans buying passage across the straits to Esha. No, he had no idea how this would affect Entori's business interests . . .

It was Vari, looking back to keep track of the baby, who noticed that Sulun wasn't part of the goggling crowd. He was still sitting on the bench where they'd left him, ignoring his half-eaten bread and cheese, looking up at the sky as if hunting for omens. He looked not at all surprised. Vari watched, thought, then paced closer.

"You knew," she said quietly, "You knew it would happen. That's why you've been so strange and furious these past few days. How did you know?"

"From Zeren." Sulun dropped his glance back to the food in his hands, but didn't eat. "He guessed. He told me. We must complete the bombard soon, very soon, or there'll be no city to defend with it. Do you understand?"

Vari nodded, staring at him, then bit her lip and went quietly away to talk to Omis.

Dinner was tense and strange. The master didn't appear, and Eloti put in only a brief appearance. The number at the servants' table seemed smaller too, though it took Sulun a while to realize who was missing.

"Where," he asked the housekeeper, "have our three great watchmen gone?"

There was a moment's silence, and then everyone started talking at once.

"They've run off, haven't you heard?" said the scullery maid. "What with all the refugees, the big houses fear thieves. There've been criers in the streets asking for trained house guards to come work up the hill, offering much better terms than the old vulture here does. That's where our three louts have gone, I can tell you."

" 'Tis the end of the world," the housekeeper gloomed. "The barbarians could come any day, breach the walls, rape and slaughter us in our beds."

"You've small need to fear that," the porter muttered.

"My spells will protect us," the house wizard mumbled into his cup.

"We'll starve first," the cook grumbled. "No food from the northlands, and there'll be less and less from the river valley as the Ancar come south. Nowhere to buy but from Esha across the water, and their prices are terrible."

"They can hardly feed their own people and us too,"

Arizun noted. "Best to cross the water, I think, and not stop in Mez, but keep on going."

That started everyone talking about flight, gathering up one's hoarded coppers and taking passage on the next boat. Sulun's party looked at each other and huddled closer, thinking much along the same lines. Sulun shook his head, disgusted at their naiveté.

"Do you think you'll be welcome in Esha?" he commented, mostly to his own people but loudly enough that the rest could hear him. "They've too many refugees already, and most of them starving. In Mez, I'll wager, you can find beggars in the streets and slaves on the block who were once rich folk here in Sabis. Go down the coast to Tari, and you might find the rich folk keeping out of the gutter—but what about poor folk like us? Hah! You'd have to run further than that. And how far will your copper bits take you? You'd do better to go inland, work for the farmers and herdsmen if they'll have you. Or go all the way to the towns at the Bay of Naydres—if you can speak the language, or learn it quickly. You might keep from starving thereby, but don't expect to ever be richer than you are in this house, right now."

He drained his cup and waited, wondering what the reaction would be.

After a moment's silence, the servants went back to discussing passage to Mez. As far as Sulun could tell, the only effect of his words was that some of the servants seriously considered how they would make a living in Esha, a land they'd never seen and knew little about.

Sulun pushed his plate aside, got up and went out. After a moment's hesitation, the apprentices and Omis and family rose and followed him.

They clustered in Sulun's room, even the children, crowding it unbearably though no one complained. Omis asked first where they could realistically plan to go, if not Mez.

"Could we get as far as Tari?" Arizun asked, guessing that none of them could afford passage to the Naydres Bay cities.

"I doubt it," Doshi answered, consulting a scribbled wax board. "I'm guessing that anyone in the south with so much as a donkey wagon to rent will be charging top prices, with so many refugees on the roads. There are, what, ten of us? Never. Perhaps we should go inland, find a farming town that needs us and our, uh, wares . . ." He shrugged, guessing as well as any of them that their particular wares commanded a poor market.

"Back to where we began when Shibari's house burned," Omis groaned. "At least now we have our tools, but I'd need a wagon to carry my anvil."

"If you had the anvil, and the rest," Sulun pondered, "could you build another forge?"

"I could, but it would take a good moon and a half—besides paying some potter to fire the bricks. Have we the money for that?"

"If we could reach Sakar, our trade would be welcomed," Yanados put in.

"The problem is reaching Sakar," Arizun pointed out. "We haven't the money to hire a ship."

"South," Vari pronounced. "It's all we can reach. How we'd live after . . . Who knows the most about the southlands?"

Everyone looked at Arizun, who only shrugged. "Why ask me? I was only a baby when we left there. All I know is that my mother had reason to leave."

"Zeren," Sulun murmured, drawing their attention back. "Zeren fought there. He'd know."

"Well, by all the gods, ask him!" Omis snorted. "Ask him tomorrow."

"We will." Sulun straightened up, rubbing kinks out of his back. "Arizun, tomorrow take Yanados and some stout sticks in case of trouble, and carry a letter to Zeren's house. Meanwhile . . ." He looked to Omis. "How soon can we start moving our necessities to the riverside shop?"

11

Zeren pondered the question long and hard, letting his gaze wander over the cracks in the ceiling. He looked, Sulun noted, worse than last time. "Nowhere in the south," he finally said. "Nowhere you could reach. Neither could you get safe passage to any of the isles. It's hopeless."

"There must be somewhere!" Sulun insisted. "And no, before you ask, I've not lost hope for the bombard. Given time, I can make it work. If not given time, I ask you, where can I take us to be safe?"

"Us?" Zeren looked at the little gathering clustered in his dining room. "You've never considered going your separate ways?"

"No," said Omis, Sulun and Vari together.

Vari added, "How would we take care of the children?"

"So it comes to that." Zeren looked at all of them for a long moment. "You may be right, you know. As a family, most especially a family of tradesmen, you could live better than any single man alone—if you could once find a place beyond the reach of the war."

"Where?" Sulun insisted. "Name a place."

Zeren leaned forward, rested his elbows on the table and his chin on his hands. "Behind the lines," he answered. "Could you once get past the army of the Ancar, find a place where they've long since passed, you'd be left alone. Doshi—"

The youth flinched, sat up. "Yes?"

"You know the northlands. Behind the Ancars' lines, what's the land like? What sort of folk live there?"

"Farmers, as I remember." Doshi scratched his arm nervously, unused to being asked for advice. "There were villages, small villas, all over that land before the invaders came. I don't know what's there now."

"I doubt that the Ancar destroyed every village they found," Zeren considered, "or that they found all of them. There's my advice, friends, for whatever good it may do. Go become the blacksmiths and brass smiths of some town behind the Ancars' march—and the further behind, the better. Go up beyond the Gol, if you can, and if you can abide the northern winters. Ah, hell, if Sabis falls, I might even come with you." He poured himself some more wine, seeming in a much better humor.

The others looked at each other, wondering if that was a joke.

Yanados paced back and forth along the work-table, studying the engine model as Sulun assembled it, frowning and muttering to herself until Sulun couldn't ignore her anymore.

"Do you have some complaint?" he asked, setting his tools aside.

"I was thinking . . ." Yanados shuffled from foot to foot.

"If such a ship were to meet with pirates, well . . . pirates hire magicians too, you know, to ill-wish their victims."

Sulun shrugged. That made sense, but he couldn't see the relevance.

"Sulun, if a full-sized engine of this sort were ill-wished, what could it do wrong?"

"I don't know," Sulun admitted, peering at his model. "The valves might fail, perhaps. We'll have to make them strong. . . ."

"What else?" Yanados tapped a finger against the tiny boiler tube set over its miniature brazier. "Fire and water, and the fierce pressure-power of steam. Could it . . . explode?"

Sulun dutifully thought about that, thought of the water poured down the funnel, through the trap-door valve, into the heated brass tube above the brazier, then through the hollowed—and moving—ball-and-socket joint, then into the spinning chamber. What weakness? Where?

The heating tube? Too little water, too little steam, and the jetted chamber wouldn't spin. Too much water would cool the tube, make too little steam, and again the chamber wouldn't spin. Fill the brazier too scantily and you'd have not enough heat; again, no steam, no spinning. Fill it too full, let the flames or even the coals overlap the tube . . .

"The tube might soften, melt, warp," he admitted, "but that would require so much heat, so much wood—"

"Believe me, if it can be done wrong, some fool sailor will do it. It will not be Natural Philosophers who use this engine at sea."

"True, true . . ." Sulun studied the assembly for a long moment, then abruptly smiled. There was indeed one simple way to keep some fool of a sailor from overloading the brazier. He reached for the metal snips.

"What are you doing with the brazier?" Yanados asked, peeping over his shoulder.

"Making it smaller and shorter," Sulun smiled, plying the heavy shears.

Snip, snip, snip—and the brazier's legs were shortened. Snap, snap, snap—and the bowl of the brazier lost its original rim. Sulun carefully tucked the little model back to its place in the assembly. He scratched some notes on a nearby tablet.

"What would that do?" Yanados asked.

"Small brazier, small fire," Sulun explained. "Load the brazier full as you can, the coals still won't reach the tube and melt it. Hmm, it wouldn't hurt to make the tube thicker, too . . ." He scribbled more notes.

"Just be certain no fool can work it wrong," said Yanados padding toward the door.

Not until after she was gone did Sulun think to wonder how she knew so much about the habits and failings of sailors.

The moon wore away her horns, and nothing improved. Morning reports with Entori grew ever more difficult and unpredictable; his shipping interests did marvelously well on the short Sabis–Mez run, carrying refugees south and food north, but elsewhere on the Inland Sea the trade was dangerous and the old man's temper likewise. Always he exhorted Sulun to hurry with the engine.

At least, Sulun told himself after leaving the master's study in a shower of abuse, the engine model was finished. It worked after a fashion; the tiny valves clearly weren't very efficient, but the rotating platform and gears managed well enough. No sense putting it off; he should begin making the full-sized engine for Entori's ship, as he'd promised.

That meant that Omis would have to put aside work on the bombard to cast and shape the brass fittings for the engine.

"Ah, well," Sulun consoled himself as he entered the courtyard, "It shouldn't take more than a day or two. . . ."

He noticed, as he walked past the end of the morning-report line, that one of the maids was missing.

"Ran away," snorted the housekeeper, when asked. "That lazy slut must have had a better offer from some uphill house. Didn't leave word, either; just out the door and gone."

"Went out shopping yesterday," the porter said, "and never came back."

Sulun left them arguing and went off to see Omis, but the permanent unease in the back of his mind grew another degree thicker. It would be wise, he decided, to start moving as much gear as possible to the river workshop. Starting today.

* * *

"The heat's awful," Doshi grumbled, slapping the reins irritably across the lagging mules' rumps. "Only fools go hauling loads about at noon."

"Only fools go out without guards at any other time," Arizun snapped, casting a quick look around the almost empty street. "You haven't seen much of the city since the bad times came, have you?"

"Oh, I know there are more thieves and beggars about, but good gods, there are three of us. And we're armed." Doshi tapped his toes on the hatchet hidden under the cart's seat. "And we're not on foot. No need for this."

"Wagoners have been robbed before, and you should keep that closer to hand." Arizun tapped the bulge at his belt under his light cloak. "And three of us wouldn't be enough against a good-sized gang."

"Keep your voices soft," Yanados warned from her perch at the back of the cart. "Don't draw any more attention than we must."

"You've both gone mad with suspicion," Doshi scoffed, in a near whisper. "That or gone silly for the ungodly fun of carrying weapons about. I swear, you're turning barbarous yourselves. Nobody goes armed unless they're looking for trouble—"

"Or expecting it to look for them," Arizun growled. "Keep your eyes on the street, fool."

"Be careful who you call a fool," Doshi muttered, steering the mule team around a corner. "You haven't read half the books—now, what's this mess?"

Several buildings down, the street was half blocked with a tumble of broken furniture and assorted garbage. A man on foot could have passed it, but the mule cart would have considerable trouble.

Arizun saw it, gasped, seized the reins from Doshi and yanked the mules to a hoof-clattering halt. "Back up!" he hissed. "Back the way we came, fast!"

"What—"

"Damnation!" Yanados yelled, making them both turn and look, as she yanked her hatchet free.

Behind them, perhaps half a dozen ragged bravos—some of them quite young, a few older men—slid out of the doorways to block the street. They carried assorted bludgeons and short knives. They stalked toward the halted cart, smiling grimly, not even bothering to give the traditional stand-and-deliver challenge.

"Back up!" Arizun repeated, shoving the reins at Doshi. Then he scrambled into the back of the cart and fumbled at something under the sacks.

Yanados hissed through her teeth, crouched at the cart's tail and swung her hatchet in a slow, warning arc. The approaching gang slowed and spread out, still smiling.

Doshi might have argued about backing into a fight, but just then his eye caught motion near the trash pile ahead. Three more club-wielding boys were slinking out of cover, coming toward the mules. Doshi gulped, wasted a precious second fumbling for the hatchet under the seat, and began hauling furiously on the mules' reins. The mules, finally understanding that there was danger ahead, squealed and backed. The toughs ahead moved faster, starting to run.

The six thugs behind the cart stopped where they were, crouched, waited for the prey to come to them, waited to jump for the tailgate.

Yanados reached out and swung at the nearest, making him hop backwards. He recovered and tried to lunge in under her arm, but she caught him backhand on the return stroke. The back of the hatchet head thwacked meatily against his head, dropping him to the ground with a shocked yell and a sudden spurt of bright blood.

The other toughs yelled in outrage, and charged the cart.

Right then, Arizun came up from the cart bed with a short bow in one hand and an arrow in the other. He loaded, snap-aimed and fired past Yanados, catching one of the boys high in the chest. The boy screeched, dropped his club and knife, stumbled to his knees and began tugging at the arrow. The others skidded to a stop, unwilling to face arrows. Yanados whooped and swung her hatchet at the nearest, making him dance away.

The thugs ahead of the wagon ran toward the mules, the nearest reaching for the bridles. Doshi, guessing what they meant to do, hauled furiously on the reins, shouting incoherently at the mules. The frightened beasts reared, braying, flailing the air with their hooves, making the attackers scramble out of the way. Doshi used the instant's respite to clutch the reins in one hand and fumble under the seat for the cart-whip with the other.

Arizun aimed and loosed another arrow, this one gouging a path across a half-turned man's ribs and finally lodging itself in his arm. The man howled and jumped away, dropping his knife and club.

The mules dropped back to all fours, and two of the young toughs lunged for their reins. Doshi came up with the whip and lashed out at the nearer, catching him squarely across the face. The thug screamed and stumbled to his knees, pawing at his face, but the other two jumped past him to grab at the mules.

One of the mules reared again, lashing out with its hooves and catching one boy with a resounding thump in the belly. The other mule snapped, but missed. The remaining tough grabbed the bridle and hauled the mule's head down, hefted his club and thwacked the mule about the ears. Doshi snapped out the whip and welted the boy's clubbing arm, making him drop the bludgeon and duck down below the mule's chest, but not shaking him loose. Doshi flailed again with the whip and yelled for help.

Arizun loosed another arrow, puncturing a man's leg. The other two, seeing the odds change drastically, turned and ran. The wounded man limped after them, cursing.

"Back up!" Yanados shouted. "We're clear, Doshi. Back up!"

"I can't!" Doshi yelled, pointing.

Arizun turned around, aimed carefully, and fired. The arrow whizzed past Doshi's ear, through the tangle of reins and harness, and buried itself in the attacker's forearm. The youth screeched and let go of the reins.

Doshi was too frozen to react, but the mules, kicking and braying in outrage, backed up of their own accord. The attacking tough, exposed now, turned and ran.

Arizun, swearing, dropped the bow, clambered back into the seat, grabbed the reins and pulled the mules further back. A dozen paces and they were at the mouth of the crossing street. Arizun hauled the mules' heads toward the turn, slapped the reins on their rumps and let them go. The beasts, willing enough, turned and scrambled into the open, empty road.

"No pursuit," Yanados announced from the tail of the cart.

"We'll try again at the second street over," Arizun decided. "It's a good bit wider, no room for traps."

"You had a bow," Doshi squeaked.

"I always do, these days. Lucky thing, eh?"

"You could have shot me!"

"Nonsense, I went right past you. Don't you think I know how to shoot?"

"It's unlawful to carry bows in the public streets!"

"It's unlawful to rob folk, too. Does the law prevent robbers? Hey, pull to the right here; there's our street."

"Is there any blood on me?" Yanados asked, wiping her hatchet clean on some sacking. "And nice shooting, Ari."

Doshi bit his lip and reined the mules toward the turn.

"It might not be that bad everywhere," Sulun considered, remembering his old teacher's endless advice to see a problem from all sides. "This was down toward the river, in the poor section."

"Not that close to the river, not that poor a neighborhood, and in broad light of noon," Yanados glowered, looking up from her long knife and sharpening-stone. "It's that bad, Sulun."

"Very well. We'll have to send out more people with every run to the old workshop. How much do we have there now?"

"Blankets, two changes of clothing, some dried fruit," Vari ticked off on her fingers, her shadow dancing on the yellowed wall behind her. "Sulfur, charcoal, some spare tools (Arizun would know which), some medicinal herbs (not enough), three kitchen knives, four short knives—"

"Not enough," Omis growled. "As soon as I've finished with these cursed brasses, I'll make long knives and arrowheads for the lot of you."

"It might be quicker to go and buy some," Arizun considered. "If enough of us go out together, we should get to the market and back safely."

"We can't spare the money," Sulun pointed out. "We'll just have to make more noon visits to the workshop. You left it closed up tight, I trust?"

"Oh yes," Doshi said, his voice still shaky. "Everything buried, locked, barricaded . . . Do you all intend to carry bows?"

"I can make enough for all of us." Yanados smiled, examining the edge of her knife.

"Was there any sign of tampering about the doors or windows?" Sulun asked.

"A little." Arizun snifed. "Omis' good iron locks and hinges thwarted them. Hah."

"Well enough. Now supposing we don't have to flee, how much more time before we can get back to work on the bombard?"

"Another tenday, at least," Omis groaned. "All that damned brass, and the gears, and the driving-axle . . . and then the polishing and fitting and assembling . . . Gods, the engine model won't be ready until the end of the month."

Everyone looked at Sulun.

"Gods," he sighed, "What can I tell Zeren?"

Nobody had any suggestions.

"What's that shouting outside?" Ziya piped up, surprising everyone. "Is that robbers?"

Arizun dived for the narrow window, Yanados half a step behind him. "I don't know," he complained. "I can't see a thing from this side. It's toward the front of the house, in the street."

"Go and look then," Sulun ordered them impatiently. "To get on then, Omis, once the engine's complete and we've put it on Entori's damned ship—Watch your feet!"

Arizun, Yanados and Ziya ignored him in their rush for the door. They scurried out into the dim corridor, hugged the wall as they scampered through the darkened courtyard and clung to the shadows of the main hall as they raced toward the stairs and the front windows. There they pulled up short, seeing two of the maids and the porter there ahead of them. Most of the front windows were taken, but the three apprentices managed to wriggle between the maids for a good view.

Shadows leaped in the street, thrown by torches set on top of a huge, box-shaped wagon. Guardsmen stood at the barred rear door of the wagon, and held the heads of the oxen drawing it. Still other guards hurried up the street, driving a knot of complaining men at spearpoint.

As the servants of Entori's darkened house watched, the guardsmen threw open the wagon door and pushed the wailing civilians inside. The door thudded shut, followed by the slam of a heavy bolt. Then came shouts, the clatter of boot heels, and a creaking and rumbling as the wagon rolled off down the shadowed street. The protesting

wails of the men locked in the wagon took longest to fade
from hearing.

"Why did they take all those men?" Ziya asked of anyone who could answer.

"Press gang," the porter spat "They're snatching poor
folk off the streets to go join the army and fight the
Ancar."

"We'd best not be seen abroad after dark," Yanados
muttered, sliding down from the window. "Still, this might
thin out the street robbers."

"Will our walls really keep them out?" Ziya asked.

Nobody answered.

"No sense in delay," Sulun announced, making a last
critical inspection of the gear train. "Light the coals and
let's pour the water."

"I still don't like the bedding of this axle," Omis muttered, giving the bearings a last squirt of greasenut oil.

"It turns, it turns! Come light the coals."

"All right." Omis poured a few drops of distilled wine
spirits on the coals, lit the fumes with flint and steel, and
stepped back to watch. The wine spirits burned with a
brief blue flame and the coals caught, glowing at the edges
first. Omis eyed the copper boiling-tube stretched above
the brazier, tapped it to check its heat, then went to the
upright funnel at the near end. "Give it another tick of the
waterclock, then pour in the water," he decided. "Then, if
the valves and tubing can withstand pressure enough to
turn the jetwheel, and if the gears don't slip off the
paddle wheels' axle, and if the paddle wheels aren't too
heavy to turn, this fool thing just might work. Does the
old vulture have the paddle wheels constructed yet?"

"Oh, yes." Sulun peered up and down the length of his
contraption for the hundredth time, shaking his head over
its bizarre shape: the turbine (more like an upright disk
than its original globe shape) with its angled escape jets,
the copper boiling-tube and brass steam-feed line with
their carefully fitted valves and sockets, the short axle with
its sturdy gearwheel waiting to engage, the fussy little
forest of supports, the bolted-down brazier and the platform they all rested on. It looked utterly eccentric and
ridiculous, but he knew it would work. This part of the
assembly would, anyway. "He's been nagging me for days

about the cost of keeping that expensive gear stored and idle."

"I just hope his carpenters got all the measurements right," Omis worried. "Proper fools we'll look if we get this set on the paddle wheel axle, take it all down to the ship, and the sockets in the deck don't fit."

"Then he can belabor the ship's carpenters, not us. Ah, I think it's warm enough. Pour in the water."

Omis shook his head, lifted a pitcher of water and poured, carefully, into the upright funnel.

Both men took a few steps back, and waited.

Water gurgled down the funnel, through the first valve, and into the heated copper tube. There was an angry hiss, more gurgling, near-human belches as the steam tried and failed to escape back up the valve, then a faint groan of protest and a puff of steam from the turbine's jets.

Sulun and Omis held their breath and made assorted handsigns for luck. They had made all the parts to triple strength, but still . . .

Slowly, then faster, the turbine moved. It turned, rolled, spun, wreathed in a cloud of dissipating steam like a dimmed sun among roiling clouds. Its attached axle spun with it, and the final gearwheel too.

"It works!" Sulun whooped. "Praise all the gods I ever heard of, it works!"

"And the supports are holding! Look, they're not even shaking! We've done it!"

By the time their combined noise brought the apprentices running in to look, Sulun and Omis were dancing a clumsy version of the Vulgar Hop-Step around a workroom full of warm fog to the tune of the whining, spinning engine. Even Ziya cheered.

"Those sailors will have to cut extra portholes to let out all that steam," Doshi noted, but he was grinning all the same.

"Master, the engine is ready for installation." Sulun did his best to keep his face politely expressionless.

"Excellent." Entori almost smiled, then caught himself. "It took you long enough. Fortunately, the ship is in port at the moment. Do the fitting today, and tell me how well the ship performs. You are excused."

Sulun stifled a sigh, bowed, and went out. There was,

he decided, no use expecting any further reaction from Master.

He supposed he should be grateful for having a whole day to install and test the completed assembly.

"No, no! Great gods, we needed to place the engine first, then the paddle wheels!" Sulun tugged his hair and glared at the sullen ship carpenters. "Now we may have to reset that whole damned axle. Gods! Never mind. Omis, is that platform socket the right size, at least?"

" 'Tis. No trouble there." Omis peered once more at the ironbound hole in the second deck, shrugged, and stood up. "Bring up the muscle-boys, and let's get this thing mounted."

Sulun, still pulling nervously at his hair, stood back and let the assorted crew manhandle the engine's platform into place. Omis did all the directing, complete with howls for careful handling, and the platform settled onto its mounting with a satisfying thud. Omis rotated the platform this way and that, glared for a moment at the huge iron axle cutting across the cabin, frowned at the two iron gears set on it, and finally swung the platform around to meet the right-hand gear.

Sulun squeezed his eyes shut, not wanting to see the expected failure. Surely the axle would turn out to be set too high or too low, or the drive gear from the engine wouldn't meet the gear on the axle, or the gear sizes would be wrong, or the perverse things just wouldn't engage. The house wizard was an unreliable drunk, and who could tell what the ship's wizard was up to? He'd have to go back to Entori and report another delay.

"Deese of the forge," Omis breathed. "The gears meet perfectly."

Sulun opened his eyes and stared. Sure enough, there stood Omis, smiling as if at his own children, studying the juncture of the two neatly meshed gears.

"So the ship can move forward, at least," Doshi commented at his shoulder. "Now, can it stop and move backward, too?"

"No reason it shouldn't," said Omis. He gripped two of the handles at the edge of the platform, and pulled. The platform turned smoothly, pulling the drive gear away from the wheel axle, swung in a neat half-circle, and settled against the opposite axle gear with a smug click. "See? Works fine." Omis grinned. "I'll say this much for Entori's other workmen; they can follow instructions to the last number. And his various wizards aren't all bad."

"Gods be praised." Sulun wiped his forehead with his sleeve. "Now all we need do is light the coals, pour in the water, and see if this engine will actually drive the ship."

"No trouble there." Omis went to the open hatchway in the deck above and bellowed up through it. "Captain, prepare to cast off. We're about to test the engine."

Groans and curses of dismay echoed down with the sunlight, but Omis ignored them and turned away. "Who has the coals?" he bellowed to all and sundry. "And the bucket?"

Ziya waddled up, toting a dipper and a sloshing bucket nearly as big as she was. Behind her Arizun dragged a huge sack of coals. Yanados followed with the bottle of wine spirits and the flint and steel striker. They filled the brazier, poured on the spirits, lit the coals and stood by with the water in a neat little ceremony that impressed the watching sailors.

"We're cast off," filtered down through the hatchway. "Are you ready?"

"Wait, wait," said Omis, turning the platform until the gears engaged exactly.

"Wait, wait . . ." said Sulun, watching the copper tube above the brazier. "Now. Pour."

Ziya solemnly lifted the ladle, but couldn't quite reach to the top of the funnel. Omis, smiling, took the ladle from her and poured the water himself.

The engine hissed, gurgled and belched. The sailors took several respectful steps backward. The captain poked his head down through the open hatchway to watch the proceedings. The first plumes of steam curled out of the jets; the turbine muttered, groaned, began to turn.

Sulun chewed his lip nearly raw and crossed his fingers under the concealment of his sleeves. Had they made the boiling-tube thick enough, the turbine sturdy enough, the valves strong enough?

A faint groan came from the main axle, and a heavier gurgling of water from the unseen paddle wheels outside. Slowly, ponderously, the gear and axle and grumbling paddle wheels began to turn.

Mixed yells came from topside. The captain snatched his head back up through the hatchway. A massive thumping, as of heavy oars, sounded rhythmically through the hull.

The captain stuck his head down through the hatchway once more. "We're moving!" he yelled, as if he couldn't believe his eyes. "We're moving!"

Now they could all hear it: the steady thump of the paddles and the sloshing of water moving against the hull. The sailors swapped looks, then cheered. More cheers and yells sounded from topside, along with curses from the steersman and exhortations from the captain. The apprentices hugged each other and danced clumsily around the platform. The rolling turbine shot out steam until the whole engine cabin was fogged and hot. Omis poured another ladleful of water down the funnel and smiled at his sturdily laboring engine much as the gods must have smiled at the new made universe.

Sulun only rubbed his forehead and heaved a profound sigh of relief.

Cheap but colorful banners bearing the name and sigil of Entori's house hung about the dock. A sizable crowd had gathered, and paid criers could be heard to landward summoning still more. Assorted pushcart merchants, taking advantage of the ready audience, peddled their way through the crowd. At the end of the dock, in a small roped-off section, sat chairs and couches for a cluster of Entori's invited guests.

"A good-sized crowd, if not a terribly respectable one," Vari commented from her place by the rail of the ship's top deck. "But as good as our master could manage, I suppose."

"Good enough to spread the word of our success all over the city," Omis considered, idly patting her hair. "Ah, here comes the old vulture now."

Sure enough: preceded by his porter, with his sister Eloti on his arm, followed by all the rest of his household, everyone dressed well for a change, Entori came strutting down the dock. The crowd stepped aside with no urging, murmuring in surprise; it had been many a long day since Entori the Miser had provided public entertainment for anyone. He paused at the end of the dock to make appropriate greetings and trade bits of conversation with the better class crowd assembled there, then gestured theatrically to the rest of his diminished household. The servants dutifully stopped where they were, taking respectful positions out of the guests' line of sight. Entori, with a flourish of his heavy cape, escorted his expressionless sister up the gangplank and onto the ship. A handful of sailors dutifully played a short fanfare on the ship's pacing drum and signal trumpet. Entori took his sister to their waiting chairs on the afterdeck and, with another flourish, sat down.

"Not bad, but I've seen better shows," Arizun whispered to the other apprentices. Sulun shushed him.

The ship's captain, doubtless given the task for his loud if unlovely voice, bellowed a short speech to the audience. Sulun heard a dozen references to Master Entori and not one mention of himself or his crew, but only shrugged. It wasn't fame that interested him now. He peered over the railing as best he could, but couldn't see if Zeren was in the crowd.

Entori raised a hand, the sailors responded with another drumroll, and the rest of the crew cast off lines. The steersman took a grip on the tiller as if expecting to wrestle with it. Sulun could hear the gurgling and belching of the engine below; he wished he were close enough to the hatchway to sneak a quick look down into the engine cabin.

A creaking groan came from the paddle wheels, then a slurging of water as the wheels began to move. The crowd on the deck shouted in amazement. Entori for once beamed from ear to ear. It was not a pretty expression.

The wheels turned faster, bringing the paddles up dripping. Water slid under the keel, and the ship shuddered, then slid away from the dock. The steersman, looking martyred, leaned heavily on the sweep. The crowd on the dock howled in shock, wonder, delight; Entori the Miser had at last put on a real show for them, a marvel such as no one had ever seen before, a bit of history to tell their children and neighbors about. They cheered, stamped, applauded and threw odd items of clothing and food into the air.

"I think our master will be pleased with his reception," said Doshi, wincing a little at the noise.

"Let's hope he's grateful, too," Sulun muttered, keeping

a covert eye on Entori. He knew what today's schedule would be: a leisurely sail across the harbor, a brief circle through the calm sea beyond—enough to test the engine's speed and the ship's maneuverability—then back to the dock for a quick examination of the mounts, valves, gears and bearings before going home to a victory dinner. Somewhere in that period he must catch Entori in a good mood and entice his permission to work fullspeed and fulltime on the Bombard Project.

Meanwhile, seeing that Entori had begun to relax, order wine and enjoy the voyage, Sulun thought he and Omis should spend some time watching the operation of the engine. He signalled to the blacksmith and made his way unobtrusively down to the engine deck.

The engine's cabin resembled the steamroom at the public baths, making figures indistinct but carrying sound. Two burly sailors were arguing in the fog while Arizun danced around them, ignored by both, insisting that he would dip the water and load the coals, thank you, but they would have to rotate the platform. Another sailor stood by the porthole, dolefully wagging a palm frond fan, trying to drive out some of the steam.

"Who's oiling the gears?" Sulun shouted, cutting off the argument in mid-yell. "And who's watching the axles for vibration? This is supposed to be a test of the engine, and which of you fools is watching the *engine?*"

The sailors looked guilty. Arizun snickered. Sulun rolled his eyes, flapped his hands in desperation, and got busy with the observations. He made a point of explaining every detail to the sailors at considerable volume, in hope that they'd remember how to do this once the test was over and the ship back to regular work. It occurred to him that he should suggest to the captain that some reliable man be permanently assigned to tend the engine, someone capable of reading the descriptions, understanding the drawings and making any necessary repairs. He toyed with the idea of a whole guild of ship-engine tenders while he peered at gears, oiled moving parts and noted water levels.

Soon enough came the captain's bellowed order to reverse course. Sulun pointed imperiously to the two sailors, then to the handles on the platform. "Pull," he commanded. "No, no, you fools! The other way! That's right.

Now wait, wait until the axle stops turning . . . There. Now pull it the rest of the way."

The sailors pulled, the platform turned, the gears engaged with a minimum of protest and the big axle began turning the other way. Cheers came from above, mixed with wails of complaint from the steersman. The sailors in the engine cabin studied the spinning axle, gears and turbine with growing admiration. Arizun smirked as he dumped on more coals. Sulun, noting everyone's sodden clothes and hair, made a quick recommendation for oiling and waxing the decks and bulkheads, and got out of there.

Back on the main deck, he found reason to be grateful for his steambath. The sun was high, the weather burning hot, and everyone but the sailors was wilting visibly. Entori and his sister sat under a hastily erected awning, sipping cups of chilled wine. The others passed around an ewer of lukewarm beer. Sulun strolled quietly to the railing and watched the captain put the ship through its paces: backing straight, backing and turning, ordering full stop and then forward while timing with a small sandglass how long the changes took. The man seemed to familiarize himself quickly with the uses of the engine. Impressed, Sulun waved him a salute. The captain smiled, nodded acknowledgement and went back to his tests. Best to talk to him later. Meanwhile, observe Entori and pick a good moment to talk to him.

Yanados stood near, eyes flicking over the working sailors but always coming back to the captain. Sulun edged close to her and quietly told her his idea of specialized engine-tending sailors. She nodded agreement, not taking her eyes off the captain.

"I'll talk to the captain, if you like," she offered. "I know the proper words sailors would use, and he'll listen to me. Best if you deal with our master."

Sulun agreed with the tactic, and eased his way toward Entori, studying his target. The man seemed to be in high good humor, actually smiling for a second or two, no doubt thinking of the profits to be made with such a ship as this. No better time than now. Sulun sidled closer.

"I would say the engine is a success, Master," he began.

"Hmm, yes," Entori agreed, barely glancing at Sulun.

Eloti gave them both an expressionless look, said nothing.

"I have another invention in mind," Sulun plunged,

"which may be even more profitable. I could proceed using little more than the supplies we already have, and bring you results within another moon or less."

"Another invention?" Entori peered at him, face falling into that habitual look of suspicion. "What is it?"

Sulun took a deep breath. "A new weapon, one that could utterly rout the Ancar, even regain the lands Sabis has lost. The army would certainly pay well for such a thing, as one may guess. With your permission, Master, I will proceed—"

"Not now." Entori dismissed him with a wave of one hand. "The navy will pay well enough for these ship engines—after I've fitted my own ships with them. You will make more such engines."

"Er, these engines can be readily made, Master—by any good smiths in the city, now that we have the designs. You could hire other smiths to make the engines—far more and faster than my little work gang could do—while I work on the weapon. If you will permit—"

"None of that!" Entori snapped. "I'll not have every rude mechanic in the city knowing the secret of these engines, selling the knowledge to every shipper who asks. No, boy, the secret will remain in my house."

"Certainly, Master," Sulun gulped. "In that event, let us hire more workmen to make the engines—make many of them, and quickly—while I proceed with the weapon, likewise in secret. You'll have two fine devices to sell, and nobody else will—"

"What, more mouths to feed? And at such prices?" Entori purpled. "Your lot is expensive enough."

"But it would take us months to build another engine! The time lost—"

"My next ship sails the day after tomorrow, and will not return to port for two good moons. Take your measurements tomorrow and have the engine ready when she returns. Other than that, I see no call for haste—not enough to require hiring more help."

"The household has lost some servants," Eloti put in, surprising both of them. "For replacements, we could hire skilled mechanics from among these northern refugees. They should come cheaply enough, and be grateful for a roof over their heads."

Sulun held his breath, giving Eloti a mute look of gratitude, while Entori thought that over.

"Not now," the miser decided. "Not until my next cargo comes in. Prices have been terrible lately, and too many of my debtors have fled south. Meanwhile, Sir Philosopher, go measure the next ship and work with what you have." He waved to a passing servant. "Hey boy, more wine. Ah, servants are all whores, whining and conniving to scrape up more pennies . . . Pour carefully, you dolt!"

Eloti gave Sulun a sad, resigned smile, and turned away.

Sulun bowed briefly and wandered back to the railing. Gods, he thought, but this was unbelievable. Greed aside, how could Entori not see the importance of the Ancar invasion? Press gangs snatched levies outside his door, and the man would not risk a few silvers to make weapons. Unbelievable.

And how would he break the news to the others?

Sulun tried, quietly and gently as possible, during the long, leisurely afternoon's voyage. The day was hot but pleasant and the ship performed splendidly, but Sulun's work gang could take no pleasure in it.

"Gods," Omis groaned, "back to sneaking and penny-pinching. How will I ever finish the bombard like this? How can we disguise the work under the old vulture's very nose? Could we move everything but the forge to the river workshop, think you? It would take several wagonloads, and the streets so unsafe . . ."

"I don't see that we have any other choice," Sulun commiserated. "The tools, and supplies . . . We'll need to go all together, or perhaps if we can get word to Zeren he can arrange to have patrols passing in the right places and times. Ah, but how would we get messages to him? Arizun alone wouldn't be safe . . . Gods, I can't think. We need Yanados's wit. Where is she?"

But Yanados was nowhere to be found, either on the top deck or below with the engine. A discreet search of what areas Sulun and Omis could reach turned up no sign of Yanados—nor, Omis noticed first, the captain either. The two craftsmen considered those facts, looked at each other, and quietly went back to their places on deck.

Yanados eventually reappeared, looking ever so faintly smug, just as the ship was turning back for the harbor.

The others said nothing, only looked at her, and she returned them a cool stare. Omis shook his head and gazed out toward the approaching port, where the low sunlight danced on the sea. The ship's bell rang twice, passing messages to the crew, and its sweet tone was echoed by the harbor bell announcing the time.

Omis jumped as if he'd been stabbed. "Bells," he whispered. "Gods, I'm a fool. Bells!"

Before Sulun could ask what he meant by that, the blacksmith ran over to the ship's bell and peered up its interior. Next he grabbed the startled signalman and threw questions at him. Was this bell made in the city? Who made it? Where was his shop? The sailor told all he knew, made a quick excuse, and fled. Omis shook his head and went stomping back to the rail.

"Bells," he kept muttering, much to Sulun's and Vari's alarm. "Heavy brass, maybe heavy enough. Lower heat, easy to cast, but how? Sand molds? Where can I learn? Brass! Gods, I'm an idiot."

"Shush," Sulun whispered. "I think the old vulture's looking."

"But how thick, to contain the pressure?" Omis mumbled.

Entori glanced his way, frowning.

"Quiet, Omis!" Vari elbowed him. "Wait 'til we get home."

Omis snorted, but shut up. Entori looked away. The ship chuffed back to its dock, belching coal smoke and steam from its aft sideports, to the welcoming cheers of the remaining audience at the waterside.

"We can do it in one trip," Omis insisted as they sneaked the mule cart out the rear gate. "Just go one street over, let me out at the brassworker's, then come get me on the way home. I'll be perfectly safe, I swear!"

"Very well, very well," Sulun capitulated, closing the gate behind them. "Once again, tell me why it must be brass."

"Because I can't get sufficient heat to melt iron, of course!" Omis snorted. "Make iron flow like water? Cast it like brass? Hah, as easily catch the unicorn. Come climb on the cart, and let's make haste."

"But the force of the explosion—"

"Brass can hold it, be she cast thick enough. I tell you—"

"Get up!" Doshi cut their argument short with a slap of reins on the mules' rumps. The laden cart rolled into the street, armed apprentices watching for danger fore and aft.

"Then what shall we do with all that iron we struggled so to get?" Sulun grumbled, struggling for a comfortable position among the bundles.

"Sell it back for better money now that it's been hammered once. Ah, gods, the time wasted! But we should keep some of it for gears and mounts and axles, damn the old vulture. Hmm, also I could hammer some of it into globes to be flung from the bombard. I've long suspected that those cannisters were a problem—"

"Crowds ahead!" Arizun warned. "Great gods, I think they're running to a riot. Let's take the next street over."

"Aye, let's," said Yanados, "but I don't think it's a riot. That lot looks more to be running from a press gang."

Doshi had already turned the mules; now he slapped them into a respectably fast trot, hoping that the sounds of the running mob would cover the noise of the cart's wheels.

"It's a god's sign," Omis observed. "This way leads closer to the brassmakers' street."

The street leading to the workshop was mostly empty— only a few streetside peddlers and a parked covered wagon about—and Sulun's party took little time opening the heavy front door. Arizun noted that at least one attempt had been made to force the latch, but Omis's sturdy iron lock had held well. They brought the cart through the narrow archway and on into the back courtyard, where they set about unloading gear. Arizun went off to lock the door again behind them, and Sulun made a point of listing all the portable goods.

"Travelling clothes, dried rations for two days, our books and tools . . . Damn, it's both too little and too much," he announced. "Too little to supply us for long, too much to carry in one cartload."

"A bigger cart?" Doshi suggested.

"Where? How do we buy one?"

"Sell Omis's extra iron," said Yanados.

"Hmm, that reminds me. Do we all have hatchets, long knives, bows and sufficient arrows?"

"Also fishhooks and lines, pins, thread and needles," Vari put in. "And medicines."

Sulun shrugged and made more notes on his waxboard.

Arizun came trotting back into the courtyard, looking a bit pale. "Pardon me, friends," he announced, sounding unusually subdued, "but we have a visitor."

Everyone jumped, and turned to look. Arizun bowed low, with as much of a flourish as he could manage.

Through the archway, dressed in a quietly tasteful gown and carrying a small sunshade, strolled Eloti.

"Greetings again, Craftmaster Sulun," she said. "So pleased to find your true workplace at last."

Sulun couldn't think of anything to say, so he bowed low. Eloti smiled politely, and stood waiting.

Ziya broke the awkward silence, toddling forward and making a more elaborate bow. "Good Mistress Eloti," she said, formal as any high-city hostess, "if you would be so kind as to join us for luncheon, we should be delighted to explain everything to your satisfaction."

Eloti raised an eyebrow in respectful surprise.

Sulun, snapped out of his confusion, breathed a quick prayer of thanks to all available gods and snapped orders to the gawking apprentices: fetch table and couches or chairs, get wine and proper food and some good tableware, suitable for a gentlewoman. The others scrambled to obey. Eloti sat down on the nearest bench, fanned herself languidly with a palm-frond fan, and waited to see what would happen. She seemed intrigued, if not downright amused.

The best that Sulun's crowd could produce was a small table (covered with a clean cloak), two chairs (of which Eloti got the better and Sulun the second), some good wine in a plain jug, some coarse but fresh bread and a bit of cheese, all served in hastily cleaned mortars and mixing bowls. Ziya did the serving, offering the plates and cups in the best high-house style, with all the proper phrases. The other apprentices watched in fascination for a few minutes, then took themselves elsewhere. Ziya poured out the wine, bowed formally again, then excused herself and hurried after the others.

Sulun took the opportunity to marshal his store of facts and arguments, and incidentally raise his estimate of Ziya's intelligence. He wondered how often the child had observed her mother performing just such duties for Shibari's creditors.

"I regret that the surroundings are less than elegant," Sulun began cautiously, "but we find this location to be useful, quiet and inexpensive."

"I'm pleased to see you practicing good economy with my funds," Eloti replied, sipping the wine. She raised an eyebrow again in approval of the vintage. "I have also noted the common absence of my mule cart. Might I ask just what tools and other goods you have been transporting?"

Accounting time, Sulun realized. It would not be wise to mislead the lady. "Tools for working on our new project in secret," he admitted. "Everything except Omis's forge."

"Also, I've noticed, considerable food, clothing and household items. Were you expecting to withstand a siege here?"

"It's possible," Sulun hedged.

Eloti tapped a fingernail on her mortar cup. "Is that the only reason?"

"No," Sulun admitted. "If this project fails and the city falls, we hope to escape."

"All of you?" Eloti glanced around at the building that concealed the rest of Sulun's crew. "Your friend the blacksmith, his wife and children also?"

"Yes." Sulun couldn't begin to explain that all of them had become a sort of household, a family, in their own right. "We'll leave no one behind."

"Indeed?" Eloti took another sip of wine. "I find your loyalty strange, but commendable." Her eyes narrowed, skewering Sulun over the edge of her cup. "Could your . . . coterie possibly be expanded to include a patron?"

Sulun gulped. "Do you mean that Entori knows—plans to escape with us?"

"Not my brother. I have tried, many times, to discuss departing Sabis with him. He will not hear of it." Eloti set her cup neatly, precisely, back on the table, and clasped her hands under her chin like any merchant about to do business. "So, I wish to employ you and your students to undertake this new weapon project under my auspices. Is that formal enough?"

Sulun let out his breath in a soundless whistle. "Certainly, Goodlady. I'm honored to have you as our . . . secondary patron."

"Then surely you would not mind storing some of my . . . gear in this workshop." Eloti smiled.

"Not at all, Goodlady." Sulun refrained from asking

what gear, or how much. "I do beg you to consider, though, how much equipment we may be able to transport in case of, er, emergency."

Eloti leaned back in her chair, the classic motion of a merchant about to dicker extensively. "I would begin with a larger wagon," she said, "still capable of being drawn by two mules."

Sulun grinned. "It must also be capable of carrying two changes of clothing for each of us, plus our books, tools, sufficient food for at least three days, basic household supplies—and, of course, all of us."

"Of course," Eloti smiled, flicking her fan. "Likewise one larger travelling-chest for myself, and enough sailcloth to cover the load."

"Of course," Sulun reached for his waxboard then frowned. "I confess, I've never had to calculate the carrying capacity of mule wagons."

"Leave that to me," said Eloti, not smiling now. "Of course, I must know how far the wagon is expected to travel, over what roads, and into what sort of country."

Sulun gnawed his lip, seeing where this was aimed. He didn't really have an answer; all of them together hadn't decided. Perhaps another conference was in order. "Doshi, Arizun, all of you," he called to the innocent-looking house, "Get out here. We have . . . travel routes to discuss."

In scant seconds the little crowd came out and ranged themselves on the workbenches, all serious-faced, even the children. Sulun guessed that they'd been listening closely through the doors and windows, and needed no explanations.

"If we run," he said bluntly, "where do we go?"

Doshi surprised him by speaking up first. "To the north," he said, with surprising decisiveness. "I've copied all the maps—begging your pardon, Lady—and I know that land. Yes, we'd be hard put to get behind the Ancar lines and I confess I don't know how we'd do that—"

"Zeren might know," Arizun put in. "Going north was his idea first."

"But once past them, we'd be reasonably safe. More, those people up there are poor farmers, not very well educated, and from all accounts the Ancar aren't scholars either. They'd welcome skilled tradesfolk, mechanicals, with our knowledge. We could make ourselves welcome there."

"And how would the Ancar conquerors care for Sabisan refugees in their midst?" Eloti asked.

"We needen't say we come from Sabis," Doshi shrugged.

"We could say we come from Halas," Arizun piped up, in his native element now. "That's the other end of the world, for all the northerners would know. They've never been there, know nothing of its people or customs. We could be as strange as we liked."

"In which case," Eloti pointed out, "they might be afraid to come near us, let alone purchase our wares or work."

"Oh no, that could be an advantage," Arizun insisted, grinning like a monkey. "We could say we were magicians."

"Magicians?" Sulun choked on a mouthful of wine.

"Certainly! Ignorant folk may fear magicians, but they always want their services. I could teach you the basics—"

The others laughed. Eloti smiled widely.

"It's true, it's true!" Arizun insisted. "How do you think I lived, all those years before Sulun apprenticed me? I swear by all the gods I've ever heard of, folk will fee and placate magicians far more than honest philosophers or craftsmen. Folk love mysteries far more than knowledge."

There was silence for a long moment while everyone thought about that, seeing the grim truth in it.

In that silence they noticed the growing noise outside. From the street came sounds of shouts, trampling feet, noises of smashing wood and pottery, and more—an indescribable growl of no one source, all too well recognized after these long weeks of hard times.

"Oh gods, not another street riot," Sulun groaned, starting to his feet.

"It won't come in here," said Arizun, tugging at his sleeve. "I made sure to lock that door, and it's too thick for them to break down."

"He's right," said Yanados, listening. "If we hear them trying to break in we can go to the upper windows and drop things on them, but there's no danger yet."

"Still, we're stuck here until it passes," Vari worried. "Gods, I hope it doesn't reach to the brassworkers' street."

"Brassworkers' street?" Eloti inquired.

"Omis is there," Sulun explained. "He wants to trade

skills with a good brass smith, learn the secrets of large brass casting. It's for our other project."

"Interesting." Eloti fanned herself thoughtfully. "If your project succeeds it may save the city, you've said."

"Yes. But if it fails, we intend to escape with whole skins."

"And," Doshi added, "with enough of our tools and knowledge that we need not live like savages."

"Indeed," Eloti murmured. "Indeed."

Then they heard the familiar iron tramp of guardsmen's booted feet in the street outside, followed by bellowed orders, howls of dismay, sounds of running sandals and assorted thumpings.

"I think the riot is leaving," Eloti observed. "Now should your plan to go north fail, what secondary plans have you?"

Secondary plans? Sulun wondered, looking about him. He hadn't even refined the first one.

But then Yanados spoke up. "The captain of the *Yanira* will take us on board, no fees and no questions, and let us off at any port we ask."

Everyone turned to look at her. Sulun coughed, then asked, "Why is he inclined to be so amazingly generous?"

Yanados bit her lip for a moment. "I . . . made a quiet arrangement, the day we tested the engine. I gave him the design drawings for the engine and paddle wheels, and . . . I told him we could make more, teach others to make more. Such skills would be very useful in . . . some places."

"I . . . see." Sulun no longer had any doubts about Yanados's family or land or origin. Everyone knew about the pirates of Sakar. Ships with Sulun's engines could rule the seas. Any clever captain could add those facts and come to the obvious conclusion. "Yes, we could escape that way."

"Provided," Eloti said, "that the *Yanira* happens to be in port at whatever time we have need of her."

More silence as the conspirators considered that.

Their thoughts were interrupted by a polite but firm knocking at the outer door. Everyone looked at each other.

"I'll go," said Doshi. "None of us looks like a stout warrior, but I think I can pretend to it better than most." He was up and away before anyone could think of a better argument.

"In case of either plan being necessary," Eloti resumed, "we'll require a wagon that can transport ourselves and our goods either out of the city or down to the docks in a single load, yet isn't so vast that it would have trouble at the gates or require more than two mules." She tapped her teeth with her fan. "I think such could be provided, say, by quarter moon."

"So quickly?" Sulun marvelled.

"My dear Master Sulun, I have not lived all these years in Entori's house without learning something of the carting business."

At that point they all heard the front door slam shut, and the sound of approaching boots. Everyone froze, wondering which guardsman Doshi had let in, and why.

A moment later the mystery was resolved as Doshi came back, grinning from ear to ear, with Zeren a pace behind him. "Look what I found on the doorstep!" he announced.

"Zeren, by all the gods!" "Make room for him!" "Where's another bench?" "Do we have more wine?" Everybody chattered at once.

Zeren, a little bemused by all the attention, dropped onto the nearest bench and took off his helmet. "I'm pleased to see you're all safe," he said. "When we cleared out this street and I saw your door, I thought I should send my boys on ahead and see if you were present, and well."

"We are, we are," Sulun fairly dithered, handing Zeren a filled cup. "We've been making plans to complete the Bombard Project. Omis has some ideas about cast brass—he's up at the brassworkers' street right now—the riot hasn't reached there, has it?"

"Oh no, it's just down here, near the river. Such troubles are fewer since we started the press-gangs . . . though they're worse when they happen at all." He stared past them at Eloti. "And who's this lady?"

Once more Ziya performed the formalities. "This is Goodlady Eloti, sister of Entori, of Entori House. Our new patroness. Madame, this is—"

"Zeren of the Guard," Zeren cut in, impatient with lengthy courtesies. He couldn't seem to take his eyes off Eloti. "Begging your pardon, Lady, but . . . what are you doing down here?"

"Inspecting my investment." Eloti met his stare with a cool smile. She hadn't missed the welcome the others gave him. "We were also discussing means of departing the city, should the invasion reach this far."

"Oh." Zeren glanced at Sulun, his eyes asking: New ally? To be trusted?

"The lady's been pointing out flaws in our existing plans," Sulun explained, then added recklessly, "She's also offered to provide help with anything reasonable."

"I see." Zeren took a careful mouthful of wine, studying Eloti over his cup. "So. What flaws did you find?"

Sulun, caught between them, got the distinct feeling that he'd been assigned the role of either truce negotiator or matchmaker, and that was something new in his experience.

"First, the ship on which we might escape southward or . . . to the islands . . . might not be in port when we need her. Second, if we try to run north, how would we pass the Ancar lines?"

Zeren thought for a long moment, looking from Sulun to Eloti and back. "You'll need a boat in any case," he said at last. "Whether you have to cross the straits, catch up with your ship or bypass the Ancar lines, you'll need a boat big enough to carry all of you safely. The river's the best place to bypass the Ancar; they're not sailors. When they crossed the Azesu all those years back, they neither bridged nor sailed it. They hunted up and down the river until they found a passable ford for infantry. Same thing when they crossed the Gol a few years later. I doubt that they've changed since. Get a boat, stay on the river as long as you can, and if their arrows can't reach you, you'll be safe."

"How big a boat?" said Eloti, pulling a small waxboard from her sleeves.

Sulun noted that she didn't take her eyes off Zeren either.

By next moon-quarter the wagon arrived. It appeared quietly one day in the stable courtyard, tucked against the wall, half under the stable eaves, looking as if it had always been there. Examining it during lunch, Sulun noted that it was indeed long and wide and sturdy enough to carry all of them, plus their clothes, food, tools, and even Omis' anvil. The flooring was doublebraced, the wheels unusually sturdy, and the whole construction made of good hardwood. A large square of tightly woven, oiled sailcloth was folded up in the footwell below the driver's seat. Sulun reflected that the mistress did indeed know the carting business, and went off to lunch in high good humor.

Back in the working courtyard, he noticed that the stacks of iron ingots were much reduced and their place taken by bags of odd-colored sand. Intrigued, he went looking for Omis, and found him by the rear gate, helping two strangers in workmen's garb muscle in a load of heavy wooden panels. Sulun knew better than to say anything before the men left, but he pounced the minute the gate was shut.

"That?" Omis rubbed his hands gleefully. "That, old friend, is the makings of a sand mold."

"A sand mold?"

"Aye. Our new bombard tube will be cast from good brass, in a mold of wet sand clenched by wooden walls. Heh! Once we've cast her, we can use this trick to make more engine parts for the old vulture."

"Hmm. And what shall we use for the casting model? Wax?"

"No, wood." Omis hefted a smoothed round log as big as his leg. "We'll shape this, put it in the casting box, pour the sand around it, wet the sand and pound it nearly solid, then pull out the log to leave its shape in the sand—where we'll pour the brass. Simple, eh? Well, there are some details, but not many. The important thing is, this technique works. I watched the bellmaker do it, from start to finish. I can do it, Sulun. We'll have our new bombard in less than a tenday."

"Er, what did you give him in exchange for the knowledge?"

"The basic design of the steam engine, for which he was sufficiently grateful. So grateful, indeed, that he told me where I might purchase something truly valuable."

"Oh gods, what? And how valuable?"

"A small, portable forge, my friend. I don't intend to be caught without a forge again, not after last time."

"You bought it, of course," Sulun sighed. "How much? And where did you put it?"

"Well, I sold most of the extra iron—the rest went to purchasing the casting sand. Brass casting requires special sand, you know."

"I know. Where is it?"

"Why, right over here in the corner." Omis led the way to a squat metal cylinder half-hidden behind the sandbags. "It's iron, lined with good fireclay. I saw the brass smith using one, and I made certain it could manage small pieces of iron, too. Isn't she pretty?"

"Delightful," Sulun groaned. "How much does it weigh? Can the wagon take it? And how soon can we get it down to the river workshop?"

"Wagon? What wagon?"

"A gift from our patroness. I just found it this morning. Come, and bring your new toy; we may as well learn right now if the wagon can carry it."

"Carry it? Hah." With that, Omis picked up the little forge, straining a bit, and carried it all the way into the stable courtyard. "See?" he puffed, putting it down. "It isn't that heavy."

"Let's see what the wagon says." Sulun dropped the new wagon's tailgate. "Load it," he said.

Surprisingly enough, the wagon could and did hold the small forge, with no more than a few creaks of complaint from the floorboards.

"There, you see?" Omis grinned as he wiped sweat off his forehead. "It's light enough to carry, and doesn't take up much room. We'll take it with us when we go."

Sulun started to say that if the bombard could be made quickly enough they wouldn't have to go at all, but then he thought better of it. "Excellent. Leave it in the wagon, then; we'll take it down to the river workshop this very afternoon."

"But I haven't even tested it yet!" Omis howled, offended. "Let me use it for today, at least!"

And nothing would satisfy him but taking the forge off the wagon and carrying it all the way back to the courtyard. Further, he wanted to test the sand mold technique by casting the new engine parts therein. Sulun gave up and let him do as he wished. They'd need some finished parts to report to Entori tomorrow morning, anyway.

That evening at dinner the servants' table buzzed with gossip. There had been a big parade down the main avenue—the cook's sister's husband had seen it—of the newly levied troops going out to hold the lines in the north. The scullions were wonderfully optimistic: maybe now there's be more peace in the city, and prices would fall back to something reasonable. Sulun's crowd said nothing; they knew Zeren's opinion of the levies, their training and armament and skills. He'd had better opinion of the mercenary troops. Still, there'd been no further riots, no further advances by the Ancar as far as anyone knew, and there were rumors of further good news.

The Imperial Court, it was said, had received a welcome visitor from the north. Eylas of the presumed lost lands of Medhyras, a former hostage from a noble Medhyran family who had been brought up in the barbarous Ancari court, had escaped his captors and fled south to Sabis, full of information. He knew of the growing rebellion against the invaders in Medhyras and even Pegyras. Given a little time, the Ancar might find themselves with the new Sabisan troops before them and a full-scale rebellion behind them. The Emperor was delighted to hear of this unlooked for help, and treated the new guest very well. The aristocracy had also been impressed with Prince Eylas's nice manners and appearance, and it seemed that he'd be invited to dine all over high-town soon.

Even Eloti seemed to be in a good humor for once, as the servants noted. His comments to his sister, overheard by the serving maids, had revolved around possible improvements of trade now that Prince Eylas had come to town.

"Ridiculous," Yanados muttered into her soup. "Is Entori mad? Nothing's really changed; the Ancar are still there."

"And we'll still need the bombard," Sulun finished. He wondered what he'd tell Eloti at their brief meeting in the garden courtyard that night. Between reporting on one project to Entori every morning and reporting on the other to Eloti every night he'd soon be running short on sleep.

"Was the wagon satisfactory?" Eloti asked, gazing thoughtfully at the few nightblooming jasmine flowers that remained at this season.

"Excellent, Goodlady. It can carry all our gear—including Omis's new little forge."

"Remarkable." Eloti shook her head. "I suppose the wagon will more than earn its price, even now that escape is no longer necessary."

"Hmm, one would do well not to count the cheeses before the cow is milked." Sulun grinned a little at that phrase, one he'd picked up from Doshi. "Prince Eylas's rebellion is only promised, not guaranteed."

"True. I, of all people, should know how rarely hope ceases flying and actually comes to roost."

Sulun suddenly wondered why Eloti was unmarried. He knew better than to ask. "What do we truly know of this man, anyway? He could be a clever liar, buying his way into the favor of the nobles for his own purposes."

Eloti shrugged. "He seemed knowledgeable enough about the lands near his home. He spoke at some length of the fine cattle of Torrhyn and northern Jarrya, so he's well-travelled at least."

"Well-travelled and well-spoken." Sulun shrugged. "Still not enough to turn the tides of war. I still claim that our bombard offers greater hope."

"I will continue to fund our little enterprise." Eloti smiled faintly. "Will you do the casting here or at the river workshop?"

"At the riverside. It's a cumbersome process, not easily hidden or disguised. Also, if you'll forgive my saying so, Entori House is well-known and ill-loved by too many. I would prefer to do our work in a quieter spot."

"I understand perfectly, but is the river house secure?"

"As safe as stout walls, good locks and Zeren's watchfulness can make it."

Eloti said nothing for long moments, eyes fixed on the few remaining flowers. "Very good," she murmured at last. "I hope you will not take it amiss if I visit you there on occasion."

"Er, no, certainly not."

"Perhaps I'll come bearing good news. You may go."

"That was all she said," Sulun reported later, in the fitful light of the cubicle's one small lamp. "I can't fathom her intentions, except that she wants us to continue."

"Perhaps she's taken a liking to Zeren," Yanados yawned, shoving a drowsing Arizun off her shoulder.

"*Our* Zeren?" Sulun laughed. "It's not like you to see romance everywhere. What, are you feeling the pull of mating season already?"

"Hardly. But can you think of a better reason?"

"I could imagine dozens, and have no evidence for any of them."

"What was that she said about Jarrya?" Doshi put in, looking up from his precious maps.

"Eh? Why, nothing—except that this Prince Eylas spoke of it." Sulun shook his head. Yanados getting romantic, Doshi getting homesick, Arizun turning mystical and Ziya fascinated by fire—they were not doing well in Entori House.

"Well then, what is this prince supposed to have said?" Doshi insisted.

"Uhm, something about the fine cattle raised there and in Torrhyn, I think. Nothing of any import or detail. I'm sorry, Doshi. Now, why that odd look?"

"Cattle?" Doshi's frown deepened. "That isn't cattle country, and never has been. The winters are too harsh to keep cattle out of doors, and the buildings are all made of stone . . ."

"I think we've all been awake too long," Sulun hinted, rubbing his back.

"They have to be stone to withstand the winter storms. One can't build very large barns there, not enough to house large herds of cattle. A few milk cows, perhaps, but they're poor beasts by southern standards. Folk there mostly raise sheep."

"Time to sleep, Doshi. We all need our rest."

Yanados took the hint and stood up, dragging Arizun with her. Doshi reluctantly gathered up his maps, but kept worrying at his thought as he shuffled toward the door.

"I don't think this visiting prince ever saw Jarrya. I think he's merrily lying his way through the court. You'd best tell Zeren that when you see him again."

"I will, Doshi. I promise. Now off to bed."

"I think there's no rebellion in the north at all, and we're just as badly off as before, except worse because now the court won't pay as much attention to the northern defenses, and—"

"Good *night*, Doshi."

"We'd best continue our plans to leave," Doshi finished as Sulun closed the door on his heels.

Arizun, perched near a window as lookout for possible

mobs, was the only one to hear the soft tap at the door. He quietly slipped the bar and locks to let Eloti in. She drifted silently as a leaf through the passageway, although the noise from the workyard would have covered ordinary footsteps. Once again, Arizun wondered how the lady managed to travel so easily and unnoticed through the dangerous streets, apparently alone, dressed well enough to attract the attention of a thousand desperate thieves. As always, he thought it best not to ask her.

Zeren was already there with the others, stripped of his armor, helping to pour sand and water into the standing mold. He glanced up as the other two came in, and for a moment his eyes met Eloti's. He blinked, nodded politely, quickly, and turned his attention back to what he was doing.

"Enough water!" Omis snapped. "We don't want to wash the sand out again. There, there . . ." He inspected the wet, packed sand in the thick wooden box, poked it here and there with his fingers, grunted satisfaction and turned to study the mold itself.

Nearly buried in wet sand, the mold didn't look very prepossessing: a heavy wooden tube, no bigger than Omis' leg, sliced lengthwise. Wet sand surrounded and filled it to the top. Omis picked up a short log, fit it neatly inside the tube until it touched the sand, and leaned on it. The sand compressed a bit, and the log stayed in place by itself. Omis nodded thoughtfully, picked up several squared short logs and poked them endwise into the box, on top of the sand.

"Everyone pound together," he announced, picking up a large maul for himself. "Remember to beat them all equally."

Everyone else sighed, picked up assorted hammers, and converged on the box.

"May I ask the purpose of this exercise?" Eloti asked, dropping gracefully onto a bench.

"We have to pound the sand tight," Arizun explained, taking a light mallet for himself. "We pour it, wet it, pack it, then pray it stays in place when we pull out the mold."

"Fascinating."

"Damned hard work."

"All together," Omis warned, raising his maul. *"Now."* He struck a good solid blow on the round log. The others followed suit, almost in unison, on the logs surrounding the mold. "And *now*. And *now* . . ."

Thud. Thud. Thud.

The hammering fell into a smooth rhythm. Water began oozing from the bottom of the box. Inch by inch, the logs drove deeper as the sand compressed. Watching them, Eloti tapped first her foot and then her fingers in rhythm.

Eventually Omis called a halt, pulled out the logs and inspected the sand. "Hmm, it should do," he decided. "Pour in more sand."

Everyone put down their hammers, picked up bags and buckets, and carefully poured. When the sand level reached the top of the mold, Omis called for the water. The wetted sand sank hardly at all. Omis poked again, studied the sand for a moment, then took up the logs and hammers once more.

It was, Sulun decided, nearly as hypnotic as the droning prayers in the temples on a great holy day. Pound, pound, pound all together, half a dozen arms swinging as one, and the sodden thudding rhythmic as a temple bell. Pound, pound, pound. If concentration, devotion and perfection made the best defense against magic, not even the greatest wizard in Sabis could touch them this day. Pound, pound, pound. Now if only his well-worked muscles didn't tire and cramp and pain him enough to break his concentration . . . Pound, pound, pound.

The voice sneaked up on him, interweaving so smoothly with the hammer-rhythm that he didn't notice it as anything separate from himself, not until one corner of his mind noted that he'd never heard the words of the song before.

"*Low* lie the *stars* over *Tos*lagen's *me*mory,
 High hang the *flowers* from the *trees* of her *tomb*."

And was it strange or not that everyone else swayed and swung with the quiet song? Everyone hammering smoothly, rapt as corybantic dancers: pound, pound, pound . . .

" '*Care*,' sing the *birds* in the *boughs* of the *cyp*resses,
 '*Care*, love and *care*, win you *free* of your *doom*.' "

Just those few lines, over and over, keeping the rhythm, drawing the arms, the mallets, to swing and pound, pound, pound endlessly, hold the mind tight on the simple action, no stray thought, no deviation, steady as a perfect engine . . .

"Halt!" Omis yelled, shaking his head. "We're down."

Everyone stopped, dropped their assorted hammers, rubbed their arms and shook their heads as if coming out of a dream. Indeed, Sulun noticed, the level of the sand was down—and packed as tight as fine clay.

Magic! Sulun turned to look at the one person who could have provided that song, the only one not hammering.

Eloti sat waving her fan gently, that faint smile lingering on her face.

"Goodlady." Sulun bowed to her. "I had no idea you could sing so well."

"A largely useless skill." She shrugged. "Save on rare occasions."

"Magic!" Arizun breathed. "That was a—a protective spell, or I've never seen one."

"You've never seen one, then," Zeren snorted, rubbing his arm. " 'Twas a work spell, and rather a good one." He grinned a brief salute at Eloti.

Eloti gave an eloquent shrug, punctuated with her fan. "It merely seemed appropriate," she said. "I assure you, I've never been a wizard's apprentice."

The others laughed approvingly, trying to imagine the quiet lady of Entori House as a scampering apprentice running errands for some crotchety wizard. Impossible, indeed.

"Back to the mold," Omis insisted. "Plug the top of the log; this will be the last layer."

The rest duly took up bags and buckets again, and went back to the careful pouring of sand and water, the last layer that would fill the box to the top.

"Gods grant," Omis muttered, easing the wooden plug into the top of the bombard shape, "we can get the pouring done today."

Sulun nodded agreement, but kept only the minimum of his attention on the mold. His eyes kept straying to Eloti, calmly fanning herself while she watched the proceedings, and his head filled with wild speculation where all the facts slid into place with a click as neat as the closing of a latch.

Eloti had sorcerous talent. His mistress was, in common parlance, a witch.

No wonder Entori House could survive the malice of Entori's clients, and with no better protection than the drunken house wizard. No wonder this house, outrageously vulnerable to the ill-will of the neighbors, at least, hadn't been disturbed by thieves nor plagued with accidents, even in these bad days. No wonder the lady came and went as she chose, unbothered by cutpurses or worse, virtually unseen. No wonder she remained unmarried. Who would have a she-wizard to wife, save for another wizard who wished to breed talented sons—and family-proud Entori would never let his sister marry below what he considered her proper class.

Yet she could read, and knew how and where to listen, and learned readily. Perhaps she had cozened secrets out of the house wizard, leaving him to forget her in his cups. Perhaps she had learned everything from books and observation alone. In secret, in whatever fashion, she had learned—and practiced. Eloti was the true protector of Entori House, and now of Sulun and his unknowing friends.

Accident. Fate. Pound, pound, pound . . .

"Enough," said Omis. "Pull out."

The others drew away their logs and mallets, and stepped back to let Omis inspect the mold. The tight-packed sand covered the wooden form almost completely, leaving only the bare disk of the plug's top visible. Omis nodded and breathed a long sigh.

"All right," he said. "Now we take out the mold form."

Only Sulun noticed that Eloti began humming softly, a different tune this time, in rhythm with the languid beat of her fan.

Omis tugged carefully, delicately, at the plug. After a second's resistance it pulled free of the wooden tube, free of the sand, displacing hardly a single grain. Omis sighed again in relief, fitted the jaws of narrow tongs around one of the tube halves and pulled gently, ever so gently. The wooden half-tube slid quietly out of its bedding, leaving the deep, perfect half circular hole in the packed sand behind it. Omis set the piece aside and reached for the last one with the tongs, careful, utterly careful, whispering prayers to assorted relevant gods.

Eloti's humming purred softly in the air like the sound of drowsy bees in sunlight.

The last piece of the mold slid out smoothly, leaving its shape perfectly molded in the packed sand.

"Perfect!" Omis whispered, tiptoeing away from the mold as if too loud a noise would shatter it.

"Perfect . . ." Sulun echoed, daring a sidelong glance at his mistress.

Eloti sat unchanged, calmly fanning herself, a faint smile resting on her otherwise impassive face.

"Begin the melt," said Omis, very quietly. "And no noise."

The others turned to the forge, gently picking up tools and billets of brass.

Sulun guessed he wouldn't be needed for this part; there was something more important to do. He went into the house, rummaged through the supplies and came back with some watered wine and light bread. Very quietly, he took them to Eloti.

"Best to refresh yourself, Mistress," he said, noncommitally. "This will be long and tedious work."

Eloti looked at him for a moment, then thanked him formally and took the food.

Sulun hurried back to the group working at the forge and busied himself with odd tasks: tossing in more charcoal as the fire rose, working the bellows when Zeren's arms tired, helping to pitch brass into the heating crucible, wetting down Omis's gloves between pokings and stirrings. Often he glanced at Eloti, noting that she kept her eyes on the undisturbed mold and could be heard softly humming to herself. Despite the heat of the forge, he shivered.

At close to sundown the brass was ready, flowing like milk, glowing like the sinking sun. Omis ran two thick iron bars through the rows of rings on either side of the crucible, took the end of one bar while Zeren took the other, ordered Sulun and the three bigger apprentices onto the other bar, and they all lifted together. Carefully, carefully, they walked their glowing burden away from the forge and up to the lip of the mold.

"Gently now, gently," Omis fairly chanted, "Set the forward bar, hold it steady, steady . . . Zeren, lift with me. Lift, lift . . ."

Eloti's humming grew ever so slightly louder.

Slowly the crucible tilted, its spout descending over the deep circular hole in the packed sand. The molten brass touched the edge, slipped into the spout, seemed to pause for an instant, then spilled gracefully into the mold. For a moment everyone saw the glowing stream pooling, with scarcely a splash, at the bottom of the long circular hole. Then clouds of steam boiled up to fog the vision, driven up from the wet sand.

"Keep pouring!" Omis snapped. "Don't change position. Close your eyes if it gets too bad. There, there . . ."

Coughing and blinking in the stifling fog, Sulun watched the shining surface of the molten brass rise in the mold. Upward it crept as the crucible slowly emptied, up to the top of the central column of sand and then over it, up to the surface of the sand mold. There it stopped, a gleaming disk in the sand, while the last drops trickled from the almost upended crucible.

"Perfect!" Omis laughed in relief. "Exactly enough. Gods, I was afraid we'd have too much, have to ease this bucket back down and empty it in a drain ditch. All together now, lift that other rod and pull back. Good, good . . ."

Step by step, with only a little less care than on their advance, they pulled the cooling crucible away from the mold and set it down. The ground steamed where it touched. Everyone else stepped back, and Omis pulled the carrying rods free.

"How long till it cools solid?" Zeren asked, wiping his forehead.

"Tomorrow sometime." Omis pulled off his gloves and tossed them aside. "I'd leave it a full day, just to be safe. So, we'll come back the morning after next to break out the mold and start on the smoothing. I suppose we can spend tomorrow working on another ship's engine for the old—er, the Master." He darted an embarassed smile at Eloti.

"Should we not celebrate our success?" she almost purred. "I believe a small thank-offering to the gods would be in order."

"A good libation should do," Zeren grinned, starting toward the house. "I brought a few jugs of a very decent wine with me."

"If we wish it heated, we could mull it in yonder crucible." Eloti smiled.

Omis roared with delighted laughter. "Gods, yes! How fitting!"

Fitting indeed, Sulun thought, following Zeren into the house to fetch the cups.

*   *   *

The gears, the hated gears . . . Sulun dourly polished another of the little iron monsters, reflecting that he was beginning to hate the very thought of steam engines and ships. Bits and parts of another engine nearly completed, Entori nagging him to hurry, the bombard waiting like a treasure that could be touched only in few, precious, stolen moments: half a moon like this. *And the news from the north no better.* All Sabis might fall before they managed to finish the bombard. *Damn Entori, damn his engines, damn these interminable gears!*

Seeing no further burrs or irregularities, Sulun dropped the hated gear in a box with its companions and glanced automatically at the sunlight above the roof. *Good gods, nearly dinnertime.* The others had gone inside, leaving him here with his wretched little task, and he couldn't blame them. He rubbed his eyes, back, fingers, and stalked off to his minuscule room. Just enough time to wash his hands and face for dinner, no time or reason to change his clothes; let the old vulture see that he'd worked like a galley slave all day. He washed fast, towelled off faster, and stalked toward the dining hall still damp.

It was the silence he noticed first: the servants eating so very quietly, heads down, trying not to be noticed. Scarcely a head lifted as he shuffled into his place on the bench at the servants' table.

But one of the heads raised was Arizun's. "Keep your head down," he whispered fiercely in Sulun's ear. "Look who's visiting Master at the upper table."

Sulun duly hunched over his plate and glanced sidewise at the Master's table—from which, he now noticed, came sounds of unusually lively conversation.

There sat Entori and his sister, as always: Eloti looking politely attentive, Entori for once animated and almost jovial. Facing them, backs to the servants' table, sat two newcomers. Guests, Sulun realized, probably business acquaintances, hardly friends, knowing Entori. Reason enough for the servants not to want attention drawn to themselves. But why was Arizun so agitated? And why was Vari shooting frightened looks at him across the bread dish? In fact, why was everyone in his work gang looking so frightened? He studied the two newcomers more closely.

Both men were fat and well-dressed, though the leftmost

was decked with more jewelry and embroidery—clearly the master. He was, at the moment, almost demanding of Entori, "But gods curse it, man, I'm offering you twenty percent of my cargoes for a full year! I'm not asking for the secret of their manufacture, only for the engines themselves. Just two good engines, fit for hundred-tonners, in exchange for twenty per hundred: Where will you find a better bargain?"

Aha, Entori's little show on the docks with the *Yanira* had borne fruit, and doubtless he was haggling over the price.

Sure enough, Entori replied, "I don't expect a better bargain. It's quite an excellent bargain. It's also quite impossible. The engine is a most complex and delicate bit of work; it takes time to make one, time to mount it properly. That first one took my craftsmen two moons to build, and the second will hardly take less. As soon as my own ships are fitted, of course, I'll be free to discuss fitting others', but you must understand the delay—"

"But then, within two moons you'll have a second ship fitted out. Surely then you could set your men to making one engine—just one—for a single ship of mine. Afterwards they could make another for you, then another for me."

"The time involved . . ."

Gods, he's bartering off our services! If Entori yielded, sent the whole pack of them to some other house to make an engine elsewhere, they'd never be able to slip away to the riverside laboratorium and finish the bombard. Sulun found himself praying that Entori's miserliness would endure through dinner.

"It might be possible," he heard Eloti say, "to measure this gentleman's ship, build the engine here, then send it to him when finished."

There was a moment's silence as both men considered that, followed by more haggling over time, prices, who would pay for what.

Sulun wilted with relief. Bless Eloti's cleverness, they wouldn't have to leave the house and work for some unknown master.

Yanados, seeing his expression, nudged him with an elbow. "We're not safe yet, Sulun. Look who else is at the table."

Puzzled, Sulun peered around his shoulder at the other guest, who had said nothing audible so far. The man was fat, sleek-looking, in elegantly cut brown robes with subdued but rich embroidery, and when he turned to reach for the bowl of cut fruit, showing his profile—

Oh gods, it's Mygenos!

Sulun ducked his head down fast, praying to every god he could remember that everyone else in his work gang kept their faces averted too. His hands shook as he reached for the sour wine.

"Right," whispered Yanados. "We've all been keeping our heads down, and don't think the other servants haven't noticed. We'll have to explain later."

"Has he recognized—"

"Not yet, I don't think. None of us."

"If he sees Ziya . . ."

"She saw him first, ducked behind Vari. Gods, if only we could get out of here . . ."

Sulun ran a long look down the table. Vari sat with her back to Entori's guest, Ziya and Tamiri huddled beside her. Ziya—thank gods they'd thought to chop her hair all those moons ago—looked very much like a small boy, a very silent and pale little boy. Omis—Deese be blessed, hadn't come to dinner in his working clothes—was hunched down so far that his beard was almost dragging in his soup. Doshi, who normally drank very little, kept his face hidden behind his wine cup, though Sulun guessed it was long empty. Arizun, taking no chances, had both his back turned and his face bowed over his plate. Yanados, now that there was no more need to speak with Sulun, cleverly made a play of trying to steal kisses from the scullery maid; the maid, smiling cynically, played along.

Their gambits appeared to work. Mygenos hadn't bothered to look over his shoulder at the servants, or hadn't seen more than drab clothes and bowed backs. Gods, if they could only get out of here, quickly and quietly . . .

But it was the custom in Entori House that the servants didn't leave the room until the Master either ordered them out or left himself. Entori had never bothered to dismiss the servants from dinner, and showed no sign of doing so now. Neither did he seem inclined to depart, clearly enjoying the game at the high table.

The game, and the dinner, dragged on for ages. The

food at the servants' table disappeared, the housekeeper frowned, the maids scowled, the porter muttered, the skinny harper/sweeper mumbled weak curses in his cup, and Sulun's gang kept silent and sweated. The house mage finally snapped at one of the maids to bring more wine, and the woman thankfully hopped up from her place to comply. Sulun toyed with the thoughts of sending the children away, one by one, supposedly on errands to the kitchen, possibly carrying empty dishes away.

He froze as he heard Mygenos's voice, raised for the first time that evening.

"Bear in mind, my Lord, the difficulty of supplying magical protection for a device of whose construction we know nothing." The man's voice was more unctuous than ever. Out of all Shibari's doomed house, he'd clearly done the best for himself. "Surely such costs must be considered when estimating the price."

There was another brief silence, then more haggling. Sulun felt sweat crawling down his back, even as he realized that both Mygenos and his new master were clearly hoping to get more than just a ship engine or two; they hoped to learn the design and construction of the device, in hopes of manufacturing their own—and that fact was not lost upon Entori.

"The engines made in this house are competently protected by our own wizard, I assure you," Entori said. "Elizan, come here."

Gods! Sulun squirmed. *Don't draw attention to us!*

"Damn," muttered the old house wizard, clambering out of his seat. "Didn' even get my drink . . . Coming, Master."

Get Ziya out, somehow. Sulun glanced at the child, seeing her keep her pale face on her empty plate.

The old house wizard doddered up to the high table, executing a clumsy bow to Entori and his guests. Sulun hoped fervently that he didn't breathe too close to Mygenos and let the man know just how drunk he was. Still, Elizan had clearly played this game before.

"My Lords," he intoned, sounding merely stuffy, "despite the infirmities of age, my powers remain undimmed and indefatigable as ever in ages past. Yea, I have guarded Entori House from ill these thirty long years and more, and pray to do so for as many more. Behold, no ill befalls this house, nor its goods, nor its enterprises, nor any under its roof, as all may see and report. Yea—"

"Arizun," Sulun whispered under the cover of the fusty oration, "tell Vari: Send Ziya out with some empty dishes, tell her to run to her room and hide. Pass it on."

Arizun nodded quick acknowledgement, leaned closer to Doshi, and duly passed the message on.

"Our ships do not fail at sea, save to the malice of pirates, of course, whose attacks cannot be adequately predicted, nor does our house fall prey to robbers and riots of the streets. Our goods do not rot overmuch, nor are they consumed by vermin." Elizan could certainly provide a good speech, given cause. "Our house remains unvisited by plague, fire, earthquake, flood—"

"Yes, yes, all very well," Mygenos interrupted, winning a frown from his new master and a scowl from Entori. "But this is a novelty we speak of, a thing untried and unheard of before now. Can you deal effectively with such novelties, my good colleague?"

Quick as a cat, he set together two wineglasses—fine crystal, Sulun noticed—and carefully balanced a third on top of them. Smiling almost gleefully, he carefully filled the topmost glass to the brim.

"A small test, good colleague, of dealing with novelty." Mygenos pointed to the filled glass. "Let us contest. Do you attempt to keep this glass in place, and I will enchant it to overturn."

"On my tablecloth?" rumbled Entori.

"Waste good wine?" gasped the house wizard.

"Ah, let them proceed," Eloti murmured. "At worst, the laundress will have a bit of work."

"Hmm, well enough," Entori subsided. "Proceed."

His guest exchanged a glance with Mygenos, and smirked.

Vari whispered urgently in Ziya's ear. Ziya nodded once, picked up a handful of empty dishes and slid noiselessly out of her seat.

Good, Sulun thought. *Now, while Myggy's busy. Go!*

A bit flustered, Elizan frowned at the balanced glasses. He licked his lips, clasped his hands, stared at the balanced glasses and visibly concentrated.

Ziya, head down, carrying the pile of dishes, padded softly across the flagstoned floor toward the doorway.

Mygenos leaned back in his chair, stared at the balanced glasses though narrowed eyes, and concentrated.

Sulun, even with his eyes fixed on Ziya's retreating back, felt the slow rise of heat behind him. It was just as he'd always felt it in Shibari's house, when Mygenos was at work. Only an unexplained surge of heat, nothing more, but he'd learned to recognize it as the mark of Mygenos's power. Magery. Wizard work. The force apart from Natural Philosophy and alien to it, the force of gathered will working across the orderly patterns of the Laws of Matter. At that moment he hated it.

And he felt no answering surge from Entori's house wizard.

Gods, what would it mean if that old drunkard lost this duel, if Entori was pushed back a step on his haggling over the engines? Loss of money, loss of pride—inevitable loss of temper, and where would that outrage go save to spend itself on his servants? No doubt the first bolt of fury would drop on poor drunken old Elizan, but the second bolt would land upon Sulun and his colleagues. What form would it take?

What if this kept them from escaping the house, from getting to the riverside laboratorium, from finishing the bombard?

The fate of Sabis, resting on a balanced wineglass!

The wineglass jiggled, softly ringing.

Then, very faintly, he heard the drifting of a quiet song. A familiar song, one heard scant days ago, down by the river. With it came an equally familiar sense of calm, like a memory of bees buzzing sleepily in sunlight.

"Low lie the stars over Toslagen's memory . . ."

The crystal-ringing stopped.

Ziya, unnoticed, padded quietly out the doorway and into the shadowed corridor. Once safe in the shadows, she began to run.

At the high table no one moved. Five figures peered, motionless, at the pyramid of wineglasses. The two wizards sweated, frowned, stared, their contesting wills almost palpable in the stillness.

Eloti, unnoticed, sat with her fingers steepled and pressed lightly against her lips, apparently just a rapt observer.

Sulun dared to raise his head and watch, feeling those balanced and battling forces: the beating heat like the wind from Omis's forge, the gently buzzing song that came from no mouth—and nothing noticeable from old Elizan.

Incredible, Sulun marvelled. *He's her stalking-horse, and no one knows it!*

Mygenos clenched his fists, gritted his teeth, and the heat rose. Almost visible, darting tongues of hot power surged again and again at the balanced glass. The glass held, calmly immovable.

The old house wizard swayed on his feet, clearly growing distressed. With or without power, he was making effort—and the effort was draining him. Even to Sulun's eye it was plain that the old tippler couldn't continue this much longer. In another few ticks of the waterclock he'd collapse, and what then?

Eloti flicked her eyes sideways at the old man, then back to the glass.

Almost casually, the silent song rose higher. It soared to a clear, ringing note—then to a falcon's screech of rage and triumph.

The glass tipped over—

—straight into Mygenos's lap.

The wizard yelped and scrambled out of his chair, leaving the wineglass to fall to the floor. Miraculously, it didn't break. Entori and his guest shouted wordlessly in surprise. Elizan gave a whoof of relief and leaned heavily against the table.

Eloti broke out laughing, an amazing sound, like the ring of unbroken crystal.

The hot cloud of tension around the high table dissipated like smoke before a rising gale. Mygenos cursed generously as he wiped his wine-stained robe, ignoring the furious look his master gave him.

"Ah, yes, I think our protections are adequate," Entori smirked, actually tugging a coin out of his belt purse and handing it to the old house wizard. "Thank you, Elizan. You may go."

"Pray, dismiss the rest of the servants too," Eloti smoothly cut in, raking a brief glance over the faces at the lower table. "Best let them get to their tasks while we discuss business in privacy."

"Oh, aye." Entori clapped his hands peremptorily, scarcely looking at the other servants. "You may go. Now, concerning the date of delivery . . ."

Sulun stood up fast, the others barely a second behind him, and headed for the door as quickly as he could manage without actually running. Vari already had the other children in tow, with Omis hurrying at their heels, and the other servants pattered after them.

Sulun had some idea of running off to their rooms to search for Ziya when the porter clapped a hand to his shoulder.

"Come down to the kitchen," the elderly servant hissed. "Ye simply must tell us who yonder guests are, and what's the trouble with 'em."

Sulun complied, tossing a last desperate glance to Omis and Vari. Yes, somebody had to satisfy the household's curiosity, and it seemed he'd been chosen. At least Ziya was safe, they were all safe from Mygenos's knowing eyes. The kitchen then, and more pilfered wine and interminable gossip. Small sacrifice for their salvation. He padded dutifully down the hall to the kitchen, grateful to see the rest of his little mob hurry off to their rooms.

There was still a fire burning in the kitchen, though no pots hung over it now. There stood the cook, who had managed to escape sitting in at that miserable dinner, handing a small pastry to a girl-child huddled on a stool beside the fire.

Girl? Who? Sulun plodded to the fireside at the porter's urging, barely noticing the cup of cider thrust into his hand, wondering where the girl had come from and who she was.

Then the child raised her head and looked at him.

"Sulun?" she squeaked, the ghost of an old smile flickering over her face. "Sulun, you're *here?*"

It was Memi. Mygenos's daughter. She remembered him.

Oh, gods!

All Sulun could think to do was plaster a sickly smile on his face and press a warning finger to his lips. "Hush, Memi," he whispered, grabbing for words. "Don't tell anyone I'm here. You know how people would laugh, hearing that Shibari's old philosopher now works for Entori the Miser."

"Aha," grinned the porter, guessing at the supposed disgrace. "So that's it, eh? 'Brought low, brought low, let none of me old friends know.' Heh-heh!"

"Aww . . ." Memi's face screwed into a grimace of pity. "I won't tell anyone, I promise."

For however long you can, Sulun groaned inwardly. "Thank you much, Memi. But tell me, how have you fared since you left Shibari's house?"

The child's noncommital shrug told Sulun all he needed to know. Mygenos's fortunes might have improved, but Memi's life was no better. She might remember her old friend Sulun kindly, but eventually her father's sternness would press her too far: To save herself punishment or win herself some pathetic gain, she would let the secret out.

Eventually Mygenos would know who Entori's engineer was. Between old malice and new rivalry, the wizard wouldn't hesitate to ill-wish Sulun and his work.

And he knew Sulun worked with firepowder.

Sulun sat down beside the fire, drank the cider, gossiped gently with the pathetically grateful child and with the momentarily kind servants, knowing his time had grown drastically short. Soon enough Mygenos would send for his daughter and depart. Soon enough Memi would reveal the secret. Soon enough Mygenos would set his vengeful little disasters in motion.

It was time to get out.

Four more days before they could get to the riverside workshop again: four days of making turbine parts, supports, molds for the steam valves—and hating every miserable hour of it. Four days of sweating over Memi's discovery, wondering when she'd tell and what Mygenos would do then. Four days of wretched work that felt like idleness without its rest.

Four days of bad news: there were more retreats, more losses in the north. The Ancar were moving steadily down the east side of the Baiz river valley, rolling over the Sabirn lines like a flood. The Imperial House issued no news, but street gossip ran high. Refugees from the upper valley added to it, and none of their news was good. The traffic to Esha increased steadily.

"Perhaps Mygenos's new master will join the panic," Sulun suggested as he helped break down the box of the sand mold. "If he runs south, Myggy just may find it prudent to go with him. After that, he'll have other things to worry about than his old rival from Shibari House."

"Hope high," Omis grunted, pulling away the last board. "Ah, that sand was pounded well."

The packed, now dry sand still stood firm as dried clay. Not a grain had moved during the four days of cooling down.

"Break it," said Omis, taking up a heavy sledge.

The rest of the work gang set upon the sand with mallets and chisels, cutting it away from the buried treasure. A familiar rapping on the front door interrupted them.

"Zeren, no doubt," said Eloti, rising gracefully from her seat on the bench. "Go on with the work; I'll let him in."

Ziya was the only one to watch her go, struck by the sight of the mistress of a respectable house going to open doors like a porter. The others kept on hammering, cutting, freeing the cast tube from the mold.

A moment later, Zeren strolled in with Eloti on his arm—just in time to hear Omis's shout of triumph and warning as the last of the sand fell away. They stopped to watch, Zeren unconsciously making a luck sign with his free hand.

The exposed tube didn't look very prepossessing: rough and pebbly, covered with glassy, fused sand, its interior still choked. Nonetheless, Omis cradled it in his arms, beaming, as if it were one of his own children.

"Beautiful," he breathed. "Not a flaw in the casting. Perfect."

"It doesn't look like much," Ziya sniffed, disappointed.

"Well, of course not, boy," Omis laughed. "It still has to be cleaned out, smoothed, polished, and the fuse hole drilled. We'll start that right now. Ah, good morning, Zeren. How is it you always manage to get here when something important's afoot?"

"No mystery," Zeren smiled, graciously lowering Eloti to her seat. "I come by every morning and see if anyone's about. I've told my guards I have a valuable informant here, which isn't a lie. The news is good, then?"

"Good now, better later. Set up the drill, boys."

While the apprentices scampered to comply, Sulun went to fetch food and drink. Zeren and Eloti were chatting when he brought the food out.

"Never mind the fool wizard," Zeren was saying. "He

and his master must have better things to occupy them now. The Ancar have been halted above Lutegh."

"Halted?" Sulun crowed, setting out the cups and bowls. "Thank the gods! If they stay put only half a moon, we'll have the bombard tested and ready . . ." He paused to cross his fingers, hoping that this model, this time, would work.

"Aye, cross your fingers," Zeren smiled sourly. "It isn't our oh-so-invincible troops that have checked them; it's the river. The Dawnstream branch of the Baiz is wide, fast and deep there, and the Ancar are no sailors. They've only turned east awhile, looking for an easy way across the river. Expect they'll find it soon enough, and then turn south again."

"Surely our troops on the south bank can stop them?"

"Perhaps," Zeren shrugged. "They've had the wit to take every boat and barge from the north bank, burn every bridge, fortify every known ford clean up into the Cerinde West hills—the generals showed that much sense."

"Still," Eloti considered, "the Ancar have taken that hill country, I believe."

"It's crawling with them," Zeren sighed. "If the main horde of the Ancar can't cross any further west, they'll simply go up into the hills, cross where the Dawnstream thins out into its tributary streams, join their Cerinde West cousins and come marching back down the south bank. A few months, at best." He glanced apologetically at Sulun. "We have less time than I thought, old friend. How long to finish your new bombard?"

"Gods . . ." Sulun tugged his hair, watching the work gang setting the drill bit into the blocked tube's muzzle. "Give us three days, just three uninterrupted days to drill it out, make the powder, test it . . . How long then, you tell me, to attract enough interest at court that we can have a dozen work gangs, busy night and day, making bombards and powder and shot?"

Zeren shrugged again. "Do I use every contact I have, call in every favor, I could get interested parties to watch you fire the bombard—successfully—at the Sworddance Field within perhaps three days. After that, at best, you might have orders and assistants from the Imperial House itself the next day—or minor interest from the lesser Ministers in half a moon."

"After that . . ." Sulun calculated, allowing for the ignorance of strange craftsmen who wouldn't begin to understand the principles of the bombard. "A dozen workshops could make a dozen bombards, with powder and shot and sufficient knowledge to use them, in perhaps another half moon at best."

"So, if the Ancar can be held off for as long as one moon, Sabis might live." Zeren leaned back to look at the cloudless sky. "There be the gods' dicing floor, right over our heads."

"But we need those three days to finish the bombard, first." Sulun turned to Eloti, wild-eyed with a desperate hope. "Mistress, what if we were to disappear from Entori's house, just for three days, all of us? What would he do then?"

Eloti thought a moment, then shook her head. "He too has favors he can call in," she sighed. "He'd have his clients hunting the city for you, offering rewards far greater than any he's paid you. Too many neighbors know you come here, too many tradesmen, street loiterers, the gods know who else. I . . . couldn't protect you from everyone. Someone would talk."

Sulun groaned and looked back toward the busy group in the courtyard. "Then we still have to steal out here only when we can—perhaps one day in every five."

"Half a moon, then, just to finish this one bombard." Zeren glowered at the innocent-looking sky. "And another moon beyond that, to save our city. If I thought the gods would listen, I would beggar myself making offerings at every temple in Sabis. Gods, give us just that much time."

Out in the courtyard, Omis's drill began to whine through the packed sand in the bombard's muzzle, clearing out the bore.

Eloti, too, looked at the sky, then back at the ground, finally out toward the river. "I had almost forgot. Sulun, while your friends are thus engaged, come with me to the river."

"The river?" Sulun and Zeren gulped together, nonplussed at the change of subject.

"One reaches it through your back gate, not so?" Eloti stood, gathering her skirts and parasol.

"Er, oh, yes." Sulun hastened to lead the way through the courtyard, around the busy crew at the drill, to the

back wall and its stout gate. "Uhm, the keys should be
. . . Yes, here on the hook. I haven't opened this fool
thing in years. Pray the hinges are . . . Yes."

The long-unoiled hinges screeched in protest, momentarily startling the apprentices, though Omis's concentration never wavered. The back gate grumbled open, revealing
the thick-weeded bank of the river. The water here was
oily and thick with garbage, and the wind off the river
blew the stink into their faces.

"Ugh," muttered Sulun, pinching his nose. "It wasn't so
bad inside. Let's go back."

"It's endurable." Eloti marched resolutely through the
high weeds to the edge of the water. "There," she said,
pointing.

Sulun looked, seeing only the wreck of what looked to
be a sizable old barge tied up to ancient stakes driven into
the mud. "What's there?" he asked.

Eloti smiled that faint, secret smile. "Look closer," she
said. "It is not a wreck."

Sulun picked his way closer, hearing Zeren a few paces
behind. The thing looked wretched enough, weathered
gray hull spotted sickly green with patches of mold, deck
covered with scatterings of rotted boards and dead weeds.
The tie ropes looked frayed, but were thick enough to
hold it steady. Still, he hated to set foot on those loose and
undoubtedly rotten boards.

"Pull the top boards and weeds away," Eloti commanded,
voice ever so slightly impatient.

Sulun obediently bent down and tugged away the topmost boards, brushed off some of the dead weeds.

Weeds? A lot of them, he noticed now, were artfully
bound straw. The rotted boards were light, thin and dry.
No rusted nails threatened his hands. The assorted trash
looked . . . fake.

Under it, the deck was clean and sound.

He stepped onto it, suspicion and wonder rising, and
looked closer.

The hull and thwarts were solid too, showing little real
sign of wear. The seams were caulked tight, no board was
warped. The weathered gray color, he saw now, was deliberately toned paint. The mold patches were painted too.

"Camouflage," he whispered, impressed, hearing Zeren

whistle in respectful amazement. "No, she's not a wreck at all."

"Below decks you'll find a mast and boom, sails, oars and an awning," said Eloti. "I would suggest moving some of your provisions on board before we leave today."

Sulun straightened up to stare at her. Zeren, chuckling, replaced the disguising boards and weeds.

"In the event that we fail . . ." Eloti shrugged eloquently. "This can carry all of us, and everything, even the wagon and mules."

"Yes," Sulun agreed, not taking his eyes off his amazing Mistress. "Yes."

Zeren sat down on the deck and looked out over the water. "Win or lose," he muttered, "surer victory or better retreat than I've ever had before."

"That," said Eloti, striding nearer to him, "is exactly what I intended."

Zeren laughed shortly. "Ah, Lady, if only some kindly god had given the defense of Sabis to you! To you, and not to those fools up on the hill." He shook his head at the madness and wonder of it.

In the courtyard, Omis stopped the drill and ordered the apprentices to change the drill bit for a heavy wire smoothing brush.

PART II

Flight

1

Because a child dropped a book . . .

Memi, toting a pile of scrolls across her father's study, dropped one of them on the floor. She tried to grab it, and succeeded in losing the whole pile.

Mygenos, busy with a long list of instructions from his master, was jarred out of concentration by the sound. He jumped out of his chair, caught the erring child by the arm and smacked her soundly on the face.

Memi, flinching away from him, blindly planted a foot on one of the unrolled scrolls, leaving a smudgy footprint.

Mygenos, his temper provoked and a target ready, yanked off his belt and began flogging the girl in earnest. The girl's struggles trampled more books, fueling Mygenos's ire to a good, high blaze. He whipped her halfway across the room, finally pinning her against the wall, whipping wherever he could reach.

The child's screeches brought no help, no easing of the blows, and in desperation she scrambled for any words that would stop the pain.

"Papa, stop it! Stop it, and I'll tell!"

Mygenos, thinking only that she meant to complain to his master, laughed shortly and hit harder.

"I'll tell where Sulun is!"

Sulun? Surprised, Mygenos stopped in mid-blow. He'd scarcely even thought of the man since Shibari died.

Taking the halt in the flogging for interest, Memi tried further. "I know where Sulun is. I saw him. Just days ago. I saw."

"Where?" Mygenos demanded, twisting her arm.

"At the big house. The one where you took me, last moon-quarter. He was in the kitchen there." Memi sniffled, remembering Sulun had always been good to her. She might not have to tell Papa everything. Maybe Sulun would be safe.

"Why didn't you tell me before?" Mygenos gave her arm another yank.

"Ow! Ow! I wasn't sure. He looked different. And you've *told* me not to speak 'til spoken to . . ."

141

But Mygenos had stopped listening. "Big house, last moon-quarter . . . Gods, Entori!"

Almost absently, he let go of Memi's arm. The girl lost no time scuttling away from him and out the door. Mygenos hardly noticed, letting the belt swing lax in his hand. He chuckled slowly. "Entori's house, Firepowder. Unknown qualities. And his wizard's an old stick, set in his ways . . . No defense. Well, well, well."

Laughing aloud, Mygenos went back to his writing table and shoved the assorted wax tablets aside. Oh yes, he'd have a new plan of attack to give his new master. At a guess, Entori would capitulate before the moon reached full again.

Mygenos reached for his meditation gem and set to work.

Because the city's draftees were hastily trained . . .

The sentry sat shivering on the bank of the Dawnstream, wishing its namesake weren't yet three hours away, wishing he were back in the familiar lands nearer the Baiz, wishing he were south in warm—if hungry—Sabis. Gods, but half a moon's training, mostly fumbling with too-big equipment while armored louts yelled at him, wasn't enough to make an invincible warrior out of a shoemaker. He'd told them and told them he'd do better making boots for the army, that years of bending over lapstone and awl had done nothing to improve his eyesight—which had been none too good at distances, ever, which was why he'd been apprenticed to a shoemaker in the first place—but none of them listened to him.

So here he sat, cold and wet and miserable, on the banks of a strange river in lands he'd never seen before, watching for some sign of invading Ancar. As if he'd recognize an Ancar if he saw one; they couldn't really be tall as trees, pale as fish bellies, dressed in scale-plate armor all over, now could they? And how was he to spot them, anyway? With his shortsighted shoemaker's eyes, he'd be lucky if he could see much beyond the ford itself: and the moon covered with clouds, as usual, and no fires or torches allowed where the Ancar might spot them and pick off troops with their fabled long bows. How was he supposed to see anything, anyway?

Oh, he could hear all right—the faint endless muttering

from the entrenched camp behind him, the eternal rumbling of the water, nothing else for hours and hours, just like last night and the night before. Nothing new.

He hoped the other sentries were better at this than he was.

They weren't.

None of them heard, beneath the sound of the river, the faint splashing downstream where the water was just over waist-deep for the taller Ancari. None of them saw, in the pitch dark under the cloud-covered moon, the dark-dressed troops struggling quietly through the water.

The attack came before the first dawnlight.

The former shoemaker never heard the arrow that killed him.

Because an old miser was proud and suspicious . . .

First, the coals on the hearth went out during the night, and the cook-fire was devilishly hard to start in the morning. Then the water crock slipped out of the scullery maid's hands, shattered and splashed half of the kitchen. Then the cook sliced her thumb on a peeling knife. Then the pot boiled over.

It grew worse from there. Roaches got into the larder, followed by mice. Nails pulled out of the walls, dumping tapestries on the floor, which knocked bits of statuary off their pedestals, which inevitably broke. Inkwells spilled, always across important parchments, quill points broke and styli slipped on waxboards to mar whole columns of figures. Mildew grew on the walls and shelves, and proliferated in the laundry. Bed webbing frayed and snapped. Old chairs collapsed when sat upon. Everything that could go wrong did.

Beyond doubt, the House of Entori was under a curse.

Morning reports lasted almost until noon, and mostly consisted of lists of small disasters. Entori spent an hour locked away behind his study door, screaming threats and insults at the house wizard. Omis and Sulun, last in line, could hear the shouts through the door, and winced in sympathy for the old drunkard. They weren't at all surprised to see, when the door finally opened, a tattered and terrified Elizan come stumbling out at the best pace he could manage—followed by a thrown inkwell. The old man held a jingling purse in his hand as if it were a large

poisonous spider, and as he left he hurried down the
corridor toward the front door.

"Going to fetch some professional help, no doubt," Omis
guessed, watching him go. "Hope it comes soon. I don't
dare light up my forge while the curse is running unchecked."

"We'd best go in together to explain that," Sulun considered. "Oh gods, I just thought: if it's this bad here,
what's happening down at the river house?"

"The firepowder," Omis whispered, going pale.

"We won't know until we get down there, which we'd
best do soon."

"Make some excuse to go there."

The bell rang peremptorily, and they walked in together.

"No, of course you can't work your forge until the other
wizards get here," Entori snapped, looking more than
ever like a ruffled vulture. "I don't suppose your other
tools will be safe, either. Gods, nothing's safe but what's
watched every moment. Nobody can work like this."

"We could test how far the curse extends," Sulun offered. "We'll get out to the market—we need some supplies anyway—and see what befalls us once we're away
from the house."

"Nonsense! No one leaves the house today, not until the
new wizards come." Entori poked among his scattered
parchments and waxboards, mumbling something they
couldn't quite catch, something about desertion. He paused
and glared up at them. "Once they arrive, I'll need you to
instruct them on the proper workings of your tools so the
protections can be arranged. Ugh, more damned outsiders
knowing my business . . . Gods' curses, it can't be helped."

"But meanwhile," Omis wheedled, "perhaps we could
investigate, go out and ask in the right places, discover
who it is that put the curse on your house—"

"I know who it is!" Entori slapped his hands on the pile
of parchments, making another stylus fall off on the floor.
"It's that damned Valishni and his doubly damned wizard,
the one who wanted my steam engine. Who else? If he
can't have it, he'll see to it that I can't use it. Son of an
ape, I'll get him . . ."

Mygenos! Omis and Sulun looked at each other, shivering with dread.

"Oh, get out of here," Entori snarled. "Go keep watch on your tools and apprentices, see that nothing else breaks or disappears. I'll have you summoned when the new wizards come. Go on, leave."

The engineers did, shaking their heads, not daring to speak until they were out the door and a good way down the corridor.

"Memi told," Omis growled. "Myggy knows we're here. Gods, the curse must center on our tools!"

"Don't blame the child," Sulun insisted. "The gods only know how he got it out of her. The old vulture's right about getting new wizards to protect our gear. Hmm, wait. We should talk to the Mistress about this."

"Best find her speedily, then."

The search took not long at all; Eloti was waiting for them in the back courtyard, expressionless as always.

"Mistress, the curse comes from Mygenos, of Valishni's house," Sulun told her without preamble. "He knew us when we worked for Shibari, and hated us cordially. We need to know if the curse centers upon us, our tools, or only on Entori's house."

"But how—" Omis threw him a wide-eyed look, only now realizing that Eloti was, despite her earlier comment, the true mage of Entori House.

Eloti gave him a cold, imperious stare. Sulun met it levelly. She shrugged capitulation. "It centers somewhere in the house," she admitted. "I went out this morning, and it did not follow me. Nor do I think, for all your . . . acquaintance's malice, that it centers on you." She met Sulun's eyes again. "I myself put protection upon you and your people, and your workshop by the river. As you've seen, I have somewhat more power than your Mygenos."

"Thank you," said Sulun, vastly relieved. "But . . . that leaves our tools and gear, here in the house."

"My forge," Omis groaned. "Everything here."

"One cannot do everything," said Eloti. "I'm sorry."

"Mistress, I'm grateful for what you've done already," Sulun vowed. "If we can get to the riverside house, we could work unhindered. Entori's hired wizards can guard this place."

"But we can't leave!" Omis groaned. "Not until the new wizards come. He wants us to show them the workings of our tools, and the engine, so they can apply protections."

"A pity," sighed Eloti. "But for that, you would have a perfect excuse to absent yourself from the house and go work at the riverside shop. I could go myself, except that he specifically bade me stay too—and, knowing him, he might call on me at any moment."

"Then we're all rooted here, idle, for the day," Sulun said gloomily.

"A single day." Eloti smiled. "I doubt that our projects will suffer much for losing a single day."

2

It took three days.

The two new wizards arrived, ushered in by a much crestfallen Elizan, before lunchtime on the first day. They spent the rest of the morning and afternoon inspecting the house, muttering, making notes to themselves and generally giving an impression of serious study. Entori, stamping along two steps behind them, was not much impressed. They did manage, by dint of much muttering and chanting, to clear the curse out of the kitchen and larder so that some sort of dinner was possible that night.

The second day, much to Sulun's and Omis's relief, the visiting wizards inspected the courtyard workshop. Everyone took pains to describe their tools and the workings thereof, and Arizun took particular joy in describing the details of the steam engine's construction—much to Entori's ill-suppressed fury. After much work and two false starts, they managed to disenchant the tools to the point where Omis dared to start up his forge. Between the wizards' prolonged well-wishing and the engineers' care, a few more engine parts were cast and cut assembled without incident—but by then it was close upon dinnertime.

"Two days wasted," Omis complained over the poorly cooked evening meal. "Two days! By now I could have had the bombard smoothed and drilled and ready for its first test. Gods, if we can only get out tomorrow . . ."

"Hope the old vulture's stopped peering over our shoulders by then," Sulun commiserated. "Hope he's turned his attention somewhere else, or at least that Mygenos

has. Most likely, though, Entori will want us to make up
for lost time on the damned engine."

"And this one's taking longer because we have to make
the valves ourselves. Gods' curses! I feel like a turtle
trying to outrun a fox."

"With luck, we can get to the laboratorium tomorrow."
Sulun wondered if they could expect any luck at all, now
that they had Myggy snapping at their heels. No doubt his
master would come sniffing around Entori House soon
enough, hoping the old miser's ill luck would make him
more amenable to a deal. When he found Entori still
unwilling, he'd have Mygenos increase the pressure: more
trouble, more delays, more work for Entori's hired wizards,
more of his attention focused on his engine building, less
chance for Sulun and his company to slip away. "We have to
get out of here," Sulun muttered to no one in particular.

And on the third day, the disaster came home.

The guards opening the city gates at dawn were first to
see the dust rising on the road. After that came the first
messengers on lathered horses, with the first of the retreating troops hard on their heels. The news went up to
Imperial House first, but it reached the marketplaces less
than an hour later.

The Ancar had crossed the Dawnstream by night,
smashed the garrisons one after the other, rolled the
Sabirn army all the way back down the south shore to the
Baiz itself.

Lutegh had fallen.

The Ancar were less than five days' march from Sabis.

Panic hit the city.

Vari heard the signal tap on the rear gate, scrambled up
on the small pyramid of barrels and tossed the rope ladder
over the other side. It creaked alarmingly as Arizun, then
Sulun, and finally Omis climbed up it. They tumbled,
panting, down the barrels as Vari pulled back the ladder
and listened briefly for sounds of anyone following.

"How are the children?" was the first thing Omis asked.

"Well enough," Vari whispered. "They think its a fine
adventure, all except Ziya, who's turned quiet and morose
again. Get inside, quickly."

They hurried through the darkened courtyard, past barricades of more barrels and crates, into the silent corridor and off to Omis's room, carefully barring the doors behind them.

Yanados and Doshi, clanking softly with belt-strung weapons, half rose as the others came in. "Are you well?" Yanados asked first. "Sulun, your arm—"

"Only a shallow cut," Sulun tried to smile. "I got it ducking behind some timbers when a gang of mercenaries went by."

Vari shook her head and set to cleaning and bandaging the scratch.

"How has it gone here?" Arizun asked. "Any more rioters trying to break in?"

"Not tonight, not so far." Doshi shrugged, making his hatchet clank against the wall. "The old man has the place barricaded with damn near everything from the storerooms, swearing the house will stand until the very mountains fall. Then again, if the doors do go down, there's hardly anyone in the house who could stop them."

"Entori still hasn't hired more bully-boys, then?" Omis winced as Vari pulled the bandage tight. "With all these damned troopers-for-pay hanging about in the streets, one would think . . ."

"Even Entori wouldn't trust that lot," Omis snorted. "Gods, how right Zeren was. We saw enough of them lolling about the streets, drinking the wineshops dry, looting wherever they fancied and bashing anyone who complained. As if the starving refugees weren't enough . . ."

"What happened to their officers?" Doshi hissed between his teeth. "Why in the nine hells aren't they outside, defending the city as they were hired to do?"

"Too many of the regular army officers were killed during the overrunning of the Dawnstream." Arizun leaned his head back against the wall, as if infinitely tired. "The mercenary troops won't obey anyone but their own commanders, who claim that they no longer had anyone to report to. Now their commanders won't take orders from anyone 'not properly authorized', so they say."

"Which means no one who doesn't come from high up in the court, with gold ready to hand," Omis finished. "Nobody in the court has done that yet."

"Gods," Vari muttered, packing her remaining healing simples into a bag. "Why not? What's wrong with the high court?"

"Utter confusion." Sulun winced, and not from his minor wound. He hesitated to tell the worst of the news, wondering how the others would take it. "There seems to be . . . some manner of faction fight going on at the moment. Some gang of fools wants to send envoys to the Ancar, make terms with them. There have been . . . disappearances, mysterious sudden deaths, messages gone awry . . . No one's sure of anything. No one knows how bad it is, truly."

"Why hasn't the old Emperor done something?" Vari insisted.

Sulun heaved a profound sigh, feeling Omis' eyes on him, knowing he'd have to say it. "He hasn't appeared publicly. There are rumors that he's . . . ill, perhaps very ill."

"Maybe dying?" Yanados guessed.

Sulun only shrugged. The others looked at each other.

"And . . ." Doshi hesitated. "The rest of the city?"

"Thievings, riots, everyone running," Arizun recited wearily. "The city guards are trying to round up everyone they can, hauling folk off to the army court—not for trial, but to be pressed into service for defense of the city. You can imagine how much success they're having, especially with the mercenaries."

"Pitched battles in the streets?" Yanados murmured. "Have you heard anything of Zeren?"

"Battles, yes; Zeren, no." Omis shook his head. "He's most likely in the thick of the mess, and we stayed away from such whenever we could."

"We may never see him again—" Vari sobbed, then caught herself.

"He'll survive, if anyone can," Omis tried to reassure her. It didn't work, but everyone pretended it did.

"Well, so." Yanados tried to smile. "'Did you make it to the river house?"

"Not even near to it," said Arizun. "Where there weren't rioters or mercenaries or press gangs, there were fires. We couldn't get through unseen, had to turn back."

"More fires?" Doshi went pale in the dim lamplight.

"*More* fires?" Omis jerked his head up. "Has anyone tried to—"

"Not here," Vari assured him quickly. "Just . . . down the street."

"How far down the street?"

"Three houses down. But you know how far that is, and

it was put out soon, just a diversion, I think, while the rioters broke into the other side of the house to steal things."

"Good gods, fire!" Omis pressed his hands to his eyes. "They'll come here soon enough."

"Maybe not," Sulun tried. "By tomorrow, someone at court may settle the squabbling up there, restore order." But he couldn't really believe it.

"Sulun," Omis reminded, dropping his hands on his lap, "what about Myggy's curse on this house?"

Sulun opened his mouth, shut it again, thought fast. "I think he'll have other things on his mind now, too much to bother with renewing his ill-wish on us."

"But can you be sure of that?"

Sulun didn't say anything.

"We have to get out." Yanados finally said the words, firmly enough that no one would argue. "This very night, out. We'll go first to the river house, then down to the port."

"Why the port?" Sulun raised his head, frowning.

"Because . . ." Yanados let out a long breath. "Because that's where we'll find the *Yanira*. Her captain will take us . . . to Sakar."

Everyone stared at her dropping the veil over her secret at last. It was Doshi who had the desperation, or lack of tact, to say the words.

"He's . . . You're a Sakaran? One of the pirates?"

Yanados blinked, but otherwise didn't falter. "Yes. My father was a most successful pirate. He also knew enough of the ways of pirates that he didn't want his daughter married to one. He could have quietly bought me a respectable marriage to some respectable mainlander, but I didn't want that, and he . . . cared for me enough to listen. I had skills, wanted to use them, persuaded him that I could make my way on the mainland. He gave me the . . . supplies I needed and got me passage to Sabis."

"Where you disguised yourself as a boy and apprenticed yourself to old Abanuz," Sulun cut in, seeing the puzzle fall together.

"Yes." Yanados tossed him a fleeting smile. "I still kept some contact with my father's people, though. Imagine my joy at finding that one of them now works the *Yanira*."

"So you took him aside for a brief chat, and explained to him how useful our steam engines—and we—would be to Sakar."

Yanados shrugged eloquently, not taking her eyes off Sulun. "If—when Sabis falls to the Ancar, who will be left that could defy them?" she said.

"Gods," Sulun breathed, sagging under the weight of the vision. Sakar, the multi-island fortress in the middle of the world's heart, the Mormuz Sea: the only land safe from the land-devouring northern hordes, one place where civilization could survive, the one kingdom that could restore the sea trade—or attack any seaports the Ancar held. *Irony of the gods! Civilization preserved, even restored, by a kingdom of pirates!* "Why not?" Sulun found himself laughing. "The 'honest' folk of Sabis have served us poorly; perhaps pirates would do better."

"Two small stumbling blocks," said Arizun, stopping the laughter. "One: is the *Yanira* in port now?"

"I don't know," Yanados admitted, "But if she isn't— tonight, tomorrow at latest—her captain's a far bigger fool than I believe. With everyone who can afford passage rushing across the straits, anyone with so much as a reed rowboat is growing rich on the ferrying trade. You can wager, the *Yanira*'s captain wouldn't miss such opportunity."

"Surely not," Sulun laughed, a little light-headed. It occurred to him that such a captain, in Entori's employ at least part of the time, would be in an excellent position to know when and where valuable cargoes sailed—and to sell such knowledge to his Sakaran friends. "Heh! No wonder Entori's lost so many ships to the pirates." *And Shibari too?* a sudden thought sobered him. Had the loss that ruined his former patron been likewise arranged? If so, then the failure of the Bombard Project, the very fall of Sabis, might be laid at the feet of Sakar.

"Two," Arizun went on implacably, "what makes you think we can get to the port?"

Yanados stared at him. "Why ever not?"

"Have you see it lately?" Arizun glanced at Sulun and Omis. Omis looked away.

Once more, Sulun felt everyone's eyes on him and wondered how he'd ever got himself into this. "We got a quick look, from several streets away," he began. "It was . . . totally mad. Even at night, people crowding the docks, howling like mad things, fighting for a place on board a ship, any ship. Sailors had to beat them back to get room to unload, and then the city guard had to beat them away from the unloaded grain!" Sulun shivered.

"There were people fighting everywhere, falling into the water," Omis added. "The ships were overloaded, small boats worse. We saw one turn over . . ."

"The poor folk were begging for rides across the river," Arizun took up the tale. "Just to get west of the city, into the swamps, on rafts made of barrels and scrap-wood, some even swimming. I don't know how many drowned."

"How," Sulun finished, "would you get to the *Yanira* in the midst of that?"

Yanados thought a while, then shook her head. "I suppose it won't get any better, not with the Ancar coming, not tomorrow, not the day after. And how long could we hide out in the riverside workshop?"

"Maybe two days before the food ran out," said Omis. "We might fish on the river, could we get to clear water."

"Upstream," said Doshi. "If we stay on the river, travel only at night, we can get past the Ancar lines soon enough."

No one answered him, but everyone gave a soft, resigned sigh. That simply, it was decided.

"When?" was all Sulun asked.

"Give us some time to rest," Vari insisted. "A few hours, at least. And the streets should be emptier after midnight."

There was a general mumble of agreement. Nobody wanted to risk those perilous streets just yet. A few more questions determined that everything usable was already at the river house, or else already packed. They had only to take up their bundles and go.

Sulun was about to suggest that everyone find bed space and get some sleep while they could when they all heard the first noise at the front door: the loud crack of a stone hitting the wood, and the echoes sounding through the house.

Everyone jumped, looked at each other, listened.

Another stone, heavier, and then the sound of voices and fists and feet, that low, growling, tearing sound they'd come to know too well. Cries and thudding footfalls sounded elsewhere in the house, and Entori's voice shouting in outrage and fear.

"The door?" Vari whispered, barely audible over the growing noise.

"Not long if they keep that up," Sulun decided, climbing to his feet. "We go. Now."

It took no measurable time for all of them to take up bundles, check their assorted weapons, blow out the lamp and peer out into the corridor. Down at the front end they saw a servant run past, apparently headed for the kitchen. Omis and Vari darted into the next room, came out bare seconds later holding the two smaller children, Tamiri running silently ahead of them.

Sulun pointed to the back courtyard, and they ran—down the dark corridor, dodging around bales and barrels, pausing for long sweaty seconds to unlock doors and get through them, out at last into the sweltering night air and the open sky.

"The wagon," Sulun whispered. "Where did you—"

"By the corner of the stable," Yanados hissed back. "There . . ."

They skidded to a tangled halt, seeing the wagon standing, mules already in harness, before the back gate. The tailgate was open and waiting, nothing in the wagon bed but a single large oak chest.

Someone was sitting at the driver's box, a woman in a dark dress. She turned and smiled politely at them.

"Eloti!" Omis gulped. "Er, excuse me, Mistress. Is Master Entori . . . ?"

"He will not come, not even now. Climb aboard quickly," Eloti said, as calmly as if she were discussing a jaunt to the market. "That front door won't hold forever."

"Yes," Sulun agreed. "Everyone, get aboard. Omis, can you get the gate open fast?"

The others complied, with considerable speed and surprisingly little noise. Sulun climbed into the driver's box and took the mules' reins. They seemed restive, but still controllable. He took up the whip, just to be sure.

"Mistress," he asked, watching Omis manhandle the gate, "what weapons do you carry tonight?"

"Only my dagger," Eloti shrugged eloquently. "Gently reared ladies are not taught the uses of the bow or sword."

"Best climb in back then, with Vari and the children. Omis, climb on!"

Omis came running, leaving the gate to swing open on blessedly silent darkness behind him. He vaulted into the driver's box just as Eloti stepped neatly into the wagon box and sat down on the chest. Sulun glanced back and saw that the others were either huddled down among the baggage or else crouched along the sides and back of the wagon, bows and axes ready in their hands.

Behind them came a cracking and splintering sound as the front door of Entori House gave way.

Sulun shook the reins and cracked the whip over the mules' backs.

Willing and eager, for once, the mules leaped for the gate. Sulun hauled hard on the right reins to make the turn into the back alley, grateful that he'd practiced this maneuver a few times before. The wagon wheels growled and rumbled on the packed earth.

"Gods, the noise!" Omis hissed "In the streets, they'll hear us coming."

"Move fast," Yanados volunteered. "Move fast and shoot arrows early."

Behind her, a child's voice rose softly in a keening wail of grief; Ziya, feeling old wounds reopened. Vari murmured attempts at comfort, but had no effect.

"Don't cry; shoot!" Arizun snapped, pressing another bow into her hands.

Ziya took the bow, nocked an arrow, and fell silent.

The wagon rumbled out into the street—and into a thin crowd all running to the right, toward the street where Entori House fronted. Sulun reined the mules to the left, and lashed wildly about him with the whip. Omis whipped up a heavy bow and let fly into the street, catching the tail of somebody's cloak. At least one of the crowd thumped into the mules, fell, went under their hooves—but managed to roll away from the wheels. Sulun whispered a brief prayer of thanks for that as the scrambling mules began gathering speed. Oncoming looters jumped aside, not ready to attack fast-moving animals and a well-armed crowd on a heavy wagon. Yanados turned and shot a few arrows to the rear to discourage anyone from following. The arrows skittered off walls and pavement, but no one followed.

In a moment, the wagon was thundering down an empty street, dark save for moonlight and an occasional lamplight glow behind shuttered windows.

"Straight three streets, then right," Omis panted. "Pray the fires have died down near the river turnoff . . ."

"I know," Sulun panted. "Get ready for more mobs. Gods, keep us from the troops!"

At the third street, they saw torches—too many torches, in the hands of too many men—coming toward them from the left. Sulun hauled the mules to the right, hearing shouts behind him. Someone in that mob had a bow too, for an arrow thunked into the tailgate. Yanados and Arizun fired back together, and Sulun lashed the mules into a gallop. The mob fell behind and the wagon went careening up the street.

Two cross streets up, a handful of silent men made a dash for the wagon. Sulun hit one across the face with the whip, Omis backhanded another with his axe, and a third fell to the now panicky mules. This time Sulun *did* feel the heavy thump of a body going under the wagon wheels, and struggled not to be sick, not now, not here. The other robbers, whoever they were, disappeared back into the shadows.

A straight road then, and no other sound but the rumbling of the wheels and the clattering hooves of the mules.

But there were fires ahead. Sulun could see the fire glow in the sky above the roofs to the right, smell the smoke heavy and fresh on the air, mixed with the smell of spilled wine.

"Third vintners' street," Omis identified it. "Be sure, the troops are looting there. Turn left, next chance, then right again."

"Narrow street," Sulun remembered. "If it's blocked . . ."

"Wasn't, earlier," was all Omis could offer.

They swung left. There was another crowd here, but running away from them. Sulun guessed they expected the rioting mercenaries to come this way, and hauled to the right again as soon as a street showed itself.

There was a fire at the end of the street. A house on the left corner was blazing furiously, its roof fallen in but walls still standing. The smoke smelled of scorched wool.

"A weaver's," Sulun guessed. "How will we get the mules past it?"

The animals were already slowing down, tossing wild-eyed heads, unwilling to get close to the fire. Sulun pulled them to the right, scraping as close to the buildings as he dared, lashing furiously at the beasts and thanking any gods who could hear him that this street was wide enough;

they could get past the fire if only the mules didn't panic completely.

From behind him, Eloti rested her hands on Sulun's shoulders, leaned forward and screeched a stream of ear-searing abuse at the mules. Sulun gulped in amazement; there were a few obscenities in that litany that he'd never heard before. Where had Entori's properly reared sister learned them?

The mules, encouraged by a familiar voice, lurched ahead—past the burning house, scraping the off wheels against walls, blundering past running figures laden with bundles and baskets, out and away onto the next street. Their flanks were dark with sweat, and foam spattered from their bridles.

"Give them some rest." Eloti said, stepping back into the wagon bed. "Otherwise they'll never last to the river."

Sulun nodded agreement and let the mules slow of their own accord, down to a lumbering trot for the moment at least. So, Eloti knew much of ships, wagons and mules; there was much he would like to ask her, if they ever had the opportunity.

Twice more they turned, avoiding any sign of light or motion ahead, away from burning torches, burning houses, even lamplight. Light meant crowds: mobs, rioting mercenaries, even the city guard—none were safe to meet tonight.

Once, looking back up the rising slope of the city, they saw a whole block of buildings on fire.

"Gods," Omis groaned, "Zeren's house is up there!"

"Pray he's not in it," Sulun muttered, whipping the mules to a faster trot. "Most likely he won't be, not tonight."

But it was pain to think of Zeren out in this night of fire and ruin, fighting thieves and rioting mercenaries in a dying city, and nowhere left to go. He might stay to the last, falling in the final defense of the city—and Sabis would fall, was doomed, the weapon that might have saved her lying half-finished in the house by the river, ruined by Fate's connivance and human stupidity and malice. Sulun coughed ashes and prayed that his friend would trust instinct, run while he could, escape one more time—to Esha, or the islands, or somewhere the endless hordes from the north couldn't reach—not to give up and die with the city.

"The river!" Omis gasped. "Smell the air."

Gods, yes: the wind had shifted, and the familiar stink came rolling, welcome for once, up the darkened street. Sulun hauled left, one more time.

Oh gods, there was a small street-brawl in the way—a crowd of bravos smashing into the wineshop. No way to get past it.

"Arrows," Omis grunted, picking up his bow.

Sulun lashed the mules into a dead run, hoping that speed and surprise would serve them one more time.

The outermost of the crowd turned their heads, noticing the noise, just as the first arrows flew. Screeches of pain and shock followed, drawing the attention of the rest of the looters. Half of them scattered as the mule-drawn wagon thundered down on them, but half didn't. Too many of the crowd were wine-soaked mean, hot on the chase of plunder, and armed. Maybe a dozen of them jumped out into the street, waving assorted bludgeons and a few hatchets.

"The mules!" Sulun shouted warning, laying about wildly with his whip.

The apprentices in the wagon fired off another volley of arrows—all of which hit, hardly room to miss—and maybe four of the bravos lurched aside, cursing or screaming but preoccupied with wounds.

In the next second, the mules ran full-tilt into the crowd, braying wildly. Omis dropped his bow into the driver's box and pulled up his axe, ducking low under Sulun's flailing whip. Two more of the crowd went down under the mules, but the rest converged on the beasts, grabbing at the bridles. The mules reared, squealing, hooves finding enough targets to keep hands away from their reins, but their forward momentum was gone. The crowd closed in.

Yanados, Arizun and Doshi fired steadily and fast, arrows thinning down the mob, but now the club-swinging crowd was up to the wagon, pawing for purchase. Omis swung a ferocious half-arc with his axe, and the nearest of the looters went sprawling backward among his cronies, face redly smashed. The apprentices dropped their bows, pulled out hatchets and began chopping at the oncoming fists. The mules brayed wildly as assorted hands finally caught their bridles. Eloti, quick as a cat, stabbed her little dagger squarely into the arm of a man trying to climb the wheel, and Vari finished him with a stout chop from a kitchen cleaver.

"Too many, too many," Sulun muttered to himself, slashing the whip across three howling faces at once. Maybe only half a dozen attackers now, but enough; they'd be on the wagon soon. Better a press gang than this . . . "The Guard!" he bellowed at the top of his lungs. "Hai, the City Guard!" Maybe that would confuse the mob for a moment, long enough for him to whip those three away from the mules. "Hai, the Guard!"

Omis, not knowing what Sulun meant, thought there were actual Guards in sight. "Zeren!" he shouted, hoping to let the Guards know who their friends were. "Hai, Captain Zeren! Here!"

Further off, somebody swore. A door banged open.

The crowd wasn't confused, and the lead three held onto the mules. One of them pulled out a knife and tried to duck toward the wagon, hoping to hamstring one of the animals. Sulun flailed at him with the whip, but only succeeded in slowing the man down. Omis spotted the attacker and leaned out over the driver's box, hoping to swing the axe at him. Behind them, Doshi yelped and toppled as a well-aimed barrel stave caught him on the leg. The stave carrier started up over the tailgate, then ducked as Yanados flew at him, hatchet raised.

Sulun didn't see the first man go down, only saw the off mule rear up, its head suddenly freed. The second man half-turned, just in time to catch a long blade across the throat. He coughed and dropped, and Sulun got a clear look at the sword and the man holding it.

"Zeren!" he shouted, just as Omis swung at the bravo crouched by the mules's flank. "Did I conjure you up?"

Omis's axe thudded meatily into the third man's shoulder, dropping him to the stones.

"Yes, I suppose you did," said Zeren, quite calmly, as he trotted toward the continuing struggle at the wagon bed. With equal calm he raised his shield and ran his sword into the side of the looter climbing the nearside rear wheel.

The two louts near the tailgate, seeing the odds change so drastically, jumped away from the wagon and ran into the dark street. What was left of the crowd scattered in the other direction, or dived into hiding in the wrecked wineshop. Sulun dropped the whip and wrestled with the reins, pulling to keep the wide-eyed beasts from plunging on down the street. Zeren wiped his sword on his thigh, sheathed it, turned back and took the reins of the nearer mule.

"Inside," he said, dragging the unwilling animal toward the open doorway of the workshop. "Hurry, or they'll come back."

Omis hopped down from the seat, ran to take the other mule's bridle, and helped pull the animal toward the gate and through it.

"Zeren?" gulped Yanados, looking over her shoulder. "Where did he come from?"

"Ask later," snapped Arizun, hopping down from the wagon. "Close the doors first." He pulled the heavy panels closed and shoved the bolt home, then ran after the others into the courtyard.

"Not too bad," Vari clucked, examining Doshi's leg. "Bruise: no break. Soak it in hot water . . . Ah, will we have time for that?"

"Not now," said Eloti. "On the boat."

"Boat?" Sulun puzzled. "Oh. Yes, the boat. Do we have everything packed? Put it on the boat, by all means!"

The others, much to Sulun's surprise, did exactly that. In a moment he was alone with Eloti and the mules.

The beasts stood panting, head down and ears sagging, ribs heaving like bellows and steam rising from their sweat-darkened hides. They looked as if they couldn't move another cubit, and Sulun didn't blame them.

"What will become of these poor beasts?" he wondered aloud.

"Why, we're taking them with us, of course," Eloti snapped, getting down from the wagon. "On the boat you'll find good straw, some tethering ropes and halters, a few days' feed and some nosebags. I recommend that we get the mules and wagon on board as soon as they're fit to move again."

"The wagon, too?" Sulun tried to imagine sailing this whole menagerie down the river.

"There is no other way to take everything."

"Very well. It's worth the bother." Eloti went to the mules' heads, took their reins and patted their foamy muzzles. "We'll need it once we leave the river. The north is said to be rough country, and I can't imagine the Ancar keeping the roads in good repair."

"North . . . No hope for reaching the port and the *Yanira*, then?"

"None whatever."

Sulun nodded weary acceptance. "How do we get the mules on the boat?" he asked.

When the last of the gear had been stowed aboard, the apprentices set the planks in a short bridge from the bank to the boat deck. Omis and Eloti took the weary mules by their bridles and led them onto the creaking platform. The beasts were nervous of their footing and moved cautiously, but between Eloti's cooed urgings and Sulun's encouragement from behind with the whip, the team and wagon crawled onto the waiting boat. The moment the rear wheels rolled off the planks, the apprentices made haste to pull the boards up again. Vari hustled to the lines to untie them, but Yanados bade her wait until the mules were safely unhitched and tied in place.

As Omis and Eloti tied the mules, there was a moment of idleness for the others, time enough to look down the river toward the port. Everyone looked, and no one said anything.

Between multiple torchlights and what appeared to be a warehouse fire, the scene at the port was visible in full and ugly detail: overloaded ships crawling away from the docks, loading ships listing visibly under the weight of desperate refugees scrambling aboard, still others waiting for room to reach the docks and take on cargo, smaller boats and even homemade rafts darkening the water as they ferried frantic Sabisans across the river. Too often, ships and tiny ferry craft collided, throwing shrieking passengers into the firelit water. From here, the constant howl of countless frantic voices formed a single, eerie wail of horror and misery.

Zeren's face was a shadowed mask of grim sorrow in the dim red light. "I should be there," he said quietly.

"Nonsense," Sulun snapped, pulling at the tie ropes. "What more could you do there? The city's doomed, and you know it. Come with us, and no more such talk."

"Run again?" Zeren glared into the wind from downriver. "I've been running all my life, it seems."

"This is an age of running," said Eloti, coming up to the huddle of apprentices. "You louts, come help me put up the mast and sail."

Yanados stood up, turned a last longing glance toward the hopeless port, and came to direct the setting of the mast. The others, subdued, followed her.

"I'm no sailor." Zeren sat down on the deck and turned his brooding gaze toward the dark water. "What use will I be to you now?"

"We won't be sailing long," Sulun reminded him. "Once we're safely past the Ancar lines, we'll go inland and north. 'Twas your idea, remember? We'll need an experienced guard in that country."

"And I'm all you have?" Zeren shook his head in almost reverent wonder. "This is mad, you know."

"Less mad than staying in Sabis to die."

"True."

Zeren heaved himself to his feet and went to help with the sail.

The captain of the *Yanira* cursed in a steady, weary monotone as he steered through the crowded inlet and beat toward open sea. Gods, this was true hell on the water, worse than any pirate raid he'd ever seen. So damned many ships, small boats, unbelievable little junk-rafts, thick as fleas on the water and getting in each others' way: he'd rammed a few of the smaller ones on every trip, and this was his third straits crossing since dawn. Ye gods, the bodies in the water, bumping off the prow even this close to the sea—some of them no doubt his own doing, for he'd had to throw a good dozen off the *Yanira* for crowding too close and fouling the gear. If it weren't for that incredible engine below deck, he couldn't have done this well.

Even so, he swore this was his last run tonight. No more of this madness, no matter how good the pickings—and the Sabisans were spending their coin now as if it would be worthless in a few days, which indeed it might well be. Already there was so much gold, silver, copper and bartered goods in the hold that he doubted he'd have room for another cargo of grain. He could leave for Sakar tonight, and his crew and himself would be rich men all their days. . . .

Once again he let his eyes range over the crowd huddled on the top deck, looking—uselessly, he already knew—for Yanados and her valuable friends. She hadn't come today or yesterday, and he doubted she'd come tomorrow. How could she reach him through that howling chaos on the docks, anyway? Would she not, more likely, have taken the first available ship? If she reached Mez on some other ship, would she not wait there to get word to him, knowing how often he put in at that port? Surely there were better ways of discharging his debt than by returning to Sabis.

No, the captain decided, feeling the wind of the free ocean ruffle his hair, *I'll come back. I'll keep coming back until the Ancar arrive and all hope fails.*

The crowd groaned in relief and quieted as the fresh sea-wind told them they were safely out of Sabis. *Besides,* the captain considered, *we're growing rich beyond dreams on this run.*

And there was always the ship itself: the marvelous dragonship that spouted smoke and ran against the wind, the swift and maneuverable wonder with its secret brass and steam heart. There was none like it anywhere in the world. Once Sabis died, she would run for Sakar, sell the knowledge of her wonders to the shipmasters there, become the mother of such as fleet as all the ages had never seen. An end for Sabis, but a new beginning for Sakar.

The captain smiled as he headed into the oncoming waves and stamped a signal for more speed to the engine room below him, fully aware that he rode at the beginning of a legend. The gods knew, future ages might make of him a semi-divine hero, little less than the gods themselves.

Not a bad fate for a former cabin boy.

Too bad for Yanados. But then again, from what he knew of her, she would most probably do well for herself in any pass, whether or not she ever came back to Sakar.

3

Dawn pearled the mist while Eloti's boat was still on the delta. Yanados frowned at the sky, worriedly studied the east bank of the Baiz, and finally snapped an order to steer into the reeds of the muddy west bank. The others, sluggish with fatigue and the night's desperation, stumbled to obey.

One of the mules set up a petulant braying, and Eloti hastened to distract it with food. "We'll have to rake out this straw and replace it with reeds," she commented, noting the fresh dung piles. "The tools are in the aft locker."

Nobody hastened to take her advice. Sulun grinned wearily, snapped off a passing reed and cut it into equal length straws, one of them notched.

At length Yanados called a halt, ordered the sails taken down and the anchor dropped.

"Here?" Zeren asked her quietly. "The fog will lift sometime today."

"No matter." Yanados smothered a huge yawn. "The Ancar are still above us, and all boats are busy south."

"Still, if we're seen from the east bank—"

"We can always move deeper into this mess of reeds and channels. In any event, we're safe now. Let's get some sleep while we can, Zeren."

Vari insisted on taking the first watch, but everyone else agreed that sleep right now was a most excellent idea.

After some brief arguing, and more cutting of reeds, everyone settled more or less comfortably on the flat deck and dropped into welcome sleep. Sulun's last sight, before he rolled over and let the silence come, was of Vari sitting alert and upright near the bow, watching the land about them with a short bow and nocked arrow in her hands.

Waking was slow and lazy, to steamy heat and a clouded-brass sky, the buzzing of pesky insects and quiet voices conversing. Sulun yawned, raised his head from the piled rushes, and looked about him.

The characteristic river fogs of early summer rose high

around the boat, cutting visibility to a dozen yards or less. Doshi was mournfully shovelling out used straw and rushes, and replacing it with fresh-cut reeds. The mules munched contentedly on piled hay and reed tops, tails busily switching flies. Omis, Vari and their two elder children were ranked along the sides of the boat near the bow, dangling fishing lines in the water; baskets partly filled with mixed fish revealed their luck. The baby gurgled happily in a lined basket nearby, playing with a heron feather. Arizun, Yanados and Ziya were nowhere to be seen, but a narrow trampled track through the rushes suggested where they might have gone. Zeren and Eloti sat at the stern, talking quietly.

Boat, rushes, slow water and hot mist were all that could be seen or heard of the world. The solitude and peace were unbelievable.

Sulun sat up and rubbed kinks out of his back, wondering what he should do next. There seemed to be no reason for activity; food, water, warmth and safety were here in abundance, and the war might as well have been on the far side of the moon. For the first time in more moons than he could remember, Sulun has no pressing duties. He felt as light-headed as a pearl diver coming up from too long in the depths.

"What time is it?" he asked Doshi, simply for need of something to say.

"Midafternoon." The youth shrugged. "The fog won't lift today. Nothing much to do but rest, fish, hunt ducks— and shovel up after these damned mules."

Sulun nodded acknowledgement more than understanding, and went to sit beside Omis. After a moment the blacksmith looked up, smiled, and handed Sulun a newly made reed fishing pole. The string, Sulun noted, was some of the heavier thread that Vari had squirreled away moons ago, and the hook was one of the lot Omis had cast from brass scraps a few days before. He looked about for some bait, and Omis obligingly handed him a fat caterpillar from a small basketful. Sulun shrugged, stuck the caterpillar on the hook and dropped it overside. *Why not fish?* he thought, bemused. *One quarter hour's walk downstream a city is dying, but that no longer has anything to do with me.*

As if it were a god's sign of approval, the line promptly

tugged with a snagged fish. Sulun smiled to himself, gave the line the proper jerk to set the hook, and began hauling in his prize.

Ziya, Arizun and Yanados came back a little before sundown,. carrying a good bag of ducks, grebes, and a single, good-sized goose. Vari made fire in a large pot set on a flat stone on the deck, and a good assortment of filleted fish toasted on a grill above it. The birds and the other fish were carefully skinned, gutted, patted with salt and set to dry in the smoky air above the cookfire.

Dinner was slow and leisurely, as pleasant a feast as any Sulun could remember, though the conversation afterwards turned to serious matters.

"Should we smother that fire once it's dark?" Omis asked, wiping grease off his mouth. "Or can't it be seen from the east bank?"

"No one will see a potful of coals," Vari said. "And we'll need some heat when the night chill comes."

"We shouldn't sleep then, but sail on," Yanados recommended. "Now, should we turn a ways down one of the other forks and hide here in this lovely delta for a few days more? Or should we press on northward as soon as we can?"

"How much food do we have stored?" Zeren countered. "There seems to be plenty here. The gods know when we'll get more, once we draw close to the Ancar holdings."

"Hmm . . ." Vari surveyed the day's catch. "Another day like this, and we'll have enough to last us half a moon, do we eat lightly."

"Then I'm for staying another day at least."

"But consider," Eloti added, "that soon enough the delta will be filling with refugees from the city, also hunting food. The gods know when the Ancar will come, but I doubt they'll wait long."

"Upriver, up the Dawnstream as I recall . . ." Doshi furrowed his brow, searching for old memories. "We'll find fewer reed beds and less mist, even in this weather. The river's wide, but we'll have to go hastily to escape the Ancar."

"They're no sailors," Yanados sneered, spitting a bone into the water.

"But they've long-reaching bows," Zeren reminded her.

"We'll want to pass them by in darkness, quietly as may be."

"How will we keep the mules quiet?" Doshi asked, throwing a nervous glance toward the drowsing beasts.

"Put nose bags full of grain on their heads." Eloti smiled. "A mule would rather eat than bray, so long as he's not hurt."

"The hard part will be passing Lutegh," Zeren considered. "We'll have to plan our passage carefully to come by there in the dark."

"We've a long stretch yet between here and there," Eloti said, "Even after we leave the delta, there'll be reeds and mists aplenty. Time enough for planning when we reach the Mother Stone on the west bank. Lutegh will then be half a day's sail upstream."

The others stared at her in surprise. "You know these waters, then?" Arizun piped up. "You've sailed here before?"

"Oh, yes, many times." Eloti nibbled delicately at a fish fillet. "Still, I would recommend leaving this delightful spot before the wine gives out. The water's unwholesome to drink unless well boiled, and there's a shortage of firewood hereabouts."

The others looked at each other, shrugged, and resumed eating. Without discussion, they understood that Lady Eloti would tell them more when she chose to, and no sooner.

They spent a second day on the delta, catching more fish and birds, smoking the meat over dried reed fires. The third day brought the distant sound of drums through the mist, though from what direction no one could properly tell. They took the sound for an omen, set the sails at evening and drove upriver on the night wind from the sea.

Once the boat was under way, Yanados became master. She held the sweep, ordered sail adjustments, suggested load shiftings, and the others hastened to obey. Zeren remarked on the phenomenon of shifting command as he, Sulun and Omis sat huddled around the firepot warming their hands and some herbal tea.

"Not so surprising," Sulun replied. "Omis and I often took turns being master of the shop, depending upon what work was done and who had most experience and knowledge therewith. Likewise, Yanados knows sailing better than any of us; therefore, when the ship sails, she commands."

"And when the ship is still? Who commands then?"

Sulun scratched at his scruffy growth of beard. He'd neglected to shave lately, saving the soap for more pressing needs. Should he continue to let it grow? "The question hasn't really come up," he said. "I suppose Vari rules on matters of food, which are not to be belittled. In knowledge of the river, the Lady appears to have the last word." He glanced to the little shelter of blankets hung from the wagon that Eloti and Vari had set up as a sleeping place for themselves and the children. "On matters of warfare, I suppose you'd be the authority, Zeren."

"On matters of craftsmanship, we've nothing to do." Omis nudged Sulun with an elbow and a wry grin. "Still, our mannerly apprentices treat us as if we still had some wisdom to impart."

"Wait till we're on land and can set up our tools again," Sulun said, smiling back. "Then our apprentices' obedience will be more than mere courtesy. How is the bombard, by the way?"

"The inside needs more polishing, never mind the outside." Omis shrugged. "And we've yet to drill the fuse hole. And where could we test it?"

"Doubtless we'll find some empty land, where the Ancar have passed."

"Unbelievable," Zeren muttered, casting a long glance over the boat and its inhabitants. "Such excellent logic, such a sensible method of rule. Yet no army has ever run thus, nor city, nor kingdom, nor empire. What manner of world would it be, did they so?"

"A more efficient one, at any rate," said Eloti, padding silently up to the fire. "I think the coals could do with some more dried reeds. Friend Zeren, is the tea ready?"

"I think so." Zeren dipped out a cup of the infusion for Eloti, and one for himself. He seemed to have forgotten that the other two existed.

Omis and Sulun looked at each other, smiled, and doled out cups for themselves.

The boat worked steadily upriver, and dawn found her safely hidden in another bed of reeds.

The crew slept until late afternoon, waking to find the

sky dangerously cool and clear. They scanned the visible western bank nervously while they fished and smoked their catches over the dried reed fire, but no sign of humanity appeared. Still, everyone remained subdued and quiet, even the mules. They ate dinner early, intending to sail on again after dark.

"The Ancar must be on the east bank now," Zeren noted, around a mouthful of smoked goose. "We'll have to be careful. How much grain is left for the mules?"

"Another dozen nosebags apiece," murmured Eloti. "Enough to keep them quiet when need be. Still, they grow restless for lack of exercise."

"Once past Lutegh—" Zeren stopped, then shrugged.

No one else said anything. It was not wise, it was tempting the gods, to make any plans before encountering Lutegh. They finished dinner quickly, bedded the children below with the supplies and gear, and set sail as soon as darkness came.

Near dawn, Eloti sighted the Mother Stone: a great solitary pier of rock nudging out into the river from the west bank. Someone, long in the mists of the past, had carved a huge likeness of a woman's face at the top, and two enormous boulders somewhat lower made good representations of breasts.

"There's a reed bank right beyond her," Eloti added. "We can pull in there for the day. I believe there's still a small channel wide enough to accommodate us."

Yanados nodded, but swore as she hauled on the tiller. Crosscurrents were thick here, and treacherous, and the sea wind was no longer strong or reliable.

It was full daylight when the boat was finally ensconced in the little channel, surrounded by reeds and cattails, masked in the rising mist.

One of the mules brayed petulantly, and everyone jumped half out of their skins. Eloti, quick as a cat, leaped to the mule's head and pinched its nostrils, stifling the noise and neatly avoiding an indignant kick with a forehoof. Doshi helped her tie on the nosebags with their bribe of grain and dried peas, while the others listened for any sign of discovery.

Zeren considered a moment, then tapped Arizun and Yanados on the shoulders. "Bring your bows," he whispered. "We'd best go see if anyone's about who might have heard the brute."

A few moments later, the silent trio slipped overboard—legs bare, tunics kilted up above the knee, bows in hand and quivers filled with arrows—and waded quietly off into the reeds. The others crouched down along the gunwales, assorted weapons in hand, wondering what on earth they'd do if their best steersman, soldier and archer never came back.

Zeren led the way through the reeds until the ground firmed underfoot and the Mother Stone loomed ahead. He studied the land about him as far as the mist would allow, looked closely at the ancient monument, then signalled the others forward.

Yanados caught his look immediately. "Up there?" she whispered, pointing toward the ancient goddess' head.

Zeren nodded, and slung his bow on his back. Yanados did likewise, and stepped after him. Arizun nocked an arrow and crouched at the foot of the stone, below the track the others climbed, to make sure they weren't followed or disturbed.

The climb was long, but not difficult until the end, where Zeren and Yanados were obliged to climb around to the back of the Mother's head to find foothold in her rough stone hair. Her crown, though, was surprisingly level and smooth, as if generations of pious (or impious) picnickers had worn a comfortable platform there. Zeren and Yanados turned carefully to all sides, peering for signs of life below.

To the landward side, the mist thinned below them, showing unbroken meadow gone rough with neglect. No cattle grazed there now, only a flock of deer and another of wild goats off in the distance. The weed-grown land might have been abandoned for ages instead of mere months.

"Kula of the Wild Things reclaims land quickly," Zeren noted, unamused. "I'll wager those fields haven't been grazed, let alone farmed, since last autumn. The country folk knew the Ancar were coming, long before Lutegh fell—long before we knew, in the city."

"It could be they simply knew the war would come," Yanados said with a shrug, "and they chose to draw their cattle inland, away from the gracious attentions of any army coming along the river."

"Hmm. Think you the landsmen still thrive, back out of sight of the river?"

"Most probably, but they'll suffer soundly enough when the Ancar come down the west bank—which they'll do, sooner or later."

"Oh, aye." Zeren turned back to the river and the lands beyond it.

Below them the mist rose, pearling in the fresh sunlight, masking the water. From this height, it looked like a shining carpet that stretched almost to the edge of sight. Beyond it rose only the blue silhouettes of distant hills.

Through it came smells of smoke, dung, food cooking: faint sounds of clanking metal and wood being chopped, occasional voices: sullen glowing of orange lights amid the pearly gray, countless numbers of them, just across the river.

"Vozai," Zeren breathed, "it's a major Ancar camp! Countless thousands of them . . ."

Yanados wriggled closer to him on the rock. "Should we try to sneak past them while the mist holds?"

"No. Never trust to mist, not once the sun's up; it could burn off at any time."

"We might get past them first."

"We don't know how many there are. They could line the bank for the next several miles." Zeren shivered in the burning sunlight. "So many of them, always so unbelievably many, stripping the land like locusts as they go. Thank the gods you've never seen an Ancar horde coming toward you! No, our chances are better if we stay put."

"Speak of sleeping in the lion's den," Yanados muttered. "Well, best go tell the others. We'll do no hunting this day."

"Nor cooking, either," Zeren agreed. "Let's go."

Sulun woke suddenly to low sunlight, a clear blue sky shining between the reedtops, and a huge, undefinable sound filling the air. A quick glance showed the others awake, crouched silently under the gunwales, a few clearly praying, the rest just listening. He crawled to Ziya, who was nearest.

"What is it?" he whispered, gesturing vaguely toward the sound.

It seemed to come from the river, or beyond: rumbling,

clanking, grinding, somewhat like the noise of a looting mob back in the city, but more vast and slow.

"Ancar. On the march," Ziya whispered back, flicking a strange-eyed look at him. "Be quiet till they're gone."

"Gods." Sulun shivered, reached for his blanket and drew it up around him. "How many?"

"Don't know. Zeren said a whole army. Hush."

Sulun hushed, trying to think of how great an army would make a noise like that, how long it would take them to pass. The mist, he saw, had burned away in the full daylight. If he wanted, he might crawl through the reeds and take a peek, actually see the enemy on the march, see the plague of this age that had ruined Sabis and was on its way to destroy his city. Surely they wouldn't see him peering through reeds on the opposite side of the wide river; he could watch to his heart's content.

Sulun decided he didn't want to look. Leave the ravaging hordes as a symbol, a shadow, something—pray the gods—he would never have to deal with directly. Look not upon the basilisk. He huddled further down in his blanket, prepared to wait out the day.

Even the mules kept their heads down, and munched their reeds quietly.

The sound went on until dark, when it changed to more rattling and shouting: noises of camp being set up for the night. All day marching, and the horde had not yet passed.

Sulun's little tribe huddled in their blankets under the wagon, all but Eloti, who went about fetching drinkable water for the mules, currying them with sacking and throwing down fresh reeds, just as if the enemy weren't dining in their uncounted thousands just across the water. Dinner was smoked fish, waybread and wine cut with chilled herb tea. Everyone ate slowly, putting off the inevitable—and necessary—departure.

At length, Eloti pointed out, "We can't wait too long before leaving. We must get past Lutegh before dawn."

Everyone shivered, but nobody argued with her logic.

They waited less than an hour after dark for dinner to settle—and, hopefully, the unseen enemy to sleep—before setting out.

This time they raised no sail. Everyone took an oar, though they began with poles to slide the boat out of its safe niche in the reeds. The treacherously clear sky at least gave them good starlight for reckoning, though they clung to the shore and the banks of reeds to at least disguise their silhouette.

On the far bank, campfires glimmered like malevolent yellow stars—countless thousands of them. One look sufficed. The refugees shivered, looked no more, and bent to the oars.

The mules, muzzles occupied with well-filled nosebags, stamped and grumbled quietly. The noise was slight, but it made the rowers wince.

Omis and Zeren, matched on the two foremost oars, bent their backs with the stoic concentration of workmen at a long, hard task. Vari and Eloti, next, hauled with distinctly different styles: Vari's angular and fierce, puffing for breath to every upstroke, Eloti swaying quietly, smoothly, her gloved hands seeming to grip casually, as if this too were just another passing amusement. Arizun and Ziya, on the third pair, lifted and hauled doggedly in tight-lipped determination to do their share. Doshi and Sulun tacitly worked out a rowing cycle that gave them an acceptable weight on the oars with the best economy of motion. Yanados crouched at the sweep, holding it with her weight, hollow eyes peering at the dark water ahead.

"Stroke . . . stroke . . . stroke . . ." she half-whispered, until everyone's rhythm matched.

The black water growled and gurgled under the hull. The boat moved slowly upstream.

In the muttering darkness the rhythmic labor grew hypnotic. Sulun found himself sinking into an oar-paced reverie, thoughts rolling in stately cadences like the phrases of a holy-day temple chant. *Who else escaped from Sabis?* he wondered. *Where will they settle? What will they do?* Mez, in the end, would benefit. The refugees who fled there were not all unskilled and penniless; the craftsmen and merchants and even the clerks would put their trades to good use. No doubt many would leave the city, work their way south and east through Esha, set up in the lesser cities and even backwater towns where they'd find less rivalry for their skills and wares. Soon enough, the lands of the southern shore would find themselves gemmed with cities of wealth, knowledge and trade. Give them a generation or two undisturbed, which the Ancar, having taken all the north and east, just might be content to do . . .

And what of the poorer refugees who fled across the Baiz into the swamps of the delta? Surely they couldn't all stay there, hiding in the reeds, living on fish and water birds. Soon enough they'd march west, into the wild lands of marsh and forest, to find some means of living among the thick foliage and wild beasts. Perhaps they'd become hunters, trappers, woodcutters—trading occasionally, resentfully, with the new masters of their old city. Or perhaps they'd go far enough west, into the unknown lands, to find some place fit to build another city. Give them time, give them time . . .

And we go north, the thought circled to conclusion. *Behind the Ancar lines, into half-wild lands, to found our own little colony. What can we build there that will endure?*

He couldn't imagine it now; his mind was growing dulled with fatigue. Only the resolution remained: find a safe place to settle, some place where a blacksmith and a gaggle of engineers could make their living as they were, doing what they had always done.

Sulun shivered as a touch of wind ruffled his hair, then nudged the hood of his robe off his head.

"Down anchor," Yanados announced quietly. "Up oars and set them."

It took Sulun a few seconds to understand the words, then act on them. Oars rattled on wood as they were drawn in. The anchor splashed down into the inky water.

"Noise!" Doshi gulped. "Too loud. Yanados—"

"We're past them," Yanados panted, leaning on the sweep. "Look."

Sure enough, the far bank of the river was dark and silent. They had finally outsailed the last fringes of the marching Ancar horde.

"Hush," Zeren warned, quietly as he could while still being heard. "They must have guards on the road, messengers, post houses . . ."

"We'll be quiet," Yanados agreed, tying down the sweep and climbing to her feet. "Better rest, though, and use this wind. Up sails."

"They might be seen."

"Not likely, not at this distance, in such dark. Put up sail."

Sluggishly, the others moved to comply. In less than a quarter-hour the boat was moving again, slowly but steadily upstream. Everyone sagged on the deck, rubbing cramped arms and backs. The mules munched placidly. Weary eyes raked the water, the shores, found only blackness. Eventually Vari got up, fetched a thin wineskin out of supplies, and passed it around. Yanados inspected the sail, reset a few lines, then came back and sat down at the tiller.

"How long?" Sulun panted, amazed at the number of cramps and aches he hadn't noticed until he stopped rowing.

"The wind? Who can tell?" Yanados shrugged. "We'll have to row again in an hour, anyway. Wind alone won't take us past Lutegh in time."

Sulun groaned, thinking of the long night ahead. Best make sure the children were safely asleep and the mules bribed to silence with enough grain.

They were rowing with the wind when the first lights came into sight. Yanados, eyes ahead, saw them first.

"Approaching Lutegh," she almost whispered to Sulun and Doshi. "Keep silence. Pass it on."

Sulun, slow-witted with fatigue, duly passed the message on before its implications sank in.

Lutegh: east, on the fork of the Dawnstream, fallen to the Ancar. And they would turn there, come into the Dawnstream almost under Lutegh's walls. How could they not be seen and noted? How could the Ancar not order some captive boatman to set out after them? It was impossible, suicidal. They should make for the west bank, land, take out the mules and wagon and go overland from here—

Through a countryside crawling with Ancar troops.

Sulun said nothing, only pulled harder on his oar.

Yanados huddled at the tiller, flicking her eyes across the water ahead, the ominous glimmers of light on the distant east shore, and the sails. Keep the sails up? They were dull gray colored, not terribly visible in the dark, would add to their speed—and the boat needed speed now, speed and power to make the turn into the Dawnstream against the gods only knew what crosscurrents. According to all she'd ever heard, the Dawnstream's mouth was wide and deep. Wide enough that a boat this size couldn't be seen by torchlight from the bank? Deep enough that the major current would run low, leaving the surface placid enough to skim quickly? And how much of the night was left? Would the mists rise at dawn, or would the air and sky stay treacherously clear? If mist came, how would she find the mouth of the Dawnstream? How would she find it anyway, in all this darkness?

No help for it; she would have to steer closer to the east shore, go within sight of Lutegh.

Yanados gritted her teeth and leaned on the tiller, pulling to starboard.

More pinpoints of orange light appeared, shimmering through the night haze, on the east bank. So many of them, no visible end to them ahead. White stars dead above, evil orange stars to the right, nothing else visible in the gurgling darkness. And now there came sounds: somewhere a dog barking, distant creaking of wood, sloshing of water around moored ships' hulls or the piers of once busy docks.

Yanados pulled the tiller straight again; they were close enough.

The others didn't look up, only rowed.

And then the wind shifted.

Yanados looked up in alarm as the sailcloth flapped noisily. She swore, tied down the tiller and ran for the mast. The damp knots seemed determined to stick, but she yanked them out and dragged the sail down. She bundled and tied the heavy cloth, alternately angry and grateful that the others had stuck to their rowing.

Gods, what was the wind doing? Gusts from the south, the northeast smelling different, contending . . . Yanados smothered a laugh as she understood. The Dawnstream brought its own wind down its wide channel, the land's wind running headlong into the last breath up from the sea.

She had her guide at last; steering straight into that grass-scented wind would take them up the Dawnstream, past Lutegh.

But they would have to do it by oars alone.

Yanados went back to the tiller, cast a long glance over the dim lights of the east bank, and steered toward the cool northeastern wind.

Stroke by stroke, the malevolent yellow lights crawled by: no end to them, fatigue a growing enemy and the

current heavier now, turbulent, making the rowers fight
for headway. They must be right on top of the confluence,
the junction of waters and winds, where the rivers met
and struggled briefly. Yes, there: the shore lights seemed
to angle away in the darkness. Once past this jumble of
flowing forces, they'd be safely into the Dawnstream. But,
gods, the battle went inch by inch!

"Stroke . . . stroke . . . stroke . . ." Yanados heard herself chanting. *Baiz, Lord of Rivers, let us go!* she prayed
furiously, knowing that Baiz had never been a patron god
of herself or her people, and why should he listen? *Mav of
warriors, help us. Ioth of my kindred, help us. Kula of the
wild things . . .*

A soft singing flowed across the deck, barely audible,
sweet and level and hypnotic in its surging rhythm.

For an instant Yanados thought of mermaids, sirens,
river wights who enchanted sailors. Then she recognized
the song, and the voice.

"*Low* lie the *stars* over *Tos*lagen's *mem*ory,
    High hang the *flowers* from the *trees* of her *tomb* . . .*"

Ah, Eloti's magecraft again. That simple chant had worked
small wonders twice before; it certainly could do no harm
now. Accept its help; steer well.

Yanados rocked gently at the tiller, matching time with
the soft repetitive song, watching the water and feeling
the wind, letting all sense of time fall away.

The distant orange light-points flowed by.

An angled block of darkness cut off the pattern of stars
ahead. For a moment Yanados stared at it, wondering
what it signified. Then she guessed what it was, and
shoved hard on the tiller with a muffled curse.

The spell-struck rowers pulled on the oars without change,
and Yanados hadn't the time to warn them. She pushed
harder.

The boat swerved to port, bucking in the cross-chop of
the water, turned and pulled sideways along that looming
block of deeper darkness so suddenly huge—no, not big,
but close. Down and down its length, so close that Yanados
could hear the water smacking its side: a faintly hollow
booming. Yes, another hull: a ship, sitting lightless and
cargoless out on the water—and what that might mean was
best not to think. So damned close!

And there, there, the end of the dark patch, the ship's

stern, less than ten yards away. Gods, they had been close. Pull away now, quietly away.

Yanados looked up, saw the silhouette of a man at the stern blocking the stars. Facing them, or facing the bow of the ship? No way to tell—save that he didn't move, didn't cry out, showed no sign of having seen them.

" 'Care,' sing the *birds* in the *boughs* of the *cy*presses,
'*Care,* love and *care,* win you *free* of your *doom.*' "

The damned song—what if he heard it?

No, wait: what if he *had* heard it, heard and been ensorcelled, urged to a dreamy and intent regard for his work—which was watching the deck of the ship? Or perhaps he simply thought that a small boat, laden with passengers and mules and wagon (could he see them in this darkness?), with a mildly singing woman aboard, could surely be up to no harm, only going about its lawful business?

Shoulders hunched, waiting for the cry of notice and alarm, Yanados steered out and away from the darkened ship, steered on until the rising grumble of the water warned that she was drawing near the west bank, perhaps straight at the fork. She hauled the tiller back, turning into the Dawnstream's wind again, back against the oncoming current. Still no sound from the now invisible ship. Still the rowers pulled.

But their rowing was ragged now, breaths audible with labored panting. Eloti's singing was fainter. Fatigue, the other enemy, was winning.

For a long, despairing moment Yanados thought of putting the anchor down, letting them rest an hour before striking on up the Dawnstream, praying the darkness would hold while they idled just across the water from Lutegh's walls. How much of the night was left? Was the sky already paling, just the slightest tinge, above the city? Was that the first breath of dawn that raised the wind in her hair?

Wind—

Once more Yanados quick-tied the sweep and darted for the sails. She'd have to do this alone, no one to help her, and the resetting again soon, and the gods knew how many tacks after that. Swearing quietly, she hauled and reset the lines, tugged the boom over and tied it fast— damned, gods-beshat, back-breaking work to do alone, but she could manage.

The sails filled, swelled awkwardly sideways, ridiculously angled but workable. The boat creaked, groaned, grumbled —but began to pull away from shore. Back toward deeper water, back toward the frowning walls and treacherous lights of Lutegh, but nonetheless upstream.

Yanados leaned against the creaking mast, panting with effort and relief. "Up oars," she gasped to the faltering team of rowers. "Up oars and set them. Rest."

Eloti stopped singing, and gratefully sagged over her oar. One by one, the others fell out of the spell and followed suit. Yanados staggered down the line of the deck, helping the over-exhausted haul in their oars, finding Ziya and Arizun slumped at their stations, already asleep. She pulled the oars in for them, stumbled back to her place at the tiller, and sat down to wait.

Tack and tack, she thought, watching the sails strain. *Zig and zag, one yard sideways for every yard forward, against wind and current, but we move, we move . . . How long until dawn?*

Gods, the eastern sky was no longer black but definitely indigo. Another hour, and the boat would be visible. Another hour, and they'd be almost under Lutegh's docks. Half an hour, then, and she'd have to reset the sails, cross back to the west, hope these short tacks would keep them moving fast enough to get out of anyone's sight.

And if they were seen, would anyone raise the alarm?

If alarm were raised, how long would it take the Ancar to find a boat and a capable steersman and set out on the water?

If the Ancar pursued, would they overhaul, get to within bowshot range? Would any Luteghi boatmen serve their masters that well?

And gods' piss, why were the stars ahead blanking out so soon? They sky was still dark . . .

Yanados blinked twice, shook her head, then smothered a whoop of hysterical laughter.

Of course! Of course! The wind is turning warm!

Dark as unwashed raw wool, just rising now from the surface of the water, came the first of the morning mist. In less than an hour, it would be thick as curdled cream and taller than the mast. Oh, it was going to be a lovely, hot, steamy, foggy day!

Crooning snatches of gratitude-prayers to all the water

gods she could think of, Yanados tied down the tiller and crawled over sleeping bodies toward the mast.

Doshi woke to miserable, wet heat, hot mist thick enough to choke him, aches in his arms and back and shoulders that made him wonder if he'd been run over by an iron-monger's cart. It took two tries to roll over and exchange one set of wretched cramps for another. He struggled for sleep, felt it slip away, and resigned himself to being awake in this pitiable condition.

The boat rocked slightly to a heavier than usual wavelet. Doshi turned the gear of thought by one slow cog, and realized that the boat was moving. Moving: not anchored. And where?

He pulled gritty eyes open, and found he was looking straight at Arizun's knees. It was not, he decided, a cheering sight. By slow and tortuous degrees Doshi turned his head and looked the other way.

A huddle of robes sat crouched by the tiller, cloak hood draping a face he barely recognized. Yanados, as he'd never seen her: lips dry and cracked, cheeks hollowed and gray-pale with something beyond exhaustion, eyes dull-gleaming as in fever but set in bruise-dark lids that gave the eerie impression of tunnels . . .

"Have you been up all night?" was the first thing Doshi thought to say.

Yanados blinked at him, took intolerably long consider-ing the simple question, and finally nodded, jerkily, once.

"Gods." Doshi started to get up, though better of it, compromised by getting to his hands and knees and crawl-ing toward her. His own memories came back slowly. "Lutegh . . . Have we passed it?"

Again Yanados fumbled with the thought for impossibly long before answering. She shrugged.

"Gods," Doshi muttered again, looking around him in the steaming mist. A fat blob of sun hung three hands up from the horizon. Then he noted the odd set of the sails, the slap of the water beating slantwise against the hull, the smell of the slow but steady wind . . .

And he remembered that smell, that wind.

"We're on the Dawnstream. We have to be past Lutegh! Oh gods, Yani, put in to shore. This fog will hide us."

Yanados frowned vaguely, trying to think about that.

Doshi looked again at the water, the sails, the surface ruffling of the wind. "Which way are we going now?" he asked, very slowly and carefully.

Yanados squinted at the sail, and finally answered. "North. Mm, northeast. North shore."

"Ah, good. Wonderful. We'll just keep going until we reach the bank. We'll put in there. Indeed, I'll do it." He sat down beside her and draped one arm over the tiller's sweep. "You go lie down, Yani."

"Down?" Yanados blinked at him.

"Lie down. Sleep. I'll handle it now."

"Mm." Yanados dutifully dragged herself free of the tiller, crawled a yard or so across the deck, then stopped and simply lay down where she was.

Doshi gripped the tiller and stared straight ahead, waiting for some sign of the riverbank to show through the mist. After a time it occurred to him that unless the others woke soon, he'd have to drop the anchor and take down the sails all by himself. He groaned at the thought.

And what if, a sudden worry gnawed, there was no cover on the north bank? What if some part of the Ancar horde was there, waiting for them? What if the fog lifted, leaving them naked to any and all eyes?

Doshi glanced at Yanados, saw her lying motionless as a corpse. No help there. Sulun was nearest in reach, one leg sprawled out toward the stern, foot within jabbing distance. Doshi stretched a cramped leg toward him, trying to reach that foot. Even a kick would do, so long as it was silent—the gods knew who might be close enough in this fog to overhear even a whisper.

Then his eye caught something in the mist ahead. Doshi gulped, pulled his leg back, looked about for some way to stop the boat, saw the anchor within reach.

As he picked up the anchor the shapes drew close enough for him to recognize, and he almost whooped with relief.

Reeds.

Near noon the mist thinned, and within an hour it lifted. By then the sturdy little riverboat was safely nestled in the reed bed and all her crew, except Yanados, were awake. All of them were stiff, sore, grateful for the early summer heat, and unwilling to move.

It was Zeren who insisted that someone go out among the reeds and look at the shore, see where they were and how close the Ancar might be. No one volunteered, as he'd half expected, so Zeren took bow and quiver and set off on the task himself.

Vari then announced that the children, at least, be fed, and snagged Sulun's help in digging up supplies and handing them out.

Eloti insisted that the same courtesy be extended to the mules, as well as throwing out their used reed-straw and providing more. This time everyone drew lots for the unwelcome duty, and Arizun got the short straw. Ziya volunteered to cut the fresh reeds, but Arizun still muttered miserably about the work he had.

Two hours later Zeren returned, muddy to the waist, but grinning widely. He also carried three plump wild ducks.

"Take the mules off and let them graze on solid ground for a change," he said, tossing his catch onto the boat. "We're safe."

"Safe?" Sulun gawked. "I can't believe it. This close to Lutegh? On the north shore? Where the Ancar have already conquered?"

"They don't seem much interested in holding empty land." Zeren grimaced. "Here, go through the reeds and see for yourself."

Sulun slipped out of the boat, picked his way cautiously from tussock to tussock until the reeds thinned, and then peeked through.

Before him lay a wide stretch of placid water. Beyond that was another reed-fringed shore, and beyond that stretched wild meadows and patches of scrubby forest. There was no sign of man, as far as the eye could reach.

Sulun clambered back to the boat, dunking his sandals twice. "They came and passed," he marvelled. "There's no one out there at all."

"No doubt they were in a hurry to reach Lutegh," Eloti sniffed, "and Sabis afterward."

"They don't pay much attention to lands they've already conquered," Doshi murmured, thinking of the north.

The others said nothing, but began setting out the boards to make a landing ramp. Not only the mules yearned to set foot on solid land for an hour, or more.

*   *   *

Yanados didn't waken until the next dawn, and then she was ravenous. Fortunately, the larder had been replenished by the hunting and fishing parties. Breakfast for everyone was ample and, for once, served on solid ground.

"If it's safe, we should go on by daylight," Yanados opined around a mouthful of grilled trout. "The wind and current are against us; we'll have to row or tack. Best do that while we can see where we're going."

"In fact," Arizun added, glowering at the mules, "why not put into shore, leave the boat and go on with the wagon? If the land's empty—"

"We don't know how empty," Doshi cautioned. "We're not even sure yet just where we are."

"I have a suspicion, though," Eloti put in. "By all means, let's sail on today—and keep an eye on the south bank."

Everyone else looked at Doshi, who shrugged. He didn't know this part of the country well, and Eloti seemed to. By all means, let her be the guide.

They set off an hour later, tacking across the slow but steady water, seeing no one across the empty leagues of the shore.

4

Close on sunset, they saw the first towers of an approaching city. The others wanted to put into the reeds at once, but Eloti smiled eagerly, took hold of the mast and stood up for a better view. .

"No reeds tonight," she announced, smiling. "We'll spend the night in those ruins."

"Ruins?" Zeren questioned. "A whole city? The Ancar would hardly leave it without some garrison, however small."

"Not if they never came near it, and I doubt they would, since the Sabisan troops would have given it a wide berth, as always."

"Eh? How wide? And why? A city, ruined or not—"

"It is the City of Ghosts. Itoma. Sukkti ruins."

"Oh." Zeren didn't say anything more. Even he had heard, during his years in Sabis, of the famous haunted ruins of Itoma.

"They say it's full of plagues, pitfalls, hideous mummies, walls that fall on you without warning, and plenty of angry ghosts to push them," Omis recalled. "No safe place to take the children."

Eloti laughed. "The last tenants indeed placed a number of pitfalls, and centuries of weather have done nothing to improve the buildings, but there are safe sections, if one knows where to find them."

Sulun gave her a measuring look. "You've been here often?" he asked. "You know your way about the ruins?"

"Oh, yes. My mother's side of the family came from there, originally. Unlike my brother, I never thought the old blood a taint or a social disadvantage."

Eloti peered toward the silhouetted towers on the south shore. "Indeed, there's much advantage in not fearing old Sukkti ghosts, bothering to visit one's old home city, exploring the ruins during long summer days . . ." She sighed, then sat back down in the boat. "Steer there. You'll find that the third stone dock is quite usable.

The sun was slinking among the massive ruins when they pulled up to the third of a series of stone quays, reaching a good distance out into the river. On the upriver side were steps going down to the water, and even a few massive bronze tie rings still bolted to the stone. Yanados made fast the boat, but no one save Eloti was eager to go ashore. A broad, stone-paved avenue ran beside the river at the foot of the docks, and directly across it from their anchorage loomed a huge flat-roofed temple. The architecture looked wrong to everyone raised among Sabis's domes and arches.

Eloti marched up the water stairs, down the dock and straight toward the temple.

"Wait!" Sulun yelled, floundering after her. "Wait until I can fetch a lamp, at least! Lady—"

"Just bring lamp oil," she chirped back at him, not breaking stride. "There are lamps enough within."

Sulun shook his head, scrabbled among the supplies for oil, tinder and striker. He remembered to grab some string too, just in case Eloti's promised lamp needed a new wick. Then he ran up the stairs and down the dock after her retreating form, and no one in the boat elected to go with him.

Sulun caught up to Eloti on the wide temple stairs, and they paced through the open dark doorway together.

"Hmm, plain slab lintels, and close-set columns to support them," Sulun noted, trying not to look at the darkness beyond the doorway. "Were these folk ignorant of the arch, then?"

"They learned it in later days, but this temple is very old." Eloti disappeared into the shadows, leaving Sulun to follow as best he could. "Ah, here. Just as I remembered. The lamp oil, please."

Sulun dutifully handed over the jug of oil, then the striker and tinder. Eloti didn't ask for a wick. He saw sparks strike, then the tinder's glow, finally a clear flame that grew large enough to show the immediate surroundings —and he gaped at what he saw.

Ranged around the walls, starting near the doors and reaching as far back as the light revealed, were great square-carved granite statues of every beast, bird and fish known to man. Between their paws, or fins or talons, rested oil lamps carved from the same stone, and before these were carved depressions that must have been offering bowls. A litter of dried stalks showed that the common offering was flowers or grain. One third of the way in from the walls stood rows of columns, supporting the long stone beams that made up the ceiling. Between them lay a mosaic-tiled path depicting flowers, fruits and leaves, more species of plants than he could recognize, forming a bright pathway down the wide central aisle. Eloti meandered down the length of the temple, filling and lighting occasional lamps—at the feet of a lion, a fish, an eagle, a bull, a stag—and gradually the shape at the far end of the central aisle emerged in the light.

Foremost stood a wide stone altar, carved and tiled with images of garlands. Behind that was another stone lamp, by far the largest Sulun had ever seen, and behind that a statue easily twelve cubits tall. Despite the rigidly formal archaic pose and unfamiliar attributes carved on her robes, she was unmistakable: Kula, in her Fruitful Mother aspect, crowned with grain and starflowers. Even in the ancient, simplified carving style, her characteristic smile was familiar.

Eloti sighed faintly and poured only a bit of oil into that huge lamp, lit it, genuflected and stepped back. Sulun thought it wise to imitate the gesture.

"So," he whispered, trying to sound respectful, "the Sukkti knew Kula also?"

"Indeed, and under that very name." Eloti sniffed. "The Sabirns took up her worship with no great changes, once they settled these lands and learned they would have to farm for a living. I believe they had worshipped only water, war and weather gods before then."

"Incredible. How may other deities, think you, were originally Sukkti?"

"Quite a number of them: any that had to do with farming, herding or manufacturing. Quite often they kept the old names and rites intact."

"And . . ." Sulun felt a wild idea sprouting. "The priesthoods also?"

"The priesthoods also," Eloti smiled. "Especially those which were exclusively female."

"Family tradition!" Sulun almost laughed, staring at her.

"In my case, an exclusively female tradition." Eloti gestured another salute to the smiling statue.

'Did your brother ever know?"

"He didn't care to know."

"I see." Sulun looked up at the statue, studying it for some sign or omen, reading nothing but the encouraging smile. "Are there any other . . . little secrets of the priesthood that were passed on as tradition in the female line?"

"A few," Eloti chuckled. "Some small magics . . ."

"Toslagen!"

"A distant ancestress, reputed to be a mighty sorceress."

"Mighty enough that even her memorial chant has power?"

"More precisely, she was a poetess who discovered the uses, principles and techniques of hypnotic chant."

"I see."

"Other things . . ." Eloti glanced around the dimly lit temple. "I know the location of certain discreet chambers where we may be assured of safe rest. There is also a temple garden—long since run wild, of course, but still quite lush—where we can safely pasture the mules for the night. No, no hidden ancient treasure, I'm afraid; that was taken away long ago and put to prudent use. The women of my family have always learned certain trades and possessed their own wealth, usually quite unknown to the men."

"Family tradition!" Sulun laughed, then took a second

look at Eloti. "An excellent tradition. And . . . you are the last of the line?"

Eloti bowed her head. "Unless, at my age, I can win a husband and produce a daughter, yes, the tradition ends with me."

"That would be a great pity, Goodlady." Sulun thought of the glances he'd observed between Eloti and Zeren, and prudently held his tongue. Best let that grow without comment. Best change the subject, too. "But how did these buildings remain intact, unmolested so long? How did Itoma earn its fearsome reputation?"

"Deliberate policy," said Eloti, turning to inspect the shadowed space behind the statue. "Itoma was a long time falling, and its people had perhaps a bit more prudence than those of Sabis. When the coastal towns fell to the Sabirns, and the river trade was cut off, Itoma could no longer support a large populace. The people departed for the countryside and other river towns, carefully spreading stories about curses and evil wizardry and ghosts and the like."

"That wouldn't have sufficed without some evidence," Sulun noted. "One of the best antidotes I know to superstition is greed for loot."

"Oh yes," Eloti laughed. "There was evidence enough. The outlying areas of the city were abandoned first, and the remaining people—seeing they no longer had the numbers to withstand a siege—built artful traps all throughout the empty neighborhoods."

"No doubt enhanced with gruesome carvings, paintings and other stage trappings," Sulun added, remembering stories he'd heard. "Is there truly a palace filled with mummies?"

"There is. It was a prince's mansion, actually; the fellow was famed for squandering money on his lavish tastes, much to his own ruin. Later, defenders of Itoma thought it clever to raid the old necropolis and place the remains in odd places all over the former spendthrift's house and grounds. I'm told that the first Sabirn scouts were artfully led there, and then treated to a most dramatic exhibition."

Sulun remembered the famous story of the Palace of the Dead, and laughed heartily. "The Sabirn tale may have been embroidered a bit, but by all accounts those poor explorers were scared out of their wits."

"I should tell you the Sukkti version of that tale some time," Eloti grinned back. "In any event, the city was emptied by poverty rather than war—which is why you'll find the buildings thoroughly stripped of portable valuables, but otherwise intact. Legend protected it long after the inhabitants had gone."

"Preserved it through the rise and fall of the conquerors," Sulun mused. "What power legends have, and rumors of magic . . ."

Right there, a marvelous idea unfolded before Sulun's eyes: a completion of a pattern first sketched moons ago in Sabis, a completion so near perfection that he glanced up at the statue of the goddess to wonder if she had inspired it.

"We should go back and tell the others to come in," Eloti suggested. "Otherwise they'll think we've been eaten by the ghosts. Does that smile signify something particular?"

"Yes. Yes, it does." Sulun pulled his grin down to polite dimensions. "Do you think that even the Ancar would have heard of the Lost and Haunted City of Itoma by now?"

"Most likely, if they've spent any time at all in the northlands. The tales spread everywhere in reach of Sabis."

"And . . . was Deese of the Forge originally a Sukkti god?"

"He was that. Hmm, do you see an advantage in being Sukkti, now that Sabis has fallen?"

"Sukkti magicians, more precisely—from the Lost City of Itoma, come out of hiding now that the rule of Sabis is gone."

"Ah . . ." Eloti smiled as the idea took hold, smiled more widely than Sulun had ever seen her do before, until their delighted-idiot grins matched. They burst out laughing at the same time.

Omis and Zeren, come searching cautiously after them, heard the gales of laughter roll out of the temple, and were heartened enough to come in and see what the joke was.

They learned soon enough, and they laughed too.

5

Thanig was a small town hidden in a fold of the Jarrya hills: small in size, smaller in fame. It served the needs of surrounding farmers and herders with simple goods, most of them locally made, the rest imported once a year from Athoa, the nearest larger Jarryan town. Aside from pack merchants and tax collectors, no one had much reason to remember its name. Neither did travellers, other than the occasional tax clerk or peddler, visit it from one year to another. Since the Ancar invasion, some ten years back, even those visitors had grown few.

Therefore it was a matter of no little excitement and concern when the townspeople first observed the column of dust, and then the strange entourage causing it, approaching by the main—and indeed the town's only—road.

The townsfolk reacted swiftly: mothers hauled children indoors, craftsmen carried display tables of their wares back into their shops, older children chased family livestock safely out of the street, householders pulled doors and window shutters closed and peeped out through the cracks. Only the innkeeper left his door open, and even he took care to hastily hide his better bottles. That done, everyone watched the strangers approach.

The spectacle was indeed something to see, remember and tell one's grandchildren about. In the lead marched two big men in long iron-colored robes and hooded cloaks, carrying iron-shod staves bound with green branches. At the rear came four similar figures, slighter in stature. Between them rolled a huge wagon, covered with iron-colored sailcloth, driven by a tall man in the same dark vestments as the others while beside him sat an imposing woman garbed in green and crowned with a garland. The wagon was painted with stylized designs that suggested ancient letters, garlanded with leaves and flowers, hung with iron chains and brass bells, and drawn by a pair of large iron-colored mules. The mules' harness was hung with brass bells and luck charms of polished brass and iron, and jingled with their every step. The dark-robed figures were chanting softly, in what the more experienced townsfolk recognized as quaintly accented Sabirn, a hymn to Deese of the Forge—with proper reference to his Lady, Kula of the Wood. The procession marched into and through the village, not glancing to left or right, heading for the long building toward the far end of town whose chimney belched smoke and sparks even at this hour of day.

"Goin' to the forge, they be," the town potter noted, much to everyone's agreement. "Pilgrims might be, but priestish sure as rain."

And, right enough, the strangers drew to a precise halt at the doorway of the town's smithy. With the precision of courtly dancers, the two men in the lead stepped back to hold the mules' bridles, the four at the rear rearranged themselves at the wagon's back and sides, and one of them stepped forward to knock formally on the doorpost.

"Blessings to all within," he intoned, in only slightly accented Jarryan. "Blessings to forge and fire, roofbeam and hearthstone, in the name of Deese of the Forge."

Dunosh, the town blacksmith, carefully set down the horseshoe he'd been shaping, while his apprentices scurried for cover. "Uh, blessings to you, also," was all he could think to say. He tucked his trusty middleweight hammer into his belt, just to be safe, and edged toward the outlandish strangers at his door. "What would ye be wanting here?"

"Food and shelter for two days, and trade also," the stranger recited as if he'd practiced it a long time. "In exchange for your assistance, brother-in-trade, we'll gladly share our knowledge with you."

Dunosh blinked, taking all that in. Too much, too strange: best deal with one problem at a time. "Ah, the inn be back down t' street, six doors down on t' left. The beer be good, and the shepherd pie likewise, but touch not the stew . . . And warn 'em well t' air out the bedding." He guessed he was babbling like a fool, but better that than to seem unfriendly—especially since he had no idea what to say to the fellow's other requests.

But the speaker smiled wide and thanked him profusely, ending with an elaborate blessing in the name of the Forge Lord. "And more," the man finished, with a conspiratorial wink, "would you like a useful bit of magic to help your work?"

"Magic?" Dunosh lifted his head like a bird dog scenting

game. In his trade there was so much that could go wrong, any helpful charm would be welcome. "Eh, a spell against splashing, p'raps?"

"Better." The speaker grinned and waved one of the larger men forward. The fellow had to stoop to get in the door, and he rolled up his sleeves as he came, revealing arms as thick-muscled as an ox's leg and streaked with the identifying scars of a smith. Dunosh stepped back respectfully.

The big stranger went to the forge, mumbled something over it, took up the tongs and studied the horseshoe between their jaws. He waved his other hand over the darkening iron, mumbled something that included the name of Deese several times, then pointed to Dunosh and said something straight and clear in Sabirn.

"Er, what'd he say?" Dunosh asked of the first speaker.

The man leaned closer and whispered in his ear: "He said: 'Temper with cold oil instead of water.' "

"Ey, I should do that . . . and that's all?"

"That's all. The rest's already been spoken."

" 'Temper with cold oil' . . ."

Dunosh was still thinking that over when the strangers rolled out of his dooryard and back down the street towards the inn. Cold oil? Where could he get that hereabouts? Butter? Far too costly. Seed oil? The same. Meat fat? Now that was possible. Rendered sheep fat was cheap enough. Cold? The town boasted no ice house, but the inn's cold cellar might do. Best go ask at once; he wanted to try that spell quickly, while the strangers were still in town.

Besides, if he followed them to the inn, who could tell what other secrets and charms he might learn?

Dunosh barked an order to his apprentices to bank the fire, and hurried off after the strangers.

By late afternoon, everyone who could leave work had gathered in or around the inn, trying to look casual while ogling the strangers. The innkeeper and his serving maids, of course, had the best excuse to chat with the odd visitors and entice information from them. The strangers proved amenable to enticement, quite glad to chat with the smiling inkeeper and his buxom serving maids, past platters of tough beef, fat pork and underspiced mutton.

Oh yes, the strangers were devotees of Deese of the

Forge—see the pretty amulet pendants: stylized iron hammers inlaid with brass flames—and yes, they were on a pilgrimage to the fabled River Gol and some ancient monuments on its banks. Yes, they knew smithcraft, and engineering, and many other bits of magic besides. Why yes, they'd be happy to talk about some of it. Headaches and joint pains? Invoke Kula three times, and drink a cup of willow bark tea. Cattle plagued with worms? Dry their feed in the first light of the morning sun, bless in the names of Deese and Kula, and feed the cattle lots of raw garlic. How to improve a lady's looks? Hmm . . . Invoke Kula thrice and wash with soap, every day. How to make that marvelous ointment? Invoke Deese's aid, boil fat in water soaked through wood ashes, skim off the result and pat it into cakes.

And who were these accommodating, fascinating strangers? Ah, that was more fascinating still.

"We are the ancient Sukkti folk," explained one of them— quite young, to judge from the voice. "The lords of Sabis suppressed our worship everywhere, save in the Lost City of Itoma. There we hid, and practiced our craft, and waited. Now, with Sabis overthrown, we dare emerge again into the light of day and visit the ancient sites of our elder worship."

After that revelation, the landlord brought fresh jugs of beer without anyone's asking.

"Ey, but now the Ancar be come," said the nearer serving maid gloomily. " 'Tis new masters now, and worse than the last, if any."

"Ah well, they know nothing of us," said another visitor, a tall skinny one with curly, wild hair. "And surely they know nothing of our magic. Let us just keep this as our little secret, shall we?"

Everyone in the inn hastily agreed. The gods knew, they had secrets enough to keep from the new crop of masters. In exchange, they were happy to tell all they knew of the roads, towns and lands to the north—though precious few of them had ever travelled far from town.

The strangers were in the midst of discussing the best place to set up shop for a day or two and sell some of their metalwares when another, less welcome, racket came from outside.

The townspeople froze, recognizing the sounds.

There were multiple hoofbeats, creakings and groanings of ill-made wagonwheels, shouts and curses in a totally unfamiliar tongue—and all coming toward the inn.

The serving maids hopped off their assorted perches and ran for the kitchen. Several of the smaller and frailer patrons followed them. The innkeeper whisked his better jugs out of sight and shoved his money box into a hidey-hole in the floor.

The strangers looked at each other, pulled their cloaks and hoods closer about them, and began humming a quiet, oddly soothing, holy song.

The newcomers came tramping through the doorway, slamming the already open door all the way back to the wall, and tromped loudly up to the inn's serving counter. There were half a dozen of them, dressed in coarse home-spun wool and roughly cured leather, hung with assorted bits of horn and plate for armor, and fairly dripping with weapons: daggers, short swords, longswords, bludgeons, horn-tipped longbows and quivers grain-sheaf thick with arrows. Their hair, beards and even moustaches were braided, and the braids were strung with odd trinkets intended as jewelry. They wore identical scowls, as if they'd practiced the look, and they glared about the interior of the inn as if expecting an armed host and a pitched battle. Despite their carefully cultivated beards, they were surprisingly young; not one of them could have been over twenty.

The Deese priests made no move, only chanted softly and stared as if they'd never seen Ancar warriors before.

The apparent leader of the small invasion force, seeming a bit surprised to find his host so thoroughly outnumbered by civilians, looked around again, bristled and scowled even more fiercely, stamped up to the serving counter and slammed his fist on it, making the jugs and cups rattle.

"Bur!" he announced. "Dimme bur!"

The innkeeper blinked, gaped, and asked, "Huh?" No one could have mistaken his meaning.

The rest of his troop crowded closer to him, either for better defense against the motionless customers or to better intimidate the innkeeper. The leader grabbed the front of the innkeeper's apron and tried to yank him forward, but succeeded only in pulling the apron off. He threw it to the floor, peevish at his failure.

"*Bur!!*" he yelled again. "Von ol ugat!"

"Huh?" said the landlord again.

The squad leader stamped in frustration. He could slaughter everyone in sight if he chose, but he couldn't make himself understood; it was an embarassing situation for a proper conqueror. He took a deep breath and tried again. "Bur," he said, miming a cup in the empty air and then drinking from it. "Hu noe, *bur*."

"I think he means, he wants beer," one of the Deese priests said quietly.

"Ah!" said the landlord, and reached for a mug.

The young Ancar turned, automatically striking a fierce pose and look, to see who had spoken.

Almost as one, the Deese priests pressed their hands together and solemnly bowed. They went on with their quiet, hypnotic chanting.

The Ancar youth looked them up and down, scratched his head, shrugged, and turned back to the counter. The landlord pushed a large mug of beer at him. He whooped in satisfaction, grabbed the mug and emptied it in one long pull. His cohort looked expectantly at him. He grinned and nodded. In a moment, they were all crowding the counter, yelling for mugs.

The landlord sighed and handed out the foamy cups, clearly not expecting to be paid for this.

In the corner, the Deese priests continued to chant quietly.

Halfway through his third cup, the young Ancar squad leader hit on another thought. He snagged the landlord, shouted unintelligibly in his face and hand-mimed something bigger, then pointed at his mug. The landlord shook his head, bewildered. The youth went through the pantomime again, yelling louder.

"I think he wants a whole barrel," said one of the Deese priests again.

The Ancar warriors didn't seem to hear, but the landlord caught it. "A whole barrel?" he groaned. "Gods, you know they won't pay for it . . ."

Nonetheless, he went to the end of the counter and rolled a sloshing barrel into sight.

The Ancar troops fell on it with whoops of delight, and began rolling it toward the front door.

"My pay," the landlord tried, chasing after the yelping squad with his hands held out in the unmistakable gesture.

The last Ancar out the door only laughed, tugged one ear, shook his head, and trotted after the others.

The landlord sighed, watching them go. Everyone else in the room quietly relaxed.

One of the Deese priests got up and peeped out the door after the retreating noise of the Ancar troop. "They've got an oxcart," he noted. "They're loading it on, next to lots of other loot. I think . . . yes, they're leaving."

"Thank the gods for small mercies," groaned the landlord. "At least it was only a barrel of cheap beer."

"Could've been much worse," the Deese priest agreed. "They're going off down the southwest road."

"Oh, my sheep!" one of the locals wailed. "I graze 'em near the road these days!" He snatched up his cap and ran out the door.

"Keep to the back trails!" the landlord called after him.

The other priests of Deese stopped that soft chanting of theirs, and stood up. One of the two biggest came quietly over to the landlord, pulling something small out of his robe.

"I think we'd best leave now," he said quietly, "before those louts tell anyone else that there's a small gang of pilgrims available for robbing. Er, could you change this?"

On his calloused palm he held out a small coin, no bigger than his fingernail, but winking unmistakably golden in the candlelight.

The landlord gaped. "Gods, no! I've not seen . . . er, such a coin in years." He glanced about worriedly, watching for unwelcome ears. "Lords of heaven, I've not seen even much silver from year's end to year's end. Have ye no other coin?"

"Unfortunately, no." The priest leaned closer and spoke lower. "Give me what coin you can lay hands on, and a keg of the best wine you have, and we'll call the deal fair."

"Er, a whole keg . . . ?"

"And two sacks of grain for our mules. Keep the rest as, hmm, compensation for your lost beer."

"Ah, aye, that'll do," the landlord agreed. "And, er, not a word to any Ancar louts about seeing the lot of you, eh?"

"Not a word to the Ancar about anything." The Deese priest smiled. "A word to a wise ear: best if your folk learned to understand the Ancar tongue as soon as might be—but never let the Ancar know it."

"Aye," the landlord grinned, showing gapped teeth. "A good word 'tis. Shall I carry out the keg for ye?"

"Best I do it—hidden under the cloak," the priest smiled back.

A moment later the party of Deese pilgrims departed the inn, two carrying grainbags and one toting a keg under his cloak. The innkeeper and his customers watched them go, already framing the tales they'd tell their assorted kin that evening. Two sets of strangers in one day: quite enough excitement for a town this size.

"Strange that those barbarian lads didn't start laying about with their irons," the blacksmith noted. "Mayhap they're settling down a bit."

"More like, the chanting o' those priests had a bit to do with it," the landlord considered. "It sounded most sleepy-like, did ye note."

"Why, so it did," the blacksmith considered. "Hmm, a good magic, that, if they be going northward."

"Aye." The blacksmith nodded soberly. "They'll need all their magic there, right enough. Ancar thick as fleas . . . "

"Oh, great doings there!" the innkeeper laughed. "Ancar warriors against Sukkti wizards: yon's a fight I'd love to see—from a safe ways back."

The blacksmith nodded dreamily, thinking about that. From such beginnings were legends born; with any luck, he'd have tales to win him drinks for his whole life long.

Once out of the tavern, the dark-robed pilgrims headed for the stables at the best speed they could make under their burdens.

"The mules . . .?" the tall thin one panted.

"Safe," retorted the big man with the keg. "Vari sat on the wagon playing with the whip until the stableboys went away. Then she re-hitched the mules and took the whole lot around behind the stable. Those Ancar pups couldn't have seen them."

"Pups! If those are the puppies, Zeren, what are the wolves like?"

"Bad enough, but all gone south where the fighting is. Those were bored brats, not fit for the front lines. We'll doubtless meet more, probably house guards of older officers, petty chiefs and the like, who've settled down to enjoy the spoils. Here . . . mind your feet! Let's load these quickly."

The grain and wine went into the wagon, where Vari and Tamiri tied them down with respectable speed.

"Are we moving on again?" Tamiri wanted to know. "I wanted to sleep in a bed. It's been so long, Mama. . . ."

"I know, dearest, but it isn't safe here. Back inside, now." Vari shooed the grumbling girl back into the body of the wagon, and held the end flaps open. "Inside, fast. There won't be much room, but—"

The others scrambled in without ceremony, climbing onto whatever seats they could manage. Doshi, the last one in, retied the flaps tightly. Zeren and Sulun went to the mules, took off their now empty nosebags, led the reluctant animals out from behind the shed, then climbed up on the driver's box and flicked out the whip. The mules plodded sullenly out onto the road.

"North, but for how long?" Sulun asked, encouraging the mules with a few hints of the whip. "The sun's low."

"Just out of sight of the village, then into the first woods near the river." Zeren reached under his cloak and tugged his sword to a handier position. "We haven't time to do better. Hmm, and I don't think it will rain tonight. Bad, bad . . . We'd best take precautions."

"And hide the fire, too." Sulun hitched his shoulders in a sigh. "Well, so that was the enemy. Can they do anything besides fight and steal?"

"Not that I've seen. Gods, that was close, in there. I expected they'd start laying about with swords, drive everyone out, steal what they wanted and set fire to the rest."

"Eloti's magic seems to be improving with practice."

"Yes . . ." Zeren set his eyes on the narrow road ahead, and said nothing further for a long while.

Choma's Chargers had grown up behind the lines, never been in on the sack of any of the large cities, only heard secondhand about the Sack of Sabis, and considered themselves most ill-used by Fate. Their older brothers and cousins, they very well knew, were busy down in the fabled southlands fighting heroic battles, collecting fabulous loot, making Great Chiefs and small kings of themselves—and here were they, Choma's company, good as any warriors in all the tribes, stuck patrolling the roads in these dirt-poor backwater lands. Wasted, they were: and all because old chief Borath had taken a bad wound in the campaigns ten years ago, and had chosen to settle here and let the rest of the war go on without him. Oh yes, he'd sent troops south with the main army, but Choma and Ruek and Lumaj and their friends had been too young to go with them. Now, by Vona's Lightning Mace, it was too late; the greatest war in history had passed them by. It was the chief complaint of their lives, and they complained about it often—especially when there was, as now, enough beer to keep their voices lubricated.

As always, it was Lumaj who pointed out the necessity of keeping the ancient warrior skills sharp lest they be lost. He explained solemnly, past a few belches, that practice—even with no better foe than a bunch of dumb dirt-farmers—was a duty to themselves and their ancestors. Better to chase sheep than chase nothing: they must patrol the district regularly, as if it meant something.

Ruek added, as usual, that there were a few benefits to such circuit riding—such as this pretty good beer and that well-roasted sheep, and the occasional local wenches.

"Women? Where?" one of the Thona brothers complained. "We've hardly seen any in two days."

"There weren't even any barmaids at that tavern," their cousin Dak agreed. "Gods, you can't compare this goat-snatching to the sack of a real city. Uncle Framm will most likely come home with a dozen mule loads of gold and jewels and . . . and all kinds of loot." He took another long pull of beer, trying to imagine the loot from a fabulous city like Sabis.

"Half a moon of riding around these hills, and we haven't seen so much as one gold coin," the other Thona brother added. "Pah, not even a handful of silver."

"I'll wager those priests had some gold," Choma considered, chasing an elusive flea in his leggings. "Lots of silver, anyway. They wore good cloth, and had plenty on their table. Aye, they were rich enough."

"Priests?" Lomaj hiccuped. "What priests?"

"You remember: the ones at that tavern. They were sitting in the corner, singing some chant or other, remember?"

"Oh yes, those strange-looking ones," Ruek slapped his

knee. "They didn't come from anywhere around here. I've never seen robes like that before."

"They must have come from the south," Choma considered. "Hey, maybe they're spies from one of the river towns, maybe Sabis itself. We should go and, uh, question the lot of 'em."

"What, now?" Dak groaned. "In the dark? We don't even know where they are."

"No, not now, of course," Choma snorted, conjuring up rough plans. "Tomorrow we go back to that town, pound on a few farmers and ask 'em where the priests are."

"What if they don't know?" Dak yawned. "What if they've gone?"

"Then we track 'em." Choma put on his best glower and stared at everyone in turn. "Do you think we can't track a bunch of fat priests?"

"Don't waste time trying to get any story out of the farmers," Ruek laughed. "None of 'em understand us, anyway."

Choma glared at him, wishing he knew how to Strike Terror With His Glance, as his grandfather was said to do. "So it'll be a proper hunt," he growled, "an exercise in tracking. Gods know, we need the practice."

The others groaned, but had no real counterargument to that.

The farmers' road meandered about the feet of hills where thin patches of woodland grew. Zeren automatically noted the signs of infrequent logging, the many birds and occasional deer. Doshi, eyes bright with childhood memories, pointed out the names and uses of the various plants and animals.

"Oh, look: Constable Jays!" he noted, as a flock of crested blue birds took to the air above them, screeching protest about the invasion of their territory. "They cry like that when anyone comes near their trees. Ah, and that's a holm oak: no better wood for long fires—"

"There'll be no long fires until we find a safe place to settle," Sulun grumbled in the wagon bed behind him. "That will be a good ways north, yet."

"How shall we know a good place when we see it?" Eloti asked. "The towns we've met so far are most unpromising."

"All we've gained," Vari added, "are some small coins and a few supplies. What should we expect in the north?"

Sulun ran his fingers through his hair and tugged his curls abstractedly. He'd thought of little else since they left the river and started overland. "We'll want a town or large villa, big enough to have need of us. It will have to be close to the old mines near the Gol. . . ." He peered again at Doshi's maps, which were never out of reach these days. "And it must be long enough conquered by the Ancar that they've settled down to trade and farming, not just looting at random, as those louts back there were doing."

"Well into Torrhyn, then," Eloti considered, craning her neck to look at the map. "Perhaps on the far side of the Gol, where the Ancar have lived for two generations at least."

"I pray not." Sulun shivered in the sunlight as the wagon pulled out onto another long stretch of sheep meadow. "We don't speak the language, and I'd rather not approach the Ancar close enough to learn it."

"Somewhere along the Gol, then, or a little south of it." Eloti peered out at the long, rolling plains ahead. "How many days, think you?"

"Who can tell?" Sulun shook his head. "So many more farming towns to try, so much time in each to gather news . . . A moon, perhaps, to reach the river, the gods alone know how much time to scout the land along it. Or perhaps we'll have a sudden windfall of luck, and find what we need in the very next town."

"Not the next," Doshi put in. "There are nothing but tiny farm villages for the next forty leagues, nothing bigger this far from the river. Expect no such luck until we pass into Torrhyn."

"Can we dare seek the larger towns then?"

The discussion dissolved into a low-level, three-way argument, an intellectual game to pass the travelling time. Zeren listened with only half an ear, keeping most of his attention on the empty land around them. Poor pasturage, this: little to attract anyone. No wonder the land was so empty, the road so narrow and little used.

Behind them, the Constable Jays rose up screeching.

Zeren thought for a moment, nodded grimly, then said

quietly to the others, "Ready your bows. We're being followed."

Half a moon or half a dozen towns ago, they might have questioned, argued, otherwise wasted time, but not any more. Sulun pulled his bow and quiver up from the bottom of the driver's seat. Tamiri and the smaller children burrowed down between sacks of clothing and food. Omis and Vari rolled the bottom of the wagon's roof cloth up a handspan from the sideboards and tied it in place. Everyone else slung on quivers, wriggled down below the sideboards of the wagon, and nocked arrows to their bowstrings.

The mules plodded on, unknowing. No one watching would have seen any notable change about the wagon, only perhaps noticed that the sound of conversation had dropped off.

No attack came, no sign of followers, though keen eyes raked the open ground that widened, moment by moment, between the wagon and the last stand of trees. "Nobody . . . no sign . . ." the news was whispered back up to the driver's box. Zeren considered that carefully.

"They don't want to charge across open ground," he guessed. "They'll stay out of sight until they can get closer. Maybe in the next patch of woods."

"What if we stay in open fields?" Sulun asked, just as quietly.

"Hmm, then they'll have to wait until dark. They probably mean to attack late at night, anyway."

"We can't drive on all night. Shall we camp in the open?"

Zeren peered down the winding road ahead, calculating chances. "No. We'll need the cover of trees. Go as long as we can, then camp in the woods . . . and set traps." He turned and called softly into the wagon, "Eloti, can you bespell a party of unknowns?"

"Not well," she answered. "If I don't know who they are, I must at least know where they are."

"Where they are . . ." Sulun considered. "Could you, then, set a spell on a section of ground, so as to take effect when, hmm, out guests cross it?"

"Hah, I hadn't thought of that." The lady, Sulun noticed, sounded much more animated these days; she seemed to take on more eagerness for life with every league that grew between her and Sabis. "Yes, a sort of reversed house-blessing. Stationary . . . A trap spell, in effect. Yes, I can do it, but it will cost me some little time. I can't just cast it on the ground as we pass."

"Could you cast it in a circle around our campsite this evening?"

There was a long moment's silence, then a laugh. "Certainly. I can do it while we cook dinner."

Zeren smiled slowly. "Magic traps and common traps: aye, I think we'll live through this night."

By dusk, the Thona brothers were grumbling: they'd wasted a whole day following those pilgrims back north, never had a good chance to jump them, and hadn't collected any more food, beer, women or other goods. Lumaj insisted that one day's march was no hardship for real warriors, especially since the reward at the end would be much better than they could get out of the dirt-poor farming towns to the south, but his argument lacked a certain enthusiasm. Dak and Ruek were mostly silent, but occasionally speculated about how much food, beer and other wealth those pilgrims must be carrying; the mules and wagon alone would be worth the effort, and they could have some fun with the pilgrims, too. Choma silently noted the morale of his troops, and made attack plans.

"We stay here till they've crossed the ridge," he announced, "then we hurry up to the ridge line and watch where they go."

"Hurry? With these damed oxen?" Dak grumbled, but not loudly.

"We'll make 'em hurry." Choma glowered and smacked a fist into his other hand. "The spies go into woods, or cross another ridge, and we catch up again. We follow out of sight until they stop."

"We can't charge a mule wagon on foot," Ruek pointed out. "Nor with oxen, either."

Choma casually clouted his head. "Not by daylight, you stupid turd. We wait till they've stopped for the night, set up camp, gone to sleep. Then we take 'em."

"Oh, right," Dak grinned, showing gaps in his teeth.

"That'll be hours," one of the Thona boys gloomed.

"What, can't you hold your water that long?" Choma gave everyone his best glare. Nobody answered it.

"They're over the ridge," Lumaj announced. "Gimme the whip for these damn beasts."

The whip flailed. The pained oxen broke into a trot. The laden cart rumbled out of the cover of trees and into the open pastureland.

"Oh Mama, why do *I* have to feed Mido and the baby?" Tamiri complained. "They're so dumb, they're spilling it all."

" 'M not dumb," Mido grumbled, smearing stew across his nose.

"You have to, because everybody else is busy setting the traps." Vari studied the fire a moment, then chucked in some more wood—two good-sized logs that would burn half the night and leave a respectable bed of coals without much care or attention. "Now keep quiet, all of you, while I help Ziya with the mules."

Tamiri sighed and rolled her eyes heavenward, silently calling the gods to witness what she had to put up with. Mido shovelled more stew into his mouth. The baby grumbled, but accepted mouthfuls of the savory mess with not much bad grace.

Vari got up and went to the far side of the fire, where the mules were tethered. Ziya had filled their nosebags with a good mix of dried peas and grain, and was busy hauling a second bucket of water up from the small stream a dozen yards off. The mules hadn't been curried yet, and dried sweat tufted their gray coats. Vari took the curry-comb and brush from under the driver's seat of the nearby wagon, and started work on the nearer mule.

Ziya set down the water bucket, checked to see if the mules were still emptying the nosebags, and went to the wagon for a long weed-cutting knife. "Will we sleep first?" she asked Vari as she passed.

"Most likely, dear." Vari didn't miss a stroke with the comb as she answered. "Remember to keep your bow covered by the blankets."

"I know." Ziya went off to cut some fresh greens for the mules, somber-faced, and with no wasted motion.

Vari was just finishing with the second mule when Eloti came out of the wood, Zeren close behind. She looked flushed, tired, but smug; had Vari not known better, she would have guessed that Zeren and Eloti had been off making love in the bushes.

"Is the trap spell set?" Vari asked, setting the brush and curry-comb aside and reaching for the hoof pick.

"Set and ready, twenty-five paces out," Eloti smiled. "Here, I'll do that; the mules know me."

"Oh, tush, I'll manage." Vari lifted an uncomplaining mule's hoof to prove her claim to expertise. "After all these weeks, I've gotten a knack for it. You go get some dinner, and rest."

"She's right." Zeren tugged gently at Eloti's sleeve. "You've worked harder than any of us. Rest for the first watch."

"Very well." Eloti let herself be led away to the fire. "And you?"

"I'll take first watch, just in case our guests are the impatient sort."

"And if they're not?"

"Heh! I assure you, I've had years' practice at waking quickly to fight."

Vari watched them stroll off to the fire, and chuckled to herself between the mules' hooves.

"How much longer?" Ruek whispered, surreptitiously scratching a flea bite.

"Awhile yet," Choma growled. "Their fire's still at flame, not coals."

"So?" the elder Thona brother grumbled, easing away from a troublesome rock that poked his belly.

"That means they're still awake," Lumaj loftily explained. "Flames means new wood, fresh put on the fire, see? That means someone's still awake to've put it there."

"Oh."

"Also means someone's awake enough to need light, firelight to see by. Get it?" the younger Thona smirked. "Fire goes down t'coals, they can't see us."

"Uh, then we can't see them, neither."

"We'll have our eyes used to the dark," Dak volunteered, unsnagging a twig from one of his braids. "Besides, they'll be asleep."

"Just a matter of waiting," Ruek sighed, rolling over on his back. "Wake me when it's time."

"Don't sleep too sound," Choma grumbled, swatting him. "Another hour, maybe two, then we go in."

Slowly the fire sank down to coals. The mules, freed of their nosebags, slurped the buckets half-empty and turned their interest to the piled weeds. Very little sound came from the wagon, or the humans stretched out around the fire, or those whom the mules could smell in the woods beyond. There was no sound or scent of any preying beast larger than a fox anywhere in the small stretch of forest, and no snakes nearby.

Reassured, the mules munched their way through the herbage, then put their heads down and drowsed.

" 'S time," Choma grunted, booting and elbowing his troops into action.

"Which way?" Ruek grumbled, rolling over. "Can't see the fire . . ."

"Straight ahead, and quietly!" Choma got to his feet with elaborate care, setting an example for the others, and inched forward through the dark brush. Too bad, he considered, that they hadn't had time to scout these woods beforehand, let alone divide the company and send half around to the other side of the spies' camp. Now they'd have to do it all in one short charge: messy, no real strategy, and some chance that a few of the outlanders might escape into the woods. Still, they'd catch some; certainly they'd get the wagon and the mules and any goods laid out in the camp. But quietly now, quietly, sneak up all the way to the campsite. Thank the gods, his boys at least knew how to move quietly in the dark.

They'd gone maybe twenty paces toward the fire when they came across what felt like a bank of mist: cold, thick dampness hanging in the air and confusing the senses. But they couldn't *see* any mist.

Dak swore softly. Lumaj shushed him, and they moved on.

One of the Thona brothers put his foot wrong on a tree root and fell, clumping and clattering, right into a thornbush. His squawk of pain seemed loud as thunder in the thick dark.

"Shh!" Lumaj whispered fiercely.

Next instant, he put his foot on something that wriggled, hissed, and sank outraged fangs into his leggings. Lumaj fell backward, howling, "Snake! Snakebite!"

"Vona's balls!" Choma drew his sword and plunged forward, swearing. No hope of a good silent sneak-up now; best to charge ahead, screeching war cries, and hope that the prey would be too confused to know what was happening. "Charrge!" he bellowed, followed by a good imitation of his grandfather's favorite war whoop.

The others came yelling and rattling after him, all but Lumaj, who was still rolling around in the bushes clutching his leg and screaming about snakes.

Running through the dark forest turned out to be much more difficult than sneaking through it: overhanging branches snagged at hair and helmets, lower boughs swatted at faces and impeded hand and foot, unseen roots and rocks tripped running feet with what seemed to be calculated malice, and the wild beasts proved numerous and troublesome.

The elder Thona got a spider down the back of his neck, which made him stop to dance and squirm and jab at it with his sword until he got a nasty cut on his back. Dak put a foot squarely into a badger hole, with the badger still in it, getting not only a badly turned ankle but a good fierce bite in the foot. The younger Thona stepped on something squashy and wiggly, which made him both jump and skid—smack into a tree, which thwacked his helmet down over his eyes and snagged him unmercifully by the beard. Ruek hit a hanging wasps' nest, which made him run faster, howl louder, and pay even less attention to where he was going. Choma ran right into what he thought was a rabbit—until it proved in the time-honored fashion that it was a skunk.

Screeching, howling, rattling and clattering mightily—and stinking to high heaven—Choma's Chargers came clanging through the woods toward where they'd last seen the campfire: out of the big trees, and into the low brush.

The Ruek's foot hit the first trip-cord. He went sprawling flat—into a thornbush—and a big deadfall of a tree fell neatly on top of him. Choma, just a few steps behind him, ran into the tree and fell across it, adding to the volume of Ruek's howls. Somewhere nearby, brass carriage bells tinkled madly.

Off near the campsite, someone shouted authoritatively in an unknown tongue, possibly Sabirn.

Traps! Choma had time to think, as he pulled himself off the log. *They set up trip-cords, alarms—*

Then a trio of small, tumbling flames came whirring through the air toward him. They hit just ahead and to either side, with a sound like smashing pottery.

Then Vona's own fire lit the earth.

Flames exploded from the ground, searing the eyes, lighting up the woods like midday sun, accompanied by a roar like small thunder and clouds of heavy white smoke that stank nearly as bad as the skunk.

Ruek screamed once, impossibly shrill, then went silent. Choma fell backward, clawing at his flare-blinded eyes. Around him, the others screeched in shocked terror, turned to run, fell against unseen trees.

That same foreign voice snapped out another order, and then the arrows came: a rain to match that wizards' thunder and lightning.

The Thona brothers howled and died together, pinned to trees and earth. Dak went stumbling off blindly through the trees, trying to pluck the arrows out of his arm, side and leg; a second volley of arrows caught him amid a snare of bushes, and he fell into a waiting cloud of wasps. Choma, crawling away through brush and jabbing tree roots, heard Dak screeching for a long time.

They really were wizards, They really were . . . Choma thought inanely as he crawled through the darkness. Somewhere out there Lumaj was still alive—if he hadn't died of snakebite. Sometime the sun had to rise, the light had to come—if his eyes were capable of seeing it. Somehow the two of them could get back to the oxcart, wash and bind their wounds, come looking for other survivors—or at least ride back to Borath's holding for help. Oh gods, Borath's holding was at least five days' ride away.

Choma crawled on, listening for some sign of Lumaj, until he collapsed in exhaustion on the edge of the wood.

The team of oxen, tethered less than twenty yards off, blinked in mild surprise at the bizarre sight, and then went back to their grazing.

In the morning Zeren took Sulun, Doshi, Ziya and Arizun out to search for sign of the attackers. They all carried bows at the ready, save for Arizun who held an amulet and chanted protective countercharms against their own trap spell.

The first thing they found was an amored body pinned under a deadfall, head and hands hideously burned.

"Your firepot must have hit right on top of him," Zeren deduced, studying the burn marks all around the corpse.

Sulun turned quickly, thrust his head into a tangle of bushes, and retched hard and fast.

The others looked a while longer at the corpse, Doshi and Arizun paling and shaken, Zeren and Ziya impassive and thoughtful.

In a moment Sulun rejoined them, looking not far from dead himself. "I didn't know it would do that," he muttered to himself. "Before all the gods, I swear, I didn't know . . ."

"There should be more this way," said Zeren, turning off to his right. "We saw one of them go down here." Almost absently, he plucked the harness bells off their station on a branch and stuffed them into his belt pouch. "Right. There."

The others looked where he pointed, and saw the body of another Ancar lying in a patch of brush. Arrows studded him like the quills of a hedgehog, and every exposed inch of his skin was swollen with wasp stings. Sulun closed his eyes; Arizun and Doshi looked away. Only Ziya and Zeren gazed calmly at the body.

"Best collect our arrows," said Zeren, reaching through the brush to pull them free.

"Gods," Doshi moaned, "can't you leave them there?"

"No, we'll need them." Zeren tugged at a stubborn arrow wedged through the sodden leather armor. "Besides, if any of his friends survived they may come looking. Much can be learned from an arrow; best to keep them ignorant."

They found two more arrow-bristled bodies back beyond the burned corpse, and scrape marks on the ground where a fifth Ancar had dragged himself away.

"No blood," Zeren noted. "That one might yet survive. We'd best collect our traps and be gone soon. We should leave right after breakfast."

But nobody wanted breakfast.

* * *

They broke camp and left within the hour, pushing the mules to a steady trot, otherwise quiet and subdued. Clouds sped over the sun, and light, steady rain fell as they crossed the next stretch of meadow and mounted the next hill.

Doshi, sitting next to Sulun on the driver's seat, spread his cloak to protect the map he studied. "Another town, perhaps eight leagues west of this track," he noted. "We could reach it before night. Should we go there?"

"No," said Sulun, huddled small under his cloak.

"Just as well." Doshi folded the map and peered at the rain-grayed land ahead. "Let's leave these lands soon as might be. They're . . . ugly."

"Your old home," Sulun murmured, surprised.

"No longer." Doshi shivered. "It's all changed, nothing like what I remember. I don't want to see any more of it."

"Nor I," Sulun admitted.

"We'll be safe in Torrhyn. Safer than here, anyway. Torrhyni dialect isn't much different from Jarryan, and we've heard enough of that to understand it. There were some small cities near the old sulfur mines, should still be there, even with the mines shut down. I don't imagine the Ancar having any use for sulfur . . . but they might have kept after the black glass, mined enough for that. They'd probably use it for pretty jewelry, or surgeon's knives. Find black glass and we find the sulfur. We can settle close enough to the mines—"

"We don't need the sulfur," Sulun snapped. "All we need is a sizable town."

"But—but we need the sulfur to make the firepowder—"

"No more firepowder! Never again!" Sulun slapped the reins fiercely on the startled mules' rumps, whipping them to a faster trot. "Gods, you saw what it did, back there . . ." He drew a deep breath, and shuddered.

Doshi half-turned, suddenly aware of the listening silence in the wagon behind him. All the others, they were waiting for him to answer. Doshi shrugged off the awareness, and looked back at Sulun.

"You saw the other bodies too, didn't you?" he said. "Forested with arrows, and one of them swollen all over with wasp stings—were they any prettier? Were those deaths any better?"

"Not . . ." Sulun rubbed one hand across his forehead. "Not the same."

"No." Doshi gnawed his lip and made himself remember. "I think they were slower."

"Oh, gods!"

"I can't remember when I last saw a . . . a good death, Sulun. Not even back in Sabis: hunger, disease, drowning, death in burning buildings or riots—"

"Stop it!" Sulun almost dropped the reins, shaking so hard.

Doshi took a long, slow breath. "What I mean to say is that the only 'good' death I can imagine is a quick one: fast, painless—like a high priest knocking down a sacrificial goat. If you must kill, do it fast. It doesn't matter how the body looks afterward—not to the dead, anyway; that's only a trouble to the living. Firepowder kills faster than arrows."

"Uglier . . ." Sulun whispered, head bowed over the reins.

"So, leave that to trouble that Ancar warrior's friends. Perhaps they'll be encouraged to leave us alone."

From the wagon bed behind them came a quiet sigh. Doshi glanced that way, thinking it was Zeren. Instead he saw Ziya peering at him, face revealing nothing, as always.

Beside him, Sulun huddled over the reins and wept quietly, tears merging with the steady rain on his face.

Doshi sighed and unrolled the map once more. "The nearest sulfur mines, if we keep to our present course, should be near the old villa of Ashkell. That's on the northern slope of the Torrhyn hills, near a tributary of the southeast fork of the Gol. Nothing's been heard of it since the old war, more than fifty years ago. The gods know what it's like now, but there was once a prosperous mining town there."

The rain continued on, all that day and into the next.

PART III

Candlelight

1

Wotheng Woshka's-son, Baron of Ashkell, woke to unwelcome sunlight and a twinging hangover. He pulled the sheepskin blanket up over his head, rolled against his wife Gynallea's soft buttocks, and crept back toward sleep.

Gynallea gave him a kick, and grunted: " 'S morning."

"Don' care." Wotheng burrowed deeper into the goose-feather pillows.

"It's morning. Get *up*." Gynallea back-kicked him again. "Work to do."

"No work yet," Wotheng insisted, pulling a pillow over his head. "Yawth hasn' knocked yet."

"Yawth came earlier, knocked, said something about newcomers. We should go see."

Wotheng counterfeited a creditable snore.

Gynallea sighed, took a deep breath, tightened her belly muscles and let loose a trumpeting fart.

Under the blankets, Wotheng got the worst of it. He choked, wheezed, and erupted out of the blankets, roaring, "Gods jam your arse with a pine tree, woman! Aaagh, that was cruel."

"That was last night's beer." Gynallea crawled out of the tumbled blankets like a venerable sow from the best wallowing hole. "Tell me no sad tales of hangover, lovey; I drank as much as you."

"Well, who asked you to sit up so late?" Wotheng grumbled as he lugged himself out of bed, idly scratching his bare hide.

"You did, remember?" Gynallea plodded to the nearest carved chair, where her undershift lay. "You wanted my good wit with numbers when those poor North Hill farmers came whining about why they'd have to delay their taxes."

"Ah, right . . ." Wotheng studied his wife's broad buttocks as she tugged the shift over her head. Fart upon headache or no, he hadn't much to complain about; a good clever wife with such a fine, buxom shape was better than most men could claim. And no doubt, the headache would improve after a mug of Gynallea's bitter bark tea . . . plus

213

half a dozen fried sausages and some hotcakes and a handful of coddled eggs, and some bread with jelly, and . . . "Ah, what were those farmers whining about, anyway? Do you remember?"

"Oh yes." Gynallea batted her tangled brown locks with a pig-bristle brush. " 'Twas that Folweel again."

"Oh. Gods, not again." Wotheng knuckled the last of sleep out of his eyes. "What did he do, set a curse of fire on the poor fools' cowshed?"

"Sheepshed. We agreed to take part of the taxes in rough-roasted mutton, remember?"

"Gods. Ah, p'raps your cooks can turn it into sausage fit for siege food." Wotheng hunted the bedposts for his clothes. The underbreeches and small shift smelled suspiciously overused. He tossed them in the corner reserved for ripe laundry, went to the clothespress and hunted for fresh smallclothes. "Vona blast that pesky wizard. We have to do something about him before we all turn poor, but what, hey?"

Gynallea shrugged into a clean enough outer skirt and glanced about for her stockings. "Sneak into his holding and poison his food stores? Set *his* thatch mysteriously afire? Dig a deep pit and lure him into it? *I* don't know, lovey. My kindred raised no wizards."

"Nor did mine." Wotheng sat down to pull on his stockings and over breeches. "Don't I wish it so, my sweet moo-cow. Don't I wish I knew *any* wizard who could steal into Folweel's hold without half a dozen curses bringing bricks down on his head. Four good men died trying that. Four, remember. I'd not ask anyone to be the fifth. Give me some better plans, sweet cow, for I'm all shat out of them."

"Do I find any, lovey, and I'll tell you. Let's to breakfast, and see what Yawth's news is."

"Aye, aye. And I suppose I should go look at that old ruin Busho was whining about . . ." Wotheng paused, one foot half into its shoe, hearing faint noise at the door. "Yawth!" he bellowed. "Yawth, stop dithering about the door and come in!"

The door swung open and a gangling servant half-fell in. "As ye wish, m'lord," he dithered. "Beggin' yer pardon, but there's much to tell of, hap'nin' downstairs."

"Then tell it," Wotheng snapped, putting on his other shoe.

"Why, sir, there's these strangers come to the gate early this morning: all robed in fine gray cloth, with a big wagon and two great mules all hung with chains and bells and charms and what-not made of right good iron and brass what twinkled like gold. Most rich folks they must be, nigh a dozen of 'em, all bearin' wands and chantin' the praises of Deese of the Forge in most outlandish High Speech . . ."

" 'Deese of the Forge'?" Gynallea turned around, forgetting her half-laced bodice, which flopped down to her hips. "Who might that be?"

"They say . . ." Yawth's dark eyes grew wide and round in his long face. "That be the ancient Sukkti name for Clong, the blacksmith's god. Oh, that's put Biddon and his shop all in a dither! They be talkin' with him now, swappin' forge wit like brothers in the same trade. 'Tis a sight to see, I grant—"

"Sukkti?" Gynallea gaped. "What are these folk, to be toying with old magic names? Do they claim to be dealing with ghosts of the Elder Folk, then?"

"Er, no, Mistress. They claim . . . they say they *are* the Elder Folk. They say they hid out in the Lost City of Itoma, far away south, until the last of their old conquerors were overthrown. Now, beggin' yer pardon, they say that with Sabis fallen, they've come out of hidin' and wish to visit their old holy grounds again. That's what they say, Mistress."

"Gods!" roared Wotheng, making Yawth jump. "Not more plaguey wizards!"

Gynallea waved him silent with a quick gesture. "Sukkti? And wizards? And what have they been about since they got here?"

"As I said, Mistress: they came this morning when the villa's gates opened, and went straightway to Biddon's shop. They greeted him in the name of Deese of the Forge, and then fell to shoptalk. They've done naught else as I know, and they be there now, if ye'd care to come see."

"Indeed we will," Gynallea smiled, tapping plump fingers on her chin. "Leave them be; we'll come presently."

"After breakfast," Wotheng put in. "Go bid cook have our plates and cups ready—and I want bitter bark tea, hear?"

"Oh, aye, Master. I hear ye right well."

"Then be about it!"

"Aye, sir. Aye, goin' now." Yawth bowed clumsily, two or three times, and hurried out the door.

Gynallea closed it after him, then turned to her husband with a broad smile. "Sukkti wizards, no less? And serving Deese of the Forge?"

"More damned wizards," Wotheng snorted, hauling on the last of his clothes. "Flocking in like crows to the corpse. Gods, we'll all be eating turnips and wearing straw. Vona, what have I done to deserve—"

"Hush, lovey, and think. A fresh breed of wizards, knowing the Elder Folk's magic, and serving a forge god. Now tell me, from what god or spirit does Folweel get his powers?"

"Yotha the Fire, of all the nasty-tempered devils, though I swear 'tis a good question who serves whom. Those wicked predictions of fire that always come true—you know well it's that damned wizard's doing, whether he takes power from Yotha to do it, or sends Yotha to run the errands himself."

"Forge and fire, lovey. Think: do you see a possible rivalry there?"

Wotheng looked up, recognizing that purring tone in his wife's voice. "Ah, you have a plan, my sweet moo-cow?"

"Ah lovey, lovey, in all your mother's fine books, did you never come across the wise fable of fighting fire with fire?"

Wotheng slowly mirrored her smile. "Or, set a wizard to fight a wizard? Heh! Whichever wins, we'll be no worse off than before."

"Possibly better, lovey. Let us go visit these new wizards, shall we?"

"Right after breakfast, sweet cow. Right after breakfast."

Biddon, the villa's blacksmith, peered so close to the anvil that occasional sparks struck his nose. Gods, yes, this stranger knew his business well; if the scars on his massive arms hadn't told tale enough, the man's obvious skill with the hammer was proof. Biddon hung on the magician-smith's every word, wishing these folk were more understandable or that he knew more of the old High Speech.

"Five times," the stranger was saying. "Hammer five

times, at least, and (incomprehensible) with a bigger bellows between. This (unintelligible) iron needs plenty. Fold like this—see?—each (impossible) time. Don't bother shaping it until the last hammering. (Unguessable) sheep-fat in the flux . . ."

Biddon nodded eagerly, straining to understand and remember. He could see the axehead taking shape under the blows, its edges showing a grain as fine as oak wood. Gods, no, he'd never seen anything like that. How well would it cut? How sharp an edge could it take? How long would it last? He couldn't wait to find out. There, now: another toasting in the hard-blown coals . . .

"Ah, it's ready," said the stranger, hefting the glowing axehead in his fine set of tongs. "Where's the (incomprehensible) trough?"

"Oh, here. Here." Biddon shoved forward the stone tempering trough with its unaccustomed load of chilled hog fat. "Be it cold enough?"

"(Unintelligible) enough," said the wizard-smith. He dropped the glowing axehead into the trough and stepped back quickly.

Clouds of vaporized grease, reeking of burned bacon, filled the shop like holy incense. Everyone coughed madly and made jokes about roast pork that were barely heard through the lively sizzling.

Another, more familiar, voice coughed also.

Biddon flinched, then peered through the dissipating clouds.

Sure enough, as if the smoke had conjured him, there stood Lord Wotheng himself. Worse, Lady Gynallea stood beside him.

Biddon whispered a quick prayer to all his family gods, bowed low, and began making excuses.

"Oh, hush," Gynallea waved him off. "Tell us what this visitor is working upon so marvelously."

Biddon gulped in relief. "Why, he was but showin' me a better way to make this axehead, m'lady. And a fine piece of work it be, too. Soon as it's cooled and fitted to th' handle, ye'll surely see how nice it does."

"We'll leave that work to your hands," Wotheng grinned. "Meanwhile, let not our guests think we're poor in hospitality. Come up to the big house, visitor, and share a cup or two with us. Eh, do you folk speak Torrhyni?"

Another, more slender, stranger stepped forward and bowed low. "We speak it a little, good sir," he said, with an accent that hinted of time spent in Jarrya. "And we thank you much for your invitation. Pray give us some time to wash, and we'll visit you directly."

Wotheng and his lady exchanged looks and smiles. "Soon, then," the lady purred. The pair turned and marched graciously out of the blacksmith's shop, not glancing back.

Biddon wiped sweat and grease off his forehead. "Oh, that were a bit of luck, there. Master and Mistress both be pleased with ye. 'Twere the axehead done it, I'll wager. Eh, I keep the wash trough outside there . . ."

The wizard-smith murmured untranslated thanks and went outside. The younger wizard ran his eyes admiringly over Biddon's anvil, then leaned closer and asked conspiratorially, "What's the Master's name? And his lady? And, er, what sort of folk are they?"

Biddon was grateful enough to answer at some length.

Doshi caught up to the others at the wash trough, where they'd been idling a while to wait for him.

"The wagon's safe," Sulun murmured in his ear as they both bent over the trough. "Only you, me, Zeren and Eloti are going in; the rest are watching the gear and the mules. What did you learn?"

"Quite an earful." Doshi splashed water noisily on his face. "Our host, Wotheng, is the son of a clever old Ancar soldier named Woshka. The old man came through here a generation ago, recognized good sheep country when he saw it, and was tired of soldiering anyway. Besides, I suspect he knew he'd get little of the loot of the richer lands once the big commanders were done with them. Perhaps the deciding factor was the buxom daughter of the then master of this villa—which wasn't called Ashkell then, by the way. That happened after Askell town proper was sacked and burned, leaving this as the largest surviving settlement."

"Get on with this, Doshi."

"Ah, right. Well, the old lord volunteered to stay behind and keep the roads open when the rest of the Ancar horde moved on. He persuaded the last owner of the villa that a few trained Ancar men-at-arms would be good protection from bandits, then married the squire's daughter and settled down to protect, tax and manage the land. By all accounts, he did a fairly good job of it, and his Torrhyn-Sabirn wife took care of the rest. Wotheng was their only surviving son, though there are a couple daughters married off here and there."

"How does he handle his . . . subjects?"

"Well, Wotheng has enough practical intelligence and muscle to maintain his authority without having to fall back on his Ancar connections—in fact, he's barely spoken or written to them in all these years. This place is wonderfully isolated from the rest of the Ancar horde."

"Written? He can read and write?"

"Oh, yes; we're not dealing with a fool here. Papa saw to it that Wotheng knew how to manage and protect the land, had a good eye for petty politics and healthy sheep. Mama, who was something of a cultured lady, saw to it that Master Wotheng learned as much reading, writing and civilized knowledge as the house library provided."

"House library? How good is it?"

"How should a blacksmith know that? He's never seen it."

"Hmm, if only we can get a look at it . . . But go on, Doshi. Is this the sort of fellow we can impress with our 'wizard' act?"

"I don't think so. His mother gave him enough sophistication to take all notions of magic and religion with a healthy grain of salt. He got a good, basic level-headedness from both parents. He pays his respects to the gods, their priests, and any magician of proven ability, but he's not the sort to be pulled about by a bit of showmanship and some simple tricks. We'll have to be careful with him, Sulun."

"Understood. What other relatives must we worry about?"

"The sisters were married off to his father's old soldiers, and all have sizable farms of their own—far enough away to have no border arguments with Wotheng—and they're barely seen here except for weddings, funerals, harvest festivals and the like. They won't be a problem, I think."

"What about the mistress of the household?"

"Ah, she's quite a match for him; daughter of the second richest farm-holder in the valley, quite as well educated as Wotheng's mother—who may have arranged the marriage. In any case, Wotheng's parents managed to live long and die peacefully. He has a clutch of children, all grown and married now, likewise scattered off to various farmsteads."

"That's all, then? No wily courtiers milking power behind the throne?"

"No, just house servants, tenants, and a few men-at-arms who double as shepherds and huntsmen. This is . . . very much the country villa it always was."

"Ah. And the mines?"

"What mines?" Doshi innocently dried his face on his undersleeves, noting that Ashkell Villa lacked knowledge of such niceties as towels.

"Do-*sheee*! The sulfur mines!" Sulun tugged furiously at his dangling curls and new beard. "Or black glass mines, as they're probably called now. Don't tell me you forgot!"

"Oh, no." Doshi grinned. "It's just that the blacksmith never heard of them."

"Oh, gods, just ten leagues away by the map, and he's never—"

"It seems that the mines originally belonged to quite another family, no connection at all with the villa. The old invasion did for them, quite thoroughly; oh, no, not wrecked, just abandoned and almost totally forgotten."

"How in the name of all the gods can everyone forget about a sulfur mine?"

"By not needing, knowing or caring about it. Sulun, remember that both the villa folk and the Ancar cared mostly about farming and sheep. The former villa holders cared nothing for the mines, and Wotheng's father knew nothing of them. A good iron, gold, copper or silver mine would have held everyone's interest, but sulfur? And black glass? Even in their heyday, the mines always made their profit on the trade with the south. When the invasion stopped that, well, no trade means no profit, and no profit meant that the mines were abandoned."

"I see. But they're still there? I mean, the entrances and shafts and all?"

"I heard nothing about anyone filling in any old mine entrances. Why should these shepherds and farmers bother, pray tell?"

"Ah, very good, then." Sulun rubbed his cheeks briskly and considered the best lines of approach. "Gods, was it so few moons ago that we played this game with Entori?"

"We've all learned much since then."

"Indeed. Let's go in."

"Sweet cow, the floor's swept clean enough," Wotheng protested, easing back in the big chair.

"Should have been scrubbed. It still stinks in here. Ah, give me that, Noba; some fresh herbs in this pot, and put it on the fire to boil. There . . ." Gynallea rubbed her hands on her apron and raked her glance around the hall. it could have been better, but it looked well enough in the light through the narrow windows: floor swept, hanging banners reasonably clean, a small table (with a clean cover-cloth, thank the gods) and some comfortable chairs near the fire, a pretty jug of good beer waiting and the sweet-smelling tea heating in the fireplace. Yes, good enough. She tugged thoughtfully at the kerchief covering her hair. Leave it on or take it off? Look more the housewife or the grand lady? Appear simple and kindly, or imposing? "Hmm, these newcomers went first to Biddon and dazzled his eyes with their skill. That smells of serious craftsfolk, concerned with trade. Best we appear as simple farmer folk, Lovey. Lull them, see if they try to take advantage. We can always show our wit and authority later." She patted straying hair back under the kerchief.

"Hmm, just as you say, moo-cow. Hey, Yawth, are they come yet?"

"Just now, Master," the servant bobbed his head eagerly. "They be waitin' at the door."

"Send them in." Wotheng heaved a mountainous sigh. He hated politicking before lunch, but a chance such as this didn't come along every day. Besides, the herb tea had dispelled his headache, and he felt fit enough to take on half the earth at full charge.

The door creaked open and the little company of Deese priests, four of them, came padding down the length of the hall. They looked a bit intimidated by the size of the place, and yes, they'd dressed in good robes and washed well. Aha, they wanted something from him. Wotheng smiled benignly as Yawth made the stuttering introductions. Vona, what strange, foreign-sounding names they had!

"Welcome to the Villa of Ashkell," Gynallea purred. "Come sit, and join us in a cup of beer."

The little quartet obediently sat and took cups. Gynallea poured.

" 'Tis humble stuff," Wotheng opened, "made of our poor local barley, but 'tis kindly to the tongue." *If not to the head, next morning.* "Have you come far, then?"

"Far, yes. From Itoma, south," said the biggest, in a bizarre southern accent. "This beer is very good." He drained his cup and reached for the jug in honest appreciation.

Wotheng smiled again. "And what brings a company of pilgrims to these poor lands? We've little here to draw worship or custom." *See if that discourages them.*

" 'Tis a long story, Master," said the slender youth with a Jarryan twang to his words. "As you know, we Sukkti held the southern lands before the coming of the Sabirns. As they marched north, we lost all save Itoma—where our mightiest wizards held fast . . ."

Wotheng nodded as he listened. He'd long known, from his mother's histories, that the Elder Folk were only the first settlers of the south, not creatures of another order. They'd had a reputation for great magic, but had lost their land anyway—except for the Lost City of Itoma. "I'd always thought that city was a fable, stuff of dreams and fireside tales," he prodded.

"Oh no, sir," the lad enthused. "It stands on a stream of the great river, made of fine gray fieldstone and pale sandstone; in good sunlight, it gleams like silver and gold. The roofs are mostly flat, and held up with many columns. . . ."

Wotheng noted, as the youth went on, the numerous details that only a builder, mechanic or architect would notice. Clearly, these folk had seen a city of unusual buildings somewhere to the south. Just as clearly, they were well-trained craftsmen—and not just in smithing. Wotheng caught his wife's eye, saw her appreciative nod and smile. "Then how came you to leave so fair a place?" he prodded gently.

"Why, sir, we wished to see those ancient shrines that were so long barred to us by Sabis. Now that their crown has fallen, we dared venture out from Itoma's safety to see what had become of the land and people."

Wotheng flicked another glance at his wife. This didn't quite make sense; something was missing. "How came you safe past the fighting?" he temporized.

"The war came not nigh Itoma," the big one answered. "It passed us by, and we came north behind it."

Wotheng shrugged and looked to his wife.

"A long, hard journey it must have been," she tried.

"Oh, yes," the youth replied. "We made our way by selling small magics and forge-work. Would you care to see some of our wares?"

Wotheng noted the tallest of the four giving the lad a small nudge with his elbow. Aha, the manner of merchants hoping to make a sale—and taking care not to advertise too quickly. Craftsmen, merchants and wizards: better and better. "Oh aye, but let's not be hasty when there's a good jug yet to finish. But say, what brings you forge folk to our humble villa? We've little trade here, and I've never heard of any holy ground hereabouts."

The youth chewed his lip and looked imploringly at the tall, thin pilgrim, who leaned forward and took up the tale.

"In truth, m'lord, there is an ancient shrine some ten leagues west of here," he said, in the same heavy southland accent as the first man. " 'Tis the place where black glass is found, which has sacred uses for such as we. Do you know the place?"

Wotheng stared blankly. Ten leagues west: that was steep foothill land, stony and thin of soil, no good for farming, poor pasturage even for sheep. He'd used it occasionally for running sheep a month or two of the year, and no more. None of his relatives or tenants would take it. There were a few ruins there, but nothing of value in them. "Ey, yes I do. That's where a small town stood, back before my father came here. 'Tis my land—poor for farming, but you might graze some sheep there. I know of no shrine."

The tall stranger didn't seem disappointed. "The shrine is a . . . formation of the rocks, and mostly valued for the black glass. If it lies on your land, might we have your permission to visit there?"

Wotheng glanced at his wife again.

"Why, surely," Gynallea smiled. "We'll happily send a guide with you. Do you wish to stay awhile there, we can give you some food and drink to take—poor stuff, but filling. But of what use is the shrine, and the black glass?"

"We would make the black glass into tools and amulets," the tall one replied readily. "When cut properly, black glass takes a fine edge—suitable for small cookknives and surgeons' blades. Also it makes fair jewels, not so costly that common folk could not afford it, yet handsome enough that quality folk would not take scorn to wear it. Also, it can be made into meditation gems, useful for small magics."

Wotheng and Gynallea looked at each other and grinned. So, these pilgrim-smith-merchants hoped to set up trade, did they? Very good. But now to the serious question.

"Small magics?" Wotheng straightened in his chair. "What sort of magics, sir? We have hedge wizards and granny witches enough, the gods know. What manner of magic do you folk do?"

The tall pilgrim shifted a bit, looking almost embarassed. "Well, simple well-wishing, of course, and some healing and crop-blessing—Kula the Mother being the consort of Deese—but mostly we deal with forge work, trade craft, mechanical work, that sort of thing."

"Forge work?" Gynallea leaned nearer. "Do you then call, er, Deese to your forge fire to aid your work?"

"Er, yes, something like that. Mostly we call him to encourage excellence of work, protection, inspiration and so on." The pilgrim glanced at his fellows, giving them a quick smile. "With his help, we do produce work of fine quality—and most difficult to ill-wish or damage."

Gynallea and Wotheng exchanged triumphant looks.

"Protection?" Gynallea almost purred. "Deese, then, gives you control—er, and safety, of fire?"

"Eh? Oh, yes m'lady. We take good care to do that."

Wotheng's smile stretched wide. "How marvelous. Could you show us a bit of your magic? We have so few amusements here. . . ."

The man shrugged, almost resignedly, and reached into his robe. "In fact, I have a small spell here," he murmured, bringing out a tiny packet of folded parchment. He got up and went to the fire, waving his other hand in a circle above the packet and chanting softly in a strange tongue. To Wotheng, listening carefully, it sounded as if the pilgrim were saying: "Pie are square, pie are square, Deese make this work right, pie are square . . ."

He tossed the packet into the fire, and raised both hands in an invocatory gesture.

Behind them, Gynallea thought she heard one of the pilgrims humming softly.

The packet exploded in a poof of smoke and a shower of sparks.

Simultaneously, the teapot began whistling.

The fire flared bright and high for a moment, shot through with colored flames: red, blue, green and purple. Then it sank back to normal, not spreading, nothing changed. The teapot whistled on, throwing clouds of fragrant smoke out into the hall.

The pilgrim turned, smiling—half apologetically, it seemed—toward his hosts and comrades. He inclined his head in a brief bow, which appeared to be aimed at the smallest of his company, the one who hadn't yet spoken.

"Excellent!" cried Wotheng, clapping his hands. "Safe control of fire! And so colorful, so marvelous. Oh yes, you'll find much call for your skills here, Sir Wizard. Ah, say, where had you folk planned to spend the night? Our house is a humble thing, but we can easily fit your company under our roof."

"Well, we had hoped to go look at the shrine while the weather is good."

"Splendid, good fellow. I'll send guides to escort you— and do you need mounts for your friends? But do be back in time for dinner; you'll find the food good, if plain, and the portions generous."

The pilgrims accepted the help with mixed eagerness, but seemed quite willing to start at once and be back for dinner. A brief exchange of pleasantries—and another yell to Yawth to go fetch Tinnod from his sheep and collect some horses— and the little company departed for their pilgrimage.

As the noise and crowd faded, Wotheng and Gynallea exchanged broad and silent grins. Wotheng poured out the last of the beer for himself, and his wife took a cup of the tea from the fire.

"Lovey," she stated firmly while spooning honey into her fragrant cup, "We *must* persuade them to stay."

"I'll see to it. Do you think they can deal with Folweel?"

"They if anyone. Encourage them to buy that western pasture and settle here. Tell them tonight about the merchant caravans to the north, speak of the good prices they could get for their goods, the cheapness of food and cloth and other staples hereabouts—"

"Sell that land? Why not rent it to them? Why should I give it up?"

"Lovey, Lovey, that land is all but worthless and those folk are valuable. They may shy away from being tenants, being at a master's beck and call, after being freeholders so long in their own city—oh, we must ask them more about the Lost City, when there's time. The land may not draw them strongly—you've seen it, and 'tisn't attractive—so we must lure them with a bargain no one but a fool would refuse. Sell it to them, and cheaply. Give it to them outright, if you must—but however 'tis done, keep them here."

"Aye, aye . . ." Wotheng considered. "Their goods alone, never mind their magic, could add much to the wealth hereabouts. Do I tell them I—heh! and I alone—can get their goods transported and sold north, at good price, and do they take up the bargain, we might gain more for such simples than we do for our wool. Hmm, perhaps I should make that part of the price for the land."

"Dangle what lures you can, lovey, but get them to stay."

An hour before noon the odd little company arrived at the site of the old mine. Tinnod, a wizened tenant shepherd, rode on a borrowed donkey beside Doshi on a shaggy pony, grumbling about weather and rents and bad luck with sheep. Doshi pretended to listen raptly while running his eyes over the surrounding land. Omis and Zeren, on scrawny horses kindly loaned from Wotheng's stables, rode next in line, murmuring quietly to themselves. Everyone else rode the wagon, Sulun driving and Eloti beside him.

"What did you make of our host?" Eloti asked. "I suspect there is more to him, and his wife, than they showed us."

"To all accounts they're no fools," Sulun considered. "They were intrigued by our, er, magic, but not frightened of it. They do seem pleased with us, possibly for the promise of goods to trade, and I think it would not be difficult to get their permission to settle here."

"Indeed, they seemed pleased to have us . . . hmm, and if this is the land you asked about, I think I know why."

The barely visible dirt road led between low hills to a steep one, with some few ruined buildings climbing its slope. A sullen stream meandered down from higher hills beyond, promising drinking water but little else. The soil was thin, poor, showing tan and bald between clumps of coarse grass and brush. As the slope rose the soil thinned further, showing outcroppings of lichened rock like bones emerging through the sunken hide of a corpse.

"Not a pretty place," Sulun agreed. "No good for farming, as our host said. Neither do I see much graze for sheep. To a man mainly concerned with those activities, such land would surely seem worthless. If the mines are still here, not blocked nor worked out, it would be worth the effort to persuade Lord Wotheng to sell."

"Remember to look reluctant when you ask him," Eloti smiled. "Or would you prefer that I undertake the negotiations?"

"Lady, no one of us could do it better. Hmm, but where, now, is that mine?"

Ahead, Doshi turned his pony toward the ruins. His eyes flicked back and forth between the stony hill and the unrolled map in his hand. Tinnod rode reluctantly after him, voicing disquiet about the unnerving ruins and the possibility of ghosts, even in broad daylight.

"I think that's it," said Sulun. "Let's see how close we can get the wagon."

The road actually improved as they approached the ruins, showing traces of ancient paving suitable to heavy loads. Its course led past roofless shells of old houses, up to the largest ruin at the high end of the former town. Here the stream had been diverted, through still intact stone-lined ditches and pipes, to pass under the remains of a millhouse attached to the chief building. The road ended there, but still there was no sign of a mine opening. The old building was as big as a good-sized barn, with a doorway more than wide enough to accommodate the mules and wagon. Despite Tinnod's warnings, the convoy passed inside.

The central part of the roof had come down, leaving a pile of rubble in the middle of the wide, cobblestoned floor. To either side, though, the stone walls of large workrooms had kept enough roofing to hold out the weather.

Sulun halted the wagon at the edge of the central rubble pile, set the brake and tied it. Eloti got out and went to the wagon bed to fetch tethers and nosebags for the mules. Doshi, Omis and Zeren dismounted and tied their animals' reins to assorted stones and fallen beams. Tinnod stayed on his donkey and shivered in the dusty sunlight.

The company gathered around Sulun, who cast a warning glance toward Tinnod, who didn't notice. "These ruins don't look very promising," he began, "but there may be much of value *buried* hereabout. Have we lamps? Torches? Good. Let's search, then. No less than two together."

"I be stayin' right here," Tinnod announced stoutly. "Gods know what all might lurk in old corners."

"Right you are," Sulun smiled. "Stay you here to guard the beasts, the wagon, the womenfolk and the children, and we'll—"

"Women?" Tinnod perked up. "And children too?"

"Why, of course." Eloti pulled down the hood of her cloak, revealing her notably feminine face, set in a punctiliously proper look. "Did you think the priests of Deese and Kula were forbidden to marry?"

"Eh, no, I hadn't thought that, ma'am," Tinnod blushed, tugging his forelock. "Whatever ye need, ma'am, I be glad to help."

"Fine." Eloti smiled sweetly. "Come out, children, but mind how you play."

Vari, grinning, hustled the children out of the wagon, followed by the rest of the apprentices. Tamiri and her brother promptly toddled off in all directions, delighted at the chance to stretch their legs and explore.

"Don't let them wander too far, now," Vari rumbled at their guide.

Tinnod, looking slightly poleaxed, got off his donkey, hobbled it quickly, and hurried after the children.

"That should keep him occupied," Eloti murmured to Sulun. "Take your lamps and go seek."

Sulun, grinning, broke out the lamps and lit them. "Watch the flames," he warned quietly. "If they suddenly spurt, or change color, get back into open air."

The others nodded understanding, formed teams, and parcelled out the lamps. Sulun found himself teamed with Omis and Arizun. Seeing the others make for the side rooms, he led the way around the rubble pile to the back wall.

Sure enough, behind a fall of timber and masonry, there stood another doorway. Beyond lay only a vast darkness and a musty smell.

Sulun thrust the lamp within, watched as it burned tranquilly, then hitched up his shoulders and led the way inside.

Two steps past the doorway, and they saw that they were in a tunnel. The walls were roughly hewn from the dark hill-stone, but the floor was sanded smooth, save for the faint ruts of cartwheels. In a few more steps they found the remains of a cart: large, square-built, stout, but with one axle broken and the front wheels collapsed.

It was piled to the top with butter-yellow sulfur.

Omis and Arizun poked fingers into the heap of yellow gravel, their eyes met, and they smiled. "Enough here alone to keep us in firepowder for a year," Sulun marvelled. "But let's go on."

At the end of the tunnel the walls fell away on deeper darkness, with the faintest draft of a breeze flowing from somewhere unseen.

"Must have cut ventilation shafts," Omis murmured, then stopped as he noted the faint echoing of his voice.

Sulun, keeping his eyes on the smoothed floor and his lamp held high, took the first steps into the echoing dark. He heard Omis and Arizun gasp behind him, stopped, and looked up.

He stood in a hall of columns, stretching as far as the light spread and doubtless far beyond. The roof was higher than his arms could reach, rough-cut as the walls and columns.

Roof, columns and floor were sulfur-yellow, with occasional streaks of obsidian black.

Sulun carefully lowered his lamp, keeping the flame away from the butter-colored stone. "We've found it," he said, amazed that his voice was so calm. "I'll wager, if we follow the wheel tracks we'll find another cart, plenty of discarded miners' tools, and a wall of sulfur thicker than anyone can guess."

"And here," Omis whispered, "an unsuspected fortress, hidden in the earth."

"Earth Goddess temple," Arizun added. "We should make images of Kula and Deese to place by the entrance. . . ."

"We should go back to the others before we're missed," Sulun decided, "and before our talkative guide—who no doubt reports to Wotheng—guesses that we've found something of interest."

"In which case, he will doubtless raise his price." Arizun grinned and turned back to the tunnel. "Let's go, then— and plan our tale to Wotheng."

On the journey back to Ashkell villa, Omis and Arizun rode ahead with Doshi and their guide, while Sulun conferred with the others in the wagon.

"Even the outer building could be fortified," Zeren noted, "which is nothing to ignore in times, hmm, and places, like these."

"Those side rooms were shops," Yanados added. "One of them houses a mill that once turned by that stream. The stones are intact, though much of the wooden gear needs replacing—"

"Omis' ironwork would do better," Vari cut in. "We'll have to ask our host about sources of iron."

"—and we'd have to replace the paddle wheel, but once we have the mill running—"

"We could fix the house with stones from the others," Ziya piped up, surprising everyone. "Make the whole house out of stone, so it won't burn."

"Yes, good thought," Eloti answered quickly. "But where would we put the forge and the larger tools?"

"That big central room, once the roof's on—or even before," said Yanados. "We could use the other side rooms for kitchens and sleeping cubicles."

"Hmm, only with much work," Vari grumbled. "I think we'll need to add more rooms, sooner or later. And a kitchen garden. Hmm, and a surrounding wall."

"Should we bother trying to raise sheep on the surrounding land?" Zeren asked. "We'll need some animals for food, in case of . . . hmm, siege, famine, other disasters."

"Goats, more likely," Vari sniffed. "They give less wool, but more milk. A few pigs, some poultry . . ."

"How would we feed them? How much of this grudging land must we plant and coax into yielding?"

"Just a little for the birds, I think. Goats can feed themselves well on almost anything, and a few pigs could make do with slops from the kitchen, and perhaps a bit of grain."

"Is it decided, then?" Eloti asked. "Are we determined to settle here?"

Sulun looked at everyone in turn. "Do any oppose the thought?" he asked.

No one did.

"So be it, then." Eloti smiled, a little grimly. "If we bargain well, we may get the land cheaply. Restoring the buildings, however, will be more of a task than we can manage ourselves—and it will cost dearly." She patted the thick oak chest she sat on. "I suspect that our Sukkti treasure will be largely used before we're done."

"Wherever we can manage for ourselves, Lady—" Sulun began.

"No, no regrets, my friend. If we succeed, I'll count it as well spent." Eloti's smile changed to something slightly more wicked. "Now, shall we discuss tactics for bargaining with Wotheng this evening?"

Dinner that evening was a whole roast suckling pig stuffed with apples, boiled green beans with bacon, thick wedges of sheep-milk cheese, roasted grain sweetened with berries, sweet pears pickled in honey, fresh rye bread with new butter, cider, perry, beer, and berry cordial. Everyone in the household, with the exception of the two outer guards, ate at the same huge trestle table. Sulun, remembering his days in Entori House, noted that the only division between the masters' and servants' sections were the bowls of salt, pepper, nutmeg and vinegar formally arranged in the middle of the table. The servants, he noted, were well and warmly dressed—if in much plainer cloth than Wotheng and his wife—and all seemed healthy and well fed. They also talked freely, laughed loudly, and showed no particular fear of the personages at the high end of the table.

I've known worse masters, Sulun thought, stuffing himself with a clear conscience. The food was well cooked, if a trifle short on spices, and the assorted drinks were superb.

After the dishes were emptied and cleared, Wotheng dismissed the lower table diners with a brief hand clap. Sulun noticed that a few of the servants chose to stay, and that this was not remarked upon.

Wotheng called for more jugs of beer and cordial, and for his pipe: a tiny wooden bowl with an attached hollow stem, filled with some resinous chopped leaf which he lit with a spill of burning wood from the fire. The apprentices watched, wide-eyed, as Wotheng calmly inhaled the aromatic smoke and seemed to enjoy the taste. Sulun guessed that the leaf was some manner of medicinal incense, and the pipe arrangement was certainly more efficient than a Sabisan-style incense burner.

"So, my friends," Wotheng began comfortably, pipe in one hand and full cup in the other, "did you find your shrine today?"

"Ah, yes," Sulun agreed with a mournful sigh. "It's in most wretched condition: all the images gone, the building all a wreck, half buried in rubble. Simply restoring it would take, oh, moons and moons."

"Ah, but it *could* be repaired?"

"Oh yes, and the priest house as well, but . . ." Sulun rolled his eyes. "Good gods, the work! The expense! We wondered most seriously if 'twould be worth the trouble, or if we should just continue north to the next shrine."

"Ah, how sad." Gynallea cast a quick look around the cluster of guests. All of them looked mournful. Yes, they might truly consider moving on. "But how can you be certain that the next shrine will be any better? The gods know, all the lands north of here suffered far worse in the wars."

"True, true." Sulun shrugged eloquently. "But what can we do?"

"Ah, well," Wotheng waved expansively. "The rent there would be very cheap—Oof!" He threw a quick glare at his wife, and rubbed his ankle.

"Rent?" Sulun rolled his eyes piously. "Ah, 'tis hopeless, then. By our most ancient tradition, the land dedicated to the god must belong to the god—of whom we priests are but servants. We were hoping to purchase the land outright, but seeing how much work must be done there, well, the expense . . ."

"Now, now, it need not be so costly as all that." Gynallea seized Sulun's nearer hand and patted it warmly. "Much of our custom hereabouts is done by barter. I'm sure that we could arrange a fair trade for the *purchase* price—" she glared at her husband "—of the land. Your smithy work, for example. Perhaps you might purchase title to the land in exchange for, say, forging goodly blades for our household guard, or some such work, in perpetuity. 'Twould be easy enough, for folk of your skill."

Sulun was about to say yes, enthusiastically, when his memory snagged on the words "in perpetuity." While he was thinking that over, Omis spoke up.

"Ah, good Lady, how could we serve your own blacksmith so? Biddon is a fine workman, and an honest fellow. How, then, should we take his custom away from him? 'Twould be a poor service to a fellow smith."

Wotheng and Gynallea blinked over that, momentarily set back.

Eloti seized the moment to speak up. "Good hosts, 'tis true we have more of smithcraft than poor Biddon does. But how, then, if we were to repay your kindness by teaching the fellow our skills? Then you would have a smith upon your villa who could work iron as well as we, and you'd not have to journey ten leagues every time a horse threw a shoe."

"Oh, aye," Wotheng muttered. "Well for Biddon and his household, and we'd make some little gain thereby, but to purchase a whole stretch of land . . . And how much, said you, that you wished?"

There was momentary confusion while Doshi produced the pertinent map and unrolled it on the table. Wotheng raised his bushy eyebrows and peered closer.

"I've never seen a chart so fair," he commented. "What, be there towns, cities, all that hereabouts, and I never heard thereof?"

"This is a copy of a much older map," Doshi explained, surreptitiously scattering a pinch of salt over certain items on the chart. "This is how the land lay before the great invasions. Many towns and villas you see marked herein be long gone, cast to the winds of fate and war. I suppose there are many new towns now, built in the years since, that this map's makers never knew."

"A well-made copy of that chart could help make up the price of the land," Gynallea purred.

"We are always willing to share learning," Eloti smiled sweetly, "for that too is part of our trade."

"Hmm . . ." Wotheng traded significant glances with his wife. Both of them could read, write and work figures; hardly anyone else within twenty leagues could do so, which had proved a constant inconvenience. Here, now, an idea caught fire and blazed.

"Well, now, there's a bit more of a fair price," said Gynallea. "Would you make a school, also, and teach whomever we sent you, that would be worth as much as, hmm, the price of a small field."

"Here it is," Doshi cut in, pointing to the map. "This hill, and the ruins upon it, and the field below where the two lesser hills come nigh the stream. That's all the land we need or ask."

Wotheng grinned behind his pipe. That was a piddling acreage, in such poor land as that. "Ey, yes, I'd agree that a school and a goodly map would almost be worth the purchase price, even for so much land as that." He smiled at his wife's anxious look. "Cast in also a simple agreement, and I think we may call the bargain fair."

"Agreement?" Sulun worried. "Concerning what matter, m'lord?"

"Why, just that if you folk should choose to sell your wares beyond Ashkell and its holdings, you shall bring the same to me to sell for you." Wotheng winked at Gynallea, grinning. "I know the roads, aye, and the towns north, and the times when the merchants' caravans come by, and the usual prices as well. Let me arrange the selling for you, friends, and you'll profit more handsomely than ever you could by yourselves."

He held his breath, marshalling further arguments: the danger of bandits, the usefulness of his men-at-arms, his knowledge of the other lordlings to the north.

"Yes!" said Sulun, eager to close the bargain and be done. This Wotheng would make a better patron than any he'd had before. "Certainly, m'lord."

Wotheng beamed.

"Ah, but at what commission?" Eloti purred. "We should agree, before putting seal to any parchment, what part per hundred of the sales shall be yours, and what part ours."

Wotheng narrowed his eyes, but still smiled. Aha, these smith's women were quite as clever at bargaining as his Gynallea. Priests or no, these folk were good merchants, and could make his holdings prosperous. "Well, seeing that we shall share the labor—you of making, myself of peddling—should we not share the profits equally? Say, half and half?"

The others looked at each other. Eloti only smiled and leaned closer, and settled in for a good half-hour's dickering —sure of her element as a bird in the air.

Wotheng closed the bedchamber door while his wife put down the candle. Then they fell upon the creaking bed, grabbed each other and rolled back and forth, giggling like mischievous children. The hysteria stopped only when Wotheng jabbed himself on Gynallea's brooch, and pulled away swearing.

"Gold in hand, lovey," Gynallea chuckled, sitting up to unfasten her clothes. "One way and another, gold in hand!"

"Umm, yes," Wotheng grinned, sucking his poked palm. "Gods, but they've good wit—and they're rich. Rich! Sweet moo-cow, we're going to be rich!"

"Hah, don't milk the cow before she's bred," Gynallea snickered, pinching his near buttock.

"Let me get out of these clothes and we'll celebrate," Wotheng snorted, tugging at pesky ties and buckles.

"Hee-hee! And you thought the bargaining was done when they signed the parchment and you gave them the deed to the land. Ho, ho!"

"Ah, my cow, you know I always sit about after a good trade, free with the jug, just in case other dealings might be offered . . . Vona's balls! Woman, can you get this knot undone?"

"Here, turn toward the light. Yes, but whose thought was it to ask them what repairs they'd need to make, what supplies and workmen needed, eh? Eh?"

"So, you got in the first word. I'd have said it soon enough. Ho, they'll have the old mill going, will they? But only for grinding ore? Hah! Do we suffer a siege, or the new mill take storm damage again, we'll have another mill to use at need."

"And where else would they purchase timber, and raw iron? Where else to get the workmen, tiles, mortar, seed and breeding stock they want? To and fro, the trade shall go—with us and our children to profit, both ways. Yes, lovey, this has been a golden evening."

"Golden, yes." Wotheng rubbed his hands together, smiling from ear to ear. "Show it to me again, dear love."

Gynallea opened her hand with a flourish, letting the candlelight fall on the gleaming gold coin centered in her palm. "A full ounce, I'll wager," she smiled. "Did you ever see the like?"

"Never, sweet cow. Who would have thought a band of pilgrims had such a coin about them? And surely that can't be the only one."

"Surely there's more to come; years' worth, with the

bargain we sealed. And all this, for our pledge of goods and workmen for barely half a year! Happy enough they were to get it, too. I'll vow, the poor things have no idea of prices hereabouts."

"Hmph, they'll learn soon enough when it comes to selling their goods. Still, once I begin selling in the north— and perhaps in the southlands, soon enough—they'll be content with the bargain. Come, blow the candle out, sweet cow. Let's to pounding the mattress."

Gynallea set the coin down carefully beside the candle, and blew out the flame.

In the creaking darkness, before plunging seriously into the task at hand, Wotheng thought to ask, "Oh, did you say aught to them about Folweel?"

"Mmm, in a manner of speaking, while you were poking up the fire."

"What manner of speaking, cow?"

"Why, lovey, I simply mentioned that other small priests and hedge witches might grow jealous of their prosperity and favor, and if any such did so, they should come complain to me. That was plain enough."

"Oh, aye . . . I suppose that suffices as warning. Move your thigh over."

Gynallea giggled. The bed creaked.

2

The burly, gray-haired man sat in the sunlight at the window seat of his study-room, drinking a cup of bark tea laced with spirits of wine and examining a waxed tablet scribbled with figures. The figures were not reassuring. The sunlight picked out a frayed thread in the gold embroidery on his red outer robe. A rough spot in the silver inlay of his brass cup snagged at his lip. Fair weather or not, this promised to be a thoroughly wretched day.

A discreet knocking sounded from the carved panels of the study's door. The man frowned, got up and went to his parchment-littered heavy oak table, adjusted his orange under-robe to show the embroidery to good advantage, and snapped, "Come in!"

A subdued maid in a plain gray dress opened the door,

ushered in the visitor, and silently closed the door behind him. The newcomer, somewhat younger, shorter and less burly than his host, wore a yellow under-robe and an orange outer one, both bearing somewhat less embroidery than the older man sported. His smile was wide, cheerful and practiced.

"Greetings, Brother Folweel," he chirped, eyes flicking to the waxed tablet lying close at his superior's elbow. "I assume you've read yesterday's tally?"

"Greetings, Brother Jimantam. Pray sit." Folweel pointed to another carved oak chair. "Yes, I've read it," he said in Murrekeen, in case the maid was eavesdropping. "Most unpromising."

Jimantam settled carefully into the indicated chair, his smile sliding away. "Attendance often falls off at this time of year," he offered, in the same tongue. "So much for the faithful to do: first harvest, second planting, shearing . . ."

"Attendance at services was quite good last summer." Folweel interlaced his fingers and tapped his thumbs together. "The temple was packed last year for the Midsummer ceremony. Yesterday there was overmuch room at the same service. Could it be that out herd is being distracted by . . . worldly concerns?"

"It does happen." Jimantam shrugged. He peered at the parchments on the table, hoping to see one in particular. "Still, the temple income is undiminished. The tally at equinox was most, er, generous."

"The tally at equinox was three moons ago!" Folweel slammed his palm on the stack of parchments. "Its figures displayed the expected increase from the temple's own livestock—at lambing time. The only sizable income we've seen since came from northern sales of wool after shearing. Of course the temple flocks and crops are doing well; we've land and servants enough for that. The problem, dear Brother, is that funds from outside the temple have fallen away. That is the precise problem I wish to discuss with you. Just why is there poorer attendance and fewer donations, pray tell?"

Jimantam shrugged again. "Some time has passed since the last miracle. People forget, they grow distracted . . ."

"We promised—and delivered—the usual miracle of the flame at the solstice ceremony. It didn't draw enough. The crowd was middle-sized at best, and the donations were small. Why, sir?"

"Well, this is coin-poor land; most trade is done by barter. If the folk simply don't have much coin on hand—"

"Coin? After first harvest and shearing? Oh, come."

"The trade caravans to the north—"

"Went out on time, came back in good time, and should have harvested the usual sufficiency of silver. Besides, even donations in goods have fallen off. Explain me that."

Jimantam spread his hands placatingly. "Worldly distractions," he murmured. "There was the usual plague of fleas, for example."

"I heard something of that," Folweel sneered. "The flea infestation was unusually mild this year—and not because of overmuch purchase of our ointment. Why, think you, was that?"

Jimantam rolled his eyes. "Perhaps some hedge wizard or granny witch has also discovered the secret of making soap, or the virtues of fleabane and garlic. Such knowledge is easy to come by, and another wizard might sell it more cheaply."

"Aha." Folweel leaned closer, eyes narrowing. "If so, then what other wizard would that be?"

Jimantam shook his head, accepting the inevitable. "This new batch of wizards off to the west," he conceded. "They have the appeal of novelty, though that should wear off soon enough."

"Yes, these new wizards." Folweel leaned back in his chair. "The Deese priests, worshippers of a blacksmith's god. They have not confined themselves to making horseshoes and praying over anvils, have they?"

"Who can tell, Brother? I know they've been selling pretty amulets of iron and brass and black glass bits, but that seems harmless enough."

"Harmless? When some of said amulets are sold specifically for protection against fire?"

Jimantam pursed his lips, said nothing.

"I have heard disturbing reports." Folweel picked up a sheet of parchment and frowned at it. "There are many of these priests, they have wealth enough that they've hired much of the local labor to build—or rebuild, as they claim—a good-sized shrine and priest house out in the old ruins. They have skills with metal work that entice a goodly amount of the local trade, and have produced enough goods beyond that to send north for sale. They have much favor with our old friend Wotheng. They have, if you please, set up a school in Ashkell villa where they teach reading, writing, figuring, healing craft and—think on this— mechanical skills. They teach this to any who will sit and listen, and with Wotheng's help and approval. Do you not see a difficulty there, Brother?"

Jimantam sighed. "We have a rival for the people's affections. Some effort will be required to sway them back again. Another prediction of fire, perhaps?"

"Too soon," Folweel snapped. "And you've utterly missed the danger of that—that school!"

"What danger?" Jimantam was genuinely puzzled. "Our own temple college teaches skills of far greater virtue: magecraft, priestcraft, estate management, merchantry—"

"For our own!" Folweel resisted the urge to tug at his impressive beard. "We teach our own initiates, and grant a bit of harmless hedge magic to our servants. These— these interlopers teach any who care to listen! Can you not see the difference, and the danger?"

"Er, we take those of more quality, better inclined to learning . . ."

Folweel sighed, remembering that he must be patient with this Brother; the man was very, very good at wringing excellent profit from the temple lands and donations. If he knew nothing of true magic, or wider applications of policy, that only kept him from overmuch ambition. One should explain as much as Jimantam needed to know.

"Dear Brother," Folweel said, very calmly, "these folk offer to teach anyone: nobles, scribes, craftsfolk, farmers or even servants. They teach skills readily useful to any- one, as even the dullest peasant may see. If all the folk have such skills, why need they come to us for service in such things?"

Now Jimantam began to see it. He frowned, counting off on his fingers. "Reading, writing, figuring . . . But they never did come to us for that. The folk always go to scribes for such. We have no competition there."

"Not there, no: but magecraft, and healing simples, and mechanics?"

"Magecraft . . ." Jimantam scratched his chin. "We've

had no trouble from the local granny witches, priests of other gods, that sort. Would these be any greater rivals?"

"They very well might be. We have no idea what their magical abilities are." That wasn't the main point, but no profit in telling Jimantam so; it might give him ideas. "Their healing simples and such spells, for example: what if they teach everyone to make and use soap, fleabane, and so on? Who will buy from us, if every shepherd's wife can make plenty?"

"I begin to see the problem, Brother." Jimantam's lips tightened. "This school must be . . . examined."

"And the cult itself," Folweel added. "We must discover what they know."

"It should be easy enough to place . . . students in the school. As to the cult, I don't know."

"That task I think I shall assign to Patrobe. Send him to see me as soon as convenient."

"Gladly, Brother Folweel." Jimantam stood, guessing that he was dismissed and eager to be about his new task, delighted to learn that the shortage of the temple's income was not to be laid at his door. "May the blessings of Yotha be upon you, forever and evermore."

"Yotha bless," Folweel waved him off, not even bothering to watch the man leave.

His eyes strayed to the image of Yotha standing against the inner wall between two bookcases. "Fire God," Folweel grumbled, in his native Halasan. If anyone overheard, they'd think he was praying or practicing magic. So be it; of recent years he'd come to think aloud at the image, for lack of more trustworthy ears. "You're very good as a sword, but this problem calls for a stiletto. Rival wizards, several of them, and well-educated by all accounts: was it pure accident they came here too? Or did they recognize a good milking herd when they saw it?"

The image made no answer, only stared broodingly at the lamp that burned perpetually in its hands.

Folweel got up and went to the bookcase, searching among the scrolls penned years ago, back in Anhalas, which no one else in this barbarous country could read. "Mechanics," he muttered, "Medicine, Natural Philosophy. Dangerous, my most useful companion. Not merely of themselves, though that's bad enough. Teach such things, and to the very peasants we need? Monstrous! Suicidal!

Are these folk utter fools, or are they keeping the greater knowledge for themselves? The latter, most like. Still, don't they realize the danger? Let common folk learn too much of the workings of the world, and they grow too confident. When peasants have faith in themselves, they lose faith in gods and wizards. Where are we then, eh?"

Yotha silently contemplated his cupped flame, giving no reply.

Folweel finally located the scroll he wanted, a large medical text. "So, so . . . Much one can learn as a doctor's apprentice in Anhalas: much of chemistry, at least, and the mechanics thereof. Mysteries of the still-room, indeed. What power hides in strong wine, triply distilled, eh? A fluid that burns, and without even a wick."

He flicked a finger playfully through the flame in Yotha's cup, making the shadows dance across the image's face, as if the fire god smiled.

"We've done very well with that one, simple trick." Folweel turned the scroll, looking for one section in particular. "Magic alone has power—well-wish or ill-wish, talent and training provide it. Natural philosophy grants knowledge that leads to power . . ." He tapped his finger on the scroll. ". . . such as our useful, most mysterious fire-fluid. But put the two together, my lad—as my old master used to say—and the results are magnified. Heh! I doubt he ever imagined I'd use that knowledge for more than medicine. But then, I doubt he ever thought that Halas could fall. Hard times, these. One must harden one's spirit to match them, use what tricks one can, take on whatever allies may be useful . . . Ah, here we are."

The section revealed in the open scroll dealt with herbs and extracts that affected the mind. Strong drink was listed first, but Folweel passed over it quickly. Opium was next, but he skipped that also; its source plant did not grow in these climes, nor was it available through local trade. The third was belladonna, the description of its properties and uses followed by a list of its herbal sources. Many such plants grew in the north. Folweel ran his finger down the list, and smiled as he read.

The bell in the pigeon tower of Wotheng's house rang twice, then rattled to indignant silence. In the second courtyard, which held the house herb garden, a dozen

children and adults of all sizes looked up, startled. Waxed
boards skittered off laps as children started to scramble to
their feet. Eloti tapped sternly on her slate tablet, and the
students hastily picked up their gear.

"Depart in an orderly fashion," she commanded, "and
don't forget the song."

The class dutifully lined up and traipsed out of the
courtyard, singing in a dozen different keys: "Ayo is for
apple, Bith is for barn . . ."

Eloti let her face slip into a smile, watching them go.

The crunch of approaching footsteps on the antique
gravel path made her turn. Gynallea, dressed in her usual
apron and headcloth, approached with a load of scrolls
under one arm and settled beside Eloti on the stone
bench.

"I've found some more texts," she said, displaying the
collection of scrolls. "One mathematics, two histories, one
compendium of medicinal plants, two poetries and a
geography—quite outdated, of course, but still useful.
How long, think you, before this lot can read them?"

"This lot? Half a year, at least." Eloti picked up the
geography first. "The second class, though, might start on
some of these in another moon."

"How have you arranged it? Beginners in the first half of
the morning, literates in the second half?"

"Just so. By year's end, I might have my whole day
filled with different grades of scholars."

"And by next year, then, will you have scholars advanced enough to enter the House of Deese as apprentices?"

Eloti smiled, seeing where this led. "That would de-
pend upon how prosperous the House of Deese becomes.
We can feed, house and clothe only so many, at present."

"Don't worry about that, dear." Gynallea grinned, patting her knee. "Those little toys you sent north fetched a
goodly price. By next year, you'll have fine trade. Surely
you can take in another by then."

"Aha." Eloti set the scrolls aside. "Biddon has been
plaguing you, too, hasn't he?"

"My dear, what could you expect? He wants to learn
more skills, all but worships the ground where you tread,
has sworn he's willing to become a lowly apprentice again
if you'll but take him in."

"He'll have to master reading, writing and figuring first.

Of course, he does his best at that—he's in the second class already." Eloti shrugged. Biddon had no head for figures and letters, but his pure determination had carried him acceptably far already. "By next year . . . well, perhaps. Certainly by the year after, if all continues as it has done."

"Ah, very good." Gynallea sat back, scratching her belly. "Now, how goes the building at the shrine?"

"Most remarkably," Eloti admitted. "The roof is on, the mill repaired, and the wall goes well. We need do some work ourselves on the plumbing, but that can wait until the forge is finished. Oh yes, Omis said to tell Lord Wotheng that we'll need another two hundredweight of firebrick and three hundredweight of clay. The, hmm, 'ladle' will need to be more stout than he'd first thought."

Gynallea shook her head in wonder. "So much brick, clay, charcoal . . . iron and brass I can understand, but the rest is a mystery to me."

"I think I can reveal that mystery to the uninitiated," Eloti laughed. "Only baked clay and firebrick, so far as I know, can withstand the heat of melting iron. The charcoal— oh, I just thought! Lady, don't let the woodcutters and charcoal burners chop down the whole forest, or there'll soon be none left. Make them plant a hundred seed for every tree they cut."

"Oh posh, daughter, we've been doing that for donkey's years. Did you never wonder why the wood on that north hill looks as neat as an orchard?"

"Ah, orchards of oaks?"

"Certainly. Even standing, they're of use; the acorns make coarse flour, or excellent pig feed. Didn't you know?"

"Ah, Lady, I'm always delighted to learn something new."

"There, dear, you may call me Gynna—at least when there are no men about."

Eloti laughed in genuine delight.

They might have spoken more, but Yawth came trotting into the garden to announce the arrival of the second class. Gynallea sighed and got up. "Back to work for both of us, daughter," she sighed. "When this class is over, come find me in the still-room. There are some arcana of equipage design I wish to ask you about."

"Hmm, that would be Sulun's field of knowledge more than mine, but I'll be glad to come. At noon, then?"

Gynallea nodded and walked away. Eloti turned to watch the incoming class, and noted that it was larger than it had been yesterday. She counted noses, discovering one extra; it belonged to a bland-faced young man dressed as a scribe, whom she hadn't seen before. Perhaps he'd kept away until now, believing his skills were adequate, for he appeared quite well fed and well clothed. He had, she noted, brought his own waxed tablets and stylus with him.

"Your name, sir?" she asked.

"Duppa, a scribe," he answered readily, smiling as if he did it often. "I live to the north, near Yedda Stream, by Topa's Lane—"

"Very good, sir," Eloti interrupted him, noting the curious looks from the rest of her class. "Take your place, and we shall proceed with exercises in mathematics."

The man dutifully sat and readied his tablets. Eloti turned away to hunt among her original basket of scrolls for the day's text, and also to hide her confusion. Magical training had made her sensitive to the presence and "feel" of other living bodies and minds; she was used to feeling the life-warmth and eager concentration of her students, and normally gave it no thought. This man was different. He seemed strangely blank, not there, a disturbing hole in the air where his body was visible, as if he were no more than a moving puppet. If he hadn't cast a shadow, she might have thought he was a very well constructed thought-sending.

Shielded, she guessed. The man was magically shielded, and so intensely that not even the "heat" of his life-force escaped. Was this pure accident, an unintended construction of the man's own mind? Or had it been done deliberately, placed on him by a competent and talented wizard? If deliberate, why? Why should a common scribe need such shields? Unless, of course, he was no common scribe? *Some local hedge wizard, studying his competition?* she wondered. *Best ask Gynallea about him.*

That decided, she took up the scroll and proceeded with the lesson.

The new forge was beautiful, clean and cold: a virgin, waiting to be initiated into the delights of her natural fire. Omis walked around her once again, eyes measuring her splendid dimensions and features, itching to fill and light her properly. There, that enormous bellows made of two whole oxhides, waiting to be geared into the driveshaft from the mill. With such a pump, in such a furnace, he could refine purest iron out of raw, red earth in a day's work or less. There, the great pulleys and chain hoist braced into the new ceiling. Once the huge ladle was finished, he could melt and pour iron by the hundredweight as easily as if it were wax in a cup. There, Sulun's precious lathe and the new grinding wheels, likewise waiting to be hitched to the mill's driving shaft. Gods, what he could make with those. He'd made little but toys since they'd settled here—farming tools, buckles, sockets for wooden wheels, even pins and needles—good quality, but such puny common things, small items readily made in the sturdy little portable forge from Sabis, on his old and admittedly worn anvil. But with tools like these, once they were ready . . .

Omis shook his head and turned away. *Patience, patience,* he reminded himself. *All goes well, better than we could have dreamed just a year ago.*

Indeed, a year ago he could never have imagined working in such a manufactory as this. Possibly there was nothing near like it in all the world. What irony to see it here, in this forgotten country estate, when Sabis and all her glory lay in ruins . . .

Omis turned away from the forge, went to a freshly oiled cabinet under the new workbench, opened it, and tugged out the cloth-wrapped shape within. He lifted the object to the bench, laid it down and pulled up a stool.

The bombard's outside was still pebble-rough and unfinished, but the interior gleamed like a mirror. She was seamless, flawless, as perfect as human skill could make her, needing only a few finishing touches. Omis didn't ask himself why he felt obliged to work on her whenever he thought of Sabis; her original purpose was long lost, fallen with the city.

Still, the Bombard Project led him on, led all of them still, had led them like a god's sign to settle here in the vestibule of a sulfur mine. Why sulfur, save for firepowder? Why firepowder, save for the bombard? Why the bombard? No answer—yet the pursuit of that idea had brought them here, to safety, protection, promised wealth, even the respect of the local people and the friendship of the local lord. Even a workshop such as this.

Omis cast a glance at the nearer of the two figures carved beside the door. "Deese, thou knowest," he said.

Then he took up a narrow circular brush and a pot of pumice paste, and began polishing the recently drilled fuse hole at the base of the bombard. After this would come the building of its carriage.

He barely heard the footsteps approaching behind him, managed to ignore them until Zeren spoke, almost in his ear.

"Where's Sulun? We have a problem."

Yanados perched on a finished section of the wall, supposedly watching the small flock of goats that foraged contentedly downslope. Under the hood of her cloak, no one could tell at this distance that she was actually watching the work crew busy on the unfinished part of the wall. Biddon sat beside her, clenching his corded hands with the effort not to point. Sulun, Zeren and Doshi came padding up behind her, climbed the broad stile to the walkway and peered toward the work gang. Zeren clapped a hand on the blacksmith's shoulder.

"Which one is he?" he asked.

"That'n, sir," Biddon pointed, just briefly. "Yonder thick-set fellow in the brown leggin's and yellow shirt. The one up on the stones, layin' mortar. I've seen him before, a'right, comin' to my shop for stone chisels, braggin' to wear me ear off. He's head stonemason of Yotha's temple, and what business, sirs, would he have here?"

"You all know more than I do," Sulun puzzled. "Who is Yotha, and why shouldn't his temple's chief stonemason come to work here?"

"Yotha, according to our friend Biddon, is an ill-tempered fire god," said Yanados, still watching. "His priests came and settled here some eight years back, built a temple some six leagues north, and have been doing well for themselves ever since. As to your second question, the chief stonemason of Yotha's temple is ordinarily paid quite well enough that he'd have no need to come work common labor on our walls. Do you see nothing suspicious there?"

"I see a mystery, and I wish you all would explain it."

"We seem to have some rivals," Zeren sighed. "Yotha's temple was the biggest and wealthiest in Ashkell Vale, before we came."

"What, simple jealousy?" Sulun asked. "How would that explain their mason working here?"

"More nor *simple* jealousy!" Biddon laughed. "See you all these folk workin' on your priest house, these many moons? Ye've *paid* 'em for their hire, day by day, not bought their service outright by the year. You folk pay well, too—in good copper and useful spells, not to mention yonder school at Ashkell House. And ye're none so haughty as Yotha's folk, nor has your Deese done harm to any. Need I tell you, then, how many folk would rather come to you than to Yotha's house?"

"We've drawn away many of Yotha's worshippers, you mean? And his priests don't like it?"

"Neither like it nor accept it philosophically, I imagine," said Doshi. "So their chief mason has shown up here: for spying, spreading disaffection, spoiling the work, or what?"

"Spying, certainly," Yanados guessed. "We may as well assume the rest, too. Now, what shall we do about it?"

"First off, I would have Arizun inspect that section of wall," Zeren put in. "See if it's made as well as the rest, or if some charm has been set into the mortar."

"Good thought," said Doshi, turning to go back down the stile steps. "I'll fetch him."

"Now wait," Sulun complained, feeling a bit left out. "What harm can a man do, setting mortar on a wall? What harm can his spying do, for that matter? Why not leave him where he is, lest these—these priests of Yotha send another spy who we don't know?"

Zeren laughed. "Sulun, my wonderfully innocent old friend, think; we've seen whole houses ill-wished, and from a distance. Why not a wall? Or the whole house, starting from the wall? That's the harm our insidious mason there can do."

Sulun thought about that, about the curse placed on Entori House, about the possible effects of such a curse in a house full of hot iron, firepowder, heavy tools—and a cellar full of sulfur. He shuddered.

"Very well, get rid of him. What will happen when his friends learn of his failure, I don't know."

"They'll know we're no fools," said Yanados. "That alone might make them behave better."

"High hopes," Zeren muttered. "More like, they'll just take another tactic. We must be watchful."

"Which is the man?" Arizun asked, climbing up behind them. "Where has he been working?"

Biddon gleefully pointed out the suspect, and the stretch of wall, adding: "There's more I could watch out for you, Masters, did I but live here. Would I not make a good initiate of Deese?"

"Soon, soon," Yanados promised, patting his shoulder. "Once Eloti says you're ready . . . Hey, the lunch bell!"

Sure enough, the iron bell so recently hung in its niche over the front door was ringing the announcement for the midday meal. All the workmen on the wall cheered happily, put down their tools, settled the last stones they'd been working on, and sat down to eat. The brown-legged spy made haste to join them.

"Doshi's idea," said Arizun. "That'll give me time enough to go look at the wall." He strode off quietly, dark robe blending with the stone of the walls.

Sulun looked around at his companions and wrung his hands in dismay. "Aren't we worrying overmuch?" he asked. "Now that we've come to a good place, I had hoped we'll stop expecting enemies everywhere."

"Were we so free of foes back in Sabis?" Yanados asked, trying not to sound bitter.

Sulun just shook his head and walked away. *Is there no peace*, he wondered, *to be found anywhere?*

Arizun strolled along the new section of wall, running one hand along the stones, keeping an eye turned toward the gang of workmen busy with their meal downslope. Did the brown-legged mason glance this way a little too often? Was he seated so as to keep an eye on the wall? One couldn't walk too slowly, then, or seem too interested.

Arizun felt it first as a subtle heat, something like warmth clinging to the shadowed stone, right in the mortared seam between two blocks. He paused to shake an imaginary stone out of his shoe, casually leaning on the wall for support, one hand pressed to the mortar. Yes, the spell was there, probably anchored in a mage sign scribbled into the mortar under the block. He could almost picture

the sign, the feeling was so clear. Yes, picture it: no more
or less than a script initial in some foreign alphabet, an
elaborate letter Y—no doubt for Yotha, very simple and
direct. Well, well. Probe further, but quickly; the man
might notice. Arizun closed his eyes and dropped, for a
moment, deeper into the Meditative State that Eloti had
taught him to attain and feel with such facility.

Oh, yes: a simple and direct curse, set in the wall,
meant to spread through the entire house, partly vitalized
already. No doubt it would increase this very night, once
the brown-legged spy got home to his friends. Ah, clever.

Arizun ground his teeth in cold, rising fury. He pulled
his shoe back on, straightened up and strolled on down
the wall for a few paces more, down to where the completed wall rose over his head and concealed him from the
work gang beyond. There he stopped, leaned against the
dark stones, reached into his second belt pouch and drew
out a faceted crystal lens. The essentials, as Lady Eloti had
told him often enough, were quite simple: concentration,
visualization, will, focus, purpose. He had will enough;
easy for this rage to power it. The crystal would help
concentration and focus. Visualization came easily too.
Purpose . . . Arizun smiled wickedly. A simple deflection,
change of target, would be so utterly fitting—and was
much easier than neutralizing the curse altogether. Yes,
just a proper deflection to a new target: he had sufficient
talent and power to do that by himself. Eloti would be so
pleased when he would tell her.

Arizun stared into the crystal, concentrating.

A second ringing of the iron bell signalled the workmen
back to their task. They tossed away crumbs, recorked
jugs, climbed to their feet and went back to the waiting
stones, derrick and wall. The senior of the work gang
poked at the trough of mortar, shrugged, added a little
water and stirred it in. The rest of the crew shoved another stone down its track of roller logs to the wooden
crane and began tying it on. A mason in brown leggings
and a yellow shirt trotted around to the back of the wall,
up a makeshift wooden stepladder to the top of the present course of stones, and prepared to guide the new block
into place.

On the way up, his foot slipped and nearly sent him

tumbling off the ladder. He swore, climbing the rest of the way with more care, too busy thinking of his task ahead to question the minor accident.

"Up!" bellowed the senior workman, and the rest of the crew hauled on the crane's tail ropes. The tail sank, the wooden fulcrum groaned as weight came on the ropes, and the tied block began to rise. "Up, up," chanted the gang's senior.

"Now right, right," shouted the man on the wall, as the block rose level with his breastbone. He reached for the trailing guide rope, missed it, leaned further out—slipped and fell flat in the spread mortar.

The work gang below laughed heartily, but didn't let the ropes slacken.

The brown-legged man pulled himself up, cursing furiously and brushing wet mortar off his no longer bright yellow shirt. "Further right, blast you all with ringworm," he shouted, reaching again for the guide rope.

The work gang obligingly swung the derrick's tail away from the wall, moving the suspended block to the right.

The brown-legged, mortar-daubed man grabbed for the guide rope, and this time caught it. Instead of pulling slowly, he yanked on it in exasperation.

The guide rope snapped taut, catching on one of the support ropes at the near corner of the block. The support rope, dragging along with the guide, pulled free.

The block shuddered for a second, then slid loose of the remaining guides and fell forward.

It tumbled straight into the brown-legged man, carrying him off the wall, and fell on top of him.

The work gang on the derrick fell flat as their ropes suddenly slackened. They all heard the short screech from behind the wall, and the grisly thud. Some cursed, some groaned, some wailed with horror. The bravest got up and ran for the wall at once; the more timorous followed slowly. Up the wooden scaffolding they ran, across the lower course of stones, through the spread mortar to the inner side of the wall—and paused there a long moment, surveying the damage.

It was impressive.

Arizun took good care to arrive after the others, to sound and look surprised. Doshi and Zeren gave him thoughtful looks as he elbowed through the crowd, but they said nothing. Biddon the blacksmith saw him coming and stepped hastily out of his path, throwing him a white-eyed look, like a frightened horse. Yanados gave him a sardonic smile and a hint of an ironic salute. Arizun ignored her, pushed to the front of the crowd, and looked.

The man was still alive, breathing in thin wheezes, fingers scrabbling aimlessly at the edge of the stone. From the waist down, his body was hidden under the tumbled block. The stone appeared to lie level on the ground, perhaps even a bit sunken into it. Blood seeped from under its edges.

"Like a berry under a brick," mumbled one of the workmen watching. A small gang of the more muscular in the crowd was trying to dig under the edges of the block and tie on ropes from the crane. None of them looked at the man under the stone, nor, for all their haste, did they seem very willing to lift the block and reveal what lay beneath it.

"Can't last the hour," one of the nearby watchers mumbled.

"Soon, soon . . ." chanted another, his tone reminiscent of prayer.

The ropes were worked under the corners, looped, tied on, drawn taut. "It's tied!" snapped the head of the work gang, keeping his eyes on the knots. "Haul it!"

On the other side of the wall, the rest of the work gang heaved at the crane's tail ropes. The derrick creaked, and the block began to rise. Sunlight spread beneath the rising stone.

The crowd groaned softly, all together.

The man under the block continued whining thinly, noticing nothing.

The gang on the crane lifted the stone until it reached its niche on the wall, then lowered it. The block slipped neatly into place, perfectly aligned, though no one drew the rope to guide it there. A film of blood on its underside stained the top of the mortar.

Arizun turned away quickly. He'd taken two steps toward the house when a hand caught his shoulder. He glanced up, and saw Sulun glaring down at him.

"No, stay and watch," Sulun whispered fiercely, in Sabirn. "That was your doing; you look at it."

"It couldn't be helped!" Arizun hissed back in the same tongue. "All I could do was deflect the curse, discharge it back on him who set it. Otherwise it would have sprung on us."

"No other choice? Nothing else you could have done?"

"No! I couldn't just wipe it away; I don't have that power, and I didn't dare wait for Eloti to come back and help me. All I could do was deflect it, send it back. Gods, I didn't know it would do *that* . . ."

Sulun dropped his hand and turned away. "Bad beginning," he muttered.

Then he saw the workmen watching him, trying not to look at the body on the ground being bundled into a stretcher improvised of cloaks. He could read their faces clearly enough, see why no one had dropped the ropes off the settled block, guess why no one now was working the crane. Time to say something. Sulun gritted his teeth, pulled his robe around him and marched up the scaffolding to the top of the unfinished stretch of wall.

"Carelessness," he intoned, "exacts a heavy price. Carelessness can slaughter more than armies. Carelessness is our enemy here—and we dare not drop our guard against it, not for a moment, not out of anger of impatience or distraction. Not ever." One quarter of his mind coolly approved the balanced shape of the speech; another cringed at its grotesque irrelevance. "You see now what harm even a moment's carelessness can do. Be warned, then. Learn the lesson well. Let us never have to learn it again."

The workmen below him nodded solemnly, accepting the words.

Sulun tried to find words to send them back to work, but couldn't think of any. The sound of the crane's ropes slapping the wood made him think of corpses hanging on gallows. No, no more of this, not today.

"Bear that poor man to his home," he said, struggling to get the words clear. "The rest of you, secure the crane, the stones and the tools, and take the remainder of the day—at full pay—to ponder this matter. Er, dismissed." He strode hastily off the stone and down the scaffolding, trying not to hear the amazed murmurs of the crowd as he passed, and headed for the new house. Somewhere among all the foodstocks there had to be some strong berry wine, and he needed a few cups of that.

Behind him, the work gang rumbled in amazement.

"Did ye hear that?" said the senior workman. "All of half the day off, and at full pay!"

"What generous folk they be," agreed the nearest. "And wise, too. His talk of carelessness be good sense."

"Aye," noted his neighbor. "Have ye seen, this is the first sore accident since the building work began? The first life or limb lost, in all these moons."

"And that on a new fellow, first day here, who didn't know the workings," another added. "'S'truth, I think he was a stranger here."

"'Tis sure, I don't know him," commented one of the men at the stretcher. "Does anyone here know where his house lies?"

"I do," rumbled Biddon, coming up on them. "'Tis far off north, by the caravan road. Yotha House, and none other."

The workmen stared at him, then at each other, then nodded knowingly.

An hour later, two riders on mules set out from Deese House. Before dusk they reached Ashkell Villa, meeting Eloti on the way and taking her back with them. Gynallea invited them in and set dinner for them at the upper end of the table, calmly as if she'd been expecting them. Wotheng, after his usual custom, asked no questions and discouraged all talk until the meal was finished and the dessert drinks brought out.

"You did say, m'lord," Sulun began, "that if any local wizards tried to harm us, we should bring our complaint to you."

Wotheng glanced sidelong at his wife, then shrugged. "Aye, so we did. What wizards have troubled you folk, and in what way?"

Sulun looked hopefully at Zeren, not certain that he could carry off this little plan. The big soldier launched into the story as smoothly as if he were giving a standard military report.

"Shortly after noon today there was an accident at the construction site on the new Deese House outer wall. A stone slipped from its cradle, crushing a workman. Upon inspection, the wall was found to have been temporarily ill-wished. The injured workman was found to have been a resident of Yotha's estate. Apparently he was attempting to set a curse on the walls when our own protective spells deflected it, causing it to discharge upon the sender."

Wotheng looked calm, mildly interested; his eyelids barely fluttered at the name of Yotha. Still, Eloti noted it.

"We wish to know," Sulun took up the complaint, "just who these people are, why they tried to ill-wish our house, and whether we may expect more of this."

Wotheng puffed at his pipe, harrumphed a few times, glanced again at his wife. "Well, Yotha's some imported fire god," he began. "Came from off to the east somewhere, no place we ever heard of. These priests of his, now, they've some sorcerous powers they claim he gives 'em; came here about eight years ago and set up to the north, maybe five leagues up along the caravan road. They say that Yotha came first, and the priests were only following where he led. What I know is that fires were seen running along the hilltops—running in lines and curliques, dancing, like. Didn't harm any but stretches of turf; stampeded some sheep, scared some folk out of their wits, and everyone came hollering to me about it."

Wotheng tapped out his empty pipe, refilled and relit it before going on.

"Next day it was, I clearly recall, these priests of Yotha showed themselves in the village. Very fierce and solemn, they were. Proud, too, as if they held themselves too high to speak to the common run of folk. Came asking to see 'the lord of this place,' which was myself, saying they knew the 'source and nature' of the fires. To be sure, I gave 'em audience."

"It was Yotha, they said," Gynallea sneered, pouring herself another berry cordial. "Their triple-damned fire god."

"Oh, aye. They said they'd been following their god's trail for moons, and now they'd found him here. They said they could entice him into a shrine, keep him appeased, keep him from doing mischief, but 'twere best if they did it quickly. Best, in truth, if they could find some empty building already standing—like the old burned mansion up by the north road. Yotha'd be drawn to that, they said, since fire had 'already frolicked there.' "

"And what of all the poor folk living there?" Gynallea

added. "Hah, never mind! Go they must, so the priests could set their god trap there."

"Now what was I to do?" Wotheng shrugged. "Here's the people all afrenzy over these fires, here's these priests saying they can put an end to it, and here's only a few poor folk in the way." He sighed and tapped out his pipe.

"What became of the poor folk who were moved out of the mansion?" Eloti asked.

"Oh, many of them weren't moved out at all—just became builders, then servants, at Yotha House. The rest, well, I granted them some sheep and some help building cottages elsewhere. Tricky juggling with land rights that was, too."

"So Yotha's priests took the house, and its lands, I presume," Eloti considered. "And the mysterious fires stopped?"

"Not entirely, no." Wotheng reached for his cup. "Now they danced all over the altar at his ceremonies there. Folk came from leagues about to attend. At other times the fires would scamper out on the bare hilltops and dance a while, and the priests would go out and chant at them a while, and they'd stop. Then the priests took to saying where fire would strike next—this one's house, that one's barn . . ." Wotheng half-turned, frowned at his fireplace and the innocent flames therein. "Folk took to paying good prices to the priests to discourage Yotha's games. See you where that led?"

Zeren, Eloti and Sulun nodded slowly. "So, Yotha's priesthood soon became rich," Eloti finished. "Now that we've come, they fear a rival for people's attention—and money."

Wotheng smiled sourly. "Be not surprised, friends, if Yotha's fire comes running up to your gates some evening soon."

"We'll not be surprised at all," Zeren growled. "Is the god truly there, think you, or is it only the priests' sorcery?"

"Who can tell? Gynallea gulped her cup empty. "I have noticed, though, that the god behaves in such fashion as to make his priests powerful and rich—more like some captive demon doing a wizard's bidding than a proper god."

"These running fires," Sulun put in, "how do they behave? Is there anything notable about their appearance that differs from ordinary fire?"

"Oh, yes," Gynallea laughed. "They burn only at night, save in Yotha House, and they run in trails all along the ground: over grass, over bare earth, over stone, even up the walls of houses to pounce upon the roof. I've seen it myself. You remember, lovey, when Poddil's cottage burned?"

"You saw this fire run across stone?"

"That I did. A most amazing sight, it was, too. I could see the fires dancing high and bright when they crossed dry grass or wood, creeping low and ghastly blue when they crawled over stone, but crawl they did: all the way to Poddil's house, up the wall and into the thatch, where they burned high and fierce."

"Wait," Sulun insisted. "Blue, did you say? When they didn't have dry grass or wood to eat, the flames were low and . . . *blue*?"

"Aye, a most ghastly color for flame."

"I . . . see." Sulun leaned back in his chair, thinking hard.

"Tell me," Eloti cut into the silence. "If you'd had such ill luck with priests and sorcerors come to settle here, why did you accept us so kindly when first we came?"

Wotheng gave her a long look, then a smile. "Because, good lady, when first you folk came hence, we saw that you went straight to the common folk—to our blacksmith, in fact—and freely gave of your skills, in exchange for no more than knowledge. Also, you offered to sell your goods to any who would buy."

"We behaved like merchants, you mean," Eloti grinned.

"Aye, dear," said Gynallea. "You claimed to be priests, but behaved like goodly merchants. Yotha's sort claimed to be priests also, but behaved more like fearsome wizards. See you the difference?"

"Also," Zeren added, fixing Wotheng with a knowing eye, "perhaps we seemed good enough wizards to drive out Yotha's folk, should it come to that."

Wotheng shrugged again, but he blushed a little.

"Well, who else?" Gynallea said stoutly. "You're skilled at such things. You can deal with Yotha and his priests far better than we."

"Perhaps we can," Sulun murmured, rousing a bit. "Perhaps indeed we can. Eloti, how long before you can return to Deese House? We'll need you to lay further protections there."

"Surely you couldn't return tonight," Gynallea protested. "All those long leagues in the dark . . ."

"No, we'll stay until after school tomorrow, and leave at noon," said Eloti. "I doubt Yotha's priests will attempt any . . . visitations of their god tonight."

"The evening still being young," said Sulun, "might I ask if your ladyship has a still-room in the house that I might observe?"

"Why, yes," Gynallea answered, surprised at the change of subject. "I showed it to Goodlady Eloti just this afternoon."

"Hmm. And would you perchance have a distillery there, and possibly some cordial that didn't come out quite right which you could spare?"

"Certainly, good priest. Ah, you have some plans already, then?"

"Perhaps."

Gort and Hobb sat a long time in the donkeycart, arguing, then finally tossing lots to see which of them would go up to the gate of Yotha House to announce the bad news. Gort lost the toss, and tiptoed, trembling, up to the bellpull. Soon enough, a yellow-robed servant opened the door and peered out.

"S-sir Priest," Gort stammered, respectfully wringing his hat in his hands, "w-we've a fellow here as belongs to yer house, what was killed today at stoneworking. Will ye not come take him inside?"

"Bide a moment," said the servant, whipping back inside.

A few minutes later he came back, accompanied by an older, stouter priest in an embroidered orange robe. The senior priest went to the donkeycart, studied the pathetic bundle inside, then signed to the servant. The junior fellow hurried back to the house, leaving Gort and Hobb alone with the corpse and the priest.

"How did this man come to die?" the priest intoned.

"B-beggin' yer pardon, sir, he were careless at the liftin', and the stone slipped its halter and fell on him." Gort got it all out in a rush.

"And where did this happen?"

"Er, why, at the wall-makin', on the new estate to the southwest."

"New estate?" the priest smiled blandly. "What new estate?"

Gort threw Hobb a desperate look. Hobb gulped twice, then took up the tale. "Why, the old house by the ruint village, what Lord Wotheng deeded t'his friends, sir. The place bein' in sad repair, they called for workmen t' mend the walls. Sure, and that must be how this feller come t' be there."

"I see. And how did you come to bring his body here?"

"Er, well, he weren't from 'round our village, sir, but a few folk said they'd seen him here, so we thought he might be one of yer servants. Please, sir, do take him in! It's five long leagues back t' the village again, and in the dark, and all . . ."

"Yes, we shall take him in."

The servant had returned with three similarly robed companions. The priest snapped his fingers, directed them to the back of the donkeycart and pointed silently to the sacking-wrapped corpse. The servants lugged the body out of the cart. The priest fumbled among his robes, looking for a coin to give the drivers, but Gort had already snapped up the whip and slapped the donkey to motion. The cart rumbled in a tight circle, then back down the road. The priest watched them go for a moment, then followed the servants inside.

Gynallea's distilling equipment was simple: a glazed, narrow-necked pot corked with boiled wood, a crudely seamed copper tube twisting out of the top and a simple catch-jar at its lower end. The pot sat on a three-legged iron ring above a small brazier full of glowing coals. The cordial which had gone into the pot less than an hour before was berry purple, but the liquid dripping from the end of the tube was colorless as water though it smelled sharp and strong.

"Wine distilled to winter wine," Sulun recited, watching the drops fall. "Winter wine distilled to cordial, cordial distilled to this. It would require much wine to begin with, or perhaps even strong beer. Does the House of Yotha purchase much wine or beer? Or does its land grow much of berries or barley?"

"Aye to both," murmured Gynallea, fascinated. " 'Tis a joke hereabouts, how much the god and his servants drink. But think you they're not just drinking it?"

"We'll know in a moment. 'Twas an experiment my old master Abanuz once showed me. The result would burn hot enough, and steady as an oil lamp, to work small bits of glass or metal. I remembered that the flame burned a most notable blue . . . Ah, I think that should do. Take away the brazier, before the leftover syrup burns. Thank you."

"Blue fire? Like oil?" Gynallea asked, shoving the brazier out from under the still-pot. "An oil that could burn without a wick? On bare stone?"

"Not an oil: spirits of cordial. Wait . . ." Sulun took a brush and carefully painted a trail of the clear liquid across a wide stone dish. He took a taper from an overhead shelf, held its wick in the coals until it caught, then touched the small flame to one end of the liquid trail.

The liquid caught fire, flared, lighted down its whole length and burned for several seconds. The flames were blue, barely tipped with yellow.

"Yotha's fire! That's it, certain as day!" Gynallea crowed. "That's what I saw, only ever so much more of it, climbing the wall of poor Poddy's house."

"And the smell?" Sulun persisted, holding the catch-bowl under her nose. "Was there a smell like this one?"

Gynallea sniffed long and hard, wrinkling her nose. "I can't recall truly, but I'll swear I've smelled that before— and in Yotha House, during one of the ceremonies where he came to the altar. I thought it but another incense, such as priests use."

"Then I think we've learned the mystery of Yotha House." Sulun frowned as he poured the liquid into a vial. "Spirits of cordial, burning fluid, more volatile than oil: wicked stuff to be playing at. Especially wicked to mix with magic. Do they dare use magic at all with such stuff lying about? Hmm, they must have protective spells all about Yotha House, against just such happenstance."

"I see it well," Gynallea growled bitterly. "They preach against some poor fellow by day, then by night come and splash trails of these spirits through his fields, up to his house or barn. 'Twould need but a spark at one end of the trail to send fire racing to the other. Gods, what a wicked business!"

"And we've threatened it." Sulun corked the vial and stuffed it in his belt pouch. "We'd best put fresh well-wishing circles all about our house, and that right soon. We'd also best finish that stout stone wall as soon as might be, and sheathe the gates with brass."

"Friend Sulun." Gynallea laid a hand on his arm. "Think you that your folk can defeat Yotha's wizards?"

Sulun gave a long sigh. "It's possible," he said. "But I wish it might not come to that."

3

Folweel was sitting at the table in his study when Patrobe entered. He waved the tall burly man to a seat without waiting on the usual formalities.

"You saw Hegg's body?" he asked without preamble.

"I did, Brother." Patrobe clasped his hands and settled into his chair with the smooth calm of a professional soldier or courtier. "We may assume it happened as those louts said: the stone slipped its harness and fell on him."

"He was ordered to anchor a curse into the mortar of the wall," Folweel explained bluntly. "The curse was deflected back at him, and that right quickly."

Patrobe held up two thick fingers. "Either his work was quickly detected and countered, or the wall was already well-wished. Hegg was skilled enough, trained enough, he should have detected a protective spell already set."

"Then there are three possibilities: first, the protective was subtly enough set that an under-priest could not detect it; second, the protective was set not on the uncompleted wall but on the entire house and grounds—"

"Damned difficult, to all accounts," Patrobe cut in. "So much area—"

"Third, the wall was not protected at all, but one or more of the Deese wizards discovered Hegg's work and counterspelled it."

"Quick work of them."

"Aye." Folweel steepled his fingers. "In any event, we are not dealing with amateurs."

Silence stretched while Patrobe considered that. "Subtlety, then. If they expect magical counterattacks, perhaps they'll not expect, say, a simple visit of Yotha's displeasure?"

Folweel smiled thinly. "Will tomorrow's weather be dry?" he asked.

The ritual in Yotha House began and proceeded much as usual. The flame on the altar leaped up from blue roots when Yotha's name was invoked, and burned there tranquilly during the hymns and the offerings. The tray full of collected coins passed through the flames harmlessly, as usual. A slightly substandard fleece (after being covertly sprinkled behind the altar) caught fire and went up in a spectacular blaze when it was offered to the flame, making the giver almost faint where he stood, but there were no other incidents.

Then came a brief memorial listing of the recently dead, which happened to include the name of Hegg Gebbi's-son.

The column of flame on the altar flared, leaped, danced, and finally shot an arm of fire to the southwest corner of the altar.

The congregation moaned, cringed and stared. The high priest chanted furiously for a long moment, and the flames finally retreated to their original size and shape. Folweel prayed loudly for understanding, then faced the flame for a long moment. When he turned to face the crowd, his face was quite calm, stern and composed.

"Thus saith the Lord Yotha, Master of Fire," he intoned. "The god is displeased at the death of his good servant. He holdeth certain of the living responsible for this good man's death, and shall not refrain from chastising them with his wrath."

The crowd groaned, knowing what that meant, and cast suspicious looks at their neighbors.

The high priest swung straightway into his sermon, as if it had been inspired by the omen of the fire: a long diatribe against sins of pride, avarice, undervaluing of the gods, disloyalty and abandonment of the path of virtue. No names were mentioned, but the congregation made its own guesses.

The noon bell rang, and Eloti stopped in mid-phrase. "Today's lesson is ended," she announced, rolling up the scroll in her lap. "Write one panel's worth of commentary to bring to class tomorrow. Gentlefolk, you are dismissed."

The little class of mixed adults, children and adolescents duly closed and stacked their tablets, tucked away their styli, and prepared to leave.

Eloti watched them sidelong while tucking scrolls into her basket. That fellow Duppa was still shielded throughly, still as bland as an apple, still utterly self-effacing at study. He was probably a spy from Yotha House. What to do about him, though? He'd certainly made no attempts at subtle spellcasting, spreading disaffection among the other students, or prying about the villa. He came, he studied, he went away, leaving as little mark of his presence as possible. Was he merely spying upon her lessons here at Ashkell Villa, or was he biding his time until some proper moment to strike? *No way to tell, not yet.* Eloti took up her basket, wrapped her cloak around her, and strolled toward the main gate, dismissing the problem in favor of the task immediately ahead. The ten league ride would take longer than the actual spellcasting, but it was unlikely she would finish before the usual dinnertime.

"Eloti, wait a bit." Gynallea caught her at the gate, plucked her sleeve and drew her aside to an untenanted corner of the courtyard. "Cook's girl went to Yotha's service this morning—on my orders, don't worry—and came back just now with a tale you'd best carry."

"What news?" Eloti lowered her voice and glanced once around the yard.

"Yotha has taken public notice of you and your friends, daughter. His flame spurted up when that dead spy's name was spoken, and the priests say 'tis because he wants vengeance for the man's death. Best watch for fires at Deese House tonight, my dear. Tell your friends that."

Eloti's lips thinned as she thought that over. "Dear Gynna, might I borrow the use of a faster horse, and perhaps a pair of your guards, for the ride home today?"

"Vari, I'll need your help." Sulun leaned in the door of the nursery, startling the children. "Tami, dearest, can you take care of the little ones for an hour or so?"

" 'Course I can," the little girl boasted. "Mama, are you going to make magic too?"

"Certainly not, dear. I've no gift for it at all. Stay here, now." Vari tugged on her cloak and followed Sulun out into the main hall. Even with the cook fires started, the big barnlike room could be chilly without the forge lit. "For that matter, Sulun, why are you still here? I thought everyone but those guards Eloti brought would be out helping her cast the spell."

"Like you, I've no talent for it." Sulun crossed to the water pipe near the millroom, shoved a bucket under its spout and turned the stopcock open. "Fill the other bucket and follow me. Ah, damn, we should have thought to buy more buckets. Well, no matter. If my guess be correct, we'll have to wet down only a single section of the wall."

"Wet down the wall?" Vari gave him a sidelong look as she shoved her bucket under the flowing spout. "That won't hasten the setting of the mortar."

"No, but it may prevent a certain nasty trick which I expect. Oof! There must be an easier way to carry these things . . ."

They dragged the sloshing buckets across the courtyard, up to the half-completed stretch of wall. In the long rays of the setting sun they could make out Eloti, standing a little ahead of the others, down by the gate. Occasional gusts of wind brought snatches of her song up to the wall. Arizun and Ziya stood just behind her, holding a fuming censer and a shielded candle, respectively. All the rest stood in a small knot further back, chanting along with Eloti. The frowns of concentration on their faces were visible even from here.

"Good, good," Sulun murmured, pacing to the end of the unfinished section. "With luck, they'll be back at the house before dark. Hmm, now Yotha's wizards won't know exactly where the accident took place, only that it was somewhere along this section. We'll have to wet down the whole thing. Damn. Ah, well . . ." He emptied his bucket over the last of the fresh-laid stones.

"I confess I've no idea what we're doing," said Vari, dutifully emptying her bucket on the stone beside Sulun's. "Do you mean to wet down this whole stretch? Gods, that's a dozen trips to the water, at least. Let's get Omis or Zeren to help us, or maybe those guards lounging about near the gate."

"Alas, we can't. The guards need watch for anyone sneaking close with kegs about them, and the others are needed to help Eloti's work." Sulun turned back toward the house for more water.

"I don't see what help they can be," Vari grumbled, following him. "Omis has no more gift for magic than I do, and I don't imagine Zeren has much more."

"No, but they can concentrate upon an image, and a magician can channel the force of that concentration for his—or her—use. Eloti explained it to me, more than once. I still can't see it. Neither can I seem to concentrate very long upon an image in my mind without playing with it, tinkering with it, which is not what a magician needs." Sulun shoved his bucket under the spout again. "I was designed by the gods to be a Natural Philosopher, a mechanic, not a magician. Let the others help Eloti; I do what I can with my own skills."

"Wetting down walls?" Vari shook her head, but loaded her bucket again.

In the thick brush by the stream Patrobe crouched in his dark brown cloak and held the pack donkey's halter rope. Waiting here in the rising chill of dusk was not his favorite duty; to be truthful, he would rather have been scouting and peering upstream with his under-priests. Still, if those two were, by some chance, seen and caught by the Deese wizards it would be far less of a calamity for Yotha House than if he were taken. Patrobe pulled his cloak tighter around him and contented himself with imagining the end of this night's work.

A soft rustle among the bushes interrupted his reverie, announcing that Gidd and Billot had returned. Sure enough, a moment later their dark-clad forms wriggled into view and slid down beside him near the stream.

"Well?" Patrobe asked quietly.

Billot recovered his voice first, while Gidd sucked on a wineskin. "Pah, dusty work," he panted. "We got within bowshot of the walls."

"No more than that?"

"They've guards out, Master; one by the front gate, one by the low part of the wall."

"And themselves are out walking the grounds," Gidd added. "I think they be spellcasting on the land. It felt that way."

"So? Did you note any manifestations?"

" 'Deed we did," Billot confirmed. "Beyond the foot of the hill 'twas suddenly cold and wet, like to a wall of mist—but there was no mist."

"Aye," Gidd put in. "We moved slow and careful, repeating the charm, but even so, we stuck our boots in mud and rabbit holes more often than not, and snagged on thornbushes, and met clouds of gnats. The very land is spell-protected, sure enough."

"Yes . . ." Patrobe interlaced his fingers and thought a while. "We must proceed very carefully, my children. Wait until full dark, then go forth with the greatest care. Move slowly as you must, knowing we have all of the night, and caution will serve you far better than speed. Use the charmed strings to guide your way back when you lay Yotha's trail; perchance they'll give you some protection against the land spell."

"What of the guards, Master?" Billot whined. "We'll not get close without they see us."

"Listen carefully: start wide apart, crawl as close as you dare. Gidd, you approach the gate, but come not so close as to be seen; lay your trail and come back, then light the fire. Billot, hear me well; wait until the first fire comes up toward the gate, and the guard at the wall goes to look at it. Then hurry you to the wall, fast as you safely can. Start the trail there, then retreat to where you'll be well hidden before lighting it. Mind the guard does not see you. Do you understand me well?"

"We do, Master," they said, almost in unison.

"Good." Patrobe got up and went to the donkey. A few quick tugs untied its pack, freeing two small kegs. He handed a keg each to his henchmen. "Be sure your tapers and flints are well tied in their pouches," he warned, "and keep repeating the charm until you're safely away.

"And be sure to make the trails thick and wide; let them not be so thin as to break or falter."

"No, Master," the men promised, already easing away into the brush.

Patrobe glanced up at the darkening sky, sat down and pulled his cloak about him again. At best, it would be a long wait.

The guards drowsed at their posts, barely sustained by warming-jugs filled with coals and smaller jugs of beer.

They glanced toward each other often, catching no more than a glimpse of silhouette or flicker of shuttered candle-lamp, wishing they hadn't been stationed so far apart. An hour ago one of the Deese priests had called down from the wall, kindly asking if they needed blankets, and that was the last they'd heard of another human presence. It was full dark now, and silent everywhere, and if not too chilly still not comfortably warm. Despite the promised pay—in silver, no less—there had to be better work than staying awake all night, waiting for an attack by wizards. Oh, this was a grim and wearing business, it was.

On the wall above, Zeren paced his circuit from the gate to the junction of wall and cliff face and back again. That cliff face bothered him; sometime in the future, they would have to wall off or sheer away all other possible slopes to the hilltop, lest some enemy get above them to throw down rocks, fire or scaling ropes on the house below. Not a problem tonight, though: he strongly doubted that anyone would attempt those steep, crumbling slopes in the dark.

At the gate top, he saw Yanados approaching. Her bow was in her hand, but her arrows still sat in the quiver. She seemed not at all tired, quite ready to walk her rounds until dawn if need be. He smiled, waving to her.

"What of the night, Captain?" she grinned, approaching. "I've heard nothing but the goats arguing in the barn."

"No more have I, but the night's far from old." Zeren turned to look down at the guard below. "Wotheng's fellows seem to know their business. I imagine we'll have some warning."

"You're sure Yotha's lads will come tonight, then? I'd hate to have to do this for the next moon or so."

"Who can predict? Still, I think they'll move tonight. Their god has a reputation for quick temper and quick action."

They leaned on the parapet, gazing out at the darkened land, hearing only the night sounds of wild creatures about their business.

"Have we changed much?" Yanados asked quietly.

"Aye." Zeren shrugged, making his cloak rustle. "We've needed to."

"And for the worse, as Sulun thinks?"

"Worse? No. Sulun broods too much over this little war."

"Ah, well, he was shaped by the gods for the scholars' tower and the laboratorium, not for such work as this."

"Third hell, were any of us born for such—Hey, look there!"

A light glimmered, far out in the dark: flame flickering, but blue as no flame should be.

The gate guard shouted and climbed to his feet. So did his companion by the unfinished wall. Zeren swore, pulled out his sword and hammered its butt on the iron gateway bell.

The flame came running toward them up the hill, crawling like a bright snake, flowing like water, straight toward the gate. Now the tips of the blue flames gleamed yellow, like spines on a dragon's back.

Running footsteps echoed in the courtyard below, Sulun's voice, mixed with Omis, demanding to know where the enemy was.

"Blue fire, running uphill toward the gate," Zeren shouted down at them. "Come up and look."

"Is it within Eloti's wards?" Sulun shouted as he scrambled up the stile to the walkway.

"Well within," Yanados pointed. "Stronger magic than hers, think you?"

Below them, the line of fire snaked up the road, making straightaway for the front gate. The guardsman there yelped and jumped to one side. His companion came running, had the sense or training to make certain his partner was unharmed, then stopped and stared at the oncoming flames. "Yotha begone, Yotha begone," he muttered, wagging his fingers in elaborate signs that had no effect whatever.

"Not magic at all," Sulun announced, watching it. "Common chemistry, not unlike our firepowder. But how could they have spread it so close . . . Wait."

Less than thirty yards from the gate the flame-trail stopped. It rose to a snapping tower of fire and danced there, lighting up the ground all around it, as if taunting the defenders of the house. One of the guardsmen covered his eyes, but after a moment dared to peep through his fingers.

"What made it stop?" asked a quiet little voice at Sulun's elbow.

He looked down, startled, to see Ziya staring at the column of fire. *Gods, this is especially cruel to her*, he thought, suddenly furious. "It ran out of fuel," he said, hearing a ring of contempt in his voice. "See there, where its tail is shrinking? That's where the fluid that feeds it has burned away. The rest will die soon enough." He leaned over the parapet and shouted at the fire column. "Shrink and die, you worthless conjurer's trick! Dry up and shrivel!"

The guards gaped up at him.

Sure enough, the fire-trail sank down and died. The column of flames grew no taller, whipped and darted for a moment in the light wind, then began to shrink. Within moments it sank to a ring of dying blue flames, then winked out. The sudden return of darkness made everyone blink and rub their eyes. After a moment, the guards sent up a ragged cheer.

"Did you make it stop?" Ziya asked.

"No, child," Sulun admitted, shivering as his anger passed. "I only guessed when it would stop of itself."

"It wasn't magic at all, was it?"

"No, not at all. Ask Eloti; magic can only well-wish or ill-wish. All the rest is elaborate tricks—like that one."

Zeren strode up, interrupting him. "Is that it, do you think? Have they done their attack for tonight?"

"Should be . . ." Sulun rubbed his forehead, trying to calculate with too many unknown factors. "They can't have much fire-fluid at any one time: too hard to make, needs too much wine for its source . . . Besides, who could come sneaking up to our walls with whole barrels full, especially unseen? And yet . . ."

"How much fluid is needed, to make that much fire?"

"Gods, I'm not sure. A kegful, at least."

"A stalking man might carry a single keg, but not more."

"True, true. They may be finished for the night. Yet, I was so sure they'd attack the wall, where the block fell."

"Hah, so that's why you set the other guard there?" Zeren leaned over the parapet and called down to the huddled guards. "You lads, did you see anyone come sneaking close to the new part of the wall?"

"No, sir," one of the guards retorted stoutly. "I been there all night, and seen none."

Zeren froze where he was, teeth showing in a sudden, unlovely smile. "All night—except for just now!"

"What, sir?"

Zeren turned his head just enough to growl at Sulun. "Diversion! Get to that wall and see who's about it right now. Hey, Yanados, go with him! You lad, hurry back to your post and tell me if you see, hear, smell or feel anything strange. Sulun, what did you say that stuff smelled like?"

But Sulun was already running for the unfinished section of wall. Yanados pounded after him, yanking an arrow out of her quiver. She almost bumped into Sulun as he skidded to a halt, sniffing fiercely, by the gap.

"Gods, it might be, but I can't be sure," he muttered, stalking forward slowly. "Keep watch; they might still be about. Where's that guard?"

"Ey, Masters," the guard called plaintively from somewhere ahead of them. "I don't know if it means aught, but I'd swear I could smell temple incense somewhere close."

Sulun looked where the voice sounded. "Gods, the scaffolding!" he yelped. "It's wood! We soaked it down but that might not be—Water! Yanados, come help me get water!"

He ran back toward the main building, cloak flapping. Yanados paused only to shove her bow and arrow back into the quiver before running after him. Vari met them at the door with two buckets and a large kettle, all sloshing full.

"You guessed, bless you," Sulun panted, picking up one of the buckets.

Yanados grabbed the other, Vari took up the kettle, and they all hurried back to the wall.

"The scaffolding," Sulun was panting as they climbed up onto the stone. "Wet it down, and the ground below it. Water, more water—Gods!"

"Here it comes again!" screeched the guard, pointing.

They could all see it: a narrow river of fire running up the hillside toward them. So fast it came, so wickedly fast.

Sulun swung his bucket in a narrow arc, splashing its contents all over the damp planks of the scaffold. "Get the ground!" he shouted. "The ground below! Hurry!"

Yanados and Vari unloaded their water at the same time, down the braces of the scaffold and onto the ground below.

The fire raced for them at windspeed, and again the guard leapt, howling, out of the way.

"More water!" Sulun shouted, dragging the others down from the wall. "If we can dilute it enough . . . Hurry!"

Vari and Yanados duly followed him, casting only brief glances back over their shoulders at the oncoming train of fire.

Zeren watched from the gate, cursing in a dozen different tongues, as the flame snake ran toward the wall. It wasn't going to stop a few yards off this time; the clever pig's-son who'd led it here had reached all the way to the wooden scaffolding, at least. Damn, that would burn like a torch if Sulun couldn't wet it enough. He pulled out his bow and nocked an arrow to the string, knowing it was futile. The sneak thief responsible would be far out of sight now, if he had any sense.

The fire-trail darted among the scatter of waiting stones and ran up to the wall, straight for the scaffolding.

And there it stopped, hissing and spouting fireballs, just out of reach of the waiting wood. Flames leapt, spat, crawled in all directions like a baffled flood halted by an invisible dam, seeking some way around it.

"Vozai, the water's stopped it!" Zeren laughed. "It can't reach—"

The cheer froze in his throat as he saw something else by the light of the frustrated flame.

A child stood on the wall, just beyond the scaffolding, almost within reach of the fire. It was Ziya, wearing a look that better belonged on a soldier in battle, and she was shaking her fist at the flames.

"Get down from there!" Zeren managed to yell. "The steam—"

And then Sulun scrambled up on the stones, lugging a bucket. He stepped past Ziya with barely a glance spared, and threw the water out over the scaffold.

The flames hissed, half-obscured in clouds of steam, and sank down to sullen blue niblets.

Yanados came up next, stared briefly, then emptied her bucket over the wall. Vari, barely a step behind, did likewise; then she swung the empty kettle on her arm, grabbed up Ziya and hauled her down from the stones.

Zeren let out a breath he hadn't realized he was holding. "Is it safe, then?" he called.

"Retreating," Sulun shouted back. "I think we've beaten it."

"Hail Deese and all his servants!" the guard crowed, daring to inch out of hiding. "Hail the Lord of the Forge, who has mastery over fire! Yotha has no power against him, nor his house, nor his servants! A very child can drive him away!"

"Oh, hush," Yanados snapped irritably. " 'Twas water did it."

"Knowledge did it," Sulun amended. "We all did it."

"Oh, yes, sir!" the guard laughed, unwilling to be cheated of his story. "Deese's wisdom, and all his wise servants: none can compare with them!"

"Oh, hell," Sulun groaned, realizing just how wet his robes were, and how cold the night. "Let's to bed, and sleep while we can."

4

By next evening, word was out all over Ashkell Vale; the wizard-priests of Deese had fought off the flames of Yotha, routed his balefires utterly, thrust him off from their walls and defied him while he slunk away. Workmen at Deese House patted the steam-blanched scaffolding for good luck as they labored—quickly, and ever so carefully—to complete the wall. Servants at Ashkell Villa made all manner of excuses, climbed into all manner of unlikely peeping spots, to look at the Wizardess Eloti while she taught her students. Enrollment in the beginners' class tripled.

Attendance at the rites of Yotha dwindled, though the fire displays thereat were spectacular enough to keep gossip running. The god was unquiet, as the priests said, because of wrongs done to him and his.

Gamblers, professional and amateur, argued lengthily over the odds that Yotha would attack again, or Deese retaliate. Ale-house conversationalists speculated merrily on what form the stroke or counterstroke would take.

Consequently, when a whole moon-quarter passed with no action taken on either side, people grew less gleeful and more fearful over the imminent battle. Gynallea noted that students at Eloti's school pressed close enough to hear her every word, yet kept distant enough to avoid any ill fate that might strike her. Wotheng, passing by Deese House while inspecting flocks pastured nearby, noted that the workmen were finishing the wall with amazing speed, as if they were eager to complete their work, collect their pay and hurry out of reach before the next blow fell.

The respective priesthoods, quite aware of the situation, kept their own council while they brooded upon these matters.

"This can't last," Zeren insisted, over the light noon meal. "Yotha's temple isn't used to losing money. The priests will take that as damage, no matter what we do, and they'll find a way to strike us."

"Our protections should hold." Sulun poked at a half-eaten bun on his plate. "They can't ill-wish us, or burn us out, or scare us with their trickery. Besides preaching against us, which hardly weighs heavy with the folk here, what harm can they do?"

"I wouldn't know, not being privy to the councils of Yotha's priests, but we can expect they'll do something as devastating as they can manage. We must take some action, something to scare them into accepting their losses and leaving us alone."

"What would you have us do? March against them with fire and sword? As I'm a true philosopher, I'll not strike first against any man!"

Zeren sighed, remembering all the times he'd had similar arguments with assorted commanders in the southlands. "What I'm trying to tell you, my philosopher friend, is that Yotha's priests believe you've already struck first—by reducing their income, killing their poor harmless observer and making a laughingstock of their god. They plot what they consider just revenge, and we'd best forestall it while we can."

Sulan tugged at his hair, disheveling it further. "We did nothing to harm their trade, that spy was far from harmless, and their 'god' attacked us. Anyone can see that."

"Anyone who chooses to, which Yotha's priests do not. This is not a case being argued in some pure and unbiased court of justice; this is more in the nature of a border war—and believe me, Sulun, I understand such things. We must take some action."

"Gods' blight! What would you have me do?"

Zeren leaned back in his creaking-new chair and looked at Omis. "The new bombard is overdue for testing, is she not?"

Omis stared at him, horrified. "You—you don't mean to attack Yotha's temple with her, do you? Great gods, we don't even know where it lies! And untested—"

"No, no," Zeren laughed. "Among other considerations, I doubt if our friend Wotheng would take kindly to a new military power at his doorstep. What I have in mind is a simple public display, something interesting, to amaze and delight our friends and . . . warn off our enemies."

Omis sat up, eyes narrowing a bit. "Just what," he asked, "do you have in mind?"

On the next afternoon, Doshi passed among the workmen at the nearly completed wall and warned them to keep away from the northern field for the next hour, for the priests of Deese would be testing a new magical device there. The work gang swore, one and all, that they had no intention of going anywhere near the northern field—indeed, had no reason whatever to go near that field, that not even goats bothered grazing in that barren field—which was quite true, especially since Arizun and Yanados had carefully herded the beasts elsewhere. Doshi expressed his delight at that news, and went back to the house. The work gang climbed the scaffolding and clustered on the new wall, straining to see the mysterious test.

Everyone saw the two largest and most muscular of Deese's wizard-priests lugging a strange object up the stile steps and onto the northern wall. The magical device appeared to be a thick, brass-colored tube, set in a sturdy wooden mount, treated with great reverence. The priests set it carefully on the top of the wall, turned it slightly here and there, raised and lowered the tube in its cradle until it was placed to their satisfaction.

Next, up onto the wall came two smaller wizards, one carrying a leather sack as if it contained powdered gold, the other bearing a heavy cannister of what looked to be well-greased, stiffened leather. The more sharp-eyed witnesses noted that the cannister was as big around as the inside of the brass-colored tube, and guessed that the one was meant to go inside the other.

Next came two very young priests, plainly apprentices. One bore an odd assortment of tools: long-handled round brushes and dashers as if for a butter churn. The other carried thin tapers or waxed-stiff cords in one hand and a tinderbox in the other.

After them, dressed in fine robes and carrying a meditation gem of black glass, came the Wizardess Eloti. Her face was stern and composed, she moved with slow and measured tread, and none could doubt the importance of her presence there.

As the workmen watched, the priests opened the sack and shovelled carefully measured handfuls of some mysterious black powder into the tube. They used the dasher-like tool to tamp the powder firmly in the bottom of the tube, then eased the greased cannister down after it. The smaller of the apprentices delicately maneuvered one of the oiled cords into a small hole at the back of the tube, working it in as far as it would go.

The wizardess rapped out a quick order, and all the other priests made a ring about the strange device and joined hands. The lady began to chant, and the others followed suit. The workmen couldn't quite hear the words, but none of them doubted that the chant was a powerful protective charm.

"Why be they doin' that, now?" Gort asked his companion. "I thought they'd bespelled all the house and grounds, even beyond the wall. Could yonder thing be especially dangersome, or would it need extra charms now that it be all put together?" His usual work was manning and repairing the derrick, and he had some skill at mechanics, as he was always quick to point out.

"Perhaps 'tis because it sits *upon* the wall," Hobb consider. His family had endured a long squabble over precise borders of sheep pastures, and he took careful note of physical boundaries. "Might be, their protection is set on the wall, and all below it, and all within it—but not on what rests *above* it. I hear spells can be particular that way."

"Like land deeds," Gort started to say, but stopped as his attention was drawn back to the wizards. The spellcasting was apparently finished, for the wizard-priests dropped hands, broke up their circle, and moved several paces away from the mounted tube. One of the priests struck a light from the tinderbox, set it to the projecting tip of the waxed cord, then hastened away to join the others. Everyone held their breath and watched as the flame sizzled redly up the cord and into the tube.

Thunder roared! Lightning flashed! Tiny storm clouds rose above the jerking tube, and a whizzing like enormous hailstones filled the air.

Out in the north field, a gout of earth leaped skyward and fountained in all directions.

The work gang cowered on the wall, jabbing quick lucky signs in the air and gulping bits of safety charms. But the priests of Deese gave a great cheer, ran closer to peer at the ravaged field and point to where the fountain had erupted. Others ran to the thunder tube and inspected it, patting it over and peering down its mouth as if it were a fretful baby. One of them took the long-handled brush and poked it down the tube, worked back and forth a while, then removed it and peered into the tube again.

"Perfect!" everyone heard the burly priest announce. "Not a sign of strain."

"She landed right within the flour circle," another shouted, peering out at the field.

Other priests whooped and hugged each other, and danced clumsy circles on top of the wall.

"Do it again," the burly wizard-priest insisted. "Another three times, at least, to be certain."

The apprentices ran back down the steps, to return shortly with more waxed cords and cannisters.

"What, again?" gulped the head of the work gang, peeping out from between his fingers. "Do they mean to plow the whole field with thunder and lightning?"

"Nay, look." Gort pointed to the field, where a small apprentice ran out and scattered flour in a circle. "I think they be testin' his aim, like an archer with a new bow."

"Be that a thunder bow, then?" the gang chief marvelled. "Gods defend, I'd hate to be struck with such an arrow!"

"I doubt not," Hobb considered, scratching his chin, "that Yotha himself would not care for it, either."

"Oho," said the chief, turning to look at his neighbors. "And do you note, he be aimed not a little in the way of Yotha's temple?"

"Aha," his audience answered knowingly.

By nighttime the tale had reached the villa, and by the next day it had spread all the length of Ashkell Vale.

"This be where the Fist of Deese struck, Master," Yawth said, pointing.

"I have eyes." Wotheng stood up in his stirrups for a better view. "A most impressive hole in the ground. Yes, well worth the ride, Yawth. See that the messenger is thanked properly."

"Aye, m'lord. There be other holes yonder. . . ."

Wotheng shook his head, still peering at the nearer hole. "One to study be enough for him with wit," he murmured. "They can aim this thing, you say?"

"Aye, Master. They were out measuring and all . . ."

Wotheng, preoccupied, didn't look up. "So great a hole, and at such a distance. Could it do thus to earth, what might it do to walls? Or to oncoming ranks of men?"

"Ey, sir," Yawth shuddered, "I wouldn't care to think."

"I daresay our most gentle and civilized friends wouldn't, either." Wotheng raised his head, lips pulling back from his teeth in a startlingly cruel smile. "They've the means, but not the will. No heads for warcraft. But if that might be changed . . ."

Yawth, knowing he was out of his depth, said nothing.

"A way can be found," Wotheng murmured. "A way to change their will, make more than one of them think like warriors. Aye, and then the northern lords might find my land less tempting."

He reined his horse around and spurred back toward home; Yawth following silently.

High Priest Folweel stood looking out the window of his study, saying nothing, his stiff back eloquent with outrage. Behind him Jimantam and Patrobe argued in furious half-whispers.

"—but your usual procedure failed! The rebound thereof has cost us badly in donations, not to mention the loss of faith among our herd."

"Well, what action have *you* taken? I haven't seen our herd giving more donations on your account."

"My account? I'm but the groundskeeper! I've delivered enough Blood of Yotha to fire half the vale; 'tis for you to put it to proper use. The Deese wizards have only the one thunder tube—"

Jimantam stopped there and bit his lip, as if he'd caught himself in an obscenity. He glanced to see if the high priest had heard.

Folweel had. He turned from the window and stalked

back to his colleagues. "Enough recriminations, please; they gain us nothing. 'Tis clear that we deal with a knowledgeable enemy—and, now, a dangerous one. Have you learned further about this thunder tube?"

Both priests looked at the floor and shook their heads.

Folweel sighed exasperation. " 'Tis also clear we must engage more subtle tools, and right quickly. Beginning tomorrow, start prophesying that the works of these new wizards are dangerous, treachous, harmful to the innocent. Also, warn the faithful that the very construction of this thunder tube is an outrage to the gods and a threat most undeserved to Yotha and his herd. Say, 'By what right do servants of Deese of the Forge steal the prerogatives of the storm gods?' Stress the impiety first, the undeserved threat to Yotha's herd second."

"Ah, Brother," Jimantam dared to interject, "a thousand pardons, but will not the weaker among the faithful assume that such warnings are simple jealousy?"

"Let them think what they will, but plant that warning well in their ears."

Patrobe noticed the hidden pattern in the instructions. "Brother, do you . . . expect . . . some disaster connected with the works of Deese's wizards?"

"Some subtle evil," Folweel admitted. "Brother Jimantam, pray fetch Brother Oralro for me. Then go fetch me an accounting from stores concerning the following herbs." He plucked a tablet from his work table and handed it to the priest, who wilted a trifle as he realized he was being dismissed.

The other two waited until he'd gone before resuming the discussion.

"Excellent for accounting, but no head for strategy, that one," Patrobe remarked toward the closed door.

"He serves his function, which has kept us from poverty." Folweel leaned closer and lowered his voice. "Still no spies established in Deese House?"

"No such fortune," Patrobe admitted. "They're a very closed lot, and the laborers at their wall aren't much better. The work will be finished soon, in any event, and the workmen dispersed, so there's no profit making further attempts among them. Bassip the Wagoner says they've even ordered less beer."

"Hmm . . . And Brother Duppa?"

"He reports regularly, that lessons proceed apace in mathematics, geography, history and literature." Patrobe snorted, dismissing such prosaic subjects. "He says the lessons on mechanics, chemistry and medicine are so simple and basic in nature that no one could mistake them for any arcane lore. At this rate, says he, they might consider him for acceptance in their order within a year, if at all. I doubt we can wait that long."

"We cannot." Folweel smacked the table in frustration. "Tell me the moment Duppa reports teachings of magic, or any art which the simple might construe as magic, or impiety . . . Hmm, bid him suborn one of the other students into asking questions on such subjects. Any answer the sorceress gives might be useful. Particularly, ask about Sukkti beliefs—but be sure to use the local word for them, to avoid suspicion. We may get something there."

"How great an excuse do we need?" Patrobe asked, pondering degrees of offense that common folk might accept.

"Enough to merit a small plague," said the high priest, glancing to the space on his table where the list of supplies had lately rested.

Patrobe raised an eyebrow. "Dangerous, Brother, to so risk our only well-placed agent."

"Place another," Folweel snapped. "Put him in the beginners' class—and make certain he be subtle, quick fingered and deft. Also send for Bassip."

Patrobe raised his other eyebrow, but said nothing.

5

The trouble began near the close of day, when the work gang were weary and hungry enough to think longingly of home and supper. The oldest of the lot, who'd been complaining of bellyache since lunchtime, succumbed first. He clutched his stomach, gasped, then howled. The workmen at the mortar trough ran to him just as he fell over. The gang on the crane and block had the training, or presence of mind, to finish lowering and setting the block before coming to see what the trouble was.

By then, some few of them had belly pains also.

When the uproar reached Sulun's ears, the problem had

spread to more than half of the work gang. Arizun rushed into the laboratorium to report widespread sickness, pains, chills, numbness of extremities, delirium and terrifying visions striking down the work gang.

Sulun slapped off the drive gear engagement of the lathe and jumped up from his bench. "Yotha!" he spat. "It has to be. Find Eloti and Vari, quick."

"They're already out in the courtyard, unless Vari's back in the storeroom hunting remedies."

"Thank the gods for that, at least," Sulun muttered, running for the courtyard.

The sight that met him was ugly: dozens of men rolling and shivering on the ground, others huddled against the wall, groaning through chattering teeth. Doshi and Yanados were just lighting a scrap-wood fire in the center of the courtyard as Ziya came running up with a sloshing kettle of water and a packet of willow bark tea. Omis and Zeren followed, bearing as many blankets, rugs and wraps as they could find. Vari and Eloti stood near the center of the crowd, peering frantically through a basketful of medical texts.

"Gods," Sulun groaned, seeing the sheer number of the afflicted. "Chills and fever—and the sun is going down." No one needed to tell him that the evenings could be chilly now that First Harvest was past. He snagged Omis on the way to hand out blankets. "Is the forge still lighted?"

"The forge? Yes, I was working on some tool-heads. But why—"

"The heat, man! That open fire won't be enough, nor those blankets for so many. Get the worst afflicted inside, close the shutters and curtains, and pump up the fire in the forge."

"Gods, of course!" Omis dropped the blankets and ran to Zeren to explain.

Sulun descended on Eloti and Vari, yanked out one of their scrolls and hunted through it, dismayed to learn that he didn't recognize half the terms therein. "Is it a curse or not?" he asked, thumbing through the scroll for some hint of an answer.

"No ill-wish: it's too specific," Eloti snapped back. "It's either plague or poisoning, and we've found no mention of any plague that attacks like this."

"Besides," Vari added, "we've taken good care to keep

the work camp clean. Those belly cramps speak strongly of bad food or bad water."

"But we drink of that stream ourselves," Sulun protested, "and none of us fell sick for it."

"Besides," Vari barely smiled, "this lot don't drink water when they've a regular ration of beer."

"Could it be their beer, then? How would Yotha's priests get at it?"

Eloti glanced up, face unreadable. "You think it's those priests' doing, then?"

"Of course it is! Zeren warned me . . ." Sulun ground a fist into his forehead. "Ah, gods, he warned they would strike, and I took no care to think how they might do it. I'm ten times a fool!"

"No, no," Vari soothed, patting his arm. "You're just too honest to think like such rogues. Now, how shall we examine their beer, if indeed they've left any?"

"The barrels." Eloti snapped her fingers and turned to look out the gate. "They keep their rations all in one shed out there, one of the ruins they haven't yet pulled down for building stone. Even the leavings at the barrel bottoms would contain any poison from the beer. Ask one of the less afflicted where they keep their rations."

"What if it wasn't the beer? The bread, perhaps, or the cheese, or—"

"Bring a dozen goats," said Eloti, already striding toward the work gang chief, who was still only in the cramps and shivering stage.

Yes, the gang chief remembered where the stores were kept—in the basement of what must once have been a wine shop, which still possessed a stout door. Yes, all food and drink for the workmen was kept there, and no one was allowed—or able, given how easily he'd be seen—to go plunder the same until proper lunchtime.

Sulun ran for the stables, shouting at Yanados to fetch out half a dozen goats from their shed. A few minutes later the big wagon came rumbling out of the stables, Sulun driving the mules in a manner that discouraged argument; Doshi, Vari and Arizun riding in the wagon bed behind him.

"Be they abandoning us, think ye?" Gort asked, between rattling teeth.

"And leaving their friends, too?" Hobb shook his head,

which made it hurt worse. "No, off upon vengeance or healing, say I."

"We'll see soon enough. Ah, gods, is that fire well lighted? Me for sitting thereabouts, do I have to crawl."

Half an hour later the mule wagon came thundering back, echoing the impact of every paving stone through the near-empty barrels in its bed. There, too, thumped sacks of bread, cheese, sausage and apples: all the stores of the looted basement.

Sulun reined the mules to a hoof-skidding stop, jumped off the wagon and ran to the nearest workman, which happened to be Gort. "Man," he asked, looking straight and guiltlessly into the bloodshot eyes, "tell me: what did you eat and drink this noon?"

"B-beer," Gort chattered, "and bread. Sausage. An apple . . ."

"Good, good." Sulun patted his shoulder and went to the next man. "And you?"

"S-same," Hobb shivered, "except I had ch-cheese instead of the apples."

"Not cheese, not apples," Sulun muttered, hurrying to the next coherent man he could find. "How shall we make goats eat sausage?"

Hobb turned to his partner and grinned as best he could. "Y-you thought they'd be l-leaving us," he jeered.

"W-was only askin'," Gort muttered, holding shaking hands out to the fire.

"Pardon me, pardon me," Omis muttered as he shouldered past them, carrying a struggling, howling derrick hauler in his arms as surely and gently as if it had been one of his own children.

Hobb peered after him through the open front doors of Deese House. "Th-they be layin' 'em down on rugs by the f-forge," he noted. "And the f-fire be blazin'. Fetchin' 'em closer t-to the god's m-magic, I expect."

"Or just g-gettin' 'em warmer," Gort muttered. "Oh, here, s-sir priest! Could we have one of th-those blankets?"

Sulun ran past, shouting, "Yanados, only two goats! Just the bread and the beer!"

"G-goats?" Hobb asked, clutching the blanket that one of the junior priests hurriedly tossed him. "Bread and b-beer?"

Gort only shook his head and reached for the other half of the blanket.

Vari came running up to the fire with a handful of shrivelled rootlets in one hand. She elbowed her way to the kettle of simmering water and threw the roots into it. "Eloti!" she shouted across the fire. "Nabian root! Nabian root! It opens the veins."

"Good," Eloti called back. "How many cups do we have?"

Yanados dragged two squealing goats to a hitching rail by the south wall and tied them there. The goats promptly started chewing on their tie ropes. She slapped their muzzles and yelled for Sulun to bring the bread and beer to her, since she couldn't leave the goats.

Omis came back out into the courtyard, looked around briefly, and went for another seriously afflicted victim.

Sulun came half-running across the courtyard, a sack of bread loaves in one hand and a sloshing pitcher in the other. He ducked and dodged past groaning and raving bodies, ran to Yanados, set down his burden and grabbed the nearest goat. "Hold it fast," he said. "How do I get its mouth open?"

Doshi, starting back for more blankets from the pile, halted suddenly with a perfectly horrified look spreading across his face. "Wotheng!" he gasped. "If they struck at our provisions, they might have struck his, too!" He changed course and ran to Sulun.

Near the forge, Zeren tackled and threw down the same raving man for the third time. "Must be a better way," he muttered. Then his eye fell on a coil or rope near the door. He hurried to it, cut a yard's length from the end, thought a bit and cut more. Trailing odd ends of rope, he went back to his charges and began tying them up. "Shut up," he explained to those who protested. "I'm trying to drive the devils out of you."

Sulun, busy pouring beer dregs down the throat of a most unwilling goat, listened to Doshi's warning without looking up. "Gods," he moaned, "it's all too possible. Take that shaggy brute Wotheng sold us—he's the fastest we have, I think—and ride straightaway to the villa. Warn them about the bread and beer, tell them we don't yet know which it is. Bring help if you can. Ask Gynallea if she knows any remedies for this sort of thing. Oh, hurry! The sun's going down!"

Doshi ran for the stables.

* * *

It was two hours after dark, and all of Yotha House was quiet and unlit save for the eternal flame on the temple altar and the high priest's study. Folweel was awake, if not overly busy. The scroll on his lap held only part of his attention; his gaze kept straying to the south window, and the smile that flickered over his face was not pleasant.

The distant sound of the gate bell ringing made him sit up so quickly that the scroll slid off his lap. He picked it up hastily, shoved it on the littered table, stood up and smoothed down his robes. "Back so soon?" he murmured, waiting for the inevitable knock on the door.

The knock came soon enough, but the figure which entered at Folweel's summons wasn't whom he'd expected.

"Pibb?" he snapped, with no preamble. "What in all the hells are *you* doing here?"

"Beggin' yer pardon, Father." Pibb bowed low, vainly trying to wipe his hands clean on his greasy leggings. "I was in the kitchen nook, gettin' a warm pint to sleep on, when her ladyship came poundin' in, yellin' for Cook. She wanted accountin' of all the bread and beer stores, and when they was brought in, and when used and all, and if anyone took sick from 'em."

"What? Lady Gynallea? Said *what*?" Folweel took two steps backward. "He couldn't have mistaken—And was anyone in Ashkell House sick?"

"None but old Nusher, and he's had the snuffles and wheezes for days, but her ladyship wanted all the bread and beer looked at anyway. 'Test 'em on the smallest pig,' says she. And then she wants some newmade sausage and a cup of hot cider for his lordship, and quick, says she, because he be ridin' out soon, and—"

"Wotheng, riding out tonight? Where?"

"That took me a bit of askin', Father, but—"

"*Where?*"

"Ey, ey, to Deese House, Father. They said 'twas either the bread or beer was poisoned there, and all the workmen sick, and they be tryin' to figure who'd done it, and they sent a messenger—one of the under-priests, I think it were, but I couldn't be sure—to warn Ashkell Villa lest it might have come there, too. His lordship was downright furious, he was: roarin' and bellowin' and haulin' his big boots on—"

"Oh, gods." Folweel slumped into the nearest chair. "How did they guess, and so soon?"

"I sneaked away when no one was lookin', guessin' ye'd want to know, and nobody saw me take leave, neither. I got a donkey from stables and came here straightaway, but 'tis my guess his lordship took his fastest horses—"

"Horses? More than one?"

"Oh, aye, Father. He took a handful of men with him, too. They went poundin' and clatterin' off down the west road, and none of 'em saw me go, so I came right here. 'Tis my guess they'll be better than halfway there by now. I wager they'll spend the night out of house. Should I go back, Father, lest I might be missed?"

"Oh, yes. Back. Here, and be careful." Folweel absently pulled a silver coin from his belt pouch and handed it to the kitchen boy, who stuffed it happily in his neck bag. "Take a pot of coals to keep you warm on the ride back, and remember to thank Yotha for his kindness."

"Aye, aye, thank ye, Father." The youth scuffed backward to the door, bowing repeatedly, and showed himself out.

"They knew . . ." Folweel muttered to himself, not watching the closing door. "They've told Wotheng, and he's riding there. . . ."

Suddenly another thought occurred to him, and he jumped to his feet. "Gods!" he shouted, lunging for the bell pull. "Dizzag, get up here!"

Repeated clangings brought a dishevelled under-priest to the door. "You wish, Father?" the man panted, eyes wide in bewilderment.

"Dizzag, take a fast horse and ride toward Deese House by the quickest route. At all cost, avoid Wotheng's party on the westward road! Find Patrobe, he'll be somewhere out in the fields near the walls, north of the road. Tell him *not* to loose the fire, you hear? My orders! Something's happened, and the fire must not be loosed. Bring him back here, bring them all back at once. Now go, and hurry!"

Dizzag bowed quickly, and fled. The door slammed behind him.

Folweel went to the south window and peered into the darkness beyond. "Gods," he groaned, "it may already be too late. As good as a signed confession. Gods, how did they guess so fast?"

He stayed at the window, watching, hope growing slowly as the night remained unbroken and black, wondering how long it would take for Dizzag's message to reach Patrobe and his men. Across fields, through sheep pastures, in the dark—or would Dizzag have the sense to take a shuttered lantern? How long? One hour? Two? He peered toward the distant nubbin on the starwashed horizon that was the hill of Deese House, hoping frantically that Patrobe would, with his usual exquisite care, take his time, enough time . . .

A pinprick of wavering blue and yellow light winked against the blackness.

Folweel slammed his hand on the windowsill and swore in three languages.

The half dozen riders had settled into a long, loping canter that ate up the miles without overtiring the horses. Wotheng cursed perfunctorily now and again, seeing it was expected of him, but his guardsmen saved their breath. They made good time, and the bouncing light of their lanterns on the road revealed landmarks that promised their goal was scant moments away.

Wotheng, riding in the center and free to look elsewhere than the road before him, noticed it first: a flare of blue-yellow light on a nearby hilltop. He shouted warning to the others, who reined in so quickly that they narrowly avoided running into each others' horses. They all turned to look, and froze where they sat.

A broad line of yellow-tipped blue fire snaked down the hill, across the shallow dip below and up the next slope. At the crest it divided, two fire tracks running parallel, then swooping away from each other, then turning back until they met and merged again. The single line of flame turned back into the middle of its previous pattern and weaved back and forth in a complex dance, for all the world as if it were a reed pen writing a letter.

The guards gasped, swore, mumbled obscure charms and gestured others. Wotheng cursed, partly at them. He might indeed have expected Yotha's priests to try spreading panic among his men. Best stop that, right now.

"Damned wizards!" he bellowed, rising in his stirrups. "What do you think you're doing, burning up pastureland? Do you kill any of my tenants' sheep, and I'll have you hanged!"

His men gaped at him in awe and amazement.

Pleased by the reaction, Wotheng swore further and more colorfully.

"Sir," one of the more level-headed interrupted him. "He—it's not moving, and the road's clear. Should we go on?"

"Hell's cesspools, yes! Since we've got such good light, let's make good time." He spurred his horse forward, obliging his men to get out of the way or ride with him. They kicked their horses forward, none willing to be last on the road.

The firelit hill fell behind them; the road snaked through a shallow valley and began to climb again. At this hill's top they could see the lights and hear the noise from Deese House. Wotheng pushed his tiring horse faster, up the rough-cobbled road and through the open gate in the wall.

He halted in the courtyard and stared, amazed.

A small horde of groaning men huddled under blankets and rugs around a roughset fire. Robed priests of Deese moved among them, giving them drink from assorted cups. Beyond the open temple doors, more men lay lightly bound and wrapped in rugs, moaning and raving, sweating in the heat from Deese's hard-blazing forge.

Tethered near the south wall were two goats, one of them backed away as far as its rope allowed, looking wide-eyed and frightened. Its companion appeared to have gone stark mad. The beast was bleating, leaping, stumbling, reeling and dancing, eyes rolling wildly in its head, flecks of foam on its jaw.

Close by stood Sulun, grimly watching the mad goat dance.

"By Vona's iron balls," Wotheng gasped. "Are you trying to magic the poison off into the goat?"

Sulun laughed, startled, and realized it was the first good laugh he'd had since noon. "No, Lord Wotheng, that's the beast I made eat the bread. The other got the beer, and it's well and sound, as you can see."

"Ah, that's good to know." Wotheng swung out of his saddle and went to tie up his horse as far from the raving goat as the hitching rail allowed. "In such case, draw me some beer and tell me what transpired."

Sulun led his eminent guest into the house, stepping carefully around the rolling bodies of the worst afflicted, through the first door on the left and into the common dining room. Wotheng's guards crowded in behind him, and they all settled at the end of the table nearest the neglected fireplace. Sulun did the fetching and serving, and lit up the fire.

"We'll have to drink from the jug, I'm afraid," he said, handing over an earthen bottle of better than average ale. "All the cups are in use outside. Did Doshi come back with you?"

"No, his horse was too tired for the return gallop—and so was he." Wotheng snagged the jug as it passed around the table end. "So the bread was poisoned, eh? I think we may guess who caused that. How was it done?"

"We're not sure. Zeren says the bread smells a bit odd, something he encountered once before, but he can't remember just what the poison was—except that it's something that can happen naturally in certain kinds of flour. That's why I wanted Doshi; his folk were farmers, and he might recognize it."

"Well, so might I. Bring me a bit of it."

Sulun went to fetch one of the offending loaves. Wotheng's men looked at him, at each other, and at the jug.

"Sir," one of them ventured, "can you be sure it's poison, as he says? Not magic? We know that was Yotha's fire, back on the hill."

"Trust a wizard to know his own business." Wotheng took a pull of the beer, then generously handed it around again. "We'll know soon enough once I've my hands on that bread."

Sulun returned, holding the heel end of a loaf almost at arm's length. "If only we knew what it was, we might find a remedy for it," he said, handing the bread to Wotheng. "At present we can do little."

Wotheng broke the bread, studied it, sniffed at it. "Coarse rye bread . . . some smell of mould . . . Hmmm."

He leaned closer to the fire, studying the color of the inner surface, then took an experimental bite. His men gasped and jumped away. Sulun started forward, then saw that Wotheng wasn't chewing. The Lord of Ashkell frowned fiercely and spat the mouthful of bread into the fire.

"Pfaww," he grumbled, wiping his tongue on his sleeve. "That's no more nor less than black rye mould! Uchh, filthy stuff. Kills horses. Aye, your folk have fevers and mad visions, do they? And belly pains? Hands and feet gone cold and numb? That's the black rye mould for you. How did that get in my good mill's bread? I'll have Feggle's hide sliced if he's ground bad flour . . ."

"The remedy!" Sulun cried. "What's the remedy?"

"Ey, the wife would know better than I. No, let me think. Jall, wasn't it two years gone that my good hunting horse came down with that? Do ye remember what the wife gave it?"

The near-left man pulled his lip, straining his memory. "I think 'twas raw beans, m'lord. Raw beans and . . . heh! Beer!"

"Those we have!" Sulun hopped to his feet and hurried out the door. They could hear him shouting to Eloti and Vari as he ran to the courtyard.

"Unmannerly of 'im," Jall huffed, "running off without a word of leave."

"Perhaps, but a good commander's instinct." Wotheng reached languidly for the almost empty jug. "You'll note, he didn't say a word about Yotha's fire. I wonder if he even saw it, being so busy caring for his men."

It was a small but grim delegation that rode out of the gates of Deese House next morning, for now they rode on the Lord of Ashkell's business, which was to determine the source of the mould-contaminated bread. From the gate itself they could all see the blackened mark burned into the next hilltop, and Wotheng swore blisteringly as he recognized it.

"All the gods assembled, that's the sigil of Vona!" he roared. "There, the lead letter of his name, within the shape of his sky hammer. How dare those Yotha dogs use it?"

He looked back fiercely to see if anyone was smiling. No one was, but his eye caught something else, something odd.

Up on the wall, sitting on top of that odd device which must be the gossip-famed Storm Tube, was a child of perhaps ten years old. The child (Boy? Girl? No telling, in those clothes) was glaring at the fire-etched mark on the hill and rhythmically patting the brass tube. *Cursing Yotha, doubtless*, Wotheng thought as he rode on down the slope. *But I'd hate to have such an expression turned toward me.*

Behind him in the rumbling mule wagon, Sulun and

Eloti were quietly arguing over possible remedies. Eloti was insisting that her collection of scrolls didn't tell enough, both rye and ergot poisoning not being common in the southlands where most medical treatises had been written, and she needed to talk to Gynallea. Sulun complained that this whole expedition might be dangerous, and she was too valuable for them to risk.

"And you're not?" Eloti retorted. "Who do you think our leader is, Sulun? Where would we all be, how would we live, without you?"

Sulun gaped at her, lost for words, ideas, or thought.

In the wagon bed behind him, Zeren chuckled. "Welcome to your new post, Commander," he said, clapping Sulun on the shoulder. "Never expected this, eh?"

Sulun only shook his head.

"Besides," Eloti smiled, "we have Zeren and Lord Wotheng and all his guards to protect us. Where would we be safer—or better needed?"

Sulun gave up the argument and turned his mind elsewhere. "The bread," he muttered. "Trace the whole track of the bread, every step. Who brought it to us? Where was it baked? Whence came the flour, and who carried it? Where it was ground, Wotheng's already told us. Where the grain was grown, he can discover also. Somewhere between the field and the workmen's stores the mould got into it, but the most likely places lie between the mill and the bakery."

"Both of which are owned by our good Lord Wotheng," Zeren added. "Don't think he's pleased with that thought."

"Indeed." Eloti considered. "Gods help those guilty when Wotheng—or his lady—lay hands on them."

What slaughters have we spawned, just being here? Sulun wondered, but did not say aloud.

"No, sirs! Never!" Feggle braced his back against the top millstone as if defending a falsely accused child. "I been top miller here these fifteen years now. Do ye think I don't know my own business? Do ye think I can't see nor smell bad grain? B'gods, m'lord, letting bad grain pass would damage my reputation and more; why, the evil would stick to my stones and poison every load to come through thereafter. Now do ye think I'd let my stones be dirtied so?" He patted the smooth, clean-cut boulder affectionately.

Wotheng and Sulun looked at each other, tacitly admitting the miller's point. Sulun thought a moment and tried another tack.

"Goodman, when was the last time you ground coarse rye flour?"

"Ey, let me think a bit . . ." Feggle rubbed his heavy chin, then went to a shelf on the nearby wall and pulled down a cord strung with tally sticks. "So, so . . . This be the last month's tally, every rod a day. This notch be one bag of barley, and that mark on t'other side be Dawp's mark—see? Now further down . . . here's four notches for wheat, with Cackle's mark." He ran expert fingers over the differing notches.

"Amazing," Sulun remarked, studying the tally sticks. "If ever you'd like to come to the new school and learn to put such marks on parchment . . ."

"Nay, I've no time for such, and these tallies suit me well enough. I'll send my boy, though." Feggle stroked rapidly through the rods, not even looking at them. Abruptly, his fingers halted. "There, m'lord." He shoved the stick forward, displaying the notches and mark. "There're five sacks of rye, and from Pibben's farm. They were the last of rye I've done. Pibben 'twas, but I know his grain's good; his grain's always been good, and I'd surely've noticed if 'twasn't."

"Pibben . . ." Wotheng's eyes narrowed in thought as he studied the tally stick. "Tell me, did he bring the grain himself or have it sent?"

"Why, he brought it himself, m'lord. He always does that."

"But did he take it away himself?" Sulun asked. "Did he wait here while you ground it and carry it off afterward?"

"Gods, no!" Feggle laughed, waving his thick hands. "Grinding takes a bit of time, it does, and there be so many wants grinding after first harvest, how should I do it all at once? No, m'lords, they bring it and leave it in the store-barn here, with their marks on the sacks, and I grinds it when I can. I barrels it after—or bags, if it be small enough—and puts it in t'other store-barn, and then the farmers come fetch it and pay me and take it home, or more likely they go straightaway to Tygg and sell t'him, and he sends his man to fetch it and pay me for the grinding."

"Tygg?" Sulun asked.

"Our baker," said Wotheng. "Would you remember, Feggle, if Pibben came and fetched his own rye or if Tygg's man came for it?"

Feggle ran his thumb over the tally stick again. "All this shows—see yonder cut in the middle?—'tis that the grinding was paid. But I know well enough Pibben sold it; his wife's a wonder at spinning and weaving, but she doesn't bake at all, no sir. He sold yonder rye to Tygg, be sure."

"I'll send a man to Pibben's just to *be* sure," Wotheng promised. "Now would your pretty stick tell us just when the rye was bought and carried away?"

Feggle shook his heavy jowls. "Nay, only when 'twas brought in, but I'll swear, m'lord, I don't keep grain overlong, lest it spoil. Yonder rye flour would've been ground within two days, no more, and gone no less'n a day later." He counted the sticks on the string, then counted further on his fingers. "It would've gone to Tygg's no more nor three days ago, and no less than two."

Wotheng and Sulun exchanged another look.

"Back to the villa, then, and to Tygg's," said Wotheng. "Let's see if his tallying is as good."

"And we'll pick up Eloti," Sulun added. "I'll guess she's learned much from Gynallea's medicine texts."

". . . these herbals to open the veins, the beer to flush the poisons out and the raw bean mash to counter the effects of the poison." Gynallea wrapped up the bundle of packets and handed it to Eloti. "How are the workmen doing?"

"When we left they were resting quietly. What simples we had did them some good." Eloti hefted the bundle, face abstracted. "This won't be the end of it, I suspect."

"No," Gynallea sighed. "You will have to settle with High Priest Folweel, in some permanent fashion, and that soon. Have you any plans?"

"Several, none of them sure." Eloti took a small polished disc of obsidian from her belt pouch and weighed it thoughtfully in her hand. "In any case, we must get into Yotha House and confront that man."

"Daughter, even my Wotheng must walk soft there! Be utterly careful of words with the high priest."

"It's not words I have in mind, dearest Gynna."

"A wizard's duel, then? At the very center of Yotha's power? Is that wise?"

"Not a duel, not there," Eloti admitted, sliding the disc back into her pouch. "We are, as you've doubtless guessed, not precisely nor entirely wizards."

"Ah, some help from your mechanical knowledge will be needed, then?" Gynallea smiled knowingly. "Choose your ground with care, my dear. Have many alternative tactics in waiting, and let everyone know their part well."

"That, unfortunately, is the problem. Sulun wants no such battle; he'll not attack."

Gynallea pursed her lip. "Commendable, but . . . difficult. Plan elaborate defenses, then. And . . . try to shape, in advance, the attack your enemy will make."

Eloti grinned humorlessly. "That," she said, "is the difficult part."

Tygg the Baker looked and spoke much like his counterpart at the mill. "Of course I inspected the flour, m'lord!" he huffed, absently patting his nearest oven. "I always inspect it myself when it arrives, if not before I buy. Great gods assembled, d'ye think I'd pay good silver for bad flour?"

"You inspected Pibben's rye, then, at the mill?" Wotheng asked. "When was that?"

"Nay, not at the mill,'" Tygg admitted, clenching his broad fists in his coarse bleached apron. "I've bought from Pibben these many years, and never had complaint. I looked at the barrelful when it came here, and 'twas good then, as always 'tis."

He ambled down the crowded bakery hall to a side room, which he opened with a heavy iron key. Within lay shelves of stacked tablets, a writing table and chair, and a large money chest bolted to the floor. He poked through the tablets, pulled one out and shoved it in front of his questioners. "There, yon's the mark for Pibben, and this for rye, and this for the amount. If 'twere bad, I'd have marked it other."

Sulun, hoping to find a literate accounting, was disappointed to see more tally marks cut in the wax. "Do you recall," he asked, "when the flour arrived? Or when it was baked? Or where you sold it?"

"Oh, aye." The baker pointed his thick finger at further

marks on the tablet. "See here: that means it came two days agone. I couldn't say when 'twas baked or sold, but it must've been right soon after. I—I bought it to bake for your work gang, m'lord wizard . . ." Tygg wilted a little. "They like the rye bread, they do, and the price is . . . well, quite fair, sir."

"Buy cheap and sell dear, I know." Wotheng grinned, making his moustache bristle. "I've no complaint with honest profit."

"Nor I," said Sulun, seeing where this led. In truth, grain prices here were astonishingly low compared to what he remembered in Sabis. "I only ask, did you send any other bread to my work gang these four or five days past?"

"Oh, no, m'lord wizard," Tygg waved his big hands in denial. "I bake and send to them but once a seven-night. My wagon man'd be too busy, else, for my other work. I send all around the vale, y'know, m'lord."

"So this was the load that was . . . tainted, and no other?" Eloti asked, stepping forward.

"M'lady, I'll swear on a dozen gods the flour was good!" Tygg wailed, almost tiptoeing a step back from her. "I looked when I bought it, and 'twas clean!"

"And how long between the time you bought it, and inspected it, and when you baked it?" Sulun asked, looking for the sequence, the timing.

"No more nor a day, I'll swear." Tygg rubbed his sweating forehead, then automatically wiped his hand on his apron. "I bought the flour 'specially because 'twas time to bake for the work gang again. One can't be late with food for that lot, y'know."

"I know." Eloti smiled, considering the uproar a gang of hungry workmen would make if their bread didn't arrive. "You bake for them once a seven-night, then, and send it out how soon after?"

"Wh-why, soon's 'tis out of the oven. It must go soon, d'ye see, for it's got to last seven days, and for all that rye bread stales but slow, in seven days 'twill be a bit stiff, so the sooner 'tis delivered, the better." The baker shrugged eloquently.

"Sir Baker," Eloti purred, well knowing the answer, "is there any means by which the ergot could have entered the bread after it was baked?"

Tygg struggled mightily with his fear and conscience,

finally had to admit, "Nay, couldna," in a defeated voice. "If it struck then, 'twould only dot the crust with black spots, easily seen and cut off."

"So the ergot entered the flour sometime between the hour when you inspected it and when you baked it?"

"Aye," Tygg almost whispered, "while 'twas here, in my storeroom . . ." Then he brightened, seeing a possibility. " 'Twas there almost a day. Anyone could have come in and traded it for bad flour while I wasn't looking."

"But wouldn't you have noticed the change when you went to bake it?" Wotheng cut in. "Surely you'd have seen, or smelled, if something were wrong when you went to measure it out."

"But—but—" Tygg bounced on his wide feet in agitation. "I confess, I didn't bake that load! I've so much to bake, y'know, m'lord, I can't do all at once. 'Twas only common rye bread, if all be told, and I'd the more dainty breads and cakes to do, as I can't trust to 'prentices, y'know." He waved a dusty hand toward the bake shop, where easily half a dozen assistants were measuring flour, rolling dough and tending the ovens. "I left the rye bread baking to . . . gods, who was it? Ey, 'twere Meep and Higgle!" He stomped to the door and bellowed, "Meep! Higgle! Get your lumbering feet in here, and be quick!"

A fat boy and a stout woman jumped as if they'd been stabbed, pulled their hands out of huge basins of flour, and came hurrying in.

"Aye, Master, what's the matter?" the woman asked, shifting from foot to foot as if her arches pained her.

"I'm hurrying with the barley bread," the boy whined. "Gods' truth, I'm hurrying, Master Tygg, it's just that—"

"Never mind you that," Tygg snapped. "Which of you baked the rye bread that went out yesterday morn?"

The two baker's assistants looked at each other, Meep woeful, Higgle smirking. " 'Twere *he* done it," Higgle pointed triumphantly to the cringing fat youth. "I lost the toss, so's *I* had to haul the wood and light it off and sweep out the oven and tend the fire and such—while *he* made the bread."

"Aw, Master," Meep whined, "I ain't never made rye bread before. The loaves looked right when they came out t'oven, crusts dark like *she* said. How's I t'know they weren't right?"

Tygg heaved a mountainous sigh—of relief? Exasperation? "And what was wrong with them?" he asked.

Meep's jaw dropped, flapped a bit, quivered. "I—I don't know, Master. Did I make the dough too heavy? Not baked long enough? Ye *said* t'leave 'em a bit moist, as they was t'last awhile. . . ."

Tygg was about to say something, probably explosive, but Eloti touched his arm and he jigged away in silence. "Listen, boy," she crooned hypnotically at the young lout, "you know who we are, do you not?"

"Y-yes, m'lady. Ye're one of the new wizards as serve Deese." His plump cheeks quivered as he tried to edge away, but Eloti caught his face neatly between her hands.

"Think, boy," she murmured, fixing his eyes with her own. "Remember well, from the beginning. When did you come to work that day?"

"T-two hours afore dawn, like always," Meep whimpered, staring.

"Were you first in the shop?"

"I came in . . . after Higgle. She'd the key."

"And what next?"

"She said t'make the rye bread, and I said—"

"Never mind what was said. What did you *do*?"

"I—we argued, and then we tossed a copper, and she lost . . . so she went t'get the firewood and I went t'get the rye flour, and—"

"How did you know which was the rye flour?"

" 'Twas in the barrel Master Tygg showed me the day afore, the one with the half-moon scratched in the wax."

Eloti shot a quick glance at Sulun, who nodded. "You went to get the flour," she said. "So you opened the barrel?"

"Nay, m'lady. 'Twas already open."

"You mean, the lid was loosened or the lid was off?"

" 'Twas off. I thought Higgle'd been there first. I took up the scoop and filled the big measure—"

"I'll fetch't," said Tygg, hurrying off.

"And did you notice anything different about the flour?" Eloti went on.

"N-no, m'lady. How would I? I'd never made the rye bread afore." Meep wrung his hands in unconscious imitation of his master.

"So you took up the measure full of flour. What did you then?"

"I brought it back t' the shop room and poured it into yonder big mixin' pot, and put in the sweetenin' and the leavenin' and then the butter and eggs, and last the milk, and then I stirred it with the big paddle, and then I let it sit and rise."

Tygg came back in, holding a measure cup the size of a half barrel. "This be the big measure, m'lady," he said, then halted as he saw that the odd interrogation wasn't finished.

"And what did you do while the bread rose?" Eloti asked.

"Ate some buns. They were left over from the day afore, would've gone t'waste, else . . ."

"*And* crackin' jokes at me, while I warmed up th' oven," Higgle added.

"And then what did you?" Eloti bored on.

"W-went back t'see how it'd risen, and it had."

"And did you notice, then, anything strange about the dough? Did it look right? Smell right? What?"

"Nay, it looked right enough—risen right well, good and high. It smelled sour, but rye bread always does, far as I know."

"So what did you next?"

"I patted it in loaves."

"You didn't punch it down and leave it to rise again?" Tygg fumed. "Ye lazy lout, I should clout yer head!"

"Hush," Sulun restrained him. "Let's hear the rest, first."

"And what then?"Eloti insisted.

"I put the loaves in the oven, and bade Higgle watch 'em."

"That he did," Higgle volunteered. "Left me t' watch, and went off t' stuff his face on more sugar buns."

"And were you alone in the shop all this time?" Eloti asked.

"Oh nay, m'lady. Swarp and Dirrot and Buj and Master Tygg came in a bit after us, and they was workin'."

"Aye," Tygg muttered. "I should've seen him nippin' the leftover buns . . ."

"But did anyone go to the storeroom before you?" Eloti insisted.

"Nay, we was first there, afore the others came in."

"That's true," Higgle agreed. "We come earliest."

"Then what became of the dough left in the big mixing pot?" Eloti asked.

Meep looked blank. "I don't *know*, m'lady," he blubbered.

"I cleaned that out." Higgle wrinkled her nose. " 'Tis the job for whoever's tendin' the fire. I lost the toss, as we said."

"Where did you wash it?" Eloti asked, releasing Meep and turning to Higgle. "And what did you do with the washings?"

"I washed it in the back yard," said Higgle, righteously holding her ground. "I threw the washings in the slops bucket, for t' take t' Mistress Tygg's pig, after."

"Aye, gods!" Tygg slapped a hand to his forehead. "So *that*'s what ailed the pig yestere'en!"

"You didn't eat any of the dough yourself?" Eloti insisted.

"Nay, m'lady," said Higgle, wrinkling her nose again. "Why eat sour old dough, when I could have leftover cakes later?" Abruptly she blushed, and looked sidelong at Tygg, who rolled his eyes heavenward and muttered about greedy apprentices eating up his profits.

"So," said Eloti, turning back to Tygg. "Meep says he used one large measure of rye flour. If that's the measure, there must still be more flour left in the barrel. May we see it, please?"

Without a word, Tygg led them to the storeroom at the other end of the bakeshop. The room was stone, windowless, with only one other door that led—as Sulun confirmed with a swift look—out to the back alley where the wagons were unloaded. The doors were stout, tight and well barred. There was no sign of rats, though a plump cat patrolled there, and the floor was quite acceptably clean.

Tygg pointed to a barrel in the near right corner, one marked with a simple half-moon cut into a splash of wax. "That be the one," he said, keeping his distance.

Sulun and Eloti approached the barrel cautiously, as if it might bite. Wotheng stayed back by the door, watching both of them and the baker. Eloti lifted off the barrel lid and peered in.

"Is it customary," she asked, "for your rye flour to be so gray in color?"

Tygg jumped as if stung, and ran to the barrel. "No, by all the gods," he said, staring into its half-filled depths. " 'Tis supposed t'be faintest hint of brown, no more." He reached in, pulled up a pinch of the flour, spread it on his palm and looked closely. "I'd be sure in better light," he whispered, "but I think I see fine flecks of black in this." He sniffed cautiously at the thin spread of flour. "It doesn't smell bad, though."

"Let us test further." Eloti scooped out a handful of the flour and walked back toward the shop room. "Please fetch me a small bowl and a bit of sweetening and milk."

Tygg practically fell over his feet, running to comply with her wishes.

It took but a moment to mix the ingredients in the right proportions. Tygg asked if she wanted oil, leavening and eggs too, but Eloti assured him it wasn't necessary.

"If this is indeed the mould I think it is," she explained, pouring out the mixture on a small plate, "then water and food is all it needs. Now let us put this in a warm place for . . . how long does it usually take for rye bread to rise, Master Tygg? Half an hour? Good. Let us take our ease for so long."

Tygg obligingly brought bench seats, cups of his own beer, and a dish of his best sweet rolls, and did his best not to look at the suspect mixture in the bowl near the oven. His staff worked furiously at their business, not daring to look lest Tygg's eye and wrath fall on them.

Wotheng drank his beer in leisurely fashion, wiped off his moustache and calmly asked, "Goodman, who was present in your shop between the time you first opened the barrel of flour and the time it was baked?"

Tygg paused, half-turned to watch his underbakers, his eyes unfocused with the effort of memory. "Hmm, ah, everyone here, of course—all my help. Also the wagoner who brought it. Many of the villa folk came in and out to buy . . . Ah, gods, I can't remember how many came and went!"

Eloti gave Wotheng a brief nod of respect, then asked, "How many of your customers came into this room, let alone into the storeroom?"

"Ey, why, none." Tygg looked relieved for a moment, then sobered as he guessed the implications. "I swear, I'd never believe any of my lot would poison their own bread!"

"I find that hard to believe, also," said Sulun. "How many of them went into the storeroom that day?"

"Gods, I can't recall!" Tygg rubbed his sweating jowls in

distress. "All of them, I don't doubt, for I had them all at work mixing and baking. I do try, m'lord, t' make 'em knowledgeable at all stages of the baking."

"But then . . ." Wotheng sat up, moustache bristling. "None of them could be sure that another 'prentice wouldn't walk in on them while they were putting the mould in the flour. Most risky work, that."

"Oh, aye!" Tygg grinned from ear to ear, seeing hope that his household was no longer suspect. "They were runnin' in and out all the day, safe for lunchtime. . ." A beatific smile spread across his sweating face. "I recall, m'lord, the barrels came from the mill just afore lunch. I tapped and 'spected 'em, paid the wagoner, and then all o' we sat down to eat together. They were all there, m'lord; none left the table afore I did. Not one of 'em got to be long alone in the storeroom: not one, sir!"

The other three exchanged glances. "How long," Eloti inquired, "would it take to empty . . ." She thought a moment, trying to remember the ratio of dark flecks to pale flour in the barrel ". . . say, a pint of mould into the flour, and stir it well enough that it wouldn't be noticed when measured out?"

The baker stopped and thought about that. He closed his eyes, measured invisible volumes with his hands, made pouring and stirring motions, then sighed. "To pour, almost no time. To stir so well . . . a good minute or two. Not long, I grant. Still, at any moment others might have come in and seen the miscreant at work." He gasped suddenly. "But wait! M'lord, m'lady, think: how would he stir the flour well, save with his hands and by reaching well into the barrel? How should he do that without daubing his arms clean up to the shoulder with flour? I'd have noticed anyone floured so far up the arms! By the gods, m'lord, I would; y'know I pride myself upon having my bake shop so clean."

"Good wit, Tygg," Wotheng approved. "Just to be sure, I would like to ask each of your lot—separately and quietly, you understand—if they noted anyone come out of the storeroom with flour up to the shoulders."

"Do so, m'lord," Tygg grinned. "Yet I think if any had seen such, they'd have told me. As ye've heard and seen, my 'prentices do rival with each other a bit—aye, and carry tales, too, hopin' for an inch more of favor."

"And sweet buns." Wotheng smiled with him. "I'll ask, anyway, but I do believe you're correct, Master Baker."

"Unless, of course," Eloti interjected, "the miscreant stirred the flour with a paddle or stick.'

"Paddle? Stick?" Tygg glowered. "Not in my storeroom. I keep the paddles out here where they be needed, near every moment. Anyone seen goin' into the stores with such would surely be noted, and 'marked upon. Besides, where would the poisoner have carried a pint measure of black mould, goin' into the stores, and it not be noted?"

"The mould might have been hidden in a bag under the clothes," Sulun considered, "but you're right about the stirring. Where could anyone have hidden even a stick that was long and stout enough to quickly mix a pint of mould into a barrel of flour?"

Wotheng frowned and rattled his fingertips on his knees, and Sulun could guess the man's thought. Either the faithful old baker was lying, which seemed very unlikely, or the poisonous mould had somehow magicked itself into the barrel. *Reconstruct the sequence*, was all he could think of.

"Try hard to remember, good Tygg," he said. "When was the first moment you saw the barrel?"

"Ey? Why, when it came off Bassip's wagon, Sir Wizard."

"What, he brought it to your door himself?" Sulun couldn't imagine any one man shifting that huge barrel alone.

"Ah, I see what ye mean. Nay, sir, I first clapped eyes on it when 'twas *on* the wagon, when the carter came knockin' at the door. I helped him roll it into stores myself. Oh, and I'll take oath, the lid was on it firm and tight then, and sealed with good wax, as Feggle always does it."

"And then you opened the lid?" Wotheng took up the thread.

"Aye sir, right then: opened and looked, and found it clean, on my oath."

"And did you pay the wagoner right then?" Eloti asked, eyes narrowing. "Had you the money in hand when you brought the barrel in?"

"Eye, not so. I went to my officium to fetch it. Then I came back and paid him and he left, and I called my lot off to lunch, and there's an end to it, for surely no one could have come into stores while I were out fetchin' the money without the wagoner would have seen 'em."

"True, true," murmured Eloti. "And are you certain you closed and barred the storeroom's outer door after the wagoner left, before you went to eat?"

"Aye, for certain, good lady. Don't I know well enough that rats and thieves get in when doors swing open?"

"Hmm. So after lunch everyone went back to work and the apprentices came in and out, and at day's end you locked up fast, I trust?"

"Oh, aye, be certain."

"And you're also certain no one could have come in again before Meep and Higgle yesterday morning?"

Again the baker struggled with his conscience, and again his conscience won. "Aye, m'lady. No door nor window forced, nothing touched. Nor none other thing. Look you all." He pointed to the doorsill, which had been recently swept clean. " 'Tis an old baker's trick I had of my father. Every night afore leavin', I sprinkle a bit of flour about the doors and under the windows. Every morning I sweeps it up to keep the rats away. If any thief, nay nor anyone, came in durin' the night, by whatever means, they'd've left tracks in the flour and on the floor beyond. No way to hide it, save by sweepin' up all the flour. Either way, I'd have noted *that* when I came in by morning."

"Marvelous!" Sulun admitted. "I must teach that trick to my people."

"Aye, would ye that?" Tygg beamed, flattered.

"So, to go on," Eloti murmured, "Meep and Higgle came in, Meep made the rye bread while Higgle tended the fire, then the loaves were packed and sent off by your wagoner. And no one else touched the dough?"

"As ye've heard." Tygg shrugged. "I swear, I cannot understand it."

"Yet someone did despoil the flour, as you can see." Eloti pointed to the warm bowl of rough dough.

They looked. They could all see that it had risen slightly, by itself, with no yeast added.

Tygg grabbed the offending bowl with a curse, and threw it into the fire. " 'Twas magicked there, good folk," he pleaded, "I'll swear, it had to be!"

"Fear nothing," Eloti smiled gently, patting his thick

arm. "I'm sure it wasn't you nor any of your people who
tainted the flour."

"Deese and Kula know it," said the baker, fervently
clasping his hands.

On the way back to their mule wagon, Sulun chewed
the problem over. "I swear," he admitted, "I don't know
where to search next. If Feggle and Tygg are honest,
and—" He threw a quick look to Wotheng. "—I'm sure
they are, then the poisoning happened in Tygg's shop, yet
no one there could have done it."

"I should go back and question the kitchen drudges
singly," Wotheng remembered, stopping where he was.

"Not necessary," said Eloti. "None of them did it."

"Eh?" Wotheng gaped at her. "How do you know?"

"Consider." Eloti ticked off on her fingers. "The flour
arrived just before lunch. The kitchen help wouldn't have
gone to fetch more flour, do more measuring, mixing or
kneading, just before lunch; no, they'd have been finishing
their tasks, not starting new ones. Any of them doing
otherwise would have been noticed, and reported to Tygg,
by his rivalrous fellows. So would anyone, after lunch,
who took a mixing stick or paddle into the storeroom—or
who came out of it with flour high up on his arms. No one
broke into the bakery during the night, or Tygg would
have seen it in his flour-trap on the floor. Meep and
Higgle tossed a coin to see who would bake and who fire
the oven, so there was no predicting in advance which of
them would go to the stores and get to the rye flour. They
might have conspired together to taint the flour, but I
doubt it, from the lack of love between them. By the time
the other apprentices came in, it was too late; the flour
was already mixed to dough, if not in the oven."

"But if none of the apprentices—" Wotheng huffed. "I
can't believe Tygg would—"

"Surely not Tygg. But who was the one person left alone
with the opened barrel of flour while Tygg went to his
officium to count and fetch the money?"

Wotheng had the presence of mind to whisper it. "Bassip
the Wagoner!"

"If, as Tygg says, he also delivered the bread, then I've
seen him coming and going at Deese House." Eloti smiled
grimly. "He could easily hide a pint measure bag under

his cloak, and he would know where the rye bread was bound."

"But," Sulun remembered, "how would he stir it in? Tygg would have noticed flour on the man's arms."

"He drives an oxcart, remember? And he always carries with him his *long-handled* driver's whip."

Zeren was no longer guarding the mule wagon when the others came up, but that wasn't necessary. Half of Wotheng's guards were watching, a few copying the motions, as he showed them one of his favorite moves.

". . . so you drop low—low as you can—as you step forward, getting under his shield. Lift your own shield, so, to block any downward chop and also to block his sight of what you're doing. Then come *up* with the sword at the exposed body. Up, you see? If the other fellow doesn't counter early, there's almost no defense against it; I've rarely seen it fail."

Wotheng raised his bushy eyebrows and turned to his companions. "How very many skills your folk have. Think you yonder large priest might be persuaded to come give his lessons more regularly?"

"I'm sure of it," Sulun agreed. "But at the moment, what shall we do about our poisoner?"

"We'll lay hands on him shortly, that I assure you." Wotheng's smile didn't reach his eyes, which were as chill as Sulun had ever seen them. "The wife doesn't bake either, having much else to do. We've our bread delivered at about this hour every morning. Ho, fellow!" he called to the nearest guard, interrupting the sword lesson. "Has Bassip the Wagoner come yet with the bread?"

"Why, yessir," gawped the nearer guard. "Has yer lordship been learning magecraft, then? Bassip's only just come his round, bein' at the tailor's shop last, and I think he be at the kitchen right now."

"Come along, then," said Wotheng between his teeth. "I've much to say to that man, and I intend he shouldn't wiggle away before I've said it."

"Er, Lord Wotheng," Sulun put in, looking pale, "If you intend to put the man to—to torture, I beg your leave to retire."

"Pshaw, not now," Wotheng almost laughed. "Torture's no good for wangling the truth from any man, I learned well enough from my father. Cause pain enough, and the pained will say whatever he thinks the questioner wants to hear. No, 'tis clever questions—and p'raps a well-timed lie or two—will get the story. But that's a tedious business, and no sense to trouble you with it. Pray, go dine with my wife while I front this wagoner. I'll speak to you soon enough."

He strolled off, whistling between his teeth, with his guardsmen shambling after. Sulun, Eloti and Zeren looked at each other.

"Doshi's inside," Zeren told them. "He and his horse are rested well enough, he can ride whenever we want. Where do we go next?"

"To lunch, as our host said." Sulun shrugged. "I think the investigation is out of our hands now, and if we've had little rest, we may as well have food."

"Besides," Eloti added, half to herself, "I've much to discuss with Gynallea—such as what, precisely, we must do about these pesky Yotha priests."

Wotheng laid his plans with some care, pausing to make a few quiet arrangements before strolling into the back of the kitchen where Bassip the Wagoner lounged against the doorpost and chatted with the cook.

"Ah, the good wagoner!" Wotheng chirped, coming up on the burly ox driver as if by accident. "What luck! Pray lend me your whip a moment."

He snatched that item out of the startled wagoner's belt and carried it back into the kitchen, whistling merrily as he uncoiled the whip's tail from its usual resting place about the handle. Bassip, both curious just what Wotheng intended and unwilling to let his primary tool get out of his sight, trotted after his lord into the kitchen. Behind him, two guardsmen quietly eased through the kitchen door, closed and barred it after themselves, and followed.

Wotheng went to a long wooden table, pulled a heavy cleaving knife off a rack above it, and—before Bassip's horrified eyes—chopped the body of the whip cleanly off the handle.

"Ah, don't fret so," Wotheng soothed the man's wailing outrage. "I'll give you a far better one soon enough." He reached for a plate that lay nearby, set the chopped whip handle upright on it, and began and unbraiding the leather straps that bound the handle's core. "I confess, I've always yearned to know what lies under all this leather. Is it bone, horn or wood? Aha, 'tis whittled bone. From an ox's thigh, perhaps? Ah, and what's this pale stuff?"

Patches and streaks of off-white powder appeared on the unbraided leather and the bone beneath, lying in little pockets where the straps had overlapped and a quick wiping hadn't reached them.

Still whistling tunelessly, Wotheng took a small paring knife and began scraping the whitish powder off the leather and bone, into the dish.

Bassip chewed his lip, mumbled something about seeing if his oxen had enough water, and began to back away.

The guards standing silently behind him clamped restraining hands on his arms.

Wotheng scraped all the available powder into the dish, cast the remains of the ruined whip aside, took a few drops of water from a nearby kettle on the tip of his knife, and mixed the thin powder and water into a flat dough.

"This odd powder on your whip stock interests me," he smiled at the now trembling Bassip. "How came it there, eh? And what is it? I daresay, I've a way to learn. Ey, Cook, pray fetch me a squab from the dovecote."

The cook scurried off. Wotheng continued to roll the thimbleful of dough about the plate until it dried and compacted into small pills. The cook came back with a young pigeon hooting mournfully in a tiny cage, set it on the table, bowed quickly and withdrew to watch.

"I've always had a fancy for stuffed squab," Wotheng commented as he seized the bird handily by the neck, pried its beak open and began shoving the pills of dough down its throat. "But how does the bird care for the stuffing, I wonder? These creatures are greedy enough for wholesome bread, I've seen. Let us see how this fellow enjoys his, hah, 'drover's meal.' "

Bassip's knees quavered and almost dropped him to the floor. The guards obligingly held him up.

Wotheng finished feeding the bird the last of the dough, tossed the dish into a wash basin, sat down at the bench and called for a cup of beer, which the cook hurried to fetch. The guards said nothing, only watched impassively. Bassip, sweating now as if he stood next to a furnace, couldn't seem to pull his eyes away from the bird.

"Have you ever noticed," Wotheng remarked cheerily around his beer, "that the smaller a creature may be, the faster it seems to live? Butterflies live but a season. Birds last scarcely a handful of years. Yet what they lack in time they appear to replace in speed. A bird, for example, eats and sleeps and sings and plays enough in a day that, were he a man, would satisfy for a seven-night. His food seems to pass through him, depositing its virtue, in scant moments. A bite of oilcake at dawn shows its sheen on his feathers by breakfast time. I'll wager this little fellow will show the good of his bread crumb feeding here within the half hour, if not sooner."

Bassip tried just once to pull away from the guards and run. Their grip loosened not a hair's width.

"Oh come, fellow, let's have no impatience," Wotheng purred. "Your oxen, being large and slow-living beasts, will surely wait. Pray, humor me? I've a fancy to learn just how much flour goes out the baker's door on the clothes and tackle of the baker's wagoner—even unto the handle of his whip. Now, by the gods, what ails that bird?"

The young pigeon was showing definite signs of distress, flapping its clipped wings, tossing its head over its back, squawking in short and high-pitched bursts.

"Why, I'd swear from looking," Wotheng commented, "that the poor creature was ill. Yet it was quite well before it ate that flour, wouldn't you say?"

Bassip moaned and sagged in his captors' grip. The squab fell on its side, kicking, as if in sympathy.

Wotheng set down his cup, stretched, and got to his feet. "Well, Bassip," he said. "Who paid you to mix the black mould into Tygg's rye flour?"

High Priest Folweel sat calm and composed before his guests, as if he received the Lord of Ashkell and a delegation of alien priests every day. Not a hair of his long beard was out of place, not a fold of his gold-embroidered red robe was wrinkled, not a single be-ringed finger trembled. Sulun stared, fascinated, at the enemy he'd never before met. However the man's thoughts inclined, he was neither foolish nor easily frightened. A learned intelligence operated behind those opaque black eyes, and a formidable will.

And the house was a well-staffed fortress, and they sat at its very heart.

"Not the least intriguing event in this case," Wotheng was saying, as calmly undisturbed as his host, "was the appearance of the Yotha fire on the hill facing Deese House. I noted, as I rode past it, that it formed the shape of the sigil of Vona." His voice hardened. "My family's patron god."

Wotheng paused a moment to let that sink in. Folweel raised an eyebrow, but said nothing.

"I wish to know," Wotheng continued tightly, "why you priests burned Vona's sigil into the turf on my land.'

"Excuse me, Lord Wotheng," Folweel purred. "It was Yotha who—"

"Bull's piss! I saw it myself!" Wotheng smacked an impatient hand on the littered table. "Don't call me ignorant, Sir Priest; that fire was fueled with nothing but distilled spirits of wine. My good wife can make it in her still-room, and I've seen it before. 'Twas you priests who set and lit that fire, sir—on my land and in the sigil of my family's god—and I wish to know why."

Folweel barely blinked at the revelation. He only smiled, shrugged, and spread apologetic hands. "Ah, I see you understand our little secret. Yes, the knowledge of fire elixir is a, hmm, trade secret among the priests of Yotha, most commonly used to feed the god's altar fire—and sometimes to send messages."

"Messages! What manner of missive was *that*, pray tell?"

"Understand, m'lord." Folweel was not to be hurried. Neither, in this dark castle, was he intimidated. "Our priesthood is to perceive and interpret the will of the god. Thought, alas, is not readily visible to the common folk; therefore we use the little trick of the fire to make visible the god's word to men. One might say, we provide the ink for the quill of the god's writing."

"I do not appreciate script which scorches my grazing land, sir. Had you a message for me, a simple letter would have done."

"This is well known, sir, but last night's message was not for you."

"Oh? For whom, then?" Wotheng asked, guessing well what the answer was.

"Why, for the rest of our guests, here." Folweel nodded politely toward Sulun's huddled quartet. "Having no other contact with the House of Deese, and no time to create any, we sent the message by the swiftest and most visible means. My regrets concerning the brief stretch of grass that was scorched, but the missive was urgent and could not wait."

"What message?" Sulun asked. *As if I couldn't guess.*

"And what had it to do with Vona?" Wotheng added.

"Why, simply this." Folweel spread his hands again. " 'Tis written in ancient tomes that the Sukkti wizards were often . . . careless . . . with their art—"

"Careless!" Zeren snorted. Sulun restrained him with a quick touch on the arm.

"In this case," Folweel said, flicking an eye toward Eloti, then away, "you folk have been most profligate with your knowledge. You have given out spells, and knowledge thereof, to any who asked—taking little care for these folks' magical ability or moral condition. Who knows to what ill uses such unfettered knowledge might be put? We received from the god the message that the Lord of Storms was displeased by such carelessness—most particularly by your, hmm, stealing his thunder, as it were, in your new magical device—and that his displeasure might soon be made manifest. That is the warning we tried to send."

Folweel bowed politely, and waited.

The reaction was not long in coming. " 'Stealing thunder?' " Sulun yelped.

"The spells we've sold are damned harmless, even beneficial!" Zeren growled.

"Do you claim my folk are unfit to learn common figures and letters, sir?" barked Wotheng. Eloti said nothing, only rubbed her shoe thoughtfully at the edge of the nearest carpet.

"Peace, peace," the high priest intoned, raising his hands as if in blessing. "I but report what the god revealed. Surely you know that Yotha has some divine agreement with Vona; elsewise, why do so many fires start from lightning strikes, despite the presence of rain?"

"Clever," Zeren snorted.

"We received the god's warning that Vona was displeased with the carelessness of Deese House, and we sent on the warning as clearly as we could. Had we but sent a letter by common messenger . . ." Folweel paused to smile blandly at each of Sulun's people in turn, "would you have believed it?"

"No," Doshi admitted, then plucked up his courage to add, "for that matter, why should we believe it now?"

"Why, then, that is your privilege." The high priest rolled his eyes heavenward. "We but reveal the word of the god. Men, in their willfulness, may refuse to believe, but we have done our part."

"At the expense of my grazing land," growled Wotheng.

"A narrow strip, no wider than your hand, easily re-grown: hardly damage worth complaint, Lord Wotheng."

"And the fires that danced along the hills, when first you folk came here?" Wotheng's eyes narrowed. "You claimed you were following the god's trail."

"And so we were." Folweel remained bland as ever. "The god did point out his track to us, and where he wished his temple built. We lit the track to show people where he had passed and where he alighted. Again, we but illustrated the god's word."

"And what of the folk who were moved out of the old manse where you wanted the temple built?"

"Not we, Lord Wotheng, but Yotha himself. Had he not sported there long before ever we came here?" The high priest shrugged eloquently. "As for the folk living there, we did offer to take them into Yotha's household. Many chose to do so, as you recall. Others did not, which was entirely their will."

"And not to be wondered at, considering the famed capriciousness of your god, Sir Priest."

"The god does as he wills; we can only interpret his will."

"Yet you cannot deny," said Wotheng, slamming his fist down on the table, "that it was your fire that burned Poddil's cottage!"

Why just that one case? Sulum wondered. *No witnesses to the others?*

"But I can, Lord Wotheng." Folweel clasped his hands calmly. "We knew from the god that Poddil's cottage *would* burn. We sent him warning, several times by word of mouth, and finally by the running fire. The first warnings he ignored, the latter came too late; his chimney had already caught fire when the running fire reached him."

"Chimney?" Wotheng bristled his moustache. "My wife *saw* your fire run to Poddil's cottage, climb right up his wall and into the thatch of his roof. Are you calling my lady wife a liar, sir?"

Aha, reliable witness. Sulun thought, drawing no comfort from it.

"Certainly not," Folweel smiled politely. "I only say that, when a warning flame runs up a wall to point at a chimney, and the chimney is also on fire and throws sparks down into the thatch, 'tis very easy to be mistaken concerning exactly which fire set the house alight. You must recall, Lord Wotheng, that witnesses saw sparks shooting out of that chimney and also saw afterward that it had fallen and was burned. The man should never have built his chimney of mere clay-daubed wattle, no matter how thick the clay. Had he not been warned of that before?"

"Poddil's chimney did indeed catch fire once before," Wotheng said slowly, "but without burning the whole house."

"Yet it could have done so, then." The high priest shook his head. "That, too, was warning. Poddil simply would not heed warnings."

"Do you attempt to tell me that Poddil's cottage simply *happened* to catch fire at the moment that your . . . *warning* . . . reached him?"

"Not at all." Folweel shook his head sadly. "In truth, his chimney caught fire a little *before* our warning reached him. We came too late, for which we pray forgiveness; we are but mortal."

"Unbelievable," Zeren muttered.

Don't provoke him! Sulun winced. *We want to get out of here alive!*

"And the fire you loosed at Deese House last night?" Wotheng rumbled. "Was that a 'late' warning, too?"

"How should it be?" Folweel raised his eyebrows, looking most honestly surprised. "Vona has not yet expressed his displeasure at Deese House, has he? Therefore, I trust our warning has reached its goal well before time."

"By all the gods!" Doshi burst out. "Do you try to tell us that you haven't heard about the poisoning of our workmen yesterday?"

"Poisoning? Workmen?" The high priest looked perfectly surprised. "Why, what's this? I've had no word of it."

"I see." Wotheng leaned back in his chair. "Then you wouldn't know that the poisoner has been seized, and has confessed?"

"You are the first to bring me this news, Lord Wotheng." Folweel bowed slightly. "I congratulate you on the speed of your justice."

"Then let me also be first to tell you that the man claimed he was paid to poison the workmen's bread—paid by one of your priests, sir." Wotheng pulled a small scroll from his belt pouch and tossed it on the table. "This is the man's confession, as I heard from his own lips."

Folweel coolly took up the scroll, opened and read it. No more than a righteous frown showed on his composed face. "Indeed a serious matter," he murmured. "This fellow—Bassip? A baker's wagoner?—claims much. Can you be certain he speaks the truth in any of this?"

"I saw with my own eyes the proof that he did the poisoning." Wotheng tapped his fingers quietly on his belt. "I heard with my own ears his confession that Twoz, under-priest of Yotha, paid him to do it and gave him the poison. I wrote with my own hands what he said, as you may read."

The high priest smiled, most gently. "Surely you know, Lord Wotheng, that a man found guilty of a serious crime will often try to shift or divide blame by accusing another. Likewise, one put to . . . serious question . . . in such a case will say whatever he thinks his questioners want to hear."

Wotheng flushed a dull red. He didn't care to have his own reasoning thrown back at him. "There is still the little question of the poison and the money. Bassip told me where in his house he'd hidden the money he got for this task; we searched and found it there. How came he by the money, pray tell?"

"Who can say? It might have been a long-saved treasure, or the result of robbery, or some windfall prize he did not care to report at tax time." Folweel raised a knowing eyebrow. "He could well have mentioned his secret hoard purely to convince you of the truth of his story."

"And the poison, Sir Priest? There was over a pint of it to poison that barrel of flour. Where came he by that?"

"He could have had that from any patch of mould-tainted

rye, field grown or wild seeded. A wagoner who deals with bakers, millers and farmers would have much opportunity to recognize such." Folweel flicked a long nail at the relevant line in Bassip's confession. "Who can guess his true reasoning for this? Perhaps the man has some grudge against the baker, or this under-priest, or someone who works on the new walls at Deese House. Perhaps, knowing that the houses of Deese and Yotha are, hmm, not speaking to each other, he hoped to raise ill will between us. Who can say?"

For a moment none of the others spoke. Eloti only shook her head in admiration for the well-woven words.

"*We* didn't start any such dissension between our houses," Sulun put in, a bit warmly. "By all the gods, we didn't even know you existed until one of your people tried to put a curse on our new walls. The first blow, sir, was yours."

"I, sir?" The high priest looked genuinely grieved. "All I know of that affair is that the crushed corpse of a man, whom one of the under-priests identified as one of our worshippers, was brought to Yotha House one night. The workmen who brought him said he'd been the victim of some magic gone awry. We buried him with proper rites, and that was an end to it. If indeed there was some ill magic done, then who suffered from it if not our poor worshipper—and, by his loss, us?"

"The man was your chief stonemason!" Sulun snapped. "He put the focus of a curse onto our walls while he worked there!"

"My dear sir!" Folweel raised his hands beseechingly. "We have not had much stoneworking done about the temple estate for many moons; if any of our masons wished to take some temporary work elsewhere, we certainly would not prevent them. As to his ill-wishing your uncompleted walls, who can say why he did so? Perhaps he hoped to gain himself more work thereby. Not all of our herd are free from the sin of greed, despite our best efforts."

"Amazing," Zeren murmured again.

Wotheng ignored him, keeping his steady stare on the priest. "And yet, sir, you loosed Yotha's fire against Deese House on the very evening of that . . . accident. The fire very nearly consumed the workmen's scaffolding. Why, Sir Priest, did you that?"

"Ah, the fire again." Folweel smiled and shook his head. "As I have already said, the god speaks of divine displeasure at the dangerous carelessness of the Sukkti wizardry, of which our stonemason died. As for the scaffolding, well, the under-priests who sent the fire may be forgiven if they were upset by their servant's death and, in their distraction, perhaps let the fire run too close to the scaffolding where the man died." He shrugged eloquently. "In any case, as I've heard, the scaffolding was not burned and no harm was done."

"Except to a bit of grass." Wotheng tapped his fingers on his belt, over and over. "Would one of those under-priests who loosed the fire that night have been this fellow Twoz, perhaps?"

The high priest frowned long in thought. "That may well have been, Lord Wotheng. I shall investigate this matter."

"I should like to investigate it myself, also. Pray bring this Twoz fellow to me; I wish to question him."

"That I shall gladly do, m'lord, as soon as he returns from the north." Folweel smiled benignly. "Twoz is one of the under-priests who went north with our last trade caravan, nearly a fortnight ago. Thus he could hardly have hired Bassip to poison your miller's flour two days ago, which is why I suspect Bassip's confession on this point."

"He might, of course, have begun the plot before he left."

"Quite possibly. We shall certainly question Twoz most carefully upon his return—and, of course, send him to you as well."

"Of course." Wotheng tapped and tapped his fingers. "And do you swear, Sir Priest, on your own altar to Yotha, that you have no malice, and have done no ill-wishing, to Deese House or any thereof?"

"Certainly I will swear so." The high priest looked utterly sincere. "Our sole complaint against Deese's priesthood is, as I've said, their dangerous carelessness with magical knowledge and application."

"If that's so," Wotheng smiled tightly, "then this Bassip fellow has done your house as much harm as Deese House, what with making either false accusations against your under-priest or else entering in a private conspiracy with him. True?"

"Quite true, m'lord."

"Why, then, I shall hand him over to your examination and judgement." Wotheng pulled himself up from the chair. "You have his confession there, and my guards have him in your courtyard. I'll also send you written account of my investigation of the poisoning, and how his guilt was discovered, if you wish."

"I shall be happy to receive them, Lord Wotheng," said Folweel, quite calmly.

"Until this Twoz returns then, I'll leave the matter in your hands. Good day, Sir Priest. Come along, good folk."

Sulun and the others had no choice but to rise, bow minimally in politeness, and follow Wotheng to the door.

At the threshhold Wotheng turned. "Only one more thing, Sir Priest."

"Yes, Lord Wotheng?"

"Don't burn so much as another handspan of my land. Is that clear?"

"Yes, Lord Wotheng."

The Lord of Ashkell tramped out, letting the door swing shut behind him.

They were well past the temple's lands before anyone spoke. Zeren leaned over the edge of the wagon to catch Wotheng's attention, and asked in as quiet a voice as he could, "Lord Wotheng, why don't you just take your men-at-arms and clean that snake's nest out? I'll be happy to help."

Wotheng laughed sourly. "There speaks a soldier, right enough. Lad, I'd have done so long before this if I could— and if I hadn't thought ahead a bit. Think you: enough folk would be glad to see that last of Yotha, perhaps happy enough to join a campaign to drive them out like wolves, aye, and even accept the combat losses.

But think a bit further down the road. In a year's time, or two, or thereabouts, the next of my lot to have any argument with me would get to thinking, 'Wotheng waited for no sure proof of crime before he turned on Yotha's priests, so what will he do to us?' Soon enough they'd find reason to grieve for Yotha's lot, and more reason to fear me. One makes secret enemies that way, my boy, great numbers of 'em. That I can't afford. No, I need proof clear and bald for all folk to see before I send swords against Yotha—or anyone. Do y'see that?"

"I . . . see." Zeren chewed his lip a bit. "However, if someone else were to make an end of Yotha's priesthood . . ."

"Then I'd have to sit in judgement on the case. Be careful, lad."

"Understood." Zeren sighed. "I'm a soldier, as you said, and no ruler. These games are a bit beyond me."

"Well, let me suggest—seeing as someone has, most definitely, tried to harm your folk—that you borrow a few of my guardsmen to watch your house and walls and workmen's camp for you. I'll hire them out cheap; all I ask is that you teach them some of the tricks you've learned in your soldiering. Like you the deal?"

"Yes," Zeren grinned. "It's a pleasure doing business with you, m'lord."

"Aye, that's what the wife says." Wotheng spurred his horse forward a few paces to hear the conversation going on in the front of the wagon.

Doshi was cursing bitterly over the whole visit. "Snake-tongued, wily monster, turning our own words back on us. Carelessness! Oh, bull's balls! He sat there and accused *us* of dangerous magic, that—that—"

"Clever old bastard," Sulun supplied. "At least he won't be setting fires so freely again."

"But what else will he do? He has so damned much power! You know that Bassip was his hireling, and could still run around poisoning people. Do we have to watch every drop of water, every crumb of food, for the rest of our lives? What if—"

"I doubt Bassip the Wagoner will do any more poisoning," said Sulun. "To keep protesting his innocence, Folweel will have to punish the man—and none too lightly. In fact . . . seeing that Bassip's clearly guilty, no longer useful, and has some damaging tales to tell about who hired him, I suspect that the poisoner hasn't many days left to live."

"Oh." Doshi thought that over, and was silent.

"I see you understand me," Wotheng put in, startling them both. "So we're all rid of a poisoner, and Folweel won't be so free with his fires hereafter, and I rather think that this fellow Twoz won't be showing his nose in Ashkell again."

"I understand, Lord Wotheng, and I thank you," Sulun

concurred. "I only worry about Folweel's next move against us."

"He might have the sense to make none." Wotheng sighed. "Well, if not, then I suspect he'll not move soon or anywhere near so boldly. I'm lending you some of my guards until next harvest comes in. No, don't thank me yet; you'll have only that long to outguess the next move from Yotha House. I trust your own house will be secure by then."

"As much as we can make it, m'lord."

"Yotha will have his own harvest to get in," Eloti recalled. "And if his donations have fallen slack of late, his priests will have to concern themselves heavily with their farming if they want to be warm and well fed this winter."

"Let's hope so," Sulun muttered.

"And if they have time left over for mischief," Wotheng added, "let's hope 'tis not much."

"Perhaps they'll have other concerns as well." Eloti smiled wickedly. "In case of any complaint, Lord Wotheng, remember that one of Yotha's admitted household *did* do a bit of ill-wishing on a bit of our property first."

"Oho?" Wotheng raised a shaggy eyebrow. "And could anyone do a little bit of ill-wishing right back? Even through Yotha House's famous magical defenses?"

"Certainly. One might cast a small curse upon a small part of Yotha House from the inside—especially while the high priest was too busy in a duel of wits to notice." Eloti smiled, smiled, like a cat with a whole bowl of cream.

"What sort of 'small' curse?" Wotheng asked quietly.

"Harmless but nagging irritations: scrolls that roll off desks and hide under heavy cabinets, inkpots that overturn, quill points that break, errors that tend to creep into the household accounts—that sort of thing."

Wotheng snorted, then whuffled, then laughed until he rocked in the saddle. "Small annoyances! Little irritations!" he whooped. "Oh, I have to tell the wife that one! A small curse . . . Aye, Vona, the slippery wizard deserves it."

Sulun chewed that over a while, giving Eloti a long look. "Falling inkpots," he murmured. "I remember that. So it was you, behind the wall of Entori's study?"

"Oh yes." Eloti smiled distantly into the wind. "My brother was a fool in so many ways. I had to keep track of his doings, or the house would have been ruined long ago."

"Lady Eloti, I'm most grateful you chose to come with us!"

"I'm grateful you gave me the opportunity."

Getting over the wall was the easy part. Yotha House stood amid an overgrown former orchard which hid both the approach and part of the side walls. There were fallen tree limbs aplenty, and the stone itself was weathered full of finger--and toeholds, and Arizun had his rope and grapnel in case those failed. Clearly the wizard-priests of Yotha never considered that any thief would dare try to climb into the god's house, or else they actually wanted hidden entrances for themselves.

Ziya and Arizun lay on top of the weathered wall, studied the hated house and planned strategy.

"We could set it on fire," said Ziya. "Serve 'em right."

Arizun winced. "Not that easy," he argued. "Besides, they play with fire themselves. Don't you think they'd have precautions against it turning on them?"

"It'd be so *right.*" Ziya hated to let the idea go.

"Maybe we could poison them right back," Arizun offered, looking half-heartedly about for the house's water supply. He cast a glance back into the orchard, where their horse was safely tied and presumably too busy eating to make any noise.

"We didn't bring any poison with us," Ziya grumbled. "We should've thought of that."

"I don't think Deese House has got any, and there wasn't time to look; not if we wanted to sneak out quick." Arizun's eye fell on something odd, something wrong-shaped, hanging in one of the trees. He looked more carefully, recognized it, and smiled to his ears. "Heyyy, I've got a better idea. Have we got a big bag?"

"The sack we brought lunch in." Ziya squirmed around to see what Arizun was looking at. "What is it?"

"Look there, that tree where I'm pointing, about halfway up. You see that thing?"

Ziya did. Her eye grew big and round, and she smothered a whoop of laughter. "Oooh, how'll we get it?"

"Some smoke, and then the bag." Arizun squirmed back

down off the wall. "Come on. This'll take time and we've got to hurry."

Ziya wriggled after him, and they ran back through the old orchard stifling giggles.

Arizun proved to be right; it took a good half-hour's careful work to build a smoky fire of just the right size, keep it from being seen while they steered the smoke upwards, and then shinny up the tree with the hastily emptied bag. Arizun did most of the latter work while Ziya kept lookout, and none of it was easy. Still, he came down grinning, mussed but unscathed, holding the reloaded bag at arm's length with the neck tied tight.

"Ick! Keep it away from me!" Ziya wrinkled her nose as she scattered and killed the fire.

"That was the easy part," Arizun warned her solemnly. "Now we've got to get this over the wall, sneak it into the house and find a good place to open it—and all that without anyone seeing or hearing us."

"We'll be real quiet," Ziya promised. "And I bet I know just where to let it loose."

They re-climbed the wall, scouted the grounds below with elaborate care, and finally sneaked down Arizun's rope to the thick-shrubbed garden.

"Why do they grow all this stuff in their kitchen garden?" Ziya whispered while they paused under a large and stinky bush. "None of it's fit to eat."

"Maybe they're poison plants. Don't touch any with your bare skin."

"Won't. Look: there's the kitchen midden, so the kitchen's got to be right there."

"The kitchen'll have people in it."

"Maybe not. Let's sneak up to the window and look."

Another ten minutes' exquisitely careful stalking brought them up to an open ground floor window. They listened for long moments before daring to raise their heads and peek in.

Inside, a solitary kitchen maid raked ashes out of the cold fireplace and shovelled them into a bucket. There was no sign of anyone else about.

The underage conspirators ducked down below the window and conferred.

"She'll go out in a minute to empty the bucket," Ziya whispered. "That's when we do it. And we shut the window after, so *they* don't get out."

"Right." Arizun carefully untied the mouth of the bag, holding it shut only with his hand. "You watch, and tell me the minute she goes."

The wait wasn't long. The kitchen maid filled her bucket, set down the hand-shovel and lugged her burden toward the rear door—with her back turned to the window.

"Now?" Ziya emphasized the signal with a light kick.

Arizun stood up, yanked the mouth of the bag wide open and hurled its contents through the window.

The cubit-long wasps' nest sailed far through the air, hit a table, bounced, and rolled under a bench. The wakened wasps came spilling out, disoriented and furious.

Arizun snatched the support pole out of the window, barely taking time to see that Ziya's head was out of the way, and let the sash fall into place.

The two of them ran like rabbits back through the garden to the dangling rope and up the wall, unseen by anyone, thanks more to luck than caution. They reeled in the rope, squirmed back among the concealing branches and peered over the wall to watch the fun.

It wasn't long in coming. The maid, her bucket emptied, turned back to the kitchen and opened the rear door. She took one step through it, froze on the threshhold, then jumped back and slammed it shut. The children nearly smothered themselves keeping quiet as they watched the maid drop the bucket, dance furiously while swatting at her hair and finally run off through the kitchen midden squalling a dozen different names or curses.

"She'll tell somebody," Ziya grumbled quietly. "They'll come smoke the wasps out before they really spread."

"Maybe not," Arizun whispered. "Look through the windows."

For all its size, the house had been built in peaceful times. It was not designed to withstand any assault, and its walls were pierced by numerous large windows to let in air and light. Through two of them the children could see a fat and well-dressed under-priest, apparently wanting a snack or drink between meals, strolling toward the kitchen. They didn't see him reach the door and open it, but they did see the result.

A screech echoed across the kitchen garden, and doubtless through the lower corridors of Yotha House. The pudgy under-priest fled back past the windows *much* faster than he'd come, swatting the air around him with flapping sleeves. What seemed to be a small cloud followed him down the corridor. The under-priest flapped and squawked through a door, shut it behind him, and then discovered that he hadn't shut out all the wasps. He danced around the unlit room, knocking over small tables and chairs, then ran out still another door and was lost to view.

The wasps left back in the corridor buzzed and swirled for a moment, briefly visible in a bar of sunlight, then began scouting the rest of the ground floor. Their progress could be traced by the screeches and thuds and slammings of doors down the length of Yotha House.

On the wall, Ziya pressed both hands over her mouth and nearly choked with the effort of keeping quiet.

Arizun tugged at her sleeve. "Let's go," he whispered. "That's all we'll get to see, and we've got to get home before we're missed."

Ziya nodded red-faced assent, and they climbed back down the wall. The howls of alarm could be heard behind them as they raced through the orchard, but the two didn't let themselves go ahead and laugh until they were on the horse and well away from the lands of the temple of Yotha. Then, of course, they giggled and whooped and howled until they nearly fell off.

Fortunately, the horse was kind-tempered and patient.

In his study, Folweel rested his elbows on the table and sagged with exhaustion and relief. Gods, that had been a close thing! How in the nine hells had those damned Deese wizards guessed so quickly that the workmen had been poisoned rather than bewitched? How had they discovered the source and nature of the poison so fast and accurately? Damn them, and damn that fat fool Wotheng's unpredictable pride, and damn his clever wife who'd discovered the nature of Yotha's Flame. Now he couldn't dare loose the Fire again, not on any land Wotheng claimed. As to other means, he'd have to be very, very careful. Putting the rye mould in the workmen's bread ration had seemed subtle enough, but clearly these Sukkti folk were accustomed to subtlety. Damn! What did that leave?

Magic? Folweel shuddered. Besides himself, the only truly competent magician in Yotha House was Oralro, and one had to be careful in handling him. Unlike the rest of them, Oralro truly *did* believe in Yotha; he wouldn't perform without convincing himself, usually by hours of meditation and prayer, that Yotha really and truly did want it done. Once decided, of course, the man was almost unstoppable; between himself and Oralro, they could cast a hefty curse. But then, who could guess how many wizards Deese House had, or how strong they were, or how trained?

For a long moment Folweel seriously considered taking the Deese wizards' warning, backing away from the conflict, letting Yotha House survive on its lands and produce and what little donations the local herd would provide hereafter.

No, that way led to poverty by slow degrees; come a bad harvest or a poor year's trading in the north, and Yotha's priesthood would be no better off than the local farmers or merchants. That was no fit ending for Folweel Gilno's-son, late of Anhalas, thank you.

So, retrench and go to the secondary plan. Keep heads down, only preach warnings, keep a good ear as close to the Deese wizards as possible, and wait for the right opportunity. Sooner or later, gods willing, a chance would come. Folweel flicked a glance torward a certain drawer in a wall cabinet, behind which a hidden compartment nestled. What lay there he would use well, and subtly, when the time came. Best pen another note to Duppa, warning him to be totally discreet. Bad enough they'd lost the use of Bassip; damn, but now they'd have to find him guilty and condemn him, the fool. Also, best warn the trade caravan to come home one under-priest the less, and make good excuse for the absence—good enough to satisfy Lord Wotheng, anyway. Let the Deese wizards suspect what they would, that fat son of an Ancar barbarian still ruled here, and any clever son of Anhalas could outwit such a creature while the sun still rose—so long as one catered to his barbarian pride and temper. Patience, patience: get on with the letters. Folweel sighed and reached for his quill pen.

He missed, and the shaved quill went rolling across the table. Folweel grabbed for it, and knocked awry a stack of tablets. The tablets slid across the desk, one of them bumping into the inkpot. The inkpot overturned, spilling a black lake across a stack of documents.

The high priest roared a pungent Halasian oath and

shoved back his chair. The chair caught on an irregularity in the rug, and tipped over, dropping Folweel unceremoniously to the floor. He landed badly, whacking his elbow, and his arm went numb down to the fingers. He grabbed the table to lever himself erect, bumped into the tottering stack of tablets, and knocked them across the table in all directions. The inkpot fell to the floor and rolled, spilling more ink across the rug.

Folweel swore and stamped. His foot hit a fallen stylus, which rolled, nearly dropping him to the floor again. He scrambled away from the table and its small disaster, intending to reach the bell pull and call the servants to clean the mess. He made two steps across the floor before the rug skidded on the polished boards and slipped out from under him. Down he went again, instinctively grabbing for the nearest support, which happened to be a chair. He hit it wrong, and the chair fell over with him, its seat back catching him a painful whack on the collarbone.

A curse! Folweel realized, as he shook pain streaks from his vision and contemplated the floor under his chin. *They sneaked a curse past our house defenses! Must have done it just now, right here . . .*

But how in the nine hells could they have done it? They'd all been talking, arguing, concentrating on trying to catch him in some slip, some contradiction or admission. Nobody could do magic in that frame of mine, but all of them had—

Wait, not all of them.

That woman! Their teacher at Wotheng's: she just sat, said nothing . . .

Folweel pulled himself up to all fours and crawled, carefully, very carefully, across the floor to the wall. He leaned on it as he got to his feet with infinite caution and reached for the bell pull, inwardly seething at how neatly he'd been tricked. Oh yes, he'd heard that the Sukkti wizards taught magic to their women too, but who could believe they'd trust a witch with something so subtle and difficult? She'd done it somehow, sitting there so politely quiet while the men argued, never giving a sign of sorcery at work. She'd done it then, while he was busy juggling Wotheng and the Deese priests: set a curse, right in this room, probably centering it right there at his work table. How? How had she done it? He'd need Oralro's help to find out. Swearing, Folweel yanked on the bell pull.

It tore loose from its moorings and dropped on top of him like a dusty snake.

"Oralro!" Folweel howled, forgetting that no one could hear very far through that thick officium door. "Oralro! Yotha's flaming balls, somebody fetch Oralro!"

Nobody answered, but he could hear thumpings and shoutings from downstairs. Could that be the racket of hauling in Bassip, and him knowing or guessing what was intended for him? Or, worse, could the curse have spread beyond this room already? Folweel make his way to the door and pulled it open.

In through the open door came the wasps.

Two days later, word was brought to Lord Wotheng that under-priest Twoz had died of plague in the north; and that Bassip the Carter had indeed been found guilty of poisoning his employer's flour, and condemned to death by Yotha's Flame.

Wotheng shivered, and shut the informing parchment away.

6

The walls of Deese House were finished by second harvest, freeing the work gang for labor in the fields. Harvest was better than average, which the Ashkell folk attributed to the beneficent magic of the new wizards, and in a sense that was true; scythes kept their edges longer, crops fumigated with "magical" herbs were less plagued by moulds and insects, people and livestock suffered fewer ailments thanks to washing ointments and herbal baths provided by Deese's consort Kula.

Attendance at Yotha's temple services dwindled steadily, although the House of Deese provided no public ceremonies to replace them. Still, requests and donations came steadily to Deese House, and enrollment in the Wizardess Eloti's school continued to increase. Biddon the blacksmith built a shrine to Deese within the villa's walls, and local folk made offerings there every day, of which Biddon took only a small share before giving the rest to Eloti to carry back to Deese House. The priesthood of Deese, after giving the matter long thought and much discussion over several dinners, agreed to cast a good man-sized statue of the god—and, later, another of Kula—for the shrine. Omis proposed casting the statue in iron, swearing that with the new furnace and bellows he could actually melt iron to liquid. Sulun complained such heat was too dangerous. The argument was still going strong at harvest time.

No further actions were taken by the priesthood of Yotha, save the oft-repeated warnings in the sermons that magic could be dangerous, that the "wizards of Deese" were too careless with it, that the gods were displeased by such carelessness and would eventually make their displeasure felt.

Wotheng counted his trade coins and his produce taxes, and smiled at his new prosperity. Gynallea totted up the household accounts and bought new winter clothes for everyone in Ashkell House. Even the weather was good— sunny days, light winds, rain frequent but light and usually well after sunset. No bandits raided from the woods, no cattle went missing, even squabbles between neighbors were few and slight.

Altogether, it looked to be a very good year.

"Too good," Zeren worried, peering down at the moonlight on the diverted millstream. "Forgive my gloom, Eloti, but I've learned never to trust too much in good luck."

Eloti hitched closer to him, tugging her cloak about her, for the wind up here on the wall could be chilly after dark. "Think, then: what direction could trouble take? What should we watch for, and guard against?"

"Gods, anything." Zeren shrugged, sliding an arm around Eloti's shoulders. "Some seasonal plague we're not accustomed to, mould in the food stores despite our care, anything going wrong with this iron-casting Omis is so determined upon . . . And Yotha's priests may not be done with us, remember. Or our good friend Wotheng may worry that we've grown powerful enough to undermine his rule, unlikely though that is . . ."

"Gynallea's a good friend to me. I'd know soon enough if her husband's mood changed."

"And I worry about the children. Ziya spends too much time playing with the bombard: raising and lowering the muzzle, turning it, sighting it, even cleaning it. Tamiri runs in and out of the workshop too much, and her little brother tags along; they may be seriously hurt, fooling with the tools, one of these days . . ."

"Zeren, my love, I think you've been so long at war that you've forgotten how to enjoy peace." Eloti interlaced her fingers with his. "Or do you regret asking to marry me?"

"No!" Zeren pulled her close, as if fearful someone would snatch her away. "I'll never regret it! Set the date sooner, if you doubt me."

"No, spring is the proper time, and solstice is best for publicly announcing the intent. I'll wait to do it properly, for I've no doubts of you."

Zeren rested his cheek against her forehead. "Thank you for that. I . . . suppose I'm only being the nervous bridegroom, and with too much soldiering to remember. I imagine threats to us, to you, around every corner. And must you go every day to the villa? When can we bring the school here? That's so long a ride, and anything could happen—"

"Oh, hush." Eloti silenced him with a finger across his lip. "We'll bring the school here in winter, once the snow makes riding difficult. As for the ride to Ashkell, don't you always send two of your best trained guards with me? Besides, for policy's sake, not to mention friendship, I prefer to see Gynallea whenever possible."

"Wotheng's guards . . ." Zeren looked down at the mill-stream and brooded again. "I've gone through all of them by now, teaching them everything I can think of. Gods, it's strange; I've fought the Armu and the Ancar all my life it seems, and here I am teaching the sons of settled-down Ancar soldiers how to fight."

"I doubt if they think of themselves as Ancar twice a year. They call themselves Ashkell Vale folk, if asked, and sometimes remember that Ashkell Vale sits in the lands of Torrhyn. The years of peace seem to have mellowed them."

"That and more. They've never faced an enemy worse than a handful of sheep thieves. I can teach them, drill them, 'til they do the proper moves in their sleep—yet I've no idea how they'd fare in battle. These aren't warriors; they're sheep wardens in armor."

"Let's be grateful for that, love, and pray none of them—or us—need ever be more."

Zeren heaved a sigh that seemed to come all the way from his boots. "And what shall I be, then? A warrior in priest robes? Perhaps I'll end my days as door warden to the House of Deese. The gods know, I'm poorer at metal-working and mechanics than the least of the apprentices!"

"Ah, so that's it." Eloti snuggled into his arm. "There are worse fates, love. Look: here you are, come through Kula knows how many wars, with a whole skin, and now a wedding before you. You could live out your days at far worse tasks than being . . . land warden of Deese House."

"Land warden . . . ?"

"Who else? Doshi knows a bit about farming, but we'll be raising goats and small gardens here. Who else knows anything of that? Did you not begin as a landholder's son?"

"So I did . . ." Zeren frowned with the effort of remembering those long-gone days. At length he laughed. "I recall too, when I was a landholder's son, I wanted to be a natural philosopher!"

"Then here's your wish, granted at last." Eloti smiled. "You've come far to get it."

"Gods, almost clear around the midworld sea!" Zeren hugged her, laughing softly. "And across nearly twenty years. The gods took their own time answering my prayers."

"They often do," said Eloti, grinning to herself. "And if you've no pressing duties tomorrow, come reassure yourself by riding with me to Ashkell Villa. Sit by while I teach, and you'll hear as much natural philosophy as your ears can bear."

"My ears," he said, kissing her, "could bear . . . your voice . . . forever."

After that, their lips were too busy for talk.

High Priest Folweel burned the candle late, grimly reading over reports. He'd saved the ones dealing with Deese House for last, wanting to chew them over in uninterrupted privacy. It had become his chief pleasure of these past few moons: studying, planning, measuring crumbs of opportunity, storing bits of useful knowledge, imagining their ultimate effect. Most often, recently, he slid into sleep cherishing a vision of Deese House wrapped in blue and yellow flames. His fingers rubbed hungrily on the parchment as he pored over Duppa's latest missive, a meticulously detailed recital of the latest lessons taught at the Wizardess Eloti's school in Ashkell villa: geometry, mechanics, drawing of mechanical devices . . .

Wait, that might be something.

Folweel interlaced his fingers and meditated upon the usefulness of drawing. Drawing of tools, drawing of devices, drawing of . . .

Yes!

Folweel sat up straight, smiling like a wolf as he set a few more plotted details in place. At length he got up and went to the bell pull. He paused there a moment, grimacing as he remembered how long it had taken both Oralro and himself to find and remove the focus of the Deese priests curse (a chip of black glass, shoved under the edge of a rug, no more), and resolutely rang the outside bell. Unconsciously he scratched at the scars of long-healed wasp stings as he waited. The soft-footed servitor came soon and quietly to the door.

"Send Duppa and Quazzil to me," Folweel said, still faintly smiling to himself.

"Father," the house servant almost whispered, "I believe they have retired."

"Fetch them anyway. This word they will want to hear."

The man bowed, turned and padded away. Folweel shut the door behind him and stalked to his cabinet, chuckling to himself at the appropriateness of this new-wrought tactic. Time indeed to use his long-hidden weapon.

How very fitting it would be, to strike down Deese House through the very witch who had dared place a curse inside the House of Yotha.

Losh, the wheelwright's son, had his hand up again. An enthusiastic boy, that: fit to travel, hopefully, to one of the great universities someday—provided any still existed now. Eloti nodded recognition to the boy, wishing she could provide better for his educational future.

"Mistress," Losh said, waving his sketch of a gear train, "if it's all right to draw pictyoors of mechanical parts, is it all right to draw other things too?"

"All right?" Eloti blinked, puzzled by the silly question. "Of course it is. You will have to draw *pictures* of many things in order to understand them properly."

"Even trees? And sheep? And . . . other things?"

Losh's neighbor, Duppa, gave him a discreet elbow in the ribs.

"And . . . people too?" Losh finished, beginning to blush.

Eloti thought she understood. She smiled knowingly. "Losh, if you wish to draw pictures of naked women for your amusement, that is a private matter between you and the woman concerned."

The class, nearly a score of them by now, erupted in a storm of laughter. Losh, blushing red as a beet, scrunched down in his clothes as if trying to disappear into the earth.

"In truth," Eloti continued as the laughter sank to a breachable level, "those of you who intend to study medicine must study detailed drawings of the human body, including all its muscles, bones, veins and internal organs. I assure you, you will see enough pictures of the human body to become heartily tired of them before you finish your course of study. Since medicine will be the next class, any who wish to see evidence of this may attend. Now, your assignment in this class for tomorrow is, using the *pictures* you already have, to make a model—in clay and sticks, or whatever else you may have ready to hand—of a 'gear train'. You may go now. The class in medicine will assemble here at the next bell."

The class shuffled to its assorted feet and scattered, most students heading out of the main hall for a few minutes of leg-stretching in the courtyard. Eloti rolled and set aside certain scrolls and hunted in her carry basket for others.

Duppa strolled out to the well, where a slight man in nondescript dark clothing had just hauled up a dripping bucket and was tugging a horn cup free of his belt.

"May I have some?" Duppa asked politely.

The other nodded and handed over the cup. "Losh takes the bait," he murmured, very quietly.

"Follow him, watch well for chances," Duppa whispered. Then he drank from the horn, handed it back, nodded politely and walked away.

The jeweler's wife watched, fascinated, as the blue fire shot up on the altar. The yellow tips of the flames reflected in her wide eyes and gilded her faintly quivering jowls. She loved fires, was utterly entranced by them, and was fiercely loyal to Yotha. She paid well for private audiences and prophecies.

In return, Yotha granted her clear messages. His fire sketched letters, sigils and simple images across the altar, plain as the writing of a quill pen. She never doubted his advice, which was always accurate.

And that takes no small doing, Folweel considered, recalling reams of observers' reports that he studied before telling the woman what she needed to hear. *Still, so loyal and generous and . . . useful a worshipper deserves the best*.

A line of blue flame ran out of the great fire bowl and ran to the far left of the altar. From there it scurried rightward, writing recognizable letters in square northern script. The jeweler's wife gasped as she recognized them.

"L . . . O . . . S . . . H. Losh! My son's name!"

"Indeed?" Folweel placed a comforting hand on her shoulder, and watched the flames finish their message.

After the letters, the fire skipped into a neat circle crossed with a vertical bar, an ancient and ominous symbol of negation.

"Death sign," the woman moaned. "Oh, gods, is my son doomed to die?"

"Peace, peace," Folweel soothed. "Remember, goodwife Nima, the sign may also be interpreted to mean only 'fatal danger.' "

While he spoke, the fire sketched one last sign—the outline of an anvil in a circle—and stopped there. The completed message burned tranquilly on the altar, plain to read.

"Anvil? What means that?" Nima couldn't pull her eyes away from the fire even long enough to glance beseechingly at the high priest. "Will my son be killed by an *anvil*?"

"I think not," Folweel murmured smoothly. "Note that the anvil is encircled, which adds much to its meaning. Not an anvil so much as one who uses it. Has your son anything to do with blacksmiths, Goody Nima?"

"No, nothing whatever . . ."

Folweel waited, letting her make the connection herself.

"Except . . . Oh gods, he goes to that school the Deese woman teaches! Could that be the danger? You've warned your herd so often that those folk are dangerously careless and profligate with magic—and my son *will* insist on going to them, learning their magic, no matter what I say to him. Oh gods, there's been no controlling him since he came of age, and he simply won't obey me, and his father thinks there's no harm in it, no matter how often I warn him it's dangerous. Gods, gods, oh beloved Yotha, is Losh going to do something dangerous with the magic they teach there? Is that it?"

The line of blue fire, its fuel exhausted, sank and died away as if on cue. The timing was perfect.

"I think your question has just been answered, Goody Nima." Long practice kept the triumph out of Folweel's solemn voice. "Say nothing of this to anyone, for you know how ill Yotha and his warnings stand in the favor of the faithless mob. Nonetheless, I should watch your son carefully, were I you. See what he does, where he goes, what he has learned and what he does with it. Perhaps vigilance can avert the danger."

"Yes. Gods, yes," said the jeweler's wife, her heavy jaw set. She fumbled in her purse for more coin, determined to show her gratitude for the warning—and the welcome advice.

No, Folweel smiled to himself. *The danger will not be averted if I have anything to do therewith.*

He bowed to the altar, to Yotha's flame and Yotha's image, with more sincerity than he'd felt in many a long moon.

"Having finished with diseases and injuries of sheep, we proceed to the study of diseases and injuries of men, their causes and cures." Eloti unrolled and hung from a lamp hook on the wall an elaborate drawing of human anatomy. It was a splendid illustration, done in several different colored inks, copied over nearly a moon from a smaller version in her best medical text. The assembled students gasped in awe, and a few of them gagged. "Be not dismayed by its complexity, for we shall learn the parts one at a time. Also, you will soon note similarities to the bodies of those animals which we have already studied."

"We're nothing like dumb animals," one of the older students grumbled.

"No?" Eloti arched an eyebrow at the woman, the daughter of a prosperous freeholder and perhaps a bit set in older ways of thought. "When injured, do we not bleed the same as they? Do our bones not break much as theirs, nor our bellies not gripe like theirs at bad food? Do we not sicken and die of disease or pests, like them? Therefore, let us learn what we can from such similarities."

"But we have speech and thought and spirit," the woman mumbled, covering her retreat. "That makes us different."

"Even so." Eloti took that in stride. "Let us begin, then, with those differences which are readily apparent in the body. Here." She pointed her long staff at the detailed drawing of the head. "You will note the brain: the seat of wisdom, home of speech and thought and spirit, master of the body. Observe that it is much larger and more detailed than that of a sheep, cow or horse, as compared to the size of the body. Here is the true difference between man and beast most clearly visible. You will note how the nerves descend from the brain through the spine, and from there to every limb and organ . . ."

The students duly bent over their tablets and drew rough copies of the human nervous system.

Duppa glanced at Losh's meticulous drawing, and smiled.

It was easy work for one with Quazzil's skills to follow Losh through the villa to his parents' shop and house, only a little less easy to find a secure and comfortable listening post in the alley behind the house. An old and fruitful chestnut tree grew there, its boughs wide enough to afford a secure rest and its foliage still thick enough at this season to conceal a listener. Best of all, from one well-concealed branch Quazzil could hear clearly through the upper and lower rear windows as well as watch the house and yard below. He folded and set his dark cloak for a mattress, stretched out on the branch and observed.

First came warm and dutiful greetings exchanged between the son and his father and older sibs. Then came a dutiful and less warm greeting between the boy and his mother. Next, hurried footsteps as the mother hustled the son into the back of the house, where Quazzil could hear more clearly. After that came a long, nagging interrogation with increasingly irritable answers. Finally the son's temper snapped.

"For the gods' sake, mother!" he shouted. "It's nothing but Natural Philosophy! She hasn't taught us a bit of magic, only stuff like mathematics and medicine and mechanics. It's harmless and useful, and nothing to be afraid of. In fact, I have to go make a model of a gear train as my assignment for tomorrow, so I can't stay here and argue with you anymore. I've got to go off and get some clay and sticks to make the model, so good *day*, Mother. I'll be back in time for dinner."

The rear door slammed and the boy could be seen stamping his way across the alley.

Smiling, Quazzil slid out of the tree and followed the boy, at a safe distance, down the alley.

Behind them, Nima's voice echoed out the door: "What in the nine hells is a 'geer trane'?"

Patrobe smiled openly as Folweel read over the report from Quazzil, knowing the high priest would find the news as useful as he could wish. Sure enough, by the time he finished reading the scrap of paper, Folweel was grinning from ear to ear.

"So," the high priest purred, leaning back in his carved chair, "Losh has a sweetheart, the daughter of a poor farmer, of whom the mother does not approve."

"His father doesn't care," Patrobe pointed out. "He wouldn't disapprove of the match."

"Which no doubt makes our dear Nima all the more irate." Folweel tapped a finger on the report. "So if the girl falls . . . ill, shall we say, Nima would do all in her power to insist her boy had nothing to do with it."

"Which means she would strive to erase any link between the boy's studies and the girl's bewitchment."

"Therefore, the link must be forged beyond any doubt. The boy has made sketches of her, and he copied on good parchment that drawing from school. The drawings *must* be found together, and with some definite smear or mar across the anatomy drawing."

"How fortunate," Patrobe grinned, "that Lady Eloti pointed out that particular body part first. Otherwise we might have had to wait long, or damage some other portion of the wench."

"Read good Duppa's hand in that," Folweel smiled. "He knows the other students well enough by now to plant the right suggestions in the right ears."

"Most clever, Brother Folweel. But even so, Nima will try to hide that evidence."

"As I said, it will be found—and announced to all the vale—by another party. Losh will appear guilty. Nima will struggle, with all her considerable will, to shift the blame elsewhere."

"And we can guess where."

"Precisely." Folweel smiled as if happy with all the world as he took up fresh parchment and ink. "This goes to Quazzil, as soon as possible."

"And Duppa?"

"Another for him, less urgent. He is only to continue observing, and to drop the proper words in the proper ears at the proper time."

As a small tenant farmer's eldest daughter, Irga had duties that made her waken early. Papa would rise at dawn to take the sheep out to pasture, usually with her brother's help. Brother Wenn would build up the fire and pack lunch for them. Mama would rise later, clean house and wash clothes, make preparations for dinner, tend the household garden and mend or sew or knit clothing for the winter. Irga had the unloved work of cleaning out the sheep barn, after which she would help Mama about the house. No one could face such a task on an empty stomach, especially not in the cold morning, so Irga would first brew a small pot of herb tea to fortify herself for the wretched work.

On this particular morning, as Irga fumbled her way down from her bed in the loft, she thought she saw someone leaving through the door. She paused to blink sleep from her eyes, guessed she had only seen the tail end of her brother leaving late, and went to put her tea on the fire. The water warmed to boiling while she washed her face and struggled into her clothes.

Perhaps she'd thrown in a bit too much of the last herbs, Irga thought as she drank the brew, for it tasted strong and a trifle bitter this morning. Perhaps she could gather some blackberry leaves to put in the new mix, if there were any good ones left so late in the year, and if she could get away from chores long enough to seek them. And perhaps, if she went berrying late enough in the

day, she could meet Losh a good way from the house and
Mama's too inquisitive eyes.

Well, best get the other chores done first. Making a
face, Irga pulled on her shawl and went out to face the
dismal prospect of a barn full of sheep droppings.

The fouled straw stank, and the cart was heavy, and the
reeking load steamed in the cold—and the cold seemed
harsher than the clear bright weather would account for.
Irga shoved the steaming cart to the compost heap, tilted
and pulled it, let the reeking load tumble out and spread
on the pile. Gods, how it steamed in this shadowed corner
of the barn wall. So thick, it seemed to form shapes of
mist.

And then it did form a shape. A gray, shifting form—
something like a bat and something like a monstrous toad—
arched up over the manure pile. At its heart, too low for
any natural face, formed vague eyes, a squat beastlike
snout, a gaping mouth.

Irga let go the cart and scrambled away, shaking with
cold to her bone marrow. She bumped into the barn wall
behind her.

The wall moved. Only a slight shivering, maybe a squirm-
ing, but the wall *moved*. Irga whirled to stare at it, and
saw that the rough texture of the field stones was chang-
ing, shivering, crawling, forming patterns like . . . like
faces, evil faces, all snarling and leering at her.

Devilry! Witchcraft! Irga thought, scrambling away from
the barn, the compost heap, the forgotten cart. She turned
to run back to the house.

The ground under her feet undulated, rippled like water on a pond.

No, not the earth too! Irga staggered, fell, landed on the
hard ground and felt it wriggle as though a thousand
worms fought a war just under its surface. She whimpered
in terror, feeling her belly cramp. Her vision smeared, but
there was no release from the horror in that, for now she
could hear sounds—whisperings full of malice, just under
the noise of the wind in the grass.

Gods, is the whole farm cursed? "Mama!" Irga screamed.
"Mama, devils! Where are you? Mama!" *What if the curse
has already caught her?* "Mama!"

But no, there, hurrying out of the cottage with a shawl

just flung over her nightgown, there came Mama running toward her.

"Irga! What's wrong? What's happened?"

The words came distorted through the evil voices in the air, on the ground, but they sounded amazed more than alarmed. More, Mama ran surefooted over earth that rolled like the sea. How could that be? How could it be that Mama couldn't see the horror unfolding all around them?

Only if the curse weren't on the farm, or the barn, nor anything else. Only if the witchery had fallen on Irga alone.

"Oh Mama, I'm bewitched!" Irga struggled forward, reaching for her mother. "Help me! Send for the wizards! I've been bewitched!"

Wotheng sneaked a quick pull from his beer mug as the last supplicant—a tenant asking permission to cut estate wood for the winter—plodded out of the hearing room. With luck, he'd have time to finish the cup before the next petition or complaint came in. Truth to tell, he'd had far more petitions than complaints this year: let me borrow more scythes, m'lord; let me hire more for harvesting, m'lord; let me expand my orchard, m'lord; and so on. Sure signs of a good year—along with the fine sales of wool and other items to the north. Vona grant it would go on this way.

No, there came the knock on the door; no time to finish the cup.

"Come in," Wotheng called.

A woman traipsed in, middling young, well fed and well clothed, somewhat prim-faced. Wotheng tried to place her: that freeholder's daughter, but damned if he could remember her name. "Yes, mistress?" There, polite and neutral enough.

"M'lord." The woman held out a grubby handful of small parchment sheets. "One of my fellow students dropped these. I don't know who it was." Her tone implied that she could guess, though. She also glanced back toward the door as if looking for someone beyond it.

Wotheng took the sheets and looked at them, puzzled frown deepening. Two of them were not bad representations of a young girl's face, quite a pretty girl, even recognizable: Irda? Irga? The daughter of one of the tenants, that fellow who'd been plagued with sheep lice last year, but hadn't that trouble gone away recently?

The third sheet showed a carefully drawn outline of a human body, and within the outline a pattern disturbing and strange. It took Wotheng a moment to recognize it for a diagram of certain human organs: there the spine, clear enough, and that must be the brain, and those lines coming out to all directions must be the nerves. Strange stuff: must be from Eloti's class on medicine. But why had the woman brought it to him rather than to Eloti?

And what meant that damned clumsy smear across the top of it, obscuring much of the carefully drawn brain?

"This is schoolwork," he said. "Why not take it to the schoolmistress?"

The woman fidgeted, glanced toward the door again. "Well, m'lord, that's what I wanted to ask y'about. Is't right to be doing such things if one isn't yet a proper master of the trade? I mean, that's making an image of a real person, m'lord, which I think isn't right, and here, y'see, it's been rolled together with that . . . picture of a body, and a body's hidden parts—and look how that's marred. It seems, well, *wrong* somehow. Mistress Eloti seems to think nothing of that, so I doubt me that she'd worry o'ermuch on it, so I come to ask you, m'lord, if this be proper work for a student."

"I see." Wotheng kept his expression distant, showing nothing, as he peered at the drawings. It could all mean nothing, of course; some fool boy making pictures of his light of love, happening to roll them together with a doctor's drawing with the ink smeared or some such. Most likely, that's all it was: pure accident, no intent whatever. If there was intent, it could be no more than a boy's silly attempt at a love charm: addle this girl's wits toward her swain. In either case, as he'd seen cause to believe, it took more than a picture and a bit of will to make magic.

But if the magical power *were* there, and the intent, and the image . . .

"Is it true, m'lord, as I've heard, that there be some law against making pictures of living folk?" The woman laced her fingers together and squirmed a bit. "There wouldn't be any, ah, trouble at law for Lo—for whoever drew them, would there?"

Oho! Wotheng glowered at the woman. "Goody, you'd best tell me who drew these pictures."

She didn't turn pale; she blushed, and squirmed further. "I . . . I think it was Losh, the jeweler's son. It looks like his way of drawing. Besides, everyone knows he's silly over that chit Irga, and I'm sure that's her picture. The gods only know why he's so mad for her, she being just some poor shepherd's girl and not educated at all nor with any wits for it either, but he *would* go running after her like a fool, though his mother could tell him there be much better prospects at the villa and all . . ."

"Enough, thank you." Wotheng could place the woman now: Pado, Hass' daughter. Rumor said she'd been hoping for a match that would tie her family to the jeweler's, but nothing had come of it. "Isn't Losh a bit young for you, Pado? Wouldn't you do better to seek another match?"

Pado blushed bright crimson. "Why-why of course he is, m'lord," she stammered. "I wouldn't have him if he were the last man in the vale!"

But you'd gladly make him sorry for refusing you. Wotheng set the three grubby parchments down on his table. "I'll see to this later," he said. "I thank you for fetching them to me. Now go send in the next petitioner."

Flustered, not sure if she wanted to complain further or escape with some shreds of her composure, the woman got up and hurried off to the door. She paused on the threshold for a moment, but couldn't think of anything fitting to say. The door thudded to behind her.

Wotheng took a hasty gulp of beer and waited for the next guest. With luck, he'd finish with this lot before noon and could talk to Gynallea before he caught up to Eloti. Of course the Sukkti wizardess couldn't have known about that old obscure Torrhynan law—few of even the local folk did—but still, she should have been more careful about possible mischief among her students. He could silence Pado easily enough, make certain no more would be said of the matter; Gynallea would help with that. A few words in private to Eloti should account for the rest. After all, drawing or no drawing, no harm had been done.

There was noise outside the door, thudding of footsteps, yelps and growls of complaint, a voice shrilling urgency.

Gods, what now? "Come in!" Wotheng bellowed.

The door flew open and a farmwife, hastily dressed in

dishevelled clothes and reeking of hard-ridden mule, almost fell into the room.

"Lord Wotheng," she panted, "I pray you, fetch a good wizard quick, oh quick! My daughter Irga, she's been 'witched!"

Behind her, in the corridor, Wotheng could see Pado watching. A malicious smile spread across her face from ear to ear.

"Vona's clanging shit!" Wotheng groaned.

There'd be no silencing the wretched business now.

Gynallea first heard the news when her husband, looking thoroughly out of his depth, hauled a weeping and wailing tenant shepherd's wife into the still-room to talk to her. Gynallea poured some brandy into the woman, took Wotheng aside and got the rest of the story from him. Next she dispatched some discreet house servants in a light cart to go fetch the afflicted girl and bring her to Ashkell House by the back doors. She also sent a rider on a fast horse to take the news to Deese House. Then she went quietly down to the hall where Eloti held her school and waited for the class to finish and depart.

Zeren happened to be present at the time, and after Gynallea's quiet explanation of the problem he refused to leave Eloti for so much as a minute.

The afflicted girl and her mother, and the delegation from Deese House, arrived at the villa almost together, and the whole howling problem wound up in the little-used guest rooms on the top floor. By dinnertime—a discreetly quiet meal, held in Wotheng's library—they had collected enough facts to discuss the situation calmly.

"It's poison again," said Gynallea, around a healthy mouthful of mutton. "I'm sure it is. The girl's eye centers were open so wide they looked all black, and her skin was flushed and hot. I'd swear 'twas delirium from a fever, save there's no other sign of sickness and no one else in the family has it. No, 'tis poison, sure as snow."

"But what kind?" Eloti nibbled indifferently on a wing of roast duck. "I don't know of any that leaves such tracks, never mind what the antidote may be."

"Is there nothing you can do for her, then?" Sulun asked, crumbling his bread small.

"We gave her willow bark tea, also beans and herb tea

to wash the blood; there's nothing else we can think of, save to keep her warm and quiet."

"She was resting when we left her," Gynallea added. "At least she's no longer so frantic, and her eyes look a trifle better. Whatever it was, it hasn't killed her yet and doesn't seem likely to."

Eloti relaxed a trifle. "With any favor of the gods, the wretched stuff will pass from her in a day or so—unless she gets more of whatever it was."

"That's one of the reasons I wanted her brought here." Gynallea grinned. "No one will sneak poison into *my* kitchen, thank you. Hmm, and once she's calm, we must ask the girl what she ate or drank before the fit came on."

"If it's poisoning again, I think we may guess who did it," Zeren growled, attacking his slab of meat as if his eating knife were a short sword. "They might be clever enough to leave no poisoned food or drink lying about to be found, not after last time."

"Still, it's worth searching the house," Sulun considered. "But how long before we know what to search for?"

"Too long," Wotheng rumbled, refilling his cup. "You're sure, sweet cow, that it's poison—and not magic?"

"Utterly sure!" Gynallea snapped. "What magic would make the girl's eyes change like that? Or give her fever without griped guts and phlegmed lungs?"

"No curse is so specific," Eloti added. "One well-wishes or ill-wishes a person or an object or a space of land. Had the girl been cursed, everything she touched or approached would have . . . gone wrong. She would have fallen into that manure pile, banged her elbow on that barn wall, stubbed her toe and stumbled on that ground—and doubtless torn her dress into the bargain. Furthermore, everyone who touched her would also have stumbled, dropped things and so forth, for as long as she was in contact with them."

"And what if . . ." Wotheng studied the depths of his cup. "What if someone placed a curse specifically on one part of the girl's body—say, her . . . brain?"

Eloti stared at him, eyebrows rising. "I doubt if it could be done at all," she said slowly. "I've never seen nor heard of any wizard who could narrow the range of a curse on a living person so tightly as that. The skill, ability, knowledge and concentration required for that . . . Well, no. No one I've ever met nor heard of, ever, could do it."

"We haven't met everyone in Yotha House," Zeren snarled, "nor observed any of them at magical work. They've had time enough to plot a work like this."

"Besides," Eloti added quickly, "a curse placed on a person's brain would affect the entire organ—and the symptoms would be utterly different. The girl would not be able to see, speak or walk at all. Most likely, she would be rendered idiot—or dead. No, lord Wotheng, we are not dealing with a curse here."

"What on earth gave you that idea, anyway?" Sulun asked. "Cursing a specific organ is rather a bizarre notion."

Wotheng sighed, reached into his belt pouch and pulled out the grubby sheets of parchment. "What else," he said, "should one make of these?"

The other four bent over the sheets, studying them.

"That's a rather poor copy of one of my anatomy diagrams," said Eloti. "Rather dirty, too. These are clearly portraits of Irga, done by a talented but totally untrained beginner."

"What connection do you see among them?" Sulun asked, turning a puzzled eye on Wotheng.

"They were found together, and brought to me by one of your lady's students."

"Oh, ho," murmured Gynallea. "Oh, *ho*. Which student was that?"

"'Twas Pado," Wotheng sighed. "She said Losh made the drawings."

"Pado? That spiteful little sow?" Gynallea snorted. "I'd not put it beyond her to make the drawings herself, then tell that tale, purely to make trouble between Losh and the girl he plainly prefers."

"Losh?" Eloti wrinkled her brow in puzzlement. "He's in my class on medicine, yes. The anatomy drawing could well be his. Indeed, he asked me but a day ago if there were any reason not to . . . draw pictures of people."

"So he drew some pictures of his sweetheart," Sulun puzzled. "What's the trouble with that?"

"More than you may think," Wotheng admitted, "seeing that the drawings were rolled together—put in contact, d'ye see—and there's a distinct smear across the brain in this one."

The others looked at each other as that sank in.

"It means nothing whatever," Eloti said firmly. "Items

put in contact have no power outside their own natures, none whatever—not unless the deliberate, concentrated will of a trained wizard is aimed at them—no more than logs piled together will catch fire of themselves."

"And . . ." Wotheng shuffled on his chair, but kept his eyes on Eloti ". . . if the deliberate will were applied?"

"You can't be accusing—" Zeren started.

Eloti tapped his hand, silencing him. "I've seen no sign whatever of magical ability in Losh," she said. "Neither has he had any such training, so far as I can see. Finally, if he loves the girl, he would certainly not harm her."

"Could it be done by accident?" Wotheng insisted. "Say, he tried to put some sort of love charm on her, something that would . . . 'turn her head,' and got it wrong?"

Eloti actually laughed. "No, no, impossible. Magic doesn't *work* that way. One can well-wish or ill-wish, and nothing more. All love spells are frauds, as I have reason to know." A flicker of some old anger darted through her eyes; passed away quickly. "And last, curse or blessing, magic done wrong simply doesn't work; one wastes one's power, nothing more. It is like—to return to that pile of logs again—trying to strike sparks in a tinderbox, and the tinder doesn't catch. One may tire out one's hands trying, but nothing else is accomplished."

Wotheng looked as grim as they'd yet seen him. "I have . . . only your word for that, m'lady, much as I wish to trust it. And I *did* see friend Sulun, here, make magic with the fire in my dining hearth, the first night we met."

"That was a simple trick with firepowder!" Sulun retorted. "A chemist's trick—just like Yotha's fire fluid."

"And the words you spoke then?"

Sulun blushed. "A bit of showman's trickery, I admit. On our travels, we've found that folk prefer their worldly marvels with a bit of show. Besides," he added with a shrug, "Deese had been good to us, and it never hurts to give him a bit of gratitude."

Wotheng chuckled briefly. "No wonder you guessed that Yotha's fire was likewise a showman's trick. One actor recognizes another, eh?"

"So it is." Sulun grinned lopsidedly. "We have real skills and goods to sell, but folk prefer to call such marvels magic. We've been, hmm, obliged to oblige them."

"Do you claim, then," Wotheng asked, very carefully, "that you have no magical powers among you at all?"

"No," said Eloti. "There are two of us—myself and Arizun—who have the ability, and the training. Neither of us, I assure you, has either the power or the wish to do what was done to that poor girl upstairs."

"Then who did?" Wotheng leaned back in his chair. "Before you ask: no, Pado spent all yesterday and the day before here in Ashkell, for she stays with her aunt during the days when you hold your classes. Other days, she stays with her family, off at the other end of the vale from Irga's house—better than half a day's journey, at best. I had my men go speak to her relatives and whatever servants they could find. Further, Pado has never been to Irga's house, would have had to ask the way there, and no one I could find recalls her ever so much as asking. And if this is indeed a case of poisoning, where would Pado find a poison that no one else in the vale knows aught of?"

"Maybe from our friends at Yotha House," said Zeren. "They've been outside the vale."

"Ah, but so have you." Wotheng grinned. "Stop sputtering, man; I only say it's possible. None of you has any reason . . . hmm, none that I know of, to harm the girl."

"None of us even knew her before this," Eloti pointed out. "She was never one of my students here."

"Nor did she ever come to Deese House," Sulun added. "I doubt if any of us ever laid eyes on her, or heard of her, before today."

"Just so." Wotheng raked his eyes around the room. "I've never heard that any of Yotha's people had aught to do with the girl, either. None in her family were worshippers, nor often went to see the ceremonies in Yotha House."

"Then this might have nothing to do with our . . . religious rivalry," Sulun offered. "It could be pure accident."

Wotheng interlaced his fingers and rested his chin on them. "That, I think, we'll learn soon enough."

"How so?"

"If nothing further comes of this incident, if Irga recovers and goes about as before, if nothing changes between her and Losh, if Yotha House does nothing to involve itself in the clamor to follow, then we may believe it was an accident. Now—"

"Clamor to follow?" Zeren caught that immediately. "What clamor? What do you expect here, Lord Wotheng?"

Wotheng hunched his shoulders and looked honestly apologetic. "I expect that Pado has yattered the tale all over the villa by now, saying that Losh magicked Irga with spells he learned at school. I also expect that Losh's mother, who opposed her son's courtship of Irga, will be doing her best to claim her son innocent of wrongdoing. I hope those two will come to blows in front of half of the villa, over the accusation. 'Twould be a disaster were they to join forces."

"Disaster? Why? Two women nattering that one boy did *not* accidentally bewitch his sweetheart—"

"I don't think you quite understand," Gynallea cut in, glancing daggers at her husband. "Lady Eloti *did* say, before her whole class, that there was no harm whatever in drawing pictures of living persons. I heard gossip of that in the kitchen, before this happened. Wager well, there'll be more such gossip now."

"Pictures?" Sulun caught that. "Whatever is wrong with *pictures*, for love of the gods?"

Wotheng sighed, avoiding his wife's eyes. "Only that it is old Torrhyn law that pictures of living persons are forbidden, lest they be used for cursing."

"What?" said Sulun, Zeren and Eloti together.

" 'Tis true." Wotheng looked from one to the other. "An old law, and one I've never enforced. I'd not enforce it now, given choice. Still, this has happened: a picture was made of a living person, and then that person fell mysteriously ill. Do you see what may happen? 'Tis the perfect answer, should those two fool women join forces over Losh: blame his teacher."

"And through her, the school—and all of Deese House," Zeren fumed. "Now I *know* Yotha's priests did this!"

"What proof, lad?" Wotheng asked mildly. "Give me proof no man can ever doubt, give me what aid you can, and I'll go clean out that snakes' nest. Without such, I needs must take care."

"Gods!" Zeren slammed a fist into his palm.

"Lord Wotheng," said Eloti, "surely this law can be abolished on grounds of its illogic. Should a wizard choose to curse someone, a picture is unnecessary. A thread from the victim's garment, his footprint, knowledge of where his house lies, even a glimpse of his face seen once and remembered—any of these will do as well, or better than, a picture. Forbidding such images is senseless."

"Much like the sword law in Sabis," Zeren laughed sourly. "The city made a law forbidding common subjects to own or carry swords, blithely thinking this would end bloodshed in its sheets. Robbers and bravos shed blood enough with knives, bludgeons and common tools. For that matter, robbers could get swords anyway, law or no law. And they faced a citizenry disarmed."

"Sabis?" Wotheng arched a bushy eyebrow at him. "You've lived there?"

Sulun and Eloti held their breath. Zeren merely shrugged. "Among many others. I'm a soldier, as you know; I've been a hired sword halfway round the Midworld Sea. Many bizarre things I've seen, too—including cities full of wizards and images of the living, and no great harm done thereby."

Wotheng shrugged. "A good argument. Remember it, if this miserable business does come to a trial."

"Why not simply abolish the damned law, then?"

" 'Tis a bit late for that." Wotheng looked to his wife. "Sweet cow, you'd best explain it."

Gynallea snorted and rolled her eyes heavenward. "Politics, my dears, all politics. Had we known this might happen, my lovey would surely have abolished the fool law right then. Now, what with an actual case, he dare not. 'Twould look to all folk as if 'twere done solely to protect favorites. D'ye see?"

"I think so," Sulun murmured. He looked sidelong at Wotheng. "You . . . can't afford to have your subjects in the vale too resentful, can you?"

Wotheng didn't precisely shrink in his chair, but he looked older and wearier than he had a moment before. "You've guessed, lad. Your friend Zeren can tell you how few men-at-arms I have, and how trained."

"Not many," Zeren agreed, "But well-trained enough to handle a mob of disgruntled shepherds, if not to storm Yotha house. You don't expect a revolt over this business, do you?"

"Pshaw, no," Wotheng laughed. " 'Tis't that I fear; 'tis the neighbors."

"Neighbors?" Eloti asked. "What neighbors, and what of them?"

"Good Lady, I'm but a small lordling compared to others." Wotheng's eyes strayed to the fire. "Vona knows, there are other sons of war captains—aye, and some present war captains as well, fresh from taking the river cities—who have far more land, wealth, men-at-arms and gear for them than do I. There are lords to the north, up where the trade caravans go, who might cast a coveting eye on my lands did they think the vale worth taking."

"With the wealth you've brought us," Gynallea said gloomily, "it just might be worth the taking now."

"Oh, they'll not give me trouble without cause." Wotheng shrugged. "They'll be needing some excuse. 'Come, me loyal boys, let's go rob another Ancar fellow of his land' isn't enough reason, and the troops would not marshal for that. But then, 'Come, me boys, Wotheng's own people rumble against him; let's go relieve them of a bad lord and put a better in his place'—now, that might get some fellows to assemble with sword in hand and hopes of good loot. If I can't keep on looking poor, and I can't raise a sizable armed host, I look a tempting target, tempting enough that any excuse will do. D'you see where my trouble lies?"

"Gods . . ." Zeren breathed, sagging in his chair. "How many could we levy? How soon?"

"Not enough," Wotheng said shortly. "The vale has few folk, being poor land, and most of those are needed for tending the sheep. Sheep are easily lost, strayed, or stolen."

"And we thought we were safe . . ." Sulun muttered.

"Tell me," said Eloti. "How would it serve to discourage such greed if it were known that you consort with powerful wizards?"

Wotheng gave her a long, unfathomable look. " 'Twould have to be proven publicly, Lady Eloti: something strong enough, and witnessed well enough, that the . . . neighbors would think it not worth their while to come troubling me."

"There was Yotha, before we came."

"Aye, and now there is Deese." Wotheng glanced into the fire again. "You've brought health, wealth and wisdom—but that may be more bait to the greedy than cause for restraint."

There was another long silence while Sulun, Eloti and

Zeren looked at each other, considering how they might have already endangered their patron.

"What can we do?" Zeren finally asked.

"I don't know," Wotheng admitted, "but it must be something that shows strength as well as your other virtues. Think on it, my friends. Pray Deese sends you a revelatory dream."

By next morning, everyone in the vale had heard the news.

The first evidence of this was Losh himself reeling, ashen-faced, through the door of Ashkell House and demanding to know where Irga was. Gynallea got to him first, and fairly dragged him off to face Wotheng. The Lord of Ashkell only pulled out the damning pieces of parchment and shoved them under the boy's nose.

"Did you draw these?" he demanded.

"Yes, I did! Oh, I did!" Losh wailed, beating his hands together. "I swear I didn't know it would do her any harm!"

"Then you did not attempt the use of magic to . . . affect the girl's mind?" Wotheng kept his voice stern, but a smile lurked under his moustache.

"Attempt? No, never! I don't *know* anything about magic, and I'd never do anything like that to Irga. Oh, where is she? I have to see her!"

"In a moment, lad. First look closely at this drawing, and tell me: did you deliberately draw that smear there?"

"Smear?" Losh looked closer, frowning in puzzlement. "No, that's not my doing. It's messed my schoolwork. It must have happened after I lost it."

"Ah. And where did you lose these drawings?"

"Somewhere at home, I think. When I looked in my schoolbag at class yesterday, they weren't there. Please, please, may I see Irga?"

"Hmm, of course, lad. Come this way."

Wotheng led the dithering boy up to the tower room, then watched the reunion with a thoughtful eye. Irga was indeed much better this morning, only a little pale and weak, and looked ethereally beautiful. Losh practically fell all over her, sobbing apologies and protestations of love and more, most of it incoherent. Irga, understanding none of it, only wanted him to hold her. Wotheng shut the door and tiptoed away, wondering how soon those two would marry. He hoped this wouldn't curtail the boy's schoolwork; from what he'd seen and heard, Losh was quite a bright young fellow when not silly with love.

Certainly there'd been no sorcery, intentional or not, on Losh's part.

Wotheng went back to his morning audiences, thinking much on the incident.

After that, the news came thick and fast, usually brought in by the morning's petitioners. A guard reported that Nima the jeweler's wife had assaulted Pado the landholder's daughter with a market basket in the middle of the villa market square; the resulting knockdown, hair-tearing brawl had overturned a pushcart and spilled several weights of fish into the street, with a total cost of two silvers and seven coppers in damage. The vintner's wagon boy reported that the high priest of Yotha had delivered a furious sermon about the dangerous carelessness of Deese's wizards, claiming—without mentioning names—that this had already led to the bewitchment of an innocent girl, and that worse would follow if such wickedness was not stopped. Biddon the blacksmith, trembling with outrage, came to report that persons unknown had thrown cow manure all over the villa's shrine to Deese and scribbled "nasty words and wild accusations" on the stones.

Wotheng treated each of these separate tales with calm, tolerance and quiet common sense, sending their tellers away with some satisfaction. To himself, he tallied and weighed and made his own plans.

Finally, another guard came in to report that a small but growing and noisy mob had gathered outside the gates of Ashkell House, shouting accusations, demanding to be let in, threatening the Lady Eloti and her students.

"Aha," said Wotheng, getting to his feet. "Tell the rest of the guards to quiet the crowd. I'll be there directly. Oh, and dispatch a messenger on a fast horse to take word of this to Deese House."

The guard saluted fast, and departed faster.

Wotheng paused a moment, fixing his eyes on the sigil of Vona painted on the near doorpost.

"Lord Vona, make this work well, and I promise you a whole ox on your next feast day," he said quietly.

Then he strode off to deal with the mob at the gate.

* * *

"Good Brother Oralro," Folweel enticed, "you know it cannot be done any other way; those Sukkti wizards are an affront to Yotha and a danger to the public morality. Already our herd of the faithful has shrunk notably." He stopped himself just in time to keep from saying: *and the donations likewise*. Let Oralro think of that for himself.

The plump Second Priest of Yotha paced back and forth across the abused rug. "I'm not sure, Brother Folweel," he muttered. "I'm not sure. Certainly this obscene magicking of a young virgin must be punished, and certainly the law is plain. Why, then, may we not openly give our support to Goody Nima's charge against the wizards? Why must we let that good and faithful woman stand alone in her hour of need?"

"Because the fickle crowd has withdrawn from us," Folweel intoned, trying not to tap his fingers with impatience. Oralro might be a splendid wizard, but he was incapable of seeing, let alone handling, matters of politics. "They regard us with suspicion and even contempt."

"Never!" snorted Oralro, pausing in mid-stride.

" 'Tis true, Brother. And worse: that fool Wotheng is likewise swayed by the pretty magics of these newcomers. Do we appear publicly in support of Goodwife Nima, Wotheng will assume we speak only out of jealousy, not righteousness."

"Yet if we speak with righteousness, we shall be heard and answered by Him whose hearing matters." Oralro thrust out his jaw, and prominent lower lip, in solid defiance. "I say, we shall be reticent only in this, Brother; we shall say nothing if not asked, but if asked, we shall answer fully."

Folweel sighed acquiescence. He had the agreement of all the others on this present bit of strategy, and this was as much agreement from Oralro as he was likely to get.

Still, best make some contingency plans in case some questioner did get to Oralro and asked him questions he was all too liable to answer.

"What is your complaint?" Wotheng roared at the sullen crowd. Goody Nima, he noted, was in the forefront of the lot, looking harassed but purposeful. "What brings you to clamor at my door in such unseemly fashion?"

"Vile wizardry!" howled an anonymous voice.

"Let us come in and clean out that nest of vipers!" yelled another, carefully distant from the first crier.

"Lord Wotheng, you have harbored serpents under your roof!" screeched a third. Clumsy, that one: "harboring serpents" was a phrase often used in sermons at Yotha's temple. Someone might notice, and make good guesses.

"Words full of wind," Wotheng snorted. "I doubt that any of you has a true charge of crime to bring me. What harm has been done, what crime committed? Have any of you a true and plain accusation?"

"I do!" Nima darted forward, waving a rolled parchment in her hand. "*I* have a charge of crime committed by that witch who teaches wizardry right inside your walls."

Wotheng waved the near guards aside and let the woman come to him with her scroll. He opened it in front of the expectant crowd and read the crabbed writing. Oh yes, the woman had been careful and thorough.

"I charge the wizardess Eloti," Nima announced to the crowd, straight from the words on the scroll, which she'd no doubt memorized. "I charge her with the crime of encouraging others to break the law against vile and harmful magic, to wit: the forbidden making of images of living persons, so as to allow the working of curses and similar evil magecraft. I further claim that such harm has in fact been done through such means—by an accidental agent—to one of your lordship's tenants." She paused, panting, triumphant at having got through the whole speech without a slip.

The crowd cheered raucously.

Wotheng raised an eyebrow, noting how quickly and neatly Nima had passed over Losh's involvement in the "vile and harmful magic." It was clear enough what direction her argument would take.

"Very well." Wotheng rolled up the parchment and shoved it in his belt purse. "Accusation of crime has been duly brought forward. I will sit in hearing on this case tomorrow, in the great hall, at second bell."

The crowd cheered wildly, with something of that undertone often heard at dogfights.

You'll have your show, Wotheng promised, casting his eyes over the now jolly mob. At the crowd's edge he saw Sulun, just riding up, looking bewildered and horrified at the scene. The man must have been on his way back here, to arrive so quickly. Too late, anyway. *The game is set and moving, my poor friend.* Wotheng stepped back in the doorway to avoid meeting Sulun's eyes. *No choice now but to play to the finish.*

Half the vale, it seemed, came crowding into the main courtyard of Ashkell House for the trial. The baker did a fine business selling smallcakes to the crowd, and the brewer would have done better if Gynallea hadn't bluntly ordered him to stop; clear heads, she explained, would be needed for this business.

Sulun, from his seat on a bench at Wotheng's left, looked about in dismay. Here, ranked behind the accused, sat Eloti's friends and household; ranged behind them, in merry disorder, were students from her school, plus their friends and some of their families. They munched small-cakes, chattered with each other, compared notes, and cheered when Eloti came out and sat in the Accused's chair—more of an arena cheering section than an audience at a trial.

Losh was not among them; he sat, looking miserable, close to his tight-lipped mother in the Accusers' seats, several rows of benches to the right of Lord Wotheng's tall chair, the official Judgement Seat.

The rest of the crowd sat or stood piled in rough ranks before the three official zones, held back by a line of Wotheng's household guards. Some of them wore ribbons or bits of cloth in Deese's familiar colors: iron gray and brass yellow. A few others, arranged closer to the Accus-ers' side, wore scraps of orange and red.

"This is a game to them," Sulun groaned quietly. "An amusement! Nobody sways an arena crowd with sweet reason. What shall we do?"

"Hush." Vari patted his arm. "We can amuse folk better than that lot."

Wotheng stood up, pulling his best cloak around him, and intoned a brief prayer to assorted gods. The crowd stayed respectfully silent until he sat down, glanced at a parchment list on the table before him, and summoned the first Accuser.

Nima stood, rustling in her starched best finery, and repeated—almost word for word—what she'd said the day before at Wotheng's gate. She would have sat down then, but Wotheng stopped her and insisted she tell her whole tale, as a witness, right then. Somewhat flustered, she related how she'd heard from the housemaid just the morning before how Pado—she flashed a veiled look at the landholder's smirking daughter—had been telling everyone that Losh had gone and bewitched Irga.

". . . So I went to see her and asked what she meant by such, and we argued somewhat." The whole crowd snickered at that, which made Nima blush furiously but didn't stop her recital. "She told me how she'd found Losh's . . . school drawings . . . and brought them to your lordship, and how she saw . . ." a brief sniff. ". . . Irga's mother come report her daughter's bewitchment. So I went to talk to Losh, and . . ." Nima paused for a deep breath, then said the rest in a rush. "He hadn't known anything about it. He was terribly upset, he was; ran right out of the house, for all I called him to wait. So then I didn't know what to do, so I talked to, er, some neighbors, and they told me to write up a Bill of Accusation, m'lord, and bring it to you, which I did." She fell silent and looked around her, as if for support.

"I notice that you didn't come alone to bring your petition," Wotheng commented. "Why was that?"

"Er, well . . ." Nima glanced about her again. "I was fearful of witchcraft, m'lord, so I asked some, er, friends and neighbors to come with me. For protection, you know."

"Protection?" Wotheng's expression was bland, mildly curious. "Against whom? And why?"

"Why, against that Deese witch that corrupted my son!" Nima shrilled, voice cracking as she pointed to Eloti. "He said she'd told him it was quite all right to draw pictures, spreading evil magic about . . . Who knows what else she could do? I wasn't safe—none of us are safe—with that sort running about, doing whatever magic they please!"

She paused, gulping for air.

Eloti raised an elegant eyebrow, turned to the crowd and spread her hands wide. "I'd never even met her before," she murmured, just audible in the moment's near silence.

"Has the Accused any questions to ask of this witness?" said Wotheng.

"Just one." Eloti turned back to face Nima, who squirmed

under her gaze. "Goodwife Nima, before you wrote your Bill of Accusation, while you were still asking neighbors for advice, did you not also ask advice of your personal priest?"

The crowd rumbled knowingly.

Nima paled. "I—I suppose so, among so many others . . ." she admitted.

Eloti leaned back in her chair and made a polite gesture of dismissal.

"You may sit down," said Wotheng. "Let the witness named Pado step forth and tell her tale."

Pado clasped her hands primly as she told of finding the three drawings, guessing whose they were, being disturbed by them and taking them to Lord Wotheng.

"As for telling folk about what I saw and heard of Irga's mother," she finished, "well, why shouldn't I? I *knew* Losh had done wrong."

"What?" said Wotheng, looking most innocently confused. "You mean, in not marrying you?"

Now it was Pado's turn to blush furiously. "That was last year!" she snapped. "No, I meant in making drawings. That's forbidden by law, you know, no matter what Mistress Eloti said."

Wotheng turned to Eloti and asked if she had any questions for this witness.

Again, Eloti had only one. "Precisely where and how did you find these three drawings?" she asked, a carrying note in her voice.

"Why . . ." Pado blinked, confused. "In truth, *I* didn't find them. One of the other students did. That clerk, Dubba? Duppa? He gave me them, said he'd found them in the courtyard, and did I know whose they were. I thought I did, so I took them."

"Lord Wotheng," said Eloti, turning toward the Judgement Seat, "I request that we summon the clerk Duppa and ask how he came by those drawings."

The crowd rumbled again; knowing laughter and speculation.

"Quite a good idea." Wotheng got to his feet, rang a handbell and announced to all and sundry, "Clerk Duppa, stand forth."

Nobody stood up.

The crowd rumbled louder.

Sulun, glancing over the small sea of faces, noticed shuffling movement toward the rear, by the wall. Who was that? A scattering of figures, robed and hooded in nondescript dark cloth, faces muffled and shadowed: who could they be?

Yotha's priests, I'll wager!

Wotheng made the summons twice more, with no result except more noise of speculation from the audience. "Does anyone here know the whereabouts of Clerk Duppa?" he shouted.

"Try Yotha House!" shouted a brawny youth, one of Biddon's apprentices.

The crowd roared agreement, with some dissent.

Wotheng gave an odd, grim smile. "Be there anyone here from Yotha House?" he asked loudly.

At the back of the crowd there was a brief argument; someone grabbed at someone else's sleeve, which was roughly tugged free. A portly man cried, "Here!" and jostled his way to the front of the throng. "I am Oralro," he announced, "Second Priest of Yotha. I know of no Clerk Duppa in Yotha House."

The assemblage muttered and hitched away from him.

"We shall make search for this Duppa," said Wotheng. "Meanwhile, let Ilna, mother of Irga, stand forth."

Irga's mother stood up among the rightside benches and duly gave her stark and pathetic account.

On the leftward benches, Yanados and Doshi conferred in whispers.

"That's done it. That's brought Yotha into it," said Yanados. "Now we'll start getting at the truth."

"Maybe good guesses, but nothing proved," Doshi said gloomily. "You can wager they blotted out their tracks. I'd say this Duppa is probably at the bottom of some well by now."

Ilna finished her tale, recounting how she'd taken her afflicted daughter to a neighbor wife and then come to ask help of Lord Wotheng. "The rest you know," she said, clasping her hands.

Wotheng scratched his chin and asked if the Accused had any questions.

"I do," said Eloti. "Goodwife, did you ask your daughter what she had eaten or drunk before this fit came upon her?"

The assemblage fell silent, surprised by that.

Ilna was clearly surprised too. "Wh—why, no. I thought nothin' of that, but only of gettin' her safe. Why?"

"And did it occur to you, at any time, that there might be any other cause than magic for your daughter's fit?"

The crowd muttered, chewing that over.

"Nay, m'lady," Ilna answered. "She said she was bewitched. What else could it be?"

"Poison," said Eloti.

The whole audience gasped, then broke into raucous argument.

Wotheng clanged his bell until the noise stopped, looking oddly satisfied.

"But who'd want t'poison my daughter?" Ilna cried. "What harm'd she ever done t'any?"

The crowd rumbled again, tossing up names like flotsam on an unquiet sea. Pado and Nima looked daggers at each other. Losh put his head in his hands. Only Oralro, standing with arms defiantly crossed in the forefront of the throng, seemed untroubled.

"Huh, he knows *he* didn't do it." Zeren muttered at Sulun's elbow. "Could be he doesn't know who did. I'll wager the high priest doesn't tell him everything."

"Goodwife!" Wotheng thundered, loud enough to make everyone shut up and listen. "Know you if this mysteriously missing Clerk Duppa ever showed an . . . interest in your daughter? Ever spoke to her? Admired her from a distance? Showed any anger toward her? Anything?"

Ilna only spread her hands and shook her head in bewilderment. Not that it mattered; the uproar from the crowd would have drowned any spoken answer.

"What's he doing?" Omis whispered to Zeren. "Is he trying to accuse this Duppa in his absence?"

"I'm not sure," Zeren admitted, rubbing his eyes. He'd spent the night sitting, armed and armored, in front of Eloti's door; he hadn't spent much or well, and that gave no edge to his wit. "Howsoever, he's opened an interesting line of thought. Did Duppa steal the drawings, magic the girl, then try to hide it by passing on the drawings to Pado?"

"Not likely, you know."

"True, but this mob will wonder about it."

Wotheng quelled the chattering horde again, and summoned forth Losh.

"Damned little we'll get out of him," Arizun muttered.

True enough, Losh had little of substance to add to the trial. Yes, he'd made the drawings, seeing that his teacher had told him there was no harm in it. The one sketch was for his class on medicine, the other two, well, simply to have pictures of Irga to look at when he couldn't be with her.

The crowd snickered. Goody Nima looked grim. Pado glared daggers at the lad.

And no, Losh went on, he hadn't tried to bewitch Irga through the drawings. Why should he, knowing she loved him as much as he loved her? How could he, when he'd never in his life studied magical arts? Besides, he'd never do anything that could possibly harm her, since Irga was the dearest, sweetest, loveliest, and so on. No one could have doubted his weepy, hand-wringing sincerity.

This time the chuckles from the audience were fewer, accompanied by sighs from the younger set and indeed from any who remembered the silly giddiness of first love. Only Nima and Pado looked as if they'd bitten sour apples.

"Why," Wotheng asked, "did you place those three drawings together?"

"I didn't intend to!" Losh wailed. "I just stuffed them in my schoolbag, along with everything else."

"And how came that dark smudge to be smeared across the anatomy drawing?"

"I've no idea! *I* didn't put it there. Why should I? It's spoiled my schoolwork."

"Hmm," said Wotheng, significantly. "Has the Accused any questions?"

Eloti did. "Goodman Losh, when and where were the drawings lost?"

Losh had to stop and think about that. "I . . . saw they were gone just the day after I made them. I opened my schoolbag at class, and they weren't there. I thought I must have lost them at home, since that's where I saw them last."

"How, then, did they come to be found at school?"

"I don't know. Maybe they fell out on my way into the hall, but I don't see how, since I don't recall that I opened the bag."

"Could anyone have light-fingered them out of your school-bag, at home or on the way to class, or even after you'd arrived?"

Losh scratched his chin and looked blank. "Well, I suppose so. But why?"

"Why indeed?" said Eloti, leaning back as if she didn't expect to be answered.

The crowd speculated in a low grumble.

Smiling tightly, Wotheng called Irga to stand forth and give her story.

Irga stood up in a halo of sunlight, still a trifle pale, dressed in the prettiest gown her mother could find for her. Her dark red hair was braided loosely down her back, and her eyes looked dark and huge in her drawn face. The whole assembly sighed rapturously at the sight of her.

"She's so pretty, they'll believe anything she says," Ziya whispered.

"Let's hope she doesn't say anything against Eloti," Arizun muttered back.

Irga seemed at a loss for what to say. Wotheng urged her to begin with when, where and under what circumstances Losh had drawn her pictures.

Irga made a few false starts, blushed slightly, and admitted it had been late afternoon of four days ago, and she was out berry-picking when Losh met her. She didn't mention, though it was obvious, that the meeting had been arranged. Yes, they talked a bit about Losh's school-work, besides this and that. Yes, Losh had said he wanted to draw pictures of her, and yes, she'd consented. No, she didn't feel any danger or distress while he'd done so— only love.

This time the crowd sighed and crooned instead of snickering.

Irga blushed again and went on. Losh had left her at about sundown. She'd gone home for supper. Nothing had happened that night. In the morning she'd wakened as usual, built up the fire and put the kettle on, dressed, and went to rake out the barn. It was while she was dumping the manure cart that the fit struck her.

She paused there, shivering. Wotheng gently urged her to continue.

Irga did, describing in chilly detail the horrors she'd seen and felt.

The listening throng groaned in sympathy.

"Bad tactics," Zeren growled. "They'll be wanting blood now, and it just might be ours."

"That would hardly suit Wotheng's purposes," Vari whispered back.

"Then why is he allowing all this . . . detail to her story?"

"I don't know, but the man's no fool. He has something in mind that will be served hereby."

Irga told how she'd cried for help, thinking the whole farm was bewitched, but when her mother came running to her showing no signs of such distress she'd guessed that the curse lay only on herself. After that she remembered little save for her mother bundling her off in the donkey cart to the neighbor's farm, hours of huddling under blankets and seeing horrors crawl the walls, then being brought to Ashkell House and tended by Lady Gynallea, after which the curse slowly wore off. Yes, she was well now. No, she was certain that Losh couldn't have done that harm to her. Yes, Lady Eloti had helped care for her and had been very kind to her. No, she didn't think the Lady Eloti had done anything to bewitch her.

"Lass, whom do you think might have bewitched you?" Wotheng asked.

"I don't *know*," Irga insisted. "I didna' think I had any enemy so cruel."

"Try Pado!" one of the students in the audience yelled.

"Or Losh's mother!" called another.

The crowd roared with unkind laughter. Pado and Nima shrunk in their seats. Wotheng rang for silence, then asked if the Accused had any questions.

"Yes," said Eloti. "Irga, did you at any time think that there might be any other cause for your distress besides magic?"

"Nay," Irga admitted, "But then, I was no' thinkin' well at all."

The audience laughed gently in sympathy.

"Now think carefully," said Eloti. "Between the time you woke and the time the fit came on you, did you have anything to eat or drink—anything not taken by anyone else in your household?"

"Why . . ." Irga thought on that for a long moment. "Just a cup of herb tea, as I always do."

A quiet ripple of gasps went through the crowd.

"Aha!" Eloti pounced. "And was that herb tea in any way different, on that morning?"

"Aye," Irga nodded, remembering. "A trifle bitter, now do I think."

The assemblage rumbled angrily.

"And is there any of that herb tea left in your house?" Eloti asked, leaning forward.

"Nay, that was the last in the jar."

The crowd sighed disappointment.

Eloti paused to think for a long moment before speaking again. "Tell me, Irga: how is your house locked up at night?"

The audience rippled with new excitement as Irga considered the question.

"Why, we but put up the door bar, with the latchstring out on chance that Papa may have to get up and tend the sheep, and aye, he might be too sleepy then to remember to put out the string by himself. I do recall a time—"

"Then anyone could have crept into the house while you slept?"

"Aye . . . they could."

The crowd was chattering loudly now, trading guesses on whom the supposed night creeper might have been. The name of Duppa kept coming up.

Eloti, eyes bright and fierce, plunged into the next question. "Have you or any of your family ever gone to the ceremonies at Yotha's temple?"

The throng hushed, all ears. Oralro flushed darkly with anger.

"Aye, once. We all went to see the flames dance at midsummer rites."

"And were there many people there? Did many of the priests and under-priests and assistants have chance to lay eyes on you?"

The crowd howled understanding, making the connection.

"I resent that question!" Oralro shouted furiously. "That has no bearing on the crime under consideration, which is image-making. This is a foul slander, m'lord! Yonder witch is trying to disguise her own guilt by flinging manure—"

"Quiet!" Wotheng roared, clanging his bell. "Witness Irga need not reply to that question. Has the Accused anything further to ask?"

"Only this: Irga, have other swains come courting you, and been turned away?"

"Aye, many." Irga blushed fetchingly again. "The lads always hoot and holler at me when I come to town for marketing."

"Any in particular? Any who have been especially . . . insistent?"

"Too many to remember," Irga admitted.

The crowd laughed knowingly.

Eloti shrugged. "I have no further questions, m'lord."

"Then—" Wotheng started.

Right there the tower bell clanged for the hour of noon, startling the listening throng.

"Then let us halt these proceedings for lunch, and reassemble at next bell," said Wotheng, rising from his seat.

The assembly cheered, and disassembled. Those who had been sitting got up to stretch and rub their cramped rumps. Those who had been standing sought dry and comfortable seats. The baker went back to selling his wares at a good rate, and the brewer—under Gynallea's watchful eye—sold pint crocks of small beer.

Assorted political factions gathered to exchange views and share lunch. Sulun's party, guessing that they'd not be dining with their judge today, sat in a rough circle at their benches, surrounded by Eloti's students. They had little chance to discuss the case among themselves, since the faction of scholars insisted on plying them with good wishes, questions and suggestions—a few of which were useful.

On the other side of the court, Losh avoided his mother's frantic clutchings at his sleeve, and went to talk to Irga; in a moment they were holding hands and murmuring at each other as if they were all alone in the world. The passing crowd had the decency not to interrupt them.

Pado glanced once at Nima, shrugged apologetically, and went off to dine with his family.

Nima glared furiously at Losh and Irga, stared sourly at Pado's retreating back, then picked her way through the crowd to the nearest visible priest of Yotha, who happened to be Oralro.

At the back of the crowd, draped in his nondescript muffling cloak, Folweel made some fast notes on a waxed board and conferred quietly with Patrobe.

" 'Tisn't going well," Patrobe was muttering. "They've suggested a fine case against Duppa."

"Did you get him safely away?" Folweel whispered without looking up.

"Aye, Brother. He must be halfway down to Gol-port by now. But what shall we do now? There'll be no muzzling Oralro, not after that witch's questioning.'

"If we can't silence him, we use him. We'll go to our second plan once the Questioning of the Accused begins." He glanced up, noted Oralro pushing toward him with Nima in tow, and smiled. "And here come our two best tools for that. Step away, Brother."

"Oh, Father, may I speak with you?" Nima gushed, drawing a few startled eyes.

"Certainly, Daughter," Folweel soothed, setting a comforting arm around the flustered woman's shoulders. "Come, let us go outside and away from the ears of the ungodly. Er, Brother Oralro, do keep an eye on that witch and her friends, lest they plot mischief."

With that, he swept Nima outside the court to put a few words in her ear. They stayed there for perhaps half the noon hour, after which Nima came back alone, smiling grimly. Folweel strolled quietly into the court a moment later, and went to find Oralro.

The tower bell rang again, the crowd reassembled, and Wotheng formally took his seat. "Let the Accused stand forth," he announced.

The throng fell so silent that distant bird cries could be heard from beyond the walls.

Eloti stood up, hands clasped loosely before her. "I have little to tell of events," she said, "but much of facts. Yes, Losh is one of my students—and an excellent student at that. He should, in time, go to some great university."

On the far bench, Losh blushed and squeezed Irga's hand tighter. She gave him an admiring look. Nima glowered at both of them.

"Yes, I use pictures as teaching devices—indeed, it would be almost impossible to teach medicine and mechanics without them. Yes, I have said to my entire class, including Losh, that there is no harm in making pictures of living persons—and indeed, there is none."

Both Nima and Oralro, back to their former places,

opened their mouths to protest. Eloti went on, giving them no time for it.

"It has been said that drawn or graven images can be used as substitutes for actual persons in operations of magic—and yes, *this is true.*"

The whole crowd gasped, including the Deese faction.

"But then, anything can be so used. The mere sight or memory of a person can be used to make him, or her, target for a curse—or a blessing. Should we then blind everyone's eyes, or blot out everyone's memory?" Eloti turned to face the assembly. "Pictures are necessary tools, and no tool is evil in itself. Objects have no will, no power, no purpose of their own, save what people give to them. Good and evil, help and harm, reside in the will and action of the user, not in the thing used."

"Blasphemy!" snapped Oralro. "Objects have power that—"

"Silence!" Wotheng retorted. "Wait until the Accused has finished speaking."

"Magic," said Eloti, "requires a most special and concerted use of will and knowledge. It requires great concentration, long study, much practice, and great knowledge of Natural Philosophy. To be quite honest, I have met no one in the vale—" she flicked a glance toward Oralro "—save in the various temples and shrines, who has the knowledge and skill needed to even begin the study, let alone the practice, of magic. No, not even among my students."

She turned an apologetic glance toward Losh, who blushed further.

"Certainly I have not taught magic to any, neither have I found any who are capable of practicing magic without such a course of study. Therefore I have told my students, when asked, that indeed there is no harm in making images—since none of them could use such images for anything but ordinary learning." Eloti cast a narrow-eyed look around the assembly. "Therefore, also, I conclude that Irga's affliction was *not* caused by anything done in my school. As you have heard, there is reason to believe that either the drawings were stolen by someone else—someone trained and capable of working magic—who then used them, for his own reasons, to ill-wish the girl—"

The crowd racketed with speculation on whom that might be. Oralro purpled with indignation.

"—or, more likely, that someone deliberately poisoned Irga and then made effort to give the impression of witchcraft, even unto casting suspicion upon Losh."

Nima squirmed on her bench, suddenly undecided. The dull-robed figure beside her patted her arm and bent close to whisper in her ear. Her face tightened again. Losh paled and gritted his teeth. Irga clenched her hand in his. Pado pursed her lips and looked vaguely elsewhere. Oralro stamped from foot to foot in steaming frustration. The rest of the throng muttered angrily.

"No," Eloti continued, "I did not know there was any law against making images of living persons, not until I was accused."

Wotheng rolled his eyes skyward. Technically, he supposed, his first questions to Eloti might in fact be called accusations. It wasn't a lie.

"Nonetheless, I maintain that this law should be more honored in the breach than in the observance, seeing that it is useless—as useless as forbidding bows in order to prevent poaching. If the law must be enforced, then let its punishment be altered to better suit the nature of the crime—such as paying a fine of, say, one flower or a pinch of grain to be placed on the nearest altar of Kula, along with a prayer that one's work will not be misused."

The student faction broke out in a cheer at the elegance of her solution. They could see in it the beginning of a pretty, romantic custom. Two old grannies who regularly tended the villa's shrine of Kula cheered likewise, thinking of the free bread they might collect from such a tradition. Wotheng smiled and rubbed his beard. Gynallea laughed outright. Eloti sat down and amid growing applause.

Wotheng quelled the noise with his bell. "Do any wish to question the Accused?" he announced.

"Me! Me!" Oralro and Nima yelled simultaneously.

Wotheng clanged his bell for order. "Let the Accuser speak first," he said.

Nima shot to her feet. "Stories!" she snapped. "Pretty tales! No shred of proof to any of this! We've only your word for it—and maybe your friends'—that your advice was harmless. You've admitted yourself that anyone *could* have stolen the drawings and used them to bewitch the girl. Who can tell but that was what you intended?"

The crowd rustled with surprise.

"Who can say," Nima plowed on, "that it wasn't yourself who stole the drawings and magicked them? 'Twould be a clever way to strike down a rival, and punish my son for preferring Irga to you!"

The assembly roared. Eloti's eyebrows shot up to her hairline; this was the last thing on earth she'd expected. Behind her, Zeren swore sulfurously and struggled to his feet through restraining hands.

Wotheng clanged for silence. "Let the Accused answer!" he bellowed.

"Well," Eloti marvelled, "this is news to me."

Her class laughed in appreciation.

"First, though I admit Losh is a handsome and clever boy, I've never had any, hmm, romantic interest in him. For one thing, he's a trifle young for me."

Pado, who'd been staring at Eloti in wide-eyed horror, now ducked her head and squirmed furiously on her bench.

"For another, I never so much as knew that Irga existed, nor knew her name or face, until she was already afflicted. I will submit to truth spell upon that." Eloti smiled sweetly out at the audience, knowing full well that there was no such thing as a "truth spell." There was only ill-wishing and well-wishing, nothing else; but let the crowd—and Yotha's wizards—believe what they liked.

"No one can truth spell a wizard!" Oralro shouted from the front of the horde. "Everyone knows that!" He glared around him defiantly, as if daring anyone to contradict him. Of course, no one did.

"For a third," Eloti continued, "I already have a lover, whom I intend to marry at spring planting."

She turned to gesture at Zeren, who got to his feet and glared daggers alternately at Losh and his mother. "That's me!" he thundered, hand visibly clenching the grip of his sword. "Does anyone want to challenge the Lady's word on that?"

No, nobody did. The throng buzzed with speculations and comparisons. A mere boy's appeal, against that of an obvious warrior-magician—and handsome, to boot—seemed very little.

"You're going to marry Eloti?" Doshi gaped, while Yanados tugged warningly at his sleeve.

"I hadn't intended to announce it this way," Zeren admitted.

The surrounding students laughed.

"For yet a fourth," Eloti went on, "when would I have the opportunity to filch Losh's drawings—assuming I even knew they existed—and place a curse on the girl? Irga was afflicted only a little after dawn; Losh did not come to school until much later. I could not have stolen the drawings when he left class the day before, since he did not make them until much later that afternoon, at Irga's farm. Neither could I have gone secretly to Losh's house to steal the drawings—again, assuming I knew he had made them, and how could that be?—because I spent the rest of that day and all the night here at Ashkell House, in the company of the Lady Gynallea."

"True," announced Gynallea, glaring around the assemblage as if defying anyone to doubt *her*.

Nima took a half-step back, still frowning. "Who knows what your magic can do?" she grumbled. "Who knows but you might have used it to spy on Losh, see where he went, whom he met, and what he did. You could have used magic to fetch the drawings—or even curse the girl without them and make him look guilty. We've only your word for it that you can't!"

Eloti rolled her eyes, but answered patiently. "*When* could I have done this? Losh claims that he went to meet Irga after school, and stayed with her until sundown. During all that time I was quite busy discussing uses of herbs with the Lady Gynallea, as well as various other members of her household, who might also be called as witnesses. After sundown, I was at dinner with all of Ashkell household—and such dinners, as many can attest, tend to run late."

Various servitors of Ashkell House laughed agreement at that.

"Afterwards, as usual, I went to the wash house with several others of Ashkell House, and thence to bed. By such time Losh was surely asleep, with his drawings safe in his schoolbag. Thus, even if I could use magic for scrying—which, I dare say, nobody in the vale can do—just when was I to spy upon Losh and discover whom he met? When, for that matter, was I to ill-wish the girl? Such things do take time, you know."

"You could have done it that night, or next morning, when no one else was awake and about," Nima insisted. "You could have scried into his schoolbag—"

"But the drawings weren't there!" Losh shouted, jumping to his feet. "I remember, I put the pictures of Irga under my pillow, so I could dream about her!"

The crowd laughed. Irga blushed prettily.

Nima glared briefly at her son. "You could have scried on his dreams, then. Or you might have scried him long before, found the girl, and waited for a good time to make your revenge. You could have done it! We've only *your* word to say you couldn't, or wouldn't!"

Eloti sighed loudly with impatience. "Why, then, when Irga was first brought to Ashkell House, did the Lady Gynallea's medicines ease this 'curse,' long before I heard anything of it?"

"Do you dare to say *I'm* a witch?" Gynallea shouted. "Or that I connived with Eloti on such a fool's venture? No, woman! That girl was poisoned, or I've never seen it."

Unnoticed, Wotheng shook his head. The crowd buzzed, enjoying the juicy fight.

"She could have set the curse to look that way," Nima grumbled, retreating. "She might have deceived you."

"Hardly," Gynallea snorted.

"You've invented a pretty tale yourself, Goodwife," said Eloti, "and with no shred of proof. From what facts we do know, 'tis far more likely that someone crept into Irga's house and poisoned the herbs she used next morning."

"Even that could have been some agent of yours!" Nima retorted.

"Who?" Eloti shot back. "Someone at Ashkell House? Ask the household if anyone stole out that night to go all the way to Irga's house, or if any were missing from the house all the night and didn't reappear until the next day."

"Someone from Deese House, more likely! Anyone there would tell tales to protect you!"

"And how would I have sent word to them, ten leagues away, that now was the time to go to Irga's house and poison her drink?"

"Magic! Magic again!"

"And would magic tell them also where to find Irga's

house, which none of us have ever visited? Would magic carry someone there, unseen and unheard by man or beast across all the farms in between? Woman, if I had magic like that, I wouldn't bother with such petty stuff; I'd have magicked Irga and Losh and you yourself straight to the bottom of the Midworld Sea. I certainly wouldn't waste time sitting here arguing with you."

The throng roared with laughter at that. One of the laborers who had worked on Deese House's walls commented loudly that with that sort of magic the wizards of Deese wouldn't have needed his help to restore their house—and could have saved themselves a good bit of money. Students speculated that, with that kind of power, Eloti wouldn't have had to spend so many moons teaching them; she could simply have magicked the knowledge into their heads.

"Sure as the nine hells," Zeren roared above the clamor, "she could have magicked your stupid mouth shut!"

That set everyone bellowing with laughter. Wotheng rang repeatedly for order, finally gave up and let the crowd laugh itself tired.

Nima, blushing red as a ripe apple, looked about her for help. No use: nothing could have been heard in that din anyway. At length she sat down, muttering bitterly to herself. Her husband huddled down in his robes and looked elsewhere.

As the noise dwindled, Wotheng rang again for silence. This time the crowd obeyed. "Has anyone else questions for the Accused?" he asked.

"I do!" snapped Oralro, striding forward. "Lady, if I dare use the term, I truly do resent the slanderous suggestions you have made against this goodwife here and against the House of Yotha besides. Slanderous, I say, to accuse any in our herd of most vilely and lecherously bewitching a young virgin!"

Several in the crowd snickered. Irga blushed furiously, and didn't look.

"Worse still to accuse us of any dealings with poison—and this is not the first such vile accusation! Nay, nor the first instance of harm come to the innocent through the careless witcheries of Deese House and its wizards. Was not our own stonemason crushed to death while working upon their walls?"

"His own damned fault!" yelled one of the workmen in the crowd.

Oralro went on as if he hadn't heard. "And more slanders: when their own workmen were poisoned with bad food, did not these Deese wizards hasten to blame our brotherhood, even though the baker's carter confessed to the deed?"

"He named one of your under-priests, too!" shouted a peeved guardsman.

Oralro sailed on, blithely unheeding. "All this harm has come to the vale with the presence of these Deese wizards! Has not Yotha warned and warned his faithful herd, repeatedly, of this danger? Have we not done our best to warn others, though they, being blinded with greed for petty wonders, have not heeded us? Have we not warned the folk of the vale that these wizards of Deese are careless in both magic and morals—allowing male and female priests to sleep under the same roof—"

"Is this your question?" Eloti snapped, spots of color showing in her cheeks.

"No it isn't, and I'm not finished!" Oralro stamped a heavy foot. "We have maintained, as Yotha bids us, that the gods are troubled by such proud carelessness. We, m'lord, are troubled also by such immoral quickness to slander others for the harm done by Deese's wizards. We are also appalled, as all good folk should be, to hear from this witch's very lips her contempt for the law! Did she not boldly admit to breaching the law against image making? And did she not blatantly claim before you all that the law itself was wrong, and should be abolished? What can we expect of those who have such contempt for law itself?"

"Common sense," Eloti answered. "Next question?"

The crowd brayed with laughter.

Oralro purpled slightly, took a deep breath, and preached on. "More, she claims, as you heard, that drawn or graven images have no power—more, that objects in themselves have no power, nor even purpose. I say before you all, this is a most blasphemous lie!"

The audience rumbled to itself, wondering.

"Of course objects have purpose! Anyone who looks at them knows that. A sword, for example, has no purpose except to kill people."

"Bull turds!" Zeren bellowed, springing to his feet. "I've used *my* sword to chop wood, make fire and stir soup!"

"A wagon," Oralro continued fiercely, "has no purpose save to draw loads."

"Or to burn for firewood, or rot and feed wood ants!" Zeren retorted.

Wotheng wearily clanged his bell, but said nothing.

"I do not say objects cannot be put to other uses than their obvious purpose," Oralro conceded, glaring daggers at Zeren. "But they rarely are. When one sees a shovel, one may safely claim that it is to be used for digging."

"Or for clanging an enemy over the head!" yelled Zeren.

"When one sees the image of a god, one may safely claim it is used for prayer and worship."

"Or for scaring money out of the gullible!"

"And when one sees an image of a living person, one may surely claim it is to be used for purposes of magic!"

"Or for kissing and sticking under one's pillow!"

Wotheng clanged the bell repeatedly, quelling both the shouting match between Oralro and Zeren and the appreciative laughter and cheers of the assembly.

"Sir Priest," he insisted, "get to your question for the Accused."

"Why, 'tis only this. Witch, does or does not the House of Deese bear ill will toward the House of Yotha?"

The crowd hushed, listening.

"Certainly," said Eloti, "and for good reason."

"Oh indeed?" Oralro smirked. "Such as our complaints against your careless use of magic? Such as our warnings against your blatant immorality? Such as our thwarting your attempts to ill-wish our priesthood? We could say much about *those* reasons."

"Not at all," Eloti replied calmly. "We have but one reason: you attacked us first."

"You've no proof of that!" Oralro shouted, stamping again. "You've nothing but your own vile slanders! Only your word, against that poor innocent woman whose son you endangered, saying there's no harm in images! You expect folk to trust in that, do you, when all knowledge and even legend say otherwise? Do you—"

"Certainly not," Eloti snapped, rising to her feet. "I can put that to proof before all this gathering. Lord Wotheng, bid Losh come forward."

The crowd hushed in shock. Wotheng rubbed his jaw and gave her a long look. "Losh, come forward," he said at last.

Clumsy with confusion, Losh did so.

"Lord Wotheng, please hand him a pen, some ink, a piece of blank parchment and a board upon which to brace it," said Eloti.

Wotheng raised both shaggy eyebrows, but handed over the requested items to Losh. "Hope you know what you're doing," he murmured.

"Now, Losh," said Eloti, smoothing down her dress, 'I pray you, draw a picture of *me*."

The whole assembly drew its collective breath. Gynallea waved frantic signals to her husband, who ignored them. Sulun and his friends looked at each other in bewilderment. Eloti smiled prettily.

"Go on, Losh. As I've said, *things* have no power—not until people give it to them."

With shaky fingers, Losh sat down and did as he was bid.

The minutes crawled. The audience crept closer, trying to peer over Losh's shoulder at the growing image. Those who could see any of it agreed that Eloti's passing judgement was right; Losh did indeed have great skill at drawing. There, that was surely the line of Lady Eloti's skirt, real as life; and there, yes, that was the very angle of her wrist. Slowly the form took shape, and then the face, smiling confidently. The crowd murmured softly in appreciation. Losh drew on, sweat beading on his forehead and trickling down his neck.

Oralro tapped his feet and jittered with impatience. Sulun and company sat quietly, sweating nearly as much as Losh. Gynallea shot puzzled glances at her husband. Wotheng alone was calm, smiling serenely, hands clasped on the table before him.

At length Losh heaved a deep sigh, set down the pen, got up and handed the drawing to Eloti. He put the board, pen and inkpot back on Wotheng's table and trudged off to his seat on the benches without a word. Irga took his hand again, radiating sympathy.

"Very good, Losh," said Eloti, studying the drawing. "Quite flattering, in fact. Now—" She turned to Wotheng. "Would you please ask Goodwife Nima to step forward."

The crowd buzzed like troubled bees as Nima bustled to the center of the courtyard.

Eloti calmly handed her the drawing. "Lord Wotheng," she said, "if, as certain parties have claimed, things have power in themselves which any person can use for ill purposes, then let Nima prove it. Let her turn her back on me, look only at the drawing, and curse *me* if she can."

The audience gasped in concert.

On the rightward bench, Folweel caught his breath in furious hope. Gods, if only he could signal to Oralro, if only the man would face him for a moment, they could use this chance to quietly cast their own curse. It would have to be something simple, done without tools or preparation—but then, a simple curse could more effectively be disguised as something Nima herself might do. Once the curse struck, everyone would think Nima had done it and that Oralro had been right. So perfect! But Oralro wasn't looking at him, couldn't be signalled. He'd have to do it himself, and wait for just the theatrically proper moment.

On the leftward bench, Arizun had just come to the same conclusion. "Gods, this is madness!" he whispered. "We don't know how many wizards they have, or what power . . . Nine hells, I'll have to help her alone." He closed his eyes and began silently chanting the meditative formulas while Ziya watched him, fascinated.

None of this was lost on Eloti. She was aware of the prickling, nonphysical pressure behind her, with that characteristic tone/color of Arizun's mind. Clever of the boy to think of it so soon, and she could certainly use the protection if this ploy failed. She silently recited the formulas herself while carefully keeping that utterly confident smile on her face, keeping it turned toward Nima. Much depended now on that silly woman's character.

Nima stared for a moment at the drawing, then glowered at Eloti. If mere target and malice were sufficient to cast an effective curse, everyone in the assembly could see that she would have done it then.

Arizun softly chanted, Folweel held his breath and waited, Eloti smiled.

Nima's assurance broke. "What nonsense is this?" she shouted, her voice noticeably shrill. "How should I put a curse on a skilled sorceress? Surely she knows means to prevent me, ward off the curse, turn it back on me, gods know what. It isn't fair, it isn't the same at all."

The crowd rumbled disappointment, speculation, contempt.

"Aughhh!" bellowed one of the former work gang. "A pigeon just splattered me! It must be the curse, deflected on the innocent. Ey, witchcraft!"

"Oooeee!" one of Eloti's students took up the game, tumbling to the ground and kicking theatrically. "I've gas pains from the beer. She must have bewitched my belches downward! Magic! Magic!" In the middle of the performance he cut a loud fart. His neighbors flinched away, holding their noses. "Praise be to all the gods," the student improvised merrily. "I've been cured!"

The audience roared with laughter. Wotheng tried quelling it with his bell, but was shaking too much with ill-held guffaws to ring properly. Oralro purpled again, stamped his feet and stuck out his petulant lip. Folweel silently cursed the lost opportunity, and bitterly hoped for another.

"It's not *fair!*" Nima shrilled in fury, her headdress slipping in disarray. "I'm no wizard! Let some real wizard do it!"

She spun on her heel, turned to the nearest of the Yotha priests—which happened to be Oralro—and thrust the parchment into his hand.

"You do it," she snapped. "You'd be a match for the likes of her."

Oralro was startled for only a moment; then a broad smile spread across his face. He glanced warily at Eloti, then set to studying the parchment.

The crowd roared, argued, railed and stared.

Folweel sat up straighter, struggling to keep his grin of victory from showing.

Eloti kept smiling, but it wasn't easy. She concentrated on the formulas, driving her mind up the levels to the plane where magic could be released, feeling her wave front spread and link with Arizun's. She hadn't, she fleetingly admitted, expected this to come so soon.

"Halt!" Wotheng roared, startling everyone. He lurched to his feet, swinging his handbell like a club, looking as ferocious as anyone had ever seen him. "I'll have no wizards' duel in my court! No, nor in my villa, either—nor anywhere on my lands. By the gods, my land's suffered too much from wizardry already."

He glared around him, ignoring his wife's amazed look. The guards, with no signal given, snapped to attention. Everyone else stared in silence.

Wotheng smiled grimly and rang his handbell three times. "Here's my judgement on this case," he thundered. "Since this matter cannot be proved nor decided save by methods of wizardry, let it so be proved. This case shall be decided in trial by combat."

Everyone gasped at that. Folweel threw caution aside and waved frantically at Oralro. Nima turned around and around, looking dazed at the sudden change. Eloti's students cheered. Sulun's coterie looked at each other and all started talking at once.

Wotheng clanged his bell once more for silence.

"I hereby decree," he announced, "that at noon tomorrow this assemblage shall gather on the field outside the walls of Deese House, there to witness said combat. The wizards of Deese shall stand before their walls and the wizards of Yotha shall face them at not less than fifty paces. Upon given signal, both shall duel with their respective skills until one or the other is defeated. Upon the victory of one or the other shall this matter be decided. So be it known and written." He clanged his bell three more times, then added, "this gathering is now adjourned."

With that, he drew his robes around him and marched back toward the doors of Ashkell House, not glancing to either side.

Gynallea gaped at his retreating back, then ran to gather up his assorted parchments and tablets and hurried after him. The two nearest guards looked at each other, shrugged, and went to pick up the table. Other guards hurried to carry in the other furniture.

"M'lord, m'lord!" Oralro was howling. "What's to keep yonder wizards from stealing a march and bewitching us, to their advantage, before combat tomorrow?"

"You have my picture, do you not?" Eloti snapped, nimbly hopping to her feet as a guard came to pick up her chair. "Keep it in surety, then. I'd advise you, nonetheless, not to try ill-wishing *me* beforetime."

"Witness!" Zeren bellowed at the guards, snagging their attention. "If any harm—*any* harm—comes to the Lady

Eloti before the combat tomorrow, you'll all know that the priests of Yotha are guilty beyond doubt!"

Oralro snorted disgust, rolled up the parchment drawing and shoved it firmly in his belt pouch. "No one shall so much as see this image beforetime," he announced, ignoring Folweel's flailing hands. "That *I* vow, by Yotha's flame."

Arizun ran to Eloti and clutched her arm. "Will you be safe until then?" he whispered.

"Once inside our walls, I will be," Eloti hissed back. "Let's get there with all haste."

The milling crowd was roaring with delight and anticipation at the coming duel, splitting into factions within factions, and already the bet makers were offering conflicting odds. The brewer pulled out his better bottles, and did a lively business. Several students formed a protective honor guard around Eloti and her friends and helped push through the throng to the gates, the wagon, and escape.

Sulun grabbed at Zeren's sleeve, utterly bewildered. "Why did he do it?" he asked, as if the brawny soldier would know. "Why did he throw us into this? I thought he was our friend."

"He planned it so." Zeren growled, glancing back toward Ashkell House in mingled fury and admiration. "That wily old wolf—he planned for this all along."

7

"Come, Brother Oralro, give me the drawing," Folweel wheedled. "You know we have much to plan, and so little time, and I need to, er, study the witch."

"I'll not," the burly Second Priest huffed. "Upon my honor and oath, I'll keep it safe and untouched until tomorrow noon."

" 'Twill be too late, then!"

"Too late for what? Do you intend some breach of honor, sir? I swore to keep the picture in surety against any such same connivance toward Yotha House."

"But there have been magical attempts already," Folweel tried. "The last just an hour ago."

"Aye, and I felt that." Oralro sneered. "That was practice work by our own under-priests, and quite poorly they did it, too. Really, Brother Folweel, after all these years of instructing our novices in basics of magecraft, did you think I wouldn't know the feel of the spirit of every mage in the house?"

Folweel sighed in frustration. "Well, then *you* deal with them! Make them practice properly in strategy for tomorrow, for I've work enough to do with the tools."

"That I'd planned to do, Brother, once I finished meditation." Oralro hesitated. "If you truly need to raise extra defenses against the witch tonight, why not simply use your memory of her as focus?"

"That I could do in any case," Folweel fumed. "I was hoping for something more concrete."

"Hm, well, it would not help you," Oralro admitted. "She's within Deese House, and the place is most thoroughly warded."

"Ah?" Folweel perked up, wondering if Oralro truly had discovered the legendary—and never proved—technique of scrying. "And how would you know that, Brother Oralro?"

"Umm . . ." The burly Second Priest looked actually embarrassed. "Because I've already tried to, er, chastise her. The attempt failed. There is effective counterspelling."

"Oh." Folweel sighed. If Oralro couldn't get through Deese House's shields, *he* certainly couldn't. "So that drawing is useless to us."

"Er, yes. And upon my honor and sworn word, I may yield it up to no man."

Easy honor, that! Folweel fumed, stamping off to see to the distillery.

Cloaked and hooded to anonymity, Gynallea stepped through the doorway of Deese's temple—and stopped to stare at what was there revealed.

The floor before her was carved with deep, narrow ditches in concentric rings, each labelled in strange letters or perhaps numbers. In their center the forge blazed, heated to eye-searing glare by a mammoth bellows. The bellows was powered by no human hand but by a complex arrangement of gears, which ran from a thick leather belt, which was turned by a whirling axle set high in the wall. Above the blazing forge hung and swayed an enormous blackened bucket of unidentifiable stone, swaying like a pendant on its thick black chains, clearly just hauled up from the roaring furnace. Its controlling chains hung also from heavy gears upon an axle running across the ceiling, and the half-naked Deese wizards hauling thereon looked like toiling trolls in the flaring light. One of them—Omis? —shouted a command, and the priests ran to pull on other chains. The rest of the crowd jumped back beyond the third ditch ring, watching tensely and wiping sweat from their faces. The huge bucket swung forward, halting just above what appeared to be a block of clay with holes in the top and a complex clay funnel with many spouts leading to the holes. As Gynallea watched, fascinated, the wizard in charge shouted another order. The others pulled on the chains, and the spouted bucket tilted slowly toward the waiting funnel.

Its contents *glowed*. Creamy white and shining like the sun at summer's noon, exhaling a blast of intolerable heat, the nameless fluid poured like milk from a pitcher. It spilled, gods' milk surely, into the clay funnel and down, down the series of spouts, into the waiting holes. The holes filled to the brim, gleaming yellow, then orange, and now Gynallea could see that they contained cores of clay, originally white, now dark by comparison. The last of the gleaming gods' milk filled the holes and covered the tops of the cores, and Omis shouted again. The emptied bucket, its pulled chains rattling, swung upright and away from the furnace. The filled holes in the clay block shone like suns in the shadow of the forge's walls.

"Ease off the fire," Omis commanded, pulling a lever by the wall. The gears of the bellows promptly disconnected, and the roar of air died away, leaving only the higher-toned wind sound of the flames. "Deese be praised: a good, clean pour!"

The other wizards cheered.

"Sorcery," Gynallea whispered. "No magic greater than this."

At that point one of the wizards noticed her and came forward wiping sweat and soot off his brow. It was Sulun, she saw.

"Lady Gynallea!" he marvelled. "What on earth do you here? Won't it prejudice the case, you being the judge's wife come visiting us?"

"Oh, pish," snorted Gynallea. "I came secretly, and no one saw me. Besides, I've noted that Yotha's priests place little regard on the doings of women . . . hmm, save when it serves them. Shall we go someplace cooler to talk? I swear, 'tis like the worst of summer in here."

Sulun gladly led her into the side dining room. A common fire twinkled on the hearth, and the air seemed wonderfully cool. Sulun fetched cups and a jug of good ale from the sideboard.

"What in all the hells was that sorcery you were performing out there?" Gynallea asked, accepting her cup. "I never saw the like."

"Metal-casting," said Sulun, pouring for them both. "Omis had set up to melt iron down to pure liquid—which, I admit, I'd thought couldn't be done. He'd intended to cast a statue of Deese for the Ashkell House shrine, but then all this business came up, and now we have to cast quickly some tubes for, hmm, firepowder and burning-mineral displays. We need them by noon tomorrow, of course. Everyone who isn't here is off making firepowder—save for Eloti and Arizun, who need their sleep, and Zeren, of course, who's busy guarding them. I swear, I don't know when I'll rest."

"Hmm, firepowder workings," Gynallea considered. "No magic in that?"

"No, m'lady: pure chemistry and mechanics. Wotheng did warn us to put on a good show." Sulun mopped his forehead again. "I don't know how much this will frighten Yotha's wizards, but it should distract their ill-wishing enough to let it fail."

"Aye, good tactics. And take care that *you* be not distracted by their tricks. You can be sure, they'll use the Yotha fire; prepare for it."

"That we've done. Also, we'll have the advantage of standing under our own walls, which are already well-wished. I suspect Wotheng thought of that when he set the conditions of the . . . wizards' duel."

Gynallea studied her cup, fiddled with it, took a deep breath. "I must confess, friend Sulun, somewhat has been kept hidden from you."

Sulun raised an eyebrow and scratched his beard. "I know that none of you warned us sufficiently when first we came here, about the sheer power and threat of Yotha's wizards."

"Well, dear, we did want you to settle here and make us rich with your skills." Gynallea gave him something nearer her usual smile. " 'Twouldn't do to scare away potential wealth-makers by saying much about local troubles, now would it?"

Sulun laughed. "I'm happy you thought so highly of us, and I must confess I've never seen better patrons than we've found at Ashkell House."

" 'T 'as been mutually rewarding." Gynallea's smile slipped away. "But we didn't warn you of the possible trouble with the neighbors, either."

Sulun rolled his cup in his hands, though it wanted no warming. "Wotheng told me he needed to appear strong if he was to become noticeably rich. Without numbers for armies, he must need to look well protected by wizardry."

"Aye, dear," Gynallea sighed. "That was another reason we tolerated Yotha for so long, besides the difficulty in ousting him."

"I see."

"Not entirely, friend Sulun, and neither do I." She set down her cup. "I confess, I don't know why he rushed both of you to this wizards' duel. Had he simply decided against Yotha on the evidence given, Yotha would have continued to dwindle away—oh, sniping here and there, perhaps, but doomed nonetheless. This way, he may rid himself quickly of Yotha, but he also risks losing *you*. He's kept his counsel tight upon that, even with me. Have you any idea why he'd take such chances?"

"No . . ." Sulun pondered long. "All I can think is that he needs this settled fast, for some reason. Perhaps he fears Yotha's continued troublemaking, or he may have cause to worry strongly about his greedy neighbors. Perhaps he fears such continued squabblings would tempt them, make us appear weak and divided. He warned me to make our 'magic' look fearful enough to discourage such hopes. That's one thing that made us decide to cast and use those fire tubes. It's also why I made such a show of testing the bombard before all the workmen. By all means, let people carry tales outside the vale of our marvelous sorcerous powers. If it helps keep Wotheng—and us—safe, then I'll be happy to add to such."

"Bombard?" Gynallea asked, an odd faraway look in her eyes.

"That large fire tube mounted on the wall." Sulun took a long pull of his cup. "The one we used to, hah! plow the

north field. The workmen took to calling it a 'storm tube,'
and the name spread."

The storm tube," Gynallea murmured, gazing off into
the darkness. "Yes . . . Hmm. Friend Sulun, I think you'd
best use that, too, to make a most spectacular display
tomorrow. You must look as fearsome as you can . . . and I
doubt not that north field could use some more plowing."

"North field? But the duel is to take place before the
east gate."

"Well, then," Gynallea said with a shrug, "move the
storm tube as close to the east gate as you may. Indeed,
I'd suggest setting it to plow the ground between your folk
and Yotha's. *That* will distract them, you may be sure."

"Distract!" Sulun gulped. "Oh, indeed it will! Have you
seen how it tears up the ground? I'd not want to risk it so
close to our folk, not ever."

"You'll have a good fifty paces, at least, between you
and them."

"Still too close!"

"Then set it to strike to one side, far enough to be safe.
Or . . . aim it closer to Yotha's priests. Measure the ground
yourself." Gynallea shrugged again and got to her feet.
"But *use* it, Sulun. Set the storm tube on the east wall and
use it, where its use may best be seen. I do not doubt this
is important, and may be what decides the victory."

"Well, if you truly believe I should . . ."

"I do most firmly believe it. And now I should go, lest
the servants at home make too free with the wine cellar.
Take care, friend wizard."

Sulun rose to show her out, and stood pondering a long
time as he watched her ride away into the dark. Her
advice had always been good, and he'd be foolish not to
take it now, with so much at stake. But what, indeed, did
Wothing intend?

The sun climbed through a rare, cloudless autumn day,
gilding the sparse-grown ground and the vast procession
on the road. Lord Wotheng and Lady Gynallea led the
horde, wearing their best robes and jewelry, in a freshly
painted cart garlanded with fir branches. Their guard surrounded them, sporting fine, sharp new swords and polished shields, dressed in their new winter livery of bronze
red and dark forest green. Behind them, on horses or

mules or in cloth-covered wagons, rode the priesthood of
Yotha; they rang chimes and chanted endlessly, and the
clear sun glittered on the embroidery of their red, orange
and yellow robes. Several paces behind the priests, giving
them a wide berth, came what seemed to be half the
population of the vale. Losh and Irga shared a borrowed
horse, and chatted as merrily as if they were going to
market. Nima rode a cart with her husband and their
other children, and studiously ignored Losh and his lady-
love. Pado, several lengths back, rode a wagon with the
other women and children of her family, glaring occasionally at Losh, otherwise keeping her eyes primly lowered.
The brewer and vintner talked business as they rode, side
by side, on two wagons loaded with barrels of their respective wares. Behind them came Tygg the baker, whistling
merrily, his assorted goods and apprentices piled into a
new wagon he'd bought just the day before. Eloti's students clung together in a raucous assemblage, those on
foot clinging to the stirrups of those fortunate enough to
have mounts. Other factions gathered, walked or rode
together awhile, fragmented and re-formed. Here and there
a gaggle of farmer's children rode in file on plow horses,
and not a few on the backs of oxen. Stuffed like sausages
into wagons or carts, riding any available beast, even on
foot, the horde plodded down the road to the valley before
the gates of Deese House.

"Kula," Sulun groaned, watching from the window, "it's
like All Gods' Day back in Sabis." He shivered, wondering
how the sacrificial goats had felt on those days. At least
those beasts had no idea, until perhaps the last instant, of
what was to happen to them. He cast another look around
the great workshop/temple/front room. "Are we ready?"
he asked.

Zeren promptly stopped fencing with shadows on the
wall, sheathed his sword, and took his planned space in
the marching formation. Arizun and Eloti, already dropping into meditative state, silently nodded. Omis, Doshi
and Yanados hefted their heavy covered baskets and stepped
awkwardly into line. Ziya looked around quickly, grabbed
a tinder box off the shelf and ran for the wall. Tamira,
huddled in a corner with the two youngest, watched them
silently with wide eyes.

"Now, just as we practiced it," said Sulun, feeling absurdly like a temple dancing master. "Wait until we hear Wotheng's summons."

The others murmured tense agreement.

Sulun rechecked the baskets for the dozenth time, knowing his worry was only what Zeren called "combat nerves," still fearful that they'd left out some small tool that would prove vital in the coming trial. *And it would be my fault,* he gnawed at himself, *if our distractions fail and Eloti or Arizun loses concentration just when we need it most. . . .*

But everything was in the baskets, even spare tools and tinderboxes, everything they'd need. Sulun chewed his lip and glanced out the door at Ziya, industriously climbing to the top of the wall and scampering along it to where the loaded bombard stood. With the spare elegance of an expert, she slid the oiled cloth covering from the bombard, so smoothly that none of the approaching crowd could have seen it done. Yes, the child was very good at her task; she'd do as instructed. Pray Gynallea was correct—but then, she usually was.

Gods, from the noise outside the crowd must be close, huge and hungry!

The procession wound up the road between the two hills, officials somber and formal, audience gazing about them with wonder and some trepidation. The combat was supposed to take place before the gates of Deese House, and that was a good way up the hill ahead. The two low hills to either side of this narrow valley would provide an excellent view at a safe distance, and the more cautious in the crowd peeled off right and left to settle there. Others, bolder, followed the Lord Wotheng's party and the priests of Yotha into the valley proper and up the rising road. As the walls of Deese House drew near though, more and more folk thought it wise to spread out to either side of the road and take positions on the sidelines. For the last hundred paces and more, up to the gates of Deese, Lord Wotheng and the Yotha priests proceeded alone.

At sixty paces out, Wotheng halted, turned, and gestured imperiously to the Yotha priesthood behind him. Everyone caught his meaning: wait here. Yotha's priests did so, halting where they were but continuing to chant and ring their hand chimes. Wotheng rode almost to the bronze-sheathed gates and signalled briefly to one of his men-at-arms. The guardsman lifted and dropped the iron rings that served as door knockers and handles, once, twice, three times.

"Let the challengers come forth!" Wotheng bellowed in a voice that could be heard to the near hilltops. Then he turned his cart, his guards neatly circling with him, and rode back to a point midway between Yotha's assembled priests and the still visible char-mark some ten strides before the gates. There he reined in and waited.

The bronze and oak doors swung open with barely a creak, pushed by two matched Deese priests, and the small procession marched out. In their forefront paced Eloti and Arizun, empty hands formally clasped, eyes deep and distant. After them, including the two who closed the doors behind the procession and resumed their place at the end of the double line, came no more than half a dozen priests of Deese.

The crowd compared the sizes of the two wizard armies, and muttered loudly.

"Gods, is that all they have?" Patrobe chuckled at Folweel's elbow. "And led by that woman and a boy? Oh, much cry and little wool!"

"Take care," Folweel shushed him. "We know not what level of sorcery they've attained."

The wizard priests of Deese advanced until they stood directly over the charred spot on the ground and stopped there, all together, with no signal given, neatly as a trained company of soldiers in some high king's guard.

The audience murmured, impressed. Wotheng raised a respectful eyebrow, then stood up in his cart and solemnly rang his judicial bell.

"Challenge has been given and accepted," he announced, in his trumpeting public-gathering voice that echoed so well from the hills. "Combatants shall not approach each other any closer than this, nor shall they depart their ground save in surrender. You shall employ no weapons save those of your wizardry, neither shall you harm any present save each other's combatants. You shall have this quarter of the hour to prepare your ground. Combat shall commence at next ringing of the bell, and shall end only when one or the other party is clearly defeated. On your lives and your honors, do you understand these terms?"

"Aye!" shouted the priests of Yotha, a trifle raggedly.

The priests of Deese only nodded their heads silently, in concert.

The crowd glanced at the Deese wizards with a touch of awe; such tight precision and utter silence were a bit unnerving.

Wotheng sat back down and steered his team to the sidelines, a good seventy paces to the south. The crowd carefully made way for him. There he turned his cart to face the field, and settled back to wait. His guards dutifully spread out along the edge of the assembly, forming a broad circle around the opposing teams of wizards. In the throng, the assorted vendors opened their wagons and set about peddling their goods. Gamblers scampered through the press, offering various odds.

Among the priests of Yotha, half a dozen of the under-priests put away their chimes, hurried to their cartload of supplies and hauled out several kegs and baskets. The remaining under-priests continued to chant hypnotically and strike their chimes, but the senior priests put their chimes away and two of them—Oralro and Folweel—drew out meditation gems as well. The two remaining priests, Patrobe and Jimantam, directed the mobile under-priests in drawing large circles of fire-fluid around the group and neatly arranging piles of covered baskets close to the circle's center.

Oralro glanced once around his knot of chanting under-priests, making certain they were well into the proper meditative level, feeling the growing wave front of their mage power. Yes, they were responding well and obediently, their power ready to be tapped and channeled where he chose to focus it. He'd need that much power, and a good tight focus, to punch through the blanketing defensive spell the Deese wizards had already placed on their house and land.

A remarkably tight and precise spell that, given the size of the area it covered; he could feel exactly where its near border lay, almost exactly between the two groups. How symbolic. Had Wotheng, in his obvious favoritism toward the Deese wizards chosen the ground of the duel for just that reason? Well, no matter; Oralro knew that with enough power and focus he could punch through it.

The real problem would be maintaining Yotha's own defensive shield, keeping his own circle safely well-wished, at the same time. That would require dividing his forces, halving his power reservoir, maintaining a second focus. Complex business for one mage; yet Folweel had skill and power sufficient to handle the second task, leaving himself free to concentrate on the first. Already he could feel the high priest's characteristic field widening, pulling in selected others from the pool of under-priests.

Oralro frowned as he noted which ones Folweel was taking: three of his strongest and best trained. Ah well, perhaps he was right; they'd need a good strong defense against the Deese wizards, who—already having a preset shield—were free to concentrate on attack. Then again, the Deese wizards were fewer in number if not in power; just one of them sufficiently distracted—or otherwise removed from the reservoir—could make a significant difference. Oralro chuckled silently as he thought of some of the "distractions" Brother Folweel had planned. Reassured, he peered into the meditation gem and concentrated on drawing his power net tighter.

The air was mild and cool, but Sulun and Vari were sweating heavily as they finished drawing the last of their three concentric rings around their base zone: the outer ring of water, the second of powdered sulfur, the inner one of firepowder. How many minutes past? How many to go? Now to set the loaded fire tubes in the holes they'd carefully dug the night before, put in the fuses and make sure they had enough air for proper burning. A quick glance to the walls showed Ziya crouched behind the bombard, ready and waiting. He hoped that the secondary protective spells they'd set last night on both Ziya and the bombard would escape the Yotha priests'. notice. What next? Oh, yes: place the buckets of water around the others, ready to use in case any of that damned fire fluid made it through the shield and hit too close to people. Now to set up the small brazier, fill it with waiting coals and pour in the lighted ones, make sure the new coals caught well and the tapers were ready to hand; it wouldn't do to be without fire when they needed it. Now to take the old bellows, make certain it was still full of water and not leaking, prop it at just the right angle to shoot the ink-dyed water into Yotha's circle—a clever idea from Omis, that—and set the handles so that a quick stamp from a hurried foot would fire it.

Fire . . . Sulun wiped his face and shivered, feeling the horrible weight of his responsibility. Eloti and the others—see, they'd joined hands now; one could almost feel the power flowing from them like heat from the forge—would do nothing but maintain shields, constantly well-wishing themselves and their ground. All the physical defense—and all the attacks—would come only from Vari and himself.

Attacks? Sulun looked around again at his preparations. *Attack is not of my nature! I'll put on a good show, startle and distract Yotha's wizards, throw enough harmless stuff into their circle to make them look foolish, make it clear they've lost . . . But truly attack? Throw firepowder, as Zeren urged me? I don't think I can do it.*

He rubbed his back, glanced at Omis, mentally reviewed the signals they'd designed, and finally went to stand beside Vari near the brazier. The shadows were so short, there couldn't be much time left now.

There wasn't. Wotheng glanced at the small hourglass set beside him on the cart, stood up and rang his bell again. "The hour has come," he bellowed to the suddenly hushed throng. "Let the combat begin."

On his word, the under-priests sparked their tinderboxes and lit their circle of fire fluid. The crowd roared as the flames sprang up and formed a ring of yellow-tipped blue fire around Yotha's priesthood.

Must be hot inside it, Sulun thought inanely as he lit a taper at the brazier, took it to the innermost ring and set off the firepowder. Again the assembly howled, seeing the snapping circle of orange-red flames run, sparking fiercely, around the priesthood of Deese.

For the next few moments nothing seemed to happen, although everyone could feel the tension. Invisible waves of will, arms of power, grappled and wrestled with each other, making no headway.

Folweel, concentrating on maintaining his net against attack, waited and waited and finally wondered why no attack came. Long moments passed, and there was no pressure of any kind on even the edges of his field. What were those Deese wizards doing? He withdrew enough of his attention to focus on the enemy. They didn't seem to be doing much of anything. Oralro, however, was clearly sweating and straining with effort. So were the obedient under-priests in his power net. Aha! So the Deese wizards were concentrating all their strength on defense! Well, he had other means to get through that, other ways to attack, and even that pompous ass Wotheng couldn't properly call them ordinary weapons.

He gestured briefly to Patrobe, then sank back into concentration. Best not leave the net weakened too long by his absence.

Patrobe nodded acknowledgement and signalled to his contingent. The half-dozen under-priests obediently reached into the waiting baskets and drew out thin-walled jugs sealed with trailing rags. They briefly upended the jugs and let the contents soak the rags, then righted them, lit the trailing rag ends, paused for a short prayer, and threw the jugs toward the center of Deese's circle.

Eloti's shield held well; the jugs all hit far from center, damaging nothing, and half their wick fires were smothered out on impact. Most of them broke, however, spreading sharp-smelling fire fluid on the ground. Two of them succeeded in catching fire, and the crowd gasped upon seeing the pools of Yotha's flames spring up, even in harmless patches. Sulun and Vari grabbed buckets, ran to the fires and doused them quickly.

"No more water than we need," Vari panted in warning. "There'll be more, and we can't go back to the stream until this is over."

Sulun nodded quickly, smothered the last fire as economically as possible and headed back to his post by the brazier.

On the way, he came across a full and intact jug. An imp of perversity nibbled. He picked up the jug, relit the rag with a taper, and threw it back.

The crowd whooped.

The jug landed and broke, just within Yotha's circle. The wick went out, but the contents splashed far enough to contact the sinking edge of the ringing fire, and catch. A blob of blue flame sprang up briefly, distorting the circle's shape. One of Patrobe's under-priests started toward it, then hesitated, unsure what to do without orders.

Not distraction enough, Sulun thought, hurrying to the nearest of the loaded fire tubes. He thrust his taper's flame against the end of the fuse, waited until it had caught well, then ducked aside and ran back to the brazier.

Nothing interfered with the fire tube's functioning. The powder ignited with a bang, shooting sparks and smoke out its muzzle—as well as a cloth-wrapped packet of sulfur. The cloth ignited also, and then the sulfur. The sizzling package erupted in mid-air on the downward arc of its trajectory, just outside Yotha's circle. Yotha's defenses still held good, but there was no way to completely avoid a widespread hail of burning sulfur, let alone its secondary effects. The ground in the forward third of the circle—and one unfortunate under-priest in Jimantam's unit—were pelted with fine grains of burning, stinking chemical. The underpriest yelped and danced and tore at his robes.

The watching assembly stood up and roared, not least with laughter.

Jimantam gestured furiously, and two more under-priests ran to their stricken fellow to help drag off his multipunctured robe and splash water on him. They coughed and gasped as the sulfur smoke rose around them, stinking to the heavens and obscuring sight.

Folweel heard the shouting, glanced up quickly and saw what was happening. *Wide-area weapon!* He cursed silently. There was only so much that even the best protective well-wishing could do against anything that splattered over a wide range. Shift probabilities as he could, some of the nasty stuff was bound to hit a target. Damn!

Well, he could respond with something similar. Folweel signalled again to Patrobe, who likewise signalled to his division of under-priests, who lit and threw more jugs.

Again, the fire jugs failed to reach their mark. Again, Vari smothered fires, Sulun found another intact jug, lit and threw it. This one, unfortunately, landed outside Yotha's circle. It broke and burned there, making no difference and no distraction.

More sulfur? Sulun considered. *No, save them. Wait, see what they do.*

Oralro, sweating and panting, came up from meditative level far enough to reach out and tug Folweel's sleeve.

"Their shield's too strong," he whispered. "Can't get through. Join me and help!"

Folweel thought for a moment, making sure there was no pressure whatever of ill-wishing on his shields, and acquiesced. Nine hells, let Yotha protect his own and keep the Deese wizards from attacking, just a few minutes more. He tapped his entranced under-priests on the wrists and hissed to them, "Join the ill-wishing!" Then he dropped back to deeper meditative level, rejoined and refocused their mingled fields. Last, he carefully joined his power net to Oralro's field, felt them interlock, expand, engage the front of the Deese wizards' shield.

Oralro smiled for the first time, feeling that enemy shield give way. He focused tighter, took the power of the net and pushed it hard, hard as he could. Degree by slow degree, the Deese field weakened.

Whatever Eloti and the others felt, they gave no sign. Sulun and Vari felt the change like a sudden change of wind, an almost audible *snap* of power in the air. They looked at each other, guessing what had happened.

As if in confirmation, the unlatched gates of Deese House swung open—and this time one of the hinges creaked.

The house has no defense! Sulun realized. He thought of what harm those Yotha priests could do to the building, its contents, his tools, if they chose—and a roused fury burned him like a hot coal.

He ran to the waiting bellows and fairly jumped on its upper handle.

The inky water shot out in a tight, hard stream, arcing high into the air before turning downward. The top of the arch was well beyond the middle of the ground between the circles. The black rain fell in a good wide circle inside Yotha's boundary ring.

Some of it fell on the leading edge of the diminishing blue fire, and put it out. The rest drew a fat black arrow-head shape on the ground, pointing straight into the knot of hard-worked wizards. A little of it caught the priests themselves: Folweel across the chest and Oralro smack in the face.

Startled out of concentration, they yelped in dismay and brushed frantically at the murky stuff. They had no idea what it was, what it would do, and they couldn't get it off them. The force of their ill-wishing attack wavered and shrank.

Everyone in Eloti's circle felt the pressure slack away. It was temptation to shift to attack themselves, but Eloti said "No," aloud and signalled to Sulun and Vari.

"Fire tubes!" Sulun shouted, running to the nearest with a taper.

They lit and fired three in quick succession before Sulun thought to conserve what was left. Three booming, whistling packets of burning sulfur sailed through the air to land neatly inside Yotha's circle, bombarding the wizards with pepper grains of fire, smoke and choking stink.

The crowd danced up and down, roaring with delight.

Only Wotheng, watching the combat through slitted eyes, showed no great joy. "Not enough," he muttered to himself, barely catching even Gynallea's quick ear. "Hit harder. More."

Within Yotha's circle, Folweel and Oralro fought yattering chaos. They yelled for Jimantam to bring water, beat flames out of their robes, coughed and choked in the reeking smoke and tried to rally their under-priests to concentration again. Jimantam's troop of servitors ran among them with water, sloshing it wildly at anyone who seemed to need it, which added further distraction.

Only Patrobe and two of his crew, to one side of the circle, missed the onslaught of water and sulfur. Snarling a curse and an order, he ran to the nearest basket of fire fluid jugs and began lighting and throwing as fast as he could. Many of the jugs flew wild, wasting themselves on neutral ground; many others landed within the circle and went out, but enough landed and burned to keep Sulun and Vari busy.

Up on the wall Ziya watched, teeth bared and breath hissing through them. Fire wakened old memories, hurtful and dark: fire thrown at her house, her friends, her family . . . Fire, from the bad people. Wicked people. The enemy. She clenched her hands on the bombard's carriage, furiously wishing that Sulun would send her the signal, let her strike at the enemy.

And not just beside them.

A coal of fury lit an idea.

He hadn't told her to *leave* the bombard aimed where it was. He hadn't told her *not* to change the setting.

Well-learned details of angle, trajectory, direction played through her head as she tugged the bombard sideways, just a trifle, just enough.

Folweel stripped off his sodden outer robe, grateful that the fire chemical hadn't burned through to the skin, and frantically dropped back to meditative level as fast as he could. There: yes, thank whatever gods, Oralro was doing the same. So were the obedient under-priests. If they could raise their defensive shields again, push back the Deese wizards' attack before it got any worse . . .

But he couldn't feel any attack.

It's all on the physical plane! he realized, with a sudden jab of hope. The Deese wizards were concentrating all their mage power on defense, come what might. That was their strategy: save magic for defense only, attack with physical means only.

They didn't have enough trained wizards for both attack and defense at once.

Folweel grabbed Oralro's sleeve. " Attack!" he hissed. "Beat down their shield and attack! Put everything into that!"

Oralro nodded, snapped out the orders to the reassembled net of under-priests, and concentrated. Folweel dropped into concentration with him. They joined and tightened focus, probed—found that suspected second shield.

Folweel almost laughed as he realized what the Deese priests were doing. They'd started with a preset, passive area defense. Under that, within their drawn circle, they now held a standing, active shield. Punch through that, and they'd have nothing. He signalled to Patrobe to keep on with the distractions, and pushed harder behind Oralro's attack.

Patrobe obligingly threw more fire jugs, and his underpriests did likewise.

Under that steady barrage, Sulun and Vari were kept hopping. Enough fires sprang up to need constant attention with the diminishing water, enough to keep them too busy to use the remaining fire tubes. The best they could do was seize unbroken jugs in passing, light them and throw them back. Hardly any landed within Yotha's circle.

"We're running out of water!" Vari gasped, smothering

one fire with her empty bucket. "How much of that stuff do they have?"

"Don't know," Sulun panted, using the last of his bucket on another. *Too much*, he guessed. That, he realized was the flaw in his strategy; Yotha's priests simply had more of everything: long-range weapons, supplies, wizards, everything. Given time, they'd wear Eloti and the others down.

Gods, there: one of the jugs broke nearby, splashing the hem of Arizun's robe. Blue flames crawled up the cloth, perilously close to his leg.

Arizun didn't move, didn't notice. His concentration was total, far from immediate physical concerns.

None of the others in the mage circle noticed the fire, either.

Vari ran up to Arizun and beat out the flames with her bare hands.

Gods, we have to break their concentration! Sulun knew it was time to bring out the last reserve, the grand distraction. Once the Yotha wizards' attack was broken, and hopefully their defenses down, he could rain them with the last of the sulfur—win time to reload the tubes and rain them further, until they gave up and ran from the targeted circle. It had to be done now.

He waved up toward the walls and shouted the code phrase to Ziya, praying the child would hear it, not freeze, do as she'd vigorously sworn she would.

"Ziya!" he shouted. *"Fire ready!"*

Ziya heard. She smiled tightly, peered once more down the bombard's realigned barrel, and touched her lighted taper to the end of the fuse.

The fuse burned, sizzling, up toward the hole and the firepowder and torn metal waiting beyond it.

On the field below, Folweel felt the first flinching, the first ever-so-slight give in the Deese-wizards' shield. *They're tiring!* he thought jubilantly, feeling Oralro's answering joy as he noted the change too. Just another few minutes of this and they'd have that last defense broken, no shield left between their furiously tight-focused ill-wishing and the target. It would probably strike that witch first. With this much power behind it, the attack might be enough to stop her heart right there. And yes, yes, their shield was definitely weakening.

Then something roared like thunder in the sky.

Folweel looked up just in time to see a cloud of smoke and sparks blossom high on the wall of Deese House, and realized it had come from the storm tube.

The watching crowd screamed together, seeing the earth shoot up like a monstrous fountain, stones and bodies and unidentifiable rags and pieces flying like leaves on the wind. Again voices wailed, seeing those unbelievable fragments fall back to earth amid a haze of smoke and dust. Then came a long, quavering, multiple groan as the smoke cleared, revealing the full sight of the damage in the unflinching sunlight.

In the center of Yotha's circle, where the knot of Yotha's priests had recently stood, lay a wide, shallow hole. Around it were scattered rags of stained cloth, bits of glass and stone, small clods of torn earth, unsightly pieces of flesh and bone, puddles and streaks of fire fluid and blood. Further out lay torn and tumbled bodies, still bleeding but too obviously dead. A lone under-priest near the far edge of the circle staggered, blood-splashed and dazed, a few steps forward. He stumbled on a tattered body, stared at it, looked wildly around him, at the earth and bodies torn to rags and ruin by the flying stones—then he fled shrieking out of the charred circle and away. They could hear him howling all the way down the road.

Sulun rubbed his stunned ears until he could hear again, and stared at the field before him in unthinking shock. *Hole . . . his mind feebly registered. Bombard. On them, not beside them . . . Oh gods, so that's what it can do!*

Vari sat down right where she was and covered her eyes; Sulun could hear her quietly cursing, and dimly marvelled that she even knew such words. Omis took a half-step forward and stared stupidly at the fresh crater as if wondering how it had gotten there. Yanados swayed, grabbed at Doshi for support, and they both collapsed together. Arizun simply and quietly fainted. Eloti, eyes wide, spread her hands and staggered like a blind man. "Gone," she whispered. "What . . . ? How?"

Zeren took her by the shoulders and pulled her close. "Will of the gods," he growled, "and will of Wotheng." He turned to face the Ashkell lord's wagon and raised his sword hand in ironic salute.

Wotheng stood up in his cart and solemnly returned the gesture. Then he lifted and rang his bell. "The combat is ended," he announced, harsh-voiced. "The priests of Deese are found innocent of all charges."

"Yes," Zeren muttered, lowering his arm. "And I hope you're satisfied."

Gynallea, white to the lips, clutched her husband's arm. "Is this it?" she hissed at him. "Is this what you wanted?"

"Aye," Wotheng growled, looking abruptly older than his years. "I knew from first report what a weapon that thing could make: fierce enough to defend the Vale, scare off greedy neighbor lords, keep us and our descendants safe. I had to make Sulun use it, would he or no: show everyone what it could do, spread the word all over the northlands. Now, by the gods, we're safe."

"Safe! Safe? With that?"

"I confess . . . " Wotheng briefly chewed his lip. "I didn't know it would . . . do quite that."

The crowd, still moaning quietly in horror, melted back from the sight of the field. The motion grew a current, slipped off the hills, out of the valley, off down the east-ward road, safely away from Deese House and its hideous new landmark and its vast and terrible power. Slowly the crowd moved, cautiously, politely—but away.

Sulun looked about him, cold with stark comprehension. Yes, he'd won, and Yotha House was no more, and Deese House was safe. But Wotheng had used him, and now the vale folk feared him, and the souls of his family and the reputation of Deese House were forever stained with a darkness. He wondered what would become of Eloti's school now, of his hopes for spreading knowledge and enlightenment, of forming the core of a new civiliza-tion in Ashkell Vale. The family of Deese had won their survival, certainly, but at what cost?

And how did it happen?

He looked up at the wall, at the bombard. No, the muzzle was not pointed where he'd seen it last; now it was aimed straight at that damning hideous hole in the field.

Beside it, straight and tall and smiling coldly in unshamed triumph, stood Ziya. She caught Sulun's eye, waved a merry salute to him, then turned and—before all the gods—began reloading the bombard.

Gods, what has she become? Sulun wondered, shivering.

Ziya finished her task, lifted her lighted taper and waved again to Sulun.

"This is not the beginning I wanted," he said, to himself as much as her. Guessing she couldn't hear him, he shook his head. "Child, can't you understand? This was a bad beginning!"

If Ziya heard, she gave no sign. She cocked her head to one side and called down from the walls, as if asking for further orders.

"Fire ready," she said.

ENTER A NEW WORLD
OF FANTASY . . .

Sometimes an author grows in stature so steadily that it seems as if he has always been a master. Such a one is David Drake, whose rise to fame has been driven equally by his archetypal creation, Colonel Alois Hammer's armored brigade of future mercenaries, and his non-series science fiction novels such as **Ranks of Bronze**, and **Fortress**.

Now Drake commences a new literary Quest, this time in the universe of fantasy. Just as he has become the acknowledged peer of such authors as Jerry Pournelle and Gordon R. Dickson in military and historically oriented science fiction, he will now take his place as a leading proponent of fantasy adventure. So enter now . . .

AUGUST 1988 65424-1 352 PP. $3.95